UNTAMABLE

A NOVEL

By Billy Sprague

Out of the Bluebell Publishing

Cover painting: Dennas Davis
Cover and Interior design: David Prendergast

Printed in the United States

Library of Congress Catalogue Card Number:
US Copyright: TXu 2-354-252

LCCN Library of Congress Control Number: 2023918319

Sprague, William Luz, 1952

Print version ISBN: 979-8- 9876883-3-5 (paperback)
Ebook version ISBN: 979-8- 9876883-4-2 (ebook)

First Edition: November 2023, Nashville, Tn

This novel is a work of fiction. The names, characters and incidents portrayed in it are the work of the author's imagination. Any resemblance to actual persons, living or dead, events or localities is entirely coincidental.

*This story is dedicated to the one who thinks love
and your magnum opus have passed you by*

and

Karla
for the look

A story is a letter that the author writes to himself,
to tell himself things that he would be unable
to discover otherwise.

Carlos Ruiz Zafón

My grace is sufficient for you,
for my power is made perfect in weakness.

2 Corinthians 12:9

How deep is your love? I really mean to learn

The BeeGees

A NOTE FROM THE AUTHOR

What's a movie without a soundtrack?

Until *Untamable* comes out as a movie (an author can dream, right?), the QR code above connects to a Spotify playlist called: **Untamable Soundtrack.** The code appears at the beginning of each chapter that includes music references. They are catalogued by chapter in the Music Addendum at the back of the book. (These titles can also be found wherever you source music.)

Here's how it works: Scan the QR code on your device and select it. This will take you to the playlist. Scroll down to a title you come across in the story. Most are only a few minutes in length. Listen and sample as you read to experience the story on a deeper level. And trust me, this timeless music will feed your soul.

I hope you enjoy and are moved by *Untamable.*

Billy Sprague

CHAPTER ONE

THE CALL

This story chose me. It drew me across an ocean to stand in one of those holy places, about to ring the bell on a door ordained completely beyond my control. How I came to that threshold pales against the story I am about to tell you. It's enough to begin - one day my phone rang.

On a clear winter morning in the first week of January, I was sitting in my car on a beach in Florida watching the Atlantic waves spend themselves rhythmically on the shore, like my thoughts. Couples walked by. The younger ones with stories still ahead of them. The older ones with most of their story behind them. Surfers, which I am not, tell me waves come in sets. Most not worth catching. On one mental wave I marveled at how life can turn on a phone call. I have had more than several of those. You probably have, too. Some bearing good news. Others delivering catastrophe.

A few weeks earlier, a call came from a longtime friend who read the fresh manuscript of my first novel. Writing fiction marked a new creative avenue after years of writing songs and a couple of non-fiction titles. Besides, I had a lot of new solitude to redeem after my divorce. My friend called to say his childhood friend, an Oscar-winning movie producer, wanted to read it. With just a phone call, I rode a wave of astonishment. It was immediately followed by several breakers of doubt and uncertainty. Who knows? It was a long shot.

Very long. But a serendipitous, perhaps ordained turn of events.

Now, sitting in my car on the beach, the next wave carried a couple of nagging questions of late: What do I write next? Or should I revive my dormant painting hobby? Having more experience and traction with a pen than a brush, I leaned toward the former. Among the half dozen ideas in various stages of ignition, fiction and non-fiction, I wrestled with which one could best redeem the season of unchosen solitude.

Indecision and inertia faced another head wind. What possible difference could another story, one more song or painting make in the world? Just as those waves of cynicism and self-pity tried to gather strength, my phone rang.

The screen read, 'Carlow, Ireland.' That had never happened. I took the call.

"Hello, Ireland," I said. A woman with an Irish accent greeted me.

"Yes, hello, sir. How're ye keepin'? My name is Zuza Miriam Petra O'Cullen."

"Very well, thank you. I like your name. But most of it doesn't sound Irish."

"You're bang on. But your names are German, Spanish and Scottish and you don't sound like any of those."

"Good point," I said.

She launched right into the derivation of her name, "Zuza is from the Hebrew "Shoshana." Like Susanna. It means 'lily'. Petra you may know is Greek meaning 'the rock.' Miriam is Hebrew also. It means, "wished-for child." It's my grandmother's name. And O'Cullen is my married name. I am born and raised in Ireland."

"Well, Ms. O'Cullen, dia dhuit." (pronounced Jee-ah ghwitch) I gave it my best try with the guttural throat-clearing sound on the dh. It means "God be with you."

"Ah, that's pretty good! You know some Gaelic."

"That's all I remember from my one trip to Ireland, besides the drinking toast, 'Sláinte.'" (pronounced: slawnchuh)

"Well, agus le do spiorad, and with your spirit, sir. I'll jump right to the reason for my call. My mother, Aneska Latva, wants you to write her story. She has told it in parts over the years at music conferences and World War II remembrances. But never the complete story. Of course, we will pay you and your expenses."

Do I need to tell you she commandeered my full attention? An out-of-the-blue call from a woman with Hebrew, Greek and Irish names offering a writing job - that pays! This was a wave worth catching.

I looked northeast at the horizon of the Atlantic toward Ireland and said, "I have two questions. Who is your mother? And why me?"

"Let me answer your second question first. After my father passed…"

"I'm sorry to hear that," I interjected.

"Thank you. After he passed a Scottish woman who took piano lessons from my mother when she was a girl sent Mama one of your books. Her name is Ruth Keenan. Apparently, you corresponded with her after her husband passed."

I remembered Ruth fondly. Her letters were kind and delightful.

"Well, your book sat in a pile of condolences for a long while. A few months ago, Mama read it. It comforted her greatly. She read it to our entire circle. I must tell you, it helped us all."

"I'm very glad to hear that."

"Mama researched you, even saw one of your paintings in an article, the blue portrait of Anne Frank. She ordered more books and all your music she could find."

"So, she's one of my dozens of fans. Sorry, go on."

"Sir, as my mother says, 'Never doubt your gift. Just keep giving it. God gives gifts as he sees fit. From Beethoven and the Beatles to the bard in the subway.'"

"She sounds inspiring."

"You cannot imagine," Zuza said.

"Ms. O'Cullen, you still haven't told me why your mother wants me to tell her story."

"Sir, my mother believes life is a symphony with recurring themes. One of those is suffering. After reading your books and listening to much of your music she told me and my brother she had found the person to write her story. She said, 'He is fellow musician, a tiefbrunnenschreiber and he has suffered. Not in the same way, but he knows deep loss.' She asked me to contact you."

I didn't know what to say except, "Is that German? What's a teefbrewninthinger?"

Zuza laughed, "Yes. A tiefbrunnenschrieber is a writer of depth, literally, a deep well writer."

"That's very kind of her. Is your mother German?"

"Yes, she speaks German, English very well, some Swedish, and a smattering of French. But her primary language is music."

Do I need to tell you I was all in? For the next half hour, Zuza told me enough about her mother to know I had to know the whole story. Ten days later, I boarded a flight on a first-class Aer Lingus ticket to Dublin to hear and tell the following story that would carry life-giving water to the dry ground in my heart, and perhaps in yours as well.

CHAPTER TWO

THE DOOR

My driver left Dublin proper heading away from the sea and the morning sun. The comfort of first-class seating mitigated jet lag some from the overnight flight. But the Irish countryside, even in winter, the birthplace of Yeats, Joyce, Shaw, C.S. Lewis and Bono, kept my face pressed to the window like a kid, as did the intrigue of my destination.

In little more than an hour, I was deposited in County Carlow in front of a black iron double gate. Stone finials resembling acorns capped tall pillars on either side. Snow dusted the ground. Delicate white blossoms around the base of the pillars defied the cold. Tall pines like ship masts lined the left side of the gravel drive, which curved to the right at about a hundred yards behind giant oaks and maples, bereft of leaves. A house was nowhere in sight. Next to the pillar on the right, a small iron gate stood open, as if I were expected. Mortared into one column, a stone sign confirmed my destination, "Snowdrop Manor." Etched into a much older stone were the words, "O'Cullen Clan." And below that, "Anno Domini 1842."

With luggage in hand, I walked down the drive, my shoes crunching on the white gravel. As the driveway curved, a house still was not visible. The vista to the left stretched across a wide valley to high hills on the far side. Another hundred yards farther, a house appeared on the right. "Mansion" better described it, in a style I later learned was Georgian with Gothic elements. It presented a storybook setting. Ivy covered the right half of the two-story red brick structure. Tall lancet windows with pointed arches trimmed in white and a latticed, half-moon glass oxeye over the entrance gave it the look of a chapel. Descending wing walls on both sides magnified the overall stature. The front façade bowed outward on either side of the main door, giving the appearance of massive castle towers. Paired, broad chimneys, each with several flues, indicated fireplaces on all floors. A coat of arms above the oxeye drew my eye. It bore the motto, "Spectemur Agendo." I took a year of Latin in graduate school but had to research a translation. "Let us be judged by our deeds."

Standing at Aneska Latva's door, I had a similar feeling as the day I hesitated in front of the bookshelf that hid the entrance to Anne Frank's hiding place, trying to take it in. That secret doorway in Amsterdam changed the world the morning of August 4, 1944, when the Nazis dragged fifteen-year-old Anne and her family and friends off to their deaths, all but the lone survivor, her father, Otto. This portal would prove no less holy than that one, but with a profound difference. I met Anne through her diary, reading it for the first time in a café around the corner from her hiding place on a sunny summer day in 1986. I tried to hide my tears over cinnamon apple crepes and espresso. But behind this dark green double door, I was about to meet in the flesh a living soul who faced the same darkness. And survived.

As I reached for the ancient door knocker, the sound of a piano came from somewhere not far inside the house. I pulled back my hand and listened. A simple melody line in three note phrases floated through the door. Rubato. With softly struck chords on each third note. It sounded like a child hunting for notes. The balanced, completed sequence paused on an unresolved note, like a bird at the peak of a climb. The phrase fell back to the beginning. Clearly established in 6/8 time, the same melody repeated, but over different chords, now arpeggiated and rolling in the left hand. It sounded characteristically Celtic, simultaneously forlorn and sweet. This was no child on the piano.

I would have listened much longer in the chilly air, but I knocked my suitcase over. It banged against the door. The playing stopped. Footsteps approached. The piano playing resumed. Both

halves of the double door swung open.

"Dia dhuit. Welcome. I'm Zuza." She offered her hand. It was as warm as her expression. "Please come in. It's so marvelous you're here."

Do I have to tell you I agreed completely? Zuza's wide-set, light blue eyes and flowing silver locks immediately brought the singer Judy Collins to mind. She radiated warmth and welcome, much like the house.

I stepped into the broad, marble-floored foyer of a home whose beauty and charm, like Zuza's, I cannot adequately describe. High ceilings, ornate crown molding, rich, wine-colored walls. A curved staircase rose elegantly to the second floor. The most striking feature was the paintings. Or I should say, the painting. Dozens of framed canvases of diverse sizes lined the walls, including the one adjacent to the stairs. The subject of every painting was a snowdrop flower in varying styles. Some mere sketches. Others caked with paint to rival Van Gogh's textures. As far as I could tell, all were signed simply, "KRL."

"Someone likes snowdrops," I said to Zuza.

"Yes, Schneeglöckchen in German. My mother renamed the estate after them, by their English name, for obvious reasons. They hold a very special place in her heart."

In the few moments I took all this in, the piano music kept playing, creating a lovely soundtrack absent in my reverent experience entering Anne Frank's sanctuary. Through an arched opening on the right, I could see the back curve of a black grand piano. But not the player.

"Is that your mother playing?" I asked Zuza.

"No, that's her protégée." She moved to the opening and pulled the two pocket doors closed. "You will meet her, too. We are all fierce happy you are here."

I was, too. Like the children in the Narnia books, I had just stepped into a whole new world.

"Let me show you to the guest house. It overlooks the river."

I followed like a rescue puppy.

"Your lunch will be brought there at noon. Feel free to rest or walk the grounds. Mother would like to meet you for afternoon tea, three o'clock, in the solarium."

Zuza led me through the remarkable home, past a lovely, half-round solarium, out a back door, across a lovely walled garden area and down a path to the guest house. As advertised, a desk in the sitting room overlooked a glassy river. The thought came, "gently winding its way through drowsing pastures dreaming of spring." I hadn't been there ten minutes and had already inhaled the poetic atmosphere breathed by Yeats and Bono. Though internally hemorrhaging poetry, I stood there in silent amazement. Zuza's humor broke the spell.

"I assume it won't irritate you too much to write in this setting?"

I tried to match her wit.

"If it does, please have me flogged and starved."

"On the contrary, mother believes it's kindness that leads to repentance. So, be prepared to repent a lot."

With that winsome warning, she left me in private awe to wonder what I could possibly have done to warrant such an adventure. I concluded this could only come from the hand of a 'beyond all we can ask or imagine' kind of God, whose ways, considering my recent shadowland, had more than puzzled and parched me. I would soon realize this was only a hint of the magnitude of what lay ahead.

I freshened up. Unpacked. The walls of every room in the guest house were crowded with a collection of more snowdrop art, but all signed by as many individuals as paintings. Next to the large window overlooking the bucolic countryside, one frame held a handwritten quote.

We can make our minds so like still water that beings gather about us that they may see, it may be, their own images, and so live for a moment with clearer, perhaps even with a fiercer life because of our quiet.

W. B. Yeats

Of course. Ireland's Nobel prize-winning poet.

Underneath the quote, a penny whistle, one of the classic Irish instruments, rested on two wooden pegs. I made a mental note to inquire about it. But in the blizzard of beauty and questions in my new surroundings, I forgot all about it. Until much later.

I grabbed my jacket and set out to explore the grounds. The entire estate would require many walks over the coming days, more likely weeks. Within a few minutes, I came upon a small graveyard surrounded by towering oaks and Douglas firs. Some of the more aged headstones went back to the 1600s. The O'Cullens were well represented. Situated just apart from the rest, a stone column stood on a raised mound. At its base, carved in granite was this inscription:

Kristers Reinhardt Latva
July 12, 1926 – June 12, 2015
Loved beyond words

KRL, obviously Aneska's husband and the artist obsessed with snowdrops. I sat for a minute on a nearby bench, placed there no doubt for contemplation. But the frosty January air cut any meditation short. A path from there brought me to the bank of the river. I stood for a short while soaking in the beauty. I felt like a few brushstrokes in a living, breathing work of art. By the time I returned to the guest house, a delicious aroma greeted me. Lunch was on the dining table. A note in the same unadorned hand that inscribed the Yeats' quote accompanied it.

My Friend,

Welcome and thank you for coming so far to our home. It's a perfect Irish day for chicken vegetable soup, honey and oat yeast loaf with clotted cream and jam. Our chef, Maja, is an artist. The cream and slice of sharp cheddar are from the dairy down the lane, my son Valor's place. As a musician and writer, I presume you enjoy beer. It's not a Guinness, but what is? But it's local like the food. I look forward to our time together.
Our hearth is your hearth. Bon Appetit. See you at tea.

Aneska Latva

I ate. Savoring every bite. The meal, gathered entirely from local sources by many hands I would never know, served with such care in the loveliest setting, fed my body and soul. I read the note again. "Our hearth is your hearth." I felt what every soul longs for – embraced. In a too often isolating world that unchooses so many, this place, these hosts, even the land itself, seemed intent on providing that essential affirmation. I raised the last of the pint to my hosts and declared, "Sláinte." Downed the last drop. Set my alarm for 2:30PM. And laid down to rest beside still waters and soon to be green pastures.

CHAPTER THREE

THE TEA

I arrived in the solarium ten minutes early armed with a notepad, digital recorder and microphone, in case we dove right in. An elegant tea service was set on a rolling white iron cart next to a round table with a cerulean blue tiled top. In the center, a crystal vase held fresh snowdrops. My eye went next to the bowl piled high with clotted cream. I salivated involuntarily. Two wing-backed Queen Anne chairs upholstered in blue sat at angles facing the windows. An impulse prompted me to secret my equipment behind the chair farther from the door. As I did, several patches of shimmering color on the floor caught my eye. I found the source of the dancing colors. High against the windows hung two rectangles of stained glass. One depicted a blue seascape with a fishing boat heading out to sea. The other, what else? A field of green dotted with snowdrop blossoms.

Footsteps approached behind me. I turned just as Zuza entered with her mother, who handed her cane to her daughter and strode to me with a steadiness not typical for her age. She extended both hands and took my outstretched hand in them. She was certainly Zuza's mother. Graceful, beaming out of the same light blue eyes and warm smile.

"Welcome, welcome, I'm Aneska Latva." She kept her grip on me as she spoke. "We are so honored that you are here. What a brave thing to answer such a call from a stranger."

I insisted the honor was all mine and tried to make a quip about it taking no bravery to win the lottery. She cast a glance at Zuza that made me wonder if I had begun with a misstep.

Her congeniality undimmed, she said, "That all depends on the prize, of course. We consider ourselves the winner in this one. Let's sit. I want to hear all about your world."

That's the last thing I expected and not why I had come. Zuza reminded her mother of a 4:30 meeting, to use her cane, which she positioned against the armrest of the chair, and excused herself.

Ms. Latva, Aneska, she insisted I call her, poured the tea. We nibbled from a three-tiered array of finger sandwiches, scones, flax seed bread with jam and clotted cream, Irish Cashel Blue cheese with dried apricots, Cadbury chocolates and strawberry cake squares. I was still overwhelmed to be sitting there, in that place, with the living witness to a time in history soon to be relegated to grainy newsreels and second-hand accounts. I was eager to hear from her, but she peppered me with questions about my children, my writing and music. She empathized with my recent heartache from divorce, commenting on the frailties and resilience of the human heart. There was no fireplace in the solarium. None was needed. Aneska was a human hearth. I finally diverted her momentum by thanking her for her interest and a reminder that I crossed an ocean to hear her story.

"Ya, of course, and so you shall. But we all have a story."

I couldn't disagree with that, and again turned the conversation to her. Anticipating the threshold of our first interview, I reached for my notebook, but her next words stopped me.

"Tomorrow morning at eight o'clock we will begin, in the study by the fireplace. Just you and me. We'll take as long as you like. As many days as necessary. However, I must ask your patience. I am committed to rehearsals here at the house and with the symphony in Dublin. I also teach and mentor at the music Academy here in

Carlow and occasionally at the Royal Irish Music Academy, in Dublin. They were so welcoming and kind to me in the early days."

'Busy woman' was my first thought. I edited my second, 'Rehearsing? At your age can you still do concerts?' And instead went with, "Rehearsing, that's marvelous. What are you working on?"

"A piano concerto. It's been a dream for a long time."

I had to ask. "Will you be playing?"

"No, my protégée, Frieda, will do me that honor."

"Zuza tells me I heard her playing when I arrived."

"Yes, she has an extraordinary gift. And her own story, too."

"It sounds like you have a very full plate."

"Yes, indeed," she said. "So, you see, we must work our fireside sessions around the rehearsals."

"I understand. Tomorrow then. How would you like to begin?"

Aneska gazed a moment out the tall windows on the sunny day, brought the teacup to her lips and returned it to the saucer. Turning her bright eyes back to me she said something a composer might say and about which she must have thought deeply.

"My friend, like most concertos, my life has three movements. Before the darkness. The darkness. And beyond the darkness. Or looked at another way, and this is how I have titled the movements of my concerto, beyond beautiful, beyond belief, and beyond words. We can begin wherever you like."

I regretted my recorder wasn't on. But her answer made the path very clear.

Glancing at her pendant watch, she brought our tea to an end, "I'm very sorry, I must go now. The Concertmaster of the Dublin symphony is arriving to review some arrangements with Frieda."

"Yes, of course."

"Zuza will have your supper brought to the guest house. Once you settle in, you're welcome to join us for meals in the dining room."

I stood as she did. She took my hand again in both of hers, "Make yourself at home, my friend. Rest well. See you fireside in the morning."

She took two steps toward the door, then turned back quickly to grab the cane. "Best not let Zuza see me without this prop." She exited like someone on a mission.

I sat down to let my body catch up to my spirit. More clotted cream on a scone seemed to help. Retrieving my notebook, I opened to a blank page and wrote Aneska's words about her life having three movements. At the top of the next page, I titled my session for the next morning: Beyond Beautiful (before the Darkness).

As I left the solarium, captivating sounds drew me to the front of the manor. A lively Celtic duet of violin and piano poured from the music room. I stood a few feet from the drawn doors to listen. These were clearly virtuosos. The vitality of the music stirred my spirit. It was innocent and triumphant. I wondered if it comprised part of the first or third movement of Aneska's life in the long-awaited concerto. It certainly reflected no darkness which I presumed must surely color the second movement. The music halted abruptly. Aneska spoke a comment partly in German I couldn't understand, followed by a female voice, also in mixed German and English, which I assumed must be Frieda. In English, Aneska said something about keeping the cadence energetic yet regal. The delight in her voice was palpable even through the door. She counted off a 6/8 bar, 1,2,3,4,5… and the players launched into the same figure again.

A voice behind me whispered, "It draws you like a flower to the sun, doesn't it?" It was Zuza. I hadn't heard her walk up.

"Yes. You caught me," I said.

"Ah, sure, look it. I do the same thing. I pull myself away because I want to be surprised the night of the first concert."

"When is that?"

"It's scheduled for April 29. The day British troops liberated her."

"Where?"

"In Sandbostel, Germany, not far from Hamburg," Zuza said.

"No, I'm sorry, I mean, where is the concert?"

"The first will be at The National Concert Hall in Dublin with the entire philharmonic. You'll be needin' to come back for that."

The thought of returning to this remarkable place for the realization of Aneska's dream washed over me again in astonishment at my good fortune. All I could think to say was, "What an honor that would be."

We listened.

I was curious. "You said 'first' concert. Is there more than one?"

"Yes, a second is scheduled three weeks later in Hamburg where Mama was born. At the famous Laeiszhalle."

"Why Dublin first?"

"Mama wants to honor the Irish people for taking her in after the war. And most of the music was written here in Ireland."

We stood a moment longer enjoying the music.

"I hope you like lamb chops and roast carrots and prata," Zuza said.

"Prata?"

"Sorry, potatoes."

"Yes, I like them very much."

"Chianti? Or a pint?"

"A pint, thank you." After all, I was in Ireland.

Zuza touched my shoulder, turned and walked quietly away. A moment later I forced myself out of the magnetic pull of the music and followed her lead, returning to the guest house.

I sat at the desk, speechless, feeling again like a few brushstrokes in the vast canvas around me. I couldn't hear it from the guest house, but magnificent music composed perhaps over many years was at that moment coming to life. Just knowing that settled a steadiness on me. The only word for it was faith. The music seemed like "the substance of things hoped for, the evidence of things not seen."

The slate blue river before me flowed almost imperceptibly. The dozing pastures dreamed. Something dormant and static inside me moved incrementally forward as well. In this place, in its embrace, I could find no reason or power to resist it.

Morning seemed too far away. Supper appeared in the guest house while I was taking another walk. I ate like the Lord of the manor. Slept like a child.

First Movement – Beyond Beautiful

CHAPTER FOUR

THE PIANO

I woke early. Instantly alert to what the day held. Like I did on fishing days with my Dad. A tray with breakfast arrived. How would I ever go back to a world without clotted cream? I ate, took my hot cup of tea outside in the cool air and stood facing the river for a few minutes to take in the beauty and choreography of the day. I could have scripted none of it.

At 7:40 a.m. I arrived at the study. A fire crackled in the broad stone fireplace.

If the large painting above the mantle was intended to draw the eye first, it worked. The canvas measured at least four feet by four set in an even larger ornate frame. It was simple. Yet masterful. Like a child painted it in a flurry, without hesitation. Two objects fought for my eye. In the center foreground, a single snowdrop flower stood against a blue sky, growing out of a snowdrift, rendered in pale blue-gray with yellow sunlit highlights. Between two narrow green leaves, one much longer than the other, the stem swept up and over in an elegant curve to a blossom of three white petals. It appeared to bow under the other object that competed for dominance. A menacing strand of burnt red and sienna barbed wire ran at an angle in a taut line across the top of the canvas. The windings on three barb clusters looked like fists. Compared to the loose, free-form strokes of the rest of the painting, the barbed wire appeared meticulously done by a steady hand and keen eye. The entire canvas had the texture and atmosphere of a Van Gogh, paint piled upon paint. Wavy, playful brushstrokes throughout made the entire painting vibrate with vitality in defiance of the barbed wire and winter scene. Even the shadow of the snowdrop on the snow seemed to move. As with Van Gogh's art, it was impossible not to attribute the source of vitality and defiance to the artist. In the lower right corner, three letters were painted in bold red, KRL, the same signature on all the paintings in the foyer. At this point, I could only wonder at the volumes the painting spoke.

Bookshelves lined nearly the entire room, the highest shelves accessible by not one, but two rolling ladders. Along the wall opposite the fireplace, a phalanx of framed photographs, many vintage black and white, crowded a long wooden table. There must have been over fifty. The only other painting in the room was a masterful portrait of a regal looking woman with kind brown eyes and a Mona Lisa smile. She held a Bible on her lap open to the book of John.

Two brown leather armchairs faced each other slightly angled toward the hearth. A small table sat just away from the fire between them, with two smaller side tables positioned next to each fireside arm. A box of tissues on each. On the center table, a glass pitcher of water and two glasses flanked a blue porcelain vase. Do I have to tell you what flowers it held?

I positioned my recorder and microphone on the center table. Tested it. Placed three notebooks and three pens on a smaller table beside one chair. At an inner prompt I removed the notebooks and pens, deciding to see which chair Aneska preferred. I turned toward the fire to take a closer look at the painting.

"One of Kristers' finest," I heard as Aneska entered the room. "The flower is a snowdrop. In German, a Schneeglöckchen,." She leaned her cane by the door and continued warmly, "Good morning. Did you rest well?"

"Yes, thank you. And you?"

She picked up a photo from the table, turned it toward me. It was a picture of her and a man, her husband I assumed, from what appeared to be many decades ago. She sighed and said, "Ya, I did, though I still sometimes reach across the bed expecting him to be there. Nearly seventy years is a long habit."

Her vulnerability seemed as natural as walking into the room.

"No doubt. That's a long time," I said. "Sounds like I may need more ink and paper."

She chuckled, from which I took great pleasure. As she moved toward the seat I vacated, she began quoting one of my favorite hymns. "Could we with ink the ocean fill, And were the skies of parchment made, Were every stalk on earth a quill, And every man a scribe by trade." She sat down. I did as well. She gazed into the fire and continued the recitation, "To write the love of God above, would drain the ocean dry." Looking up at the painting she finished the stanza. "Nor could the scroll contain the whole, though stretched from sky to sky."

"That's one of my favorite hymns," I said.

"Ya, mine, too. Kristers introduced me to it. He had a lovely voice, before…" She trailed off for a moment and then amended to, "for a mathematician."

I regretted not hitting play on the recorder when she walked in, to capture the timbre of her voice reciting the hymn, the lament in her tone about the empty bed, and her hesitation and edit about Kristers' singing voice. I made a mental note for future sessions to hit the record button as soon as possible.

"Water?" I asked.

"Ya, please."

Her use of 'Ya', besides being very charming, obviously sprang from her native tongue, even though she had been in Ireland for a very long time. During the coming days, which turned into weeks, I would find many of Aneska's intimate memories triggered a natural response in German, which she was glad to translate. She credited the Irish that her English, and even Gaelic, had come a long way, but some things are best remembered in one's native tongue.

I told her my native tongue was Texan. That I would be glad to translate into English. We began with a good laugh. I filled two glasses from the pitcher and asked, "How long do we have today?"

"All morning, though let's take a brief break after mid-tea. If rehearsals in the afternoon wrap up early, maybe another craic later?"

I said that sounded good, whatever a 'craic' was. Turns out it means a good chat or conversation. I thanked her again, expressing how honored I was to be there, and hoped I would give her story the treatment it deserved. Her grace came as naturally as her vulnerability.

She said, "Friend, I have every confidence. I am also honored to be part of your story. Now, where would you like to begin?"

The six words I said next were the longest sentence I spoke till Zuza brought tea at 10:00.

"Aneska, tell me about the light years." I pressed record and opened the first of many notebooks. Aneska sighed and began her story in simple elegance. Over the course of the morning, she requested certain photos from the long table. I brought them to her and returned them to their places as she spoke. Here is the story I came four thousand miles to hear.

* * *

My early years were beyond beautiful. I was born Miriam Aneska Pfeiffer on the morning of April 4, 1929, in Hamburg, Germany. My father, Carl Deitrich Pfeiffer, owned a fishing fleet of three boats. The largest one harbored in Hamburg to fish the North Sea. It was named "der Fischkönig." The Fish King. All the fishermen thought Papa was the best. The other two boats harbored in Lübeck, an hour northeast on the Baltic Sea. Their names were "Freiheit des Meeres," Liberty of the Sea and "Gegen den Wind," Against the Wind. I always thought their names sounded like storybooks.

Papa met my mother, Miriam, when he was forced to lay in for repairs in Malmo, Sweden. I have only that one picture of just the two of them arm in arm. *She pointed to it. I got up and brought it to her. She held it as she talked.*

Mama was a nurse. She came to the boat to tend one of the crew injured in a fight with a Swedish fisherman. Papa told me he was in love from the moment he held her hand to help her on board. He walked with her after, convinced her to stop for supper. She was part Jewish, which made no difference to Papa. One side of his Pfieffer family tree went back in Sweden. The attraction was mutual. She was tall and beautiful, well-spoken and educated. He looked like a Viking, blonde and muscular. Mama said he had a "vittrad ömhet" from a life on the sea. That's Swedish for 'weathered tenderness.' He often called her his "bester fang," his best catch. Everyone knew Papa as Kapitän Carl. Mama called him Deit.

I had two brothers, Wilhelm and Jakob. They grew up crewing the boats with Papa. And protecting me from boys and caddy girls. They adored me. They were my shining knights. I have only one picture of them together. It's there.

I retrieved it.

We were all together in this picture.

She pointed to Wilhelm, his arm around Jakob's shoulder. Then Miriam, Carl at her other side, his arm behind her, laying on Wilhelm's arm. Young Aneska stood in front leaning back on them with her arms spread across them all. Like she was presenting them to the world. She continued.

So many families lost every photo in the war. But that's not part of the light years.

Four weeks after they met, Papa crossed the Baltic to meet Mama's family and bring her to Hamburg. Her father, Jakob, refused to give his blessing. He was not pleased that Papa was German and over five years older, but furious that he was not Jewish, and even worse, a confirmed Lutheran. Mama told her parents she was doing what Ruth did in the Bible. Where Deit goes, she would go. His Gott would be her Gott and Papa's people her people. Kapitän Carl later redeemed himself in Jakob's eyes. Papa smuggled Jews across the Baltic to Sweden for four years. *She said this with great pride.* But that's a story for later.

We weren't rich but we had more than most. Besides the boats, Papa had an old car. And a truck for carrying ice and fish. My earliest memories are of the docks. Every time they pushed off and returned Papa rang the ship's bell three times, for 'ich liebe dich', I love you. It was always exciting to watch them unload the catch. The shiny mounds of herring and cod were so beautiful, like piles of silver and gold bars. My favorites were the trout and salmon. We ate fish so often Papa used to check me for gills.

Her laugh was like music.

One Christmas, Papa surprised Mama with a piano. I was not quite five. She played early on, but not so much after leaving Sweden. While the men were at sea, she taught me English, some Swedish, how to read and write. And how to read music. She recognized my passion for it. Mama told me she believed the piano was really a gift for me.

I practiced constantly. With her help, in four weeks I was playing Prelude in C by Back, "A Well-Tempered Clavier." It's mostly single whole notes in the left hand and arpeggiated chords in the right. But it got my fingers working and opened my ears with its wonderful bouquet of chords. In the next month I mastered Gymnopedie No.1 by Erik Satie. I resisted that one because it was so sad.

Mama told me, "All of life will not be a minuet, mein liebling, my darling."

Music made sense to me. I didn't know then it would help make sense of life. Before I turned six, I could play Minuet in G by Bach and the first movements of his Sonata in D Major and Beethoven's Moonlight Sonata. I even began improvising a few pieces of my own. Mama invited a Professor Nachtneder from the Hamburg Konservitorium to hear me. Isn't that an unfortunate name? It means "night fog." For the next year, twice a month, I took lessons from him there. He was stern but brilliant. My parents worried about the cost. I heard Mama tell Papa, "Aneska's gift will make a way for her, Deit." I remember so clearly, when he tucked me in that night, I told him I could just play at home and learn from Mama.

"Aneska, my angel," Papa said, "Ich werde die Boote bedienen. I will work the boats. Du bearbeitest die Klaviertasten. You work the piano keys."

In the summer after my fifth birthday, 1934, Dr. Nachtneder came to our house again. The Konservatory wanted to sponsor me. A full scholarship! I was in heaven! But the day I officially started, Herr Dr. forbade me to play Gymnopedie because it was by a French composer, not a German. It was my earliest encounter with tyranny. In my young head, I remember wondering why someone would forbid beauty. I understood why the students called him Dunkler Schatten, Dark Shadow, behind his back. Or just Dr. Nacht. Dr. Night. He also called Satie's piece 'unangemessen.' Isn't that an ugly word? It means 'inappropriate.' A friend told me Gymnopedie was French for 'nude dance accompanied by song.' We giggled. Naturally, I wanted to play it even more.

It was one of Kristers' favorites. *Aneska chuckled.* Sometimes, he would set the sheet music on top of the stack by the piano, you know, to signal he wanted, well, you know. He didn't need words.

Where was I? Oh, ya. The week after my sixth birthday, my first recital was held with other students at Laeiszhalle. Bring me that photo with my parents, please.

I did. She placed the photo on the table between us.

Imagine it. Strauss, Stravinsky and Liszt played there! Mama and I walked around the statue of Brahms in the foyer. Did you know he was born in Hamburg? And Mendelssohn, too. Miraculously, this historic hall survived the war, even the terrible firebombing the summer of '43. I discovered later it was built with the fortune of a shipowner, Carl Heinrich Laeisz. My Papa owned simple fishing boats. But Herr Laeisz owned giant ships. I love that. Sometimes life composes harmony only heaven can hear.

I immediately wrote down that statement, thinking, with that kind of elegance and aphoristic expression, she would make a good songwriter.

Mama's parents, my "farföräldrar" in Swedish, which I have forgotten most of, they came all the way from Malmo for my first recital. I wore an enormous bow in my hair like the girls did then. Dark blue, like my dress. While other students played Für Elise and Minuet in G, I played Brahms' Intermezzo Opus 118, No. 2. Very emotional. Very nostalgic. Very few composers blend love, sorrow, nostalgia, pain and hope like Brahms.

Papa cried. After the recital he handed me a large bouquet. There was a post party. Next day my name was even in the paper. Mama framed it. The review said I was the standout player of the evening, but the Brahms piece was too emotionally mature and 'nicht zugänglich,' inaccessible, for a six-year-old. Oh, mein Gott! What has age to do with longing? I knew even then music would be my life. I could not have known it would save my life.

Honestly, I basked in the praise. Mama saw that. She knew how obsessed I was with music. That I was gifted for it. She found a way to bring me back down to earth.

About a week later, Mama sat me down at our piano and talked about what an opus was. I knew the word, of course, from titles on folios. That it meant a 'work.' She explained creation was an opus of Gott. But not his Magnum Opus. Not his greatest work. Every person within his creation is a high opus. And every person has at least one opus inside them, a purpose or calling. But even we are not his magnum opus. She believed music was most likely my opus. But she insisted music is not the Magnum Opus. There is only one Magnum Opus.

Mama brought out a sign. A friend of Papa's in the Hamburg shipyard stamped words in Latin into a piece of galvanized sheet metal kept on a boat for making repairs. Papa hung it on the wall over the piano. Mama taught me how to say it.

Dei magnum opus est amor

"Mein Schatz," she said, "these words mean, 'Gott's greatest work is love.'" She reminded me that scripture says, no matter how impressive your opus is to the world, without love, it means nothing. Do you know the passage, my friend? Corinthians 1 chapter 13?

Yes, the 'love chapter,' I said.

Precisely. Well, I got the message. And kept getting it every time I sat at that piano. When you go into the front music room, you will see the sign hanging there in direct sight for anyone who sits at that piano.

I was amazed that the sign survived the war and wanted to ask about it. How it made it to Ireland. But I stifled that impulse and obeyed my instinct – let Aneska keep talking. It wouldn't be the last time my silence paid off.

My time at Konservatory increased. Mama and I rode the street cars there and back several times a week. Hamburg was a beautiful city. Bustling markets and delicious pastry shops. Stately buildings and majestic old churches with tall steeples. Papa took us to church every Sunday when the fish were not running. Mama even got confirmed and baptized with my brothers and me. Papa bought her a small gold cross on a delicate chain. She wore it every day.

It was a lovely time. I remember skating with my brothers on the frozen lakes in winter and going to the beach in summer. Though the Baltic is cold even then. During fish runs, Papa and my brothers could be gone more than a week. And only home long enough to offload the catch and set out again. In winter, they were home more. The fireplace burned day and night. I cooked with Mama. Soups in winter, pork and beef with roast potatoes, boiled cabbage and brats. I still cannot make her apple pie without tears. Zuza makes Mama's pie now, too. In the evenings we played games, sang around the piano. Mama made up funny songs on the spot. She read us stories. Papa read the news out loud. It always irritated him.

Papa followed the boxer, Max Schmeling. I remember his and my brothers' excitement to see him fight in Hamburg. But Papa came home very angry. Schmelling won but did something that enraged him. After his victory, Schmelling gave the Nazi salute. That infuriated Papa. I remember because I was preparing my first recital and Papa asked me to play Debussy's "Claire du lune" to calm him down.

Because my parents shielded me, I was nearly oblivious to most of the changes going on across Germany in 1935. Music absorbed me. I was more concerned about what color dress and bow to wear in my hair.

For instance, I had no idea in 1933, when I was only four, the government imposed a boycott of Jewish businesses. I didn't know what a boycott was. My parents shopped at many of those places. Papa sold fish to Jewish vendors.

I suppose my parents' protection is why those years still carry such delight. Of course, I had seen and heard the name Hitler. A large portrait of him hung in all my classrooms. But I think, because of my Papa's fury after the Schmeling fight, that was the first night it worried me.

Still, music and school and family were my daily world. Practicing was a pleasure. Every year I prepared two recitals. One in Fall and one in Spring. I became friends with many of the wonderful players in the orchestra, and watched them practice at Laeiszhalle with the other students. The manager of the hall, a very kind man, Herr Hans Benedict gave tickets to our whole family to attend their concerts. He would become another harmony that life would offer during the war. But I won't get ahead of myself.

Watching the philharmonic and guest artists made me dream of writing music and playing concerts with orchestras around the world. I imagined moving people. Bringing them together without words across barriers and cultures. Music brought my grandparents and parents together after a long silence. Maybe it was a little girl's dream, but it was my dream. And the way people responded to my playing fed it. I also imagined one day perhaps opening my own music academy called, "Beyond Words," which many years later we created here in Ireland after the war. It's just down the road in Carlow. We host many international students and work hand in hand with the Royal Irish Academy of Music in Dublin. And we owe it all to the compassion and generosity of Brynn O'Cullen.

Aneska pointed to the painting of the lady on the wall.

Oh, Gott shower her with blessings in glory. She's the reason we're sitting here. But I'll get to her. Let's see now.

Aneska took a drink of water, held the glass up and looked at it, pausing a long while. By the look on her face, I wondered what memory was washing over her. I waited.

I'm sorry. The simplest things, they…my mind jumped to the

moment Kristers and I first met. I was sitting at a piano. I had a little cough. He poured a glass of water and handed it to me with a small bow, but his eyes never left mine. Ah, but that comes later, too.

I was telling you about the boxer and recitals and the orchestra. Oh ya, I was preparing three of Mendelssohn's "Songs Without Words" for a Spring recital around my seventh birthday.

At this point, Zuza appeared at the door with a tray. Before enjoying midmorning tea, we took a brief break. I returned to the study first and started the recorder, not wanting to miss any nuggets. The best thing I captured was her laugh. Other than that, true to form she wanted to know about my life. After half an hour Zuza retrieved the tray. I didn't have to remind Aneska where she left off.

CHAPTER FIVE

THE SHADOWS

As I was saying, four weeks before my first recital, I had three Mendelssohn scherzos nearly memorized. This would be the Spring of 1936. Dr. Dunkler Schatten, I'm sorry, that's not very respectful. Dr. Nachtneder met my mother and me at the door and led us to his office. He informed us the Chamber of Culture in Berlin added Mendelssohn to the list of composers who were verboten, forbidden! Naturally, we were completely baff, open mouth. Flabbergasted, as you say.

Mendelssohn was a renowned German composer. Born in Hamburg! I remember it also shocked me that Herr Professor seemed pleased to announce that. He explained that Mendelssohn had some Jewish heritage and his grandfather, philosopher Moses Mendelssohn, his views were opposed to those of the Third Reich. His books were also verboten. I nearly blurted out that my grandparents in Sweden were Jewish. Mama grabbed my hand very hard and cut me off. She protested that Mendelssohn was a Christian, baptized in the Lutheran church. I was so confused.

Herr Nacht made no apology about my recital preparations. He handed us two lists. One of the approved German composers. The other of the banned ones.

If you know your history, the head of the Nazi Chamber of Culture in charge of the arts was Joseph Goebbels. A true fiend. He was the head of the Ministry of Public Enlightenment and Propaganda. They decided what films, art, music and literature were politically acceptable. And who was permitted to work in the arts. In 1934, the Chamber of Culture forbade all Jewish actors from stage or screen! Imagine how brazen to use the words "Enlightenment" and "Propaganda" together. Why not just come out and say it, "Our lies and false narratives will set you free from freedom! And your job!"

I'm sorry, for someone who claims to let the music do my talking, I am quite chatty these days about a great many things.

I told her no apology was necessary. That without her chattiness this book would be a brochure. She laughed. And continued.

For my recital, I could only choose from the approved list. My mother told him we would select a new piece. I tried to protest. Mama squeezed my hand again. We stood to leave. Dr. Nacht stood as well, stuck his arm up in the air and said, "Heil, Hitler." We left. Mama did not heil him back.

Waiting for the streetcar, Mama talked passionately about how great music rises from many cultures, but reaches beyond culture to our common humanity. Gott gives all people gifts. Nazis don't understand that. They were under the delusion that Gott placed them at the top of mankind, in every field. She also stressed that I must never say a word about our Jewish relatives. Things were changing in Germany. We must be very careful about saying certain things, even to our friends. I remember the gravity in her manner like a shadow on that sunny spring day.

That night, our family sat around the supper table and Papa explained it more. I had never seen him so grave. He said Germans had not stood against Hitler early on and now they were forced to bow. He insisted we would not bow, but we must take precautions. Jakob would begin using his first name, Papa's middle name, Deitrich. Papa tried to explain how the government defined people as Jews, not by how they practice religion, but from ancestry. Since my Opa was Jewish and Oma half Jewish, Mama was part Jewish, and so Wilhelm, Jakob and I were part Jewish by heritage, too. Even though we were all confirmed Lutherans. Imagine how disturbing for a seven-year-old!

But Papa wasn't done. He said even though the times were troubled, and evil seemed to be pushing back the light, Gott made it clear what happens to evil. He opened Mama's Bible and read Psalm 73. Most of the time, Mama read the Scriptures to us. That night, the verses in Papa's voice were the encouragement we needed. "Surely, Lord, you cast the wicked down to ruin. They are suddenly destroyed, completely swept away." Papa reassured us "Meine lieben Kinder, 'my dear children,' evil will not, cannot win."

I believed it. But we had no idea then how long that would take.

After the family talk, I wanted to hear some sad music. I played Gymnopedie No.3 by Erik Satie. The saddest of the three. Mama asked me to play it very softly. And only at home. Satie was on the verboten list. I didn't have words for it then, but in my free spirit, freedom died a little. Mama was right. Not all of life was a lively minuet.

The light years faded that night. More shadows were coming. Gott would have his work cut out to fulfill Psalm 73.

The next time we entered Konservitory, the atmosphere had completely changed. All the students were muted. Laughter felt out of place, almost verboten. There were whispered conversations. Mama and I chose Mozart's Fantasia in D Minor KV397 for the recital. Dr. Nachtneder suggested a lively piece by Beethoven. The joy in it felt like a lie. I fought him over it. He said I was free to choose any composer on the approved list. Even at age seven, I knew being free to choose any selection on the approved list was not freedom. Mama convinced him that on such short notice, the Mozart piece was within my grasp. We didn't say out loud that it spoke the way we both felt about the oppressive situation, or that I could already play Fantasia. We prevailed. But from that point we sensed Dr. Nachtneder's support for me wane.

My grandparents did not come for that recital. Or any more recitals. Papa reminded us not to talk about our disappointment or the reason they couldn't come. The cost of fear was more freedom lost. Freedom of expression. Freedom of association and travel. In my own composing, such as it was, I explored dark chords and odd melodies.

At what must have been great personal risk, Herr Benedict secreted some folios into my satchel before they were removed from the music library. Chopin, Mendelssohn, Liszt, Debussey, Tchaikovsky. That's how I discovered Béla Bartók. His Piano Sonata Sz. 80. I could tell just from the notes on the page and the subito forzando notations, he was working out something in his soul. I played it, rather, I tried to play it, only when everyone was out of the house. I inherited long fingers from both my parents, but I wasn't strong enough to play Bartók well. His discordant notes and abrupt stops spoke my own soul at the time. And his overhand technique improved mine greatly.

I learned after the war, Bartók was not Jewish, but said he would become one to protest the oppression going on in Austria and his home country, Hungary. His music sounds like someone who would say such a thing. It sounds like protest. No wonder he was on the verboten list. No wonder I liked hammering it on the piano. I still do not prefer his angular melodies, but at the time he gave voice to my angst.

Hamburg changed, too. Its beauty faded as the city became draped in long red and black Nazi banners and flags. Red like the blood most of us knew they intended to spill. Black like the hearts driving the madness. Many people on the subway didn't talk or laugh much. Except those who celebrated how Hitler was restoring Germany to greatness and would crush its enemies. The entire city grew quiet. Except the loudspeakers mounted on buildings and trucks. Announcements blared. And speeches. And sometimes Wagner's dramatic music.

One day, I remember Papa came home very upset. Hundreds of street names were being changed. Many historical names. No Jewish names allowed. Even names of second-degree mixed blood Jews. I asked if I was second or third-degree mixed blood. It makes my heart smile still what Papa said, "Schatz, we are covered by the blood of Jesus. We are first degree children of God. But if anyone asks, we are confirmed Lutherans."

About that same time, Mama framed another Latin quote and hung it over the inside of our front door. We could see it every time we left the house. You will see it in the same place in this house.

Marcet sine adversario virtus

It means, "Valor becomes weak without an opponent."

I naturally assumed that was the origin of her son's name, Valor. But waited to let her reveal that.

That summer, there was a bright spot for everyone. Even Papa. The summer Olympics came to Berlin. It gave all Germany a distraction from the growing shadows. I understood later Berlin was selected five years earlier, in 1931. Before Hitler came to power. Maybe at the time it was a gesture to welcome Germany back into the community of nations after the Great War. But the community of nations ignored Hitler's ideology. Can you imagine? If the world had known what he and his deviants were doing and planning? To oppress and exterminate an entire portion of the German people and rule Europe? And beyond? Who would turn a blind eye to that and choose such a nation to host the finest young athletes from around the world?

I remember the banners going up. I would bet money Goebbels himself came up with the motto. "Ich rufe die Jugend der Welt!" 'I call the Youth of the World!' Papa was not fooled. He said the Third Reich was targeting the youth. That Hitler himself had written, "Whoever has the youth has the future." At school, Wilhelm and Jakob came home with stories about "Race Science" being taught in biology. Everything became about race. Papa ranted that it was tearing the nation apart. That Hitler was raising up an army. And using the Olympics to show the world the superiority of the Aryan race.

Mein Freund, my friend, isn't this always the way of both good leaders and tyrants? Woo and win the children? I understand that. We do it at our own academy. But we woo and win them with freedom. Freedom of expression. We have no approved or verboten list of composers or music. Maybe that's more complex in popular music? You deal with words. Words can inspire and inflame. They can declare or twist the truth.

We had a lively discussion about whether art shapes or reflects culture. She said early on Kristers forcefully argued that science shaped culture more than art. Pointing at his painting over the mantle she said wistfully,

But he saw the light.

She paused, like a memory was playing out in her mind's eye. Apparently, that was a story for later. She picked up where she left off.

I remember our family listening to the Olympic events on the radio and seeing some of the newsreels at the theater. Papa noticed with great pleasure only the British team did not give the "Seig Heil" at the opening ceremonies. I fell in love with the British national anthem. "Gott save the Queen." It was like a regal hymn. I had to learn it.

Every time the American, Jessie Owens, a black man, won a gold medal, Papa cheered. The German band had to play a brief version of "The Star-Spangled Banner." When Owens won his fourth gold,

Papa exploded. It's one of the few times I heard foul language come out of his mouth.

"Überlegenes Rennen, mein arsch! Hitler ist ein verdammt böser idiot!" That means, 'Superior race, my ass! Hitler is a damned evil idiot!' *She chuckled.* Papa apologized for his language and put on his grave voice again. He warned us emphatically not to repeat any of that — to anyone. The consequences for all of us, including Mama's parents, would be severe.

After Papa's strong words, Mama added her wisdom, as she often did. She asked us how many kinds of flowers there are in the world? Too many to count, we answered. And how many kinds and shapes and colors of people in the world? Same answer.

She said, "Gott made all the flowers and all the people. Does he love all the flowers and all the people? Does He make all people in his image?" Yes, of course, we answered. But I had a question, too.

I asked her if God loves evil idiots like Dr. Nachtneder and Hitler. Her brow furrowed. She gave Papa a look, then smiled at us. I will never forget her answer.

"Ya, meine Schätz, 'my treasures,' but flowers cannot choose good or evil. People can. What does Scripture say? 'Hate evil, hold on to what is good. Pray for your enemies. And do good to those who persecute you.'"

The last thing I wanted to do to Dr. Nacht was good. While we all listened to the Olympics, Mama took me into the kitchen. Side by side, we made two apple pies. One for our family. And one for Herr Nachtneder and Hans Benedict. Of course, baking for Herr Benedict was a pleasure. But in my mind, Nachtneder didn't deserve a pie. Except maybe in his face.

While we baked, Mama talked. We talked a lot while we baked. She reminded me of what Pastor Weber taught us in confirmation about forgiveness and absolution. I didn't understand all those big church words, like atonement and Versöhnung, reconciliation. Mama put it simply. "We forgive. God absolves. We don't excuse Herr Nachtneder's behavior, but forgiving him frees us from the power and damage of it."

As we cleaned up the kitchen, she said we were absolving the dishes. Cleansing them from the mess. That's what Jesus does with our sin. Forgiving Nachtneder, might help him see his mess and seek the Lord's cleansing, absolution. It's not up to us to clean him up. We forgive. God absolves.

I only had one pushback. 'But Mama, the dishes didn't get themselves dirty. We make the mess.'

She didn't hesitate. "Excellent point, mein Schatz. We make our own messes. The Lord chose to wash us, atone for our sin and absolve our guilt, wash us clean with his own life blood. Our part is to confess our mess and ask him to clean us up."

I loved our talks.

The next day at noon, before my lesson, we delivered the pie to Herr Nachtneder and Herr Benedict. Mama made me hand the pie to Dr. Nachtneder. He didn't know what to say. Herr Benedict insisted we all share it together for lunch. We actually sat around a table together and ate. What a simple thing. From that moment, I felt Herr Nachtneder's tone soften a little with us. I have never forgotten the power of kindness. Or how it can strengthen valor in the face of an opponent.

I remember lying on my bed being puzzled at hate. The kind of hate for people you don't even know. The more organized the hate grew in Hamburg, the more confused I became. There was certainly anger and hate in my own heart. But mine was justified, of course. It was easy to hate evil, but how could I possibly want good for evildoers?

Despite the détente of the apple pie, the next day in my lessons I pounded the piano more forcefully. I was, after all, still very much a child. And my Papa's daughter. Dr. Nachtneder scolded me harshly to be more gentle with certain passages. So much for apple pie diplomacy. He screamed at me, "This isn't Bartok!" Even a child smells and recoils at that kind of duplicity. Be mean to insist I be gentle? Seriously? I made him an apple pie, and this is what I get? It was all I could do not to lash out at him. Knowing my mother sat outside the room kept my tongue in check. I broke down in tears. He had no idea what to do but call Mama in and take a break.

It wouldn't be long before I learned that defeating evil sometimes takes more than kindness. Sometimes it takes sacrifice and blood. The entire world would soon learn. Again.

Zuza appeared in the door again. Lunch was ready. The last hour and a half seemed like twenty minutes. She reminded Aneska that Frieda and the Concertmaster with a string quartet would arrive at 1:30. Time enough to eat and rest a bit before rehearsal.

Four of us dined together for the first time. Aneska, Zuza, me and the chef, Maja, an attractive Swedish woman whom I guessed to be under thirty. Her accent and energy were delightful. They called her Magic Maja, and I soon understood why. She served us piping hot tomato basil soup with slices of ham encrusted in breadcrumbs on the side. A Swedish Julskinka, Maja called it. Plus, three kinds of local cheeses and a flax seed loaf still steaming from the oven. The conversation centered on preferences for supper, and some issues and scheduling at the music academy. Maja inquired about Nashville. She was a big country music fan. I wanted to ask Zuza about her husband and his relation to Brynn O'Cullen. But left that for another time.

After lunch, I returned to my quarters. I spent most of the afternoon transcribing Aneska's storytelling. For ten minutes I stood in the front foyer to bask in the stirring sounds of strings and piano coming from behind the doors of the music room. At 4:45 p.m., Zuza stopped by to inform me her mother would not have time for another session till the next morning at 8:00.

For the next two weeks, this became our pattern. Except twice when rehearsals happened in the morning. On a few days, Aneska managed an afternoon session around tea in the solarium. Once, she traveled to Dublin for preparations at the National Concert Hall, which gave me a lovely day to explore the grounds.

On our fourth day together I asked only one question to start us off: Aneska, when would you say the second movement of your life began?

Second Movement – Beyond Belief

CHAPTER SIX

THE TYRANNY

If I had to point to one moment, the second movement of my life began that day at Konservitory, crying in Mama's arms. Through my tears as a child, I couldn't possibly see the big picture. And how I was being swept up in it. But I knew things would never be the same.

Aneska stared into the fireplace. Thoughts tumbled out like notes she had played many times in her mind.

When we are children, we see the world in a very narrow, near-sighted way. We only see how things affect us and those closest to us. Those we care about. We see outcomes. Not the causes out there in the big wide world. We don't know the forces set in motion long before we are born. Forces that will impact us directly, for good or ill. From out of the blue, it seems. But most of those forces are not out of the blue. They've been set in motion, intentionally. As a child, you don't know the struggle for freedom and the darkness that battles against it has been raging for centuries. That it's a worldwide struggle. And it usually takes much longer to discover the battle is not just out there. It's in every human heart.

Like all the children of my youth, I had no idea detention and death camps like Dachau were being built while I was learning to read and practicing piano. Or that verboten books were being burned at universities. All this happened immediately after Hitler became Chancellor, in 1933. I was four. In my heart and family, I was born into the freedom of Christ. In my country, I inherited tyranny.

You, my friend, are the recipient of great freedom in your country. Established long before you were born. Freedom of speech, religion, assembly and more. I have studied and watched your country, founded on the freedom and the rights Gott grants. I traveled there once. To Philadelphia. To speak at a music school conference. I visited Independence Hall and saw your cracked Liberty Bell. I'm aware of your country's ongoing struggle against forces that oppose freedom. This struggle is a human thing. Even your brilliant founders set forth ideals many of them did not fully live by. But liberty rings true even from cracked hearts.

Obviously, I jotted that down.

The child born to be your first president and the child born into slavery both longed for freedom. Both knew slavery was not right in the eyes of Gott and not in line with his design written on their hearts. It took great sacrifice and blood to align your country with its founding ideals. Those ideals are why your nation and your Lady Liberty have always held out a light to those yearning to be free. It still does.

The struggle for freedom and adherence to those ideals continues through endless legislation and conflict. Here in Ireland as well. And around the world. But ultimately, alignment with Gott's ideals by nations can only be done on the inside of a human heart, by Christ. Law and force will never accomplish what only love can do.

There it was. A song idea. 'What Only Love Can Do.' It would not be the last one. I already knew better than to interrupt her flow.

Sadly, there are always people who would rather have control than freedom. To those who prefer power, freedom is threatening. It's an obstacle. So, the struggle continues all around the world, between the light of God's ideals and the stubborn, scheming hubris in the hearts of people craving power.

The forces pulling my country into the darkness of that time were strategically set in motion before I was born. In 1920, just two years after Germany's defeat in the Great War, the Nazi party defined its mission. To establish a nation, a world, built on the Aryan race. Instead of "all men are created equal," they brazenly believed all Aryans are created superior. In fact, Hitler believed Gott created Aryan blood spiritually superior. It's in his writings and speeches - that race is the key to world history, all conflict and all human culture. He proclaimed the elite were destined to dominate the world and rule over the masses of inferior races.

Too many in my nation could not resist the lure of being part of that elite, the chosen, the powerful. Hitler appealed to the darkest nature in humanity, a false nobility that gave them value and identity based on genetics. And a false spirituality and might, not based on the Gott-breathed value of every human life. For Hitler and his deluded tribe, it was not, "For Gott so loved the world." It was, "For Gott so loved the Aryans."

As the world can attest, the results were beyond belief. Drunk on that hubris, they launched a world war that ruthlessly deprived millions of life, liberty and the pursuit of their own destinies.

It was obvious she had done a lot of thinking about these things. I couldn't help wondering if these cascading thoughts and emotions would be reflected in her concerto. I asked her.

I'll let you decide that for yourself. All I will say now is I would rather play you what I just said than speak it. But there is a time when these things must be spoken as well. The sooner the better. When fear makes good people silent, darkness gains strength. And fear has always been the dominant weapon of tyrants. Many of my countrymen kept silent and exonerated themselves from complicity. But even those who never fire a bullet, if they make speaking freely dangerous or censor and punish the fearless for speaking out, they play a duet with evil. Even as a seven-year-old girl, I began to feel and see that fear and evil all around.

I was born into a family that loved Gott and tried to honor his ways. Honestly, at the time I loved music more than Gott. Until the music was stripped from us, I saw Dr. Nachtneder as merely a stern, unhappy man and a great nuisance. A threat to my personal freedom. I had no idea that an army of Nachtneders and worse, was being gathered against all that we believed.

Not long after the verboten list of composers appeared, two students, Ben and Hannah Blum, were gone. They were teenagers. Ben was an extraordinary violinist, destined for greatness. His sister, a pianist like me. She even tackled some Rachmaninov. And not just his "Daisies." That's the caliber player she was. Of course, that Russian composer made the verboten list. We were told Ben and Hannah moved to another city. But a few weeks later, Mama and I saw Ben and his mother on a streetcar. She told us Ben and Hannah were removed because of their Jewish relatives in Latvia. The Blums were not even practicing Jews!

Like I said, as a child I only saw the outcomes of the dark forces mutating Germany. I often overheard my parents talking in the kitchen about troubling things. That Papa was not supposed to do business with people who were our friends or a nearby shop that closed because of a boycott. I only knew the word 'boycott' because of shopping with Mama. The Deutsches Jungvolk, boys too young to join the Hitler Youth, they linked arms in front of Jewish businesses to keep people from shopping there. One of Jakob's friends even bragged that his mother bought his uniform, a brown shirt and black shorts, at a Jewish clothing store that he blockaded!

During that time, many of my brothers' friends joined the military. Herr Nachtneder proudly announced that one of his sons was training to be a fighter pilot. Papa said none of it was voluntary. The young men were all drafted. I didn't know what that meant either. But I learned the sting of it in when Wilhelm and Jakob, Deiter as we then called him, were forced to join the Hitler Youth.

In 1937, the Boy Scouts became verboten and at age fourteen all boys were required to join the Hitler Youth. Papa managed an exemption for my brothers, and from the required six months of service with the Reich Labor Service. As fishermen, they were essential to feed the German people. They were still required to attend a Hitler Youth camp for three weeks for physical and paramilitary training. They came home with cruel stories of harassment and long marches and rituals. In small groups they took turns reading aloud Hitler's manifesto, "Mein Kampf." Everyone had to box someone till blood flowed. Every boy was required to shout an oath of complete allegiance to the Führer. Papa went into the basement. We heard shouting and things breaking.

At my school the shadows grew darker, too. Some books disappeared, and new ones arrived, praising the Aryan race and Hitler. There were books denigrating Jews. I vividly remember "Der Giftpilz." The Poisonous Mushroom. A blond German mother and her young, blond son go into the forest to collect mushrooms. The good mother warns him about the poisonous ones. She tells him mushrooms are like people. Good and bad. And the most poisonous people are the Jews.

Even without the guidance of my parents, I knew that was sehr stinkend, very stinky. Papa was never one to hold back. He told me, "Mein Shatz, the real poison is the one who wrote that book. And your teacher for trying to poison your mind."

I liked the title of another book, "Never Trust a Fox on the Green Heath." But the title was deceiving. On one page, it had a picture of a tall, shirtless, healthy young man standing in a field. He was leaning on a shovel. On the opposite page was a short, very fat, cigar smoking man with a valise. He looked like he was limping down the street. My teacher, Herre Krause, drew a vertical line down the blackboard. She asked us to point out the differences. Students eagerly raised their hands with observations. The teacher wrote them on the board. Tall/Short. Blonde/Bald. Muscular/Fat. Handsome/Ugly. Healthy/Crippled. Clean shaven/Stubbly beard. Working the land/Doing a deal. One student laughed and said even the fat man's red polka dot tie was ugly.

When our teacher asked, "Who is the man on the left?," a chorus of voices answered, 'a true German.' "And the man on the right?" Same chorus, 'an ugly Jew.'

Indoctrination and hatred were not subtle.

Herre Krause was much more than a stocky woman, to put it kindly. I made the mistake of raising my hand and asked if there was a weight limit to being a good German. The whole class laughed. I knew my motive. I sinned once when I asked it, and again when I enjoyed the laughter. I had to stay after school. Herre Krause lectured me on disrespecting and questioning authority. She wrote a note to my parents. Can you guess my Papa's reaction? He threw the note in our fireplace.

At Schule, school, first thing every morning we were required to stand, face the portrait of Hitler, lift one arm and say in unison, "Sieg Heil." All my teachers talked about complete obedience to the state and the Führer. They all wore a Frauenschaft badge of the Nazi group for women. I can still see it on their lapels. A black triangle with a white cross and red swastika in the middle of the cross. I didn't know that all across Germany teachers joined the Nazi party more than any group, shaping young minds into bigots and fanatics. I only saw the behavior of my own teachers.

Maybe you've heard it said, "Racists are not born. They are made." My teachers tried every day to make us racists by making everything about race.

One day, I came home from school and asked my mother what a 'bastard' was. Needless to say, she was shocked and wanted to know where I heard that word. I told her my teacher said Jews and some other groups were bastard races. That night, I heard Mama tell Papa about it in the kitchen. As the Irish say, he made a holy show of himself.

The tone in Aneska's voice reflected the anguish of the retelling.

Like Hamburg, I changed. I became less friendly. Less talkative. It was safer. I tried to keep my head down in my studies and focused on my music. I began composing some of my own music. To get things out. I'm sure you understand that, my musical friend. Mama loved playing hymns, so I'm sure that influenced my early piece called "Lieber Herr Jesus, Nimm Meine Hand." Dear Lord Jesus, Take My Hand. Unlike a hymn, it has no words. Very simple. It was my unspoken prayer. And it helped me explore melody and mood. Kristers loved it. Zuza thinks I should play it myself at the end of the concerto. Like a denouement or encore. I'm considering it. I'll play it for you some time.

Do I have to tell you how much I looked forward to that?

I was too young to be required to join the League of German Girls until my tenth birthday in April 1939. That summer, it was mandatory to attend some events and activities. Would it surprise you to know the leaders reprimanded me repeatedly in front of the other girls for my lack of enthusiasm? *She chuckled.* But Mama was right. My musical ability made a way for me. With a bit of acting, I played the rousing songs meant to instill fervor for Germany and its glorious future.

There were several firm "invitations" to perform at the birthday parties of high-ranking Nazi officials. But always with a group of singers. No piano solos. I didn't see the reason for this. But Papa did. He said solo performances focused too much on the individual. Songs were used by the Reich to create solidarity. I didn't know that word at the time. But I witnessed it in the meetings and festivals. There was such high energy, emotion and national pride.

She recited a bit of one of the songs.

Onward, onward, fanfares are joyfully blaring.
Onward, onward, youth must be fearless and daring.
Germany, your light shines true, even if we die for you.

I was my Papa's daughter. And I had no intention of dying for the third Reich.

As a child, how was I to know the force behind it all believed the state was far more important than the individual. That the state was an instrument to build a pure Aryan culture. And building the spirit of National Socialism could not be left up to parents. The schools and mandatory youth programs took on that role. I was just one little girl in a sea of change. I felt so false playing that music. Papa told me, "Aneska, play along with your fingers, but not your heart." So, I did. At the time, I didn't think of it as playing a duet with evil.

But let me back up some. The summer before that, I heard my father shouting for joy in the sitting room. My brothers were confused, too. Papa had just heard that the American boxer Joe Louis knocked out Germany's champion, Max Schmelling. In the first round! In America. At Yankee Stadium. Just before the Olympics in 1936, the Nazis touted Schmelling as a prime specimen of the Aryan Race after he beat Louis, a black man, on American soil, also in Yankee Stadium. Papa loved Schmelling but he celebrated his loss to Louis.

"It's a sign," Papa said. "Don't you see? Just like Jesse Owens, this madness can be beaten!" But it would take more than a one round knockout. Far worse was yet to come.

In November of that year, 1938, the darkness roared. I was nine.

You've probably heard about the Night of Broken Glass, Kristallnacht. I saw and heard it. We all did. The fires. The smoke. The shouting and gunfire. Papa predicted it. On a Wednesday, November 9, Mama and I came home from my afternoon lesson at Konservitory. Papa called a family meeting. He told us not to go out. There was going to be trouble. A German diplomat had been assassinated on Monday in Paris by a student, a Polish Jew. That night near midnight, a noise woke us up. Men running and shouting in the streets. We heard windows being smashed. Papa looked. The Jewish businesses down the street were being destroyed. Places we shopped. Someone knocked on our door. It was a Jewish family of five who owned one of the shops. They lived above it. Papa let them in. They stayed the night. I helped Mama make beds on the floor. The synagogue near us burned. The light from the flames flickered through the curtains in my room.

Riots went on for two days. We couldn't see this was happening all over Germany and Austria. More than a thousand synagogues burned. Jews were killed by mobs. No one knew that by order of the Gestapo, the police did nothing. Firemen were instructed to watch synagogues burn. And protect only Aryan buildings that might catch fire. The violence was staged to look like spontaneous demonstrations. Also out of our sight, across the country, thirty thousand Jewish men were rounded up and shipped to Dachau and Buchenwald. They were put to work expanding the camps.

My mother told me later Kristallnacht was the last straw for Papa. Unknown to me, he began smuggling Jews to Sweden in his boats. My brothers were in on it. So were my Opa and Oma across the Baltic. I was the only one who didn't know.

For the next year, Mama and I continued as much a normal routine of school and piano lessons as we could. But normal was gone. So were some people. Some of them our neighbors.

Papa always had a sixth sense about these things. One morning in February of the next year, Papa woke us up. But not for school. It was a Tuesday. We were excused from school because "the devil himself," that's what Papa called Hitler, was in Hamburg to christen a battleship. We had seen the Führer two years before, when he christened a large ocean liner. But we couldn't get very close that time. Papa wanted us to see and hear the monster leading Germany to ruin. A metalworker at the shipyard, one of Papa's friends, got us within fifty meters of Hitler.

The ship was enormous. With massive guns. Sailors lined the railings. Flags fluttered all over it. Hitler made a speech in front of it about why he chose the name Bismarck. I didn't understand. He just sounded angry and full of pride. Papa told me Bismarck went to war with other countries to unify Germany, and our current madman claimed he himself would unify Germany's power even more.

When we got home from seeing Hitler…

When she said that, I had one of those indelible moments that connected me to the world stage and made history 3D. Like the time my friend Hardy and I shook Margaret Thatcher's hand as she made her way up the aisle after she spoke at Vanderbilt University. Or the night with the same friend and fellow musician, we met one of the creators of the soundtrack of our lives, Ringo. We had backstage passes after his All-Starr Band concert. He signed my pass and handed me an autographed pair of drumsticks for my drummer son, Will. All I could think to say was, "Thank you for all the music." Ringo looked me in the eye and in his Liverpool accent, in the same voice that sang, "I get by with a little help from my friends," he simply said, "Ooh, you're welcome."

But this moment with Aneska went to a new height and depth. How many people left on the planet can say "When we got home from seeing Hitler?" Looking at Aneska I had the profound, time-pausing sense that I was in the presence of an eyewitness to one of the most horrific upheavals in human history. The light blue eyes looking into my own had seen and heard the evil architect of it all. By contrast, the serenity of our setting felt close to miraculous. I knew I hadn't heard the worst of it. The magnitude and pathos of it must have registered on my face somehow. Aneska asked,

Are you alright? Would you like to take a break?

She poured me a glass of water. I took a drink and told her no, I was fine. Just trying to take it all in. Please continue.

When we got home from seeing Hitler, Papa said to us, "Kinder, a man like Hitler doesn't build a warship that big to keep the peace."

The next week, he and Mama began storing dry goods in the basement. This was to be another family secret. Mama bought us clothes we didn't need. Papa said we were stocking up because Hitler was taking Germany to war. In late August, when official rationing of food began Papa said, "Here it comes." Less than a week later, September first of 1939, Germany invaded Poland. Papa was right. He was right a lot. But even he couldn't see it all.

On the same day, hidden from us and most of Germany, Hitler gave doctors the power to euthanize anyone suffering from a physical or mental handicap. Including children! Anyone who the Nazis considered "not worthy of life." Which included all Jews. Hitler called many groups "subhuman." It sounds monstrous even to say it. Who knows how many Itzhak Pearlmans the world lost! Thank Gott Itzhak's parents left Germany before the war.

Aneska was incensed and visibly upset, like I hadn't seen before. I poured more water in her glass. It struck me how keen her memory was. After a moment I asked her about how that was.

I assume you have scars. And you can tell me how you got each one, right? All my scars have stories, too. Most of them are on the inside. But let's not forget, our blessings have stories, too. And besides, I've had seven decades to see in hindsight what I couldn't see then. To remember and discover how that darkness captured so many and shook the world.

My friend, there is so much. More than a single book can hold. Please, feel free to separate the wheat from the chaff.

I thanked her and told her it's a good thing I don't need a gluten-free diet because in my view, every word she spoke was whole wheat. She laughed and said,

Kind and funny are good side dishes.

It was my turn to laugh. She said,

Maybe you should write that down?

I guess I don't have to tell you I did. She continued.

The war occupied our daily lives. Identity papers were issued to everyone. Every time we left the house there was the anxiety of being stopped. Soldiers were everywhere. More and more regulations governed our lives. Especially the Jews. Their identity cards carried a large J. They couldn't attend schools, own a bicycle, go to a movie or sporting event. There were even signs in the parks to remind Jews they were not permitted to sit on the benches! Can you imagine?

Well, maybe you can. The same thing went on in parts of your country during the same time. Black people couldn't eat in certain places or sit in the front of buses. Or use the same water fountains as white people, right? The Third Reich took it even farther. Papa said they would regulate our breathing if they could. For Jews and many others, this proved to be a deadly truth.

For the next two years, the loudspeakers around Hamburg announced the brilliant victories of the Führer, usually followed by Wagner's music. Attending public celebrations was mandatory. But the fervor grew less in volume and sincerity. Apparently, we were not the only ones faking it. Or tired of food and gas rationing and curfews.

At the end of the summer, 1941, the infamous yellow Star of David appeared. All Jews over the age of six were required to wear it in public. At all times. We got a pamphlet from Ministry of Propaganda and Enlightenment instructing German citizens how we should respond to neighbors wearing the yellow star. That's another time foul words erupted from Papa's mouth. He burned the pamphlet in the fireplace like that letter from my teacher.

The first time I saw Ben and Hannah Blum on the street with their stars, let's just say, like Papa, I nearly made a holy show of myself. Only Mama's painful squeeze on my hand prevented it. She and Papa kept assuring me Ben and Hannah would be fine. I wondered how they could be sure.

Papa and my brothers continued to fish. And smuggle Jews apparently. I heard him tell Mama that seventy-five percent of their catch was confiscated at the docks for the war effort. But Papa often returned with more than fish. Cheese, venison jerky, lamb, sausages, and my favorites, butter and sugar. Things none of our neighbors could get easily. Papa told us he traded fish to other fishermen for those things. Once he brought home pastries. When I noticed they were just like the ones Oma baked with me, he said he got them from Swedish fishermen. Years later, I understood where he got all those provisions.

One day, Papa came home from the boats with a dark bruise around his eye. A Nazi officer backhanded him for not returning his "Sieg Heil." I told Papa, "Play along with your hand. Just don't salute with your heart. I have to every day at school." Like my Papa's animosity to the Third Reich, the Bartok rebel rose in me, a trait which would eventually bring my biggest trouble and most profound blessing.

The mounting casualties of the war became hard to hide. More than a few times, military cars drove into our neighborhood. Soldiers with black arm bands rang at a door. Everyone knew they brought hard news. I imagined the same was happening in Britain and America and many countries. The pride of sacrificing for the

Fatherland began to crumble under the weight of grief. Reports of successes became fewer.

Because Mama was a nurse, she volunteered at a hospital. Some nights, I snuck downstairs and listened to her tell Papa about the horrible wounds she saw. I wrote a piece called "Reflection in A" thinking about all the wounded soldiers. On both sides. It was adagio, nearly rubato. A very sparce, delicate melody, like Eric Satie, with some improvisation over the same repeating four chords in the left hand. The main figure reprised in octaves. Next rainy day when you're missing your children, I'll play it for you.

I told her it doesn't have to rain for me to miss my children.

Of course. I feel the same about mine.

At my parents' insistence, I kept up my piano studies. One day at Konservitory, Dr. Nachtneder arrived a few minutes late. I was at the piano playing "Reflection." When he came in, I stopped. To my surprise he asked me to keep playing. He sat behind me. Across the room. I heard him crying softly. When he finally spoke, all the gruff was gone. He actually said the piece was lovely. I kept playing. He asked without derision if it was Eric Satie.

"Nein," I said. "It's just a kritzeln, a scribble, mein Herr. One of mine."

He asked what I called it. "Reflexion in A, mien Herr."

The next thing that happened reconfirmed my life's mission.

He stood beside me and asked, "Darf ich?" 'May I?'

I scooted over on the bench. He sat down on my right. That had never happened. If he wanted to show me something I always stood up and let him be seated. This time he prompted me to keep arpeggiating the chords below middle C.

Imagine my astonishment when Dr. Nachtneder, that hardened, severe taskmaster, played my simple theme exactly. Tenderly. The same bristly tyrant who seemed glad to banish much of the world's beautiful music played my little song. With a fragile touch. Like he was finding his way down a path never taken. I knew he was brilliant. We kept playing, his face still wet from crying. He didn't even wipe the tears away. Time evaporated. He played notes only the two of us and heaven will ever hear. We played maybe three or four minutes. Without speaking, we retarded together. I let an A chord ring over octave Ds. The silence still felt like music. An indefinite rest.

When he finally spoke, all he said was, "Danke, Aneska. I will see you Wednesday."

After I closed the door, the arpeggiated chords began again.

On the streetcar going home, Mama told me one of Herr Nachtneder's sons was killed in a dogfight over France. The war would never be distant again.

I was twelve.

The next year, in the Spring of 1942, the war came closer. The British bombed Lübeck, not an hour from Hamburg. It was the first German city to feel the impact of a large air assault. Three weeks earlier, like he knew it was coming, Papa sold his big boat, "der Fischkönig," and moved the two in Lübeck east to a small harbor near Wismar. Papa was sure the Hamburg docks, U-Boat bunkers and armaments on the west side would be targeted. Its defenses were stronger than Lübeck's, but it was only a matter of time. A month or so later, bombs dropped on our hometown for the first time.

It was very pretty in Wismar. But farther from home than Lübeck. The Navy drafted Papa's other crew. So, with only one boat, he and the boys were gone more. We visited and stayed with them a lot. Wilhelm, Jakob and I slept on one boat. Papa and Mama took the other one. It was like camping. Except on the nights we heard the drone of aircraft in the distance. And the thunder of explosions. We spent fewer nights all under the same roof that year. Our house in Hamburg was on the northeast edge of the city, toward Lübeck. Miles from the main harbor and U-Boat pens, but we never knew if it was going to be there when we returned. Papa had a plan.

From what I knew already, that didn't surprise me. Kapitän Carl seemed like a man with a plan.

CHAPTER SEVEN

THE PLAN

As with a lot of other things, I was the last to know Papa's plan. Mama said he read the signs of the war like the sea and weather. And the signs were everywhere. In the fall of '42, the pompous announcements about the Eastern front stopped. Mama heard injured soldiers at the hospital talking about how bad it was. Stalingrad would not fall. Winter was setting in. Allied bombing raids on Hamburg focused on the north and west sides toward the submarine bases and port.

My piano studies with Dr. Nachtneder were only once a month. He agreed to meet at our house for those. But that didn't last long. Herr Benedict was gone. Drafted.

I was thirteen. Growing up in war.

I didn't know Papa's plan was for all of us to escape to Sweden. Sink the boat, Liberty of the Sea, then make our way to Britain. He was waiting for the right window. In the meantime, he and the boys lived on the boats. Mama and I spent time there, too.

In February of 1943, the Eastern Front collapsed. Stalingrad held. I remember Papa announcing sarcastically, "The superior Aryan army is in retreat. Let them broadcast that!" He believed the war was lost. But not over.

In April, just after my fourteenth birthday, he arranged for me and Mama to stay with his cousin, Petra Neumann. She had a two-story farmhouse on twenty acres just outside Sandbostel, a small town ninety kilometers southwest of Hamburg. There was a large POW camp there, too. Papa reasoned the Allies would not likely bomb POWs. His plan would get us all out of danger.

I protested. I wanted to live on the boats with the men. And all of us stay together. But Papa said they had work to do. Petra's husband Rolf had been drafted. He drove a petrol truck behind the lines somewhere in France. They had no children. We could help her around the house and farm. And Petra found Mama a job as a nurse at the camp, Stalag X-B.

We loaded the remaining provisions from the basement in the truck. I played one last piece on the piano Mama taught me to play on. Bach's Minuet in G. None of us were as happy as that music. But it felt hopeful.

The POW camp had another plus. Petra told Papa the International Red Cross inspections kept the conditions less harsh. "At least during their visits," Papa said. Apparently, Germany and most countries were part of the Geneva Convention. An agreement he had to explain to me. About humane treatment of prisoners.

But Papa said tyrants don't keep agreements. They break the rules and make up their own. His anger ramped up talking about it. Er flippte komplett aus, as we say. He freaked out completely.

I told Aneska we say, 'he went off.'

Ya. Papa went off like a rocket.

He said, "Hitler broke the Treaty of Versailles! He broke the Munich Pact with Britain. The Non-Aggression with the Soviets. Hell, Miriam, he even signed a pact with the Pope and broke that! For tyrants, ink is just another way to lie. The only language they understand is strength. And those who think otherwise will be trampled with a treaty in their hands. Good people must do more than spill ink and give speeches. They must act! Thank Gott for Herr Churchill."

We made the drive to Sandbostel mostly in silence. It was more like a village than a town. It had one Lutheran church. One funeral home. One bank. Half a dozen shops on main street, including a pharmacy where Petra helped develop photographs. She was an excellent photographer. There was one school and a town hall. Most of the residents were farmers. It hosted a produce market every Saturday. The best part – there was only one loudspeaker. On the town hall. Thank the Lord it was silent most of the time.

Besides being safer and quiet, Sandbostel held another blessing. Petra had a very fine upright piano. And she knew how to keep it in tune. I brought stacks of music with me to keep practicing. Including verboten music. Mama made me promise to play those pieces softly. That left out Bartok.

The Stalag was immense. It held over ten thousand POWs. Soviet, Polish, French, Belgian, American, British and even some Germans considered "enemy civilians."

Mama described the SS Commandant, Colonel Hugo Blixt, as a Nachtneder type, only worse. Portly, with a pencil moustache and round glasses, who leaned his head back to look down his nose at everyone. He referred to himself as a medical scientist. But he was not a doctor. Very intellectual. Godless. Mama secretly called him Herr Geist. Mr. Mind. He believed humans are merely the sum of all our parts. And that someday scientists would map all the parts and be able to fix or replace whatever breaks. He was bitter about being stationed as a prison warden out in the middle of nowhere instead of central command in Berlin. Mama thought he took it out on the prisoners, especially the Russians.

That didn't surprise Papa. The Third Reich considered Russians an inferior race. To be dominated. He said the Soviets didn't sign the Geneva Convention. So, the Germans took advantage of that. Colonel Blixt used that technicality to keep the Red Cross from legally visiting the Soviet section of the camp. Even Mama was not permitted there. She was told that section had its own medical staff. We found out later many of the Soviets starved.

Papa called Blixt a viper, like the one in the Garden of Eden. He warned Mama to keep her distance.

As usual, Mama turned it on him. She asked Papa to bring the Commandant some nice fish on his next trip.

"Deit," she said, "Jesus told us 'feed your enemies'."

Papa reminded her that scripture includes, "*IF* they are hungry." But on his next trip, he brought extra fish.

Sure enough, Papa's plan protected us. In late July of '43, bombers rained hellfire on all of Hamburg. For eight days and nights. And we were not there. Most of the beautiful city I grew up in was in ruins. Including our house. And Mama's piano. Papa and the boys dug through the rubble. They found a few silver coins the boys hid. Three kitchen pots. The iron skillet Mama cooked so much in. Including her apple pies. And miraculously, the metal sign over the piano. It slid down behind the piano and survived. They brought what was salvaged to Petra's.

Curiosity satisfied: that's how the Latin sign survived the war.

That skillet is hanging here in our kitchen. The sign is in the music room. No pictures survived the Hamburg bombing. Except the few Mama brought with her before. When we were liberated, I got them from Petra's. That one of me at the piano was taken in our house in Hamburg. I think I was seven. You can see part of the metal sign in the background.

I got up and retrieved the picture.

See the big bow in my hair. Mama tied it.

Aneska paused. Gazed at the picture. I left the moment alone, unable to even guess what was replaying in her head. She set the photo on the little table beside her. Peered into the fireplace. And continued.

The war carried on all around us. The allied forces were hitting back very hard. We got most of our war news from the POWs under Mama's care. Papa secretly celebrated every Allied victory in North Africa and Italy that summer. And the naval battles. We knew the war was going on in the Pacific, but news of it was scarce. The loudspeaker on the town hall fell silent. Mama said the arroganz of the Nazis - you have nearly the same word in English. The arrogance of the Nazis was replaced by agitation and more aggression, especially toward Russian prisoners and the British and American airmen who had dropped bombs on Germany.

Of course, the POWs loved Mama. You would have, too. She wasn't just beautiful. She was so kind and caring. She smuggled food to them. Bread and sausages and chewing gum and candy. Sometimes even fruit. They talked to her. Mama's English was good, and she spoke a little French. She came home with their stories. She knew their names and where they were from.

That fall, Papa and the boys fished all the time. They visited us in Sandbostel when they could. We spent Christmas '43 there. All together. Late Christmas Eve we huddled around a candle. I'll never forget it. Papa prayed for Gott to protect us all and bring Hitler to his just reward in hell. And soon. The boys agreed with 'Amens.' Mama prayed for Petra's husband and the POWs. I prayed for Ben and Hanna Blum. And a childish prayer about world peace, that still hasn't been answered. Papa reassured me my prayer about the Blums was as good as answered. I asked him how he knew. He said, "A little fishy told me, mein Schatz." I didn't know he had already smuggled the Blums to Sweden.

I was supposed to be asleep but couldn't because the next morning was Christmas. I overheard Mama in the kitchen tell Papa she suspected Herr Blixt was badly mistreating the Soviets. Her offers to help were always denied. Papa insisted she just do her job and stay clear of him. He also said something about a date for some "trip" in March while the nights were still longer. With a good southerly tailwind we could make it to Trelleborg, Sweden in less than ten hours under cover of darkness. That's when I found out the plan. But I didn't tell Mama I knew.

On Christmas morning, I woke everyone up playing Mozart's Rondo Alla Turca from his Sonata #11. It's so lively. That was the happiest I'd been in a long time. Before exchanging gifts, Papa read Luke 2 like he always did. His present to me was the sheet music for Bach's Christmas Oratorio. All six parts! Petra and Mama and I baked Franzbrötchen. They're like a cinnamon roll. Petra added raisins when she could get them. I'll ask Maja to make some. They taste like, well, like Rondo Alla Turca makes you feel.

As you can imagine, I couldn't wait for March. I felt like a seed waiting for Spring. Only less patient.

Mid-February 1944, news came about the bombing of Leipzig and other industrial cities. I hoped Papa might launch the plan sooner. But February 20, it was a Sunday. I'll never forget.

Papa and Jakob showed up without Wilhelm. The Navy revoked his fishing exemption, and drafted him for his skill with boats. We were devastated. Papa was enraged. But strangely quiet. One of his trawlers, Liberty of the Sea, was seized, too. To be refitted as a patrol and weather boat. No compensation. Just the gratitude of the Führer. Wilhelm was given the rank of Korvettenkapitän, Lieutenant Commander of the new vessel.

Papa seemed lost. Jakob told me Wilhelm urged Papa to get the rest of us to Sweden. He would find a way to join us. But Papa wouldn't go without him. Germany was taking a beating. So, we had to find another way and hope the war was turning. Wilhelm promised to write once a week to us in Sandbostel. With just two to crew the boat, Papa had to resort to gill net fishing instead of the big drag nets.

Fishing still kept Jakob from being drafted. We were thankful for that.

I turned fifteen in April. It was not the happiest birthday. I know I was blessed beyond so many other girls my age. Many daughters saw their brothers and fathers leave for war, never to return. At that same time, Anne Frank was in hiding, couped up in a few rooms for nearly two years. She would turn fifteen June 12. Still invisible and anonymous to the world. A whole generation of seeds were waiting like us for Spring. For a new world after the war.

By the way, I host a little birthday party every year for Anne on her birthday, ever since I first read her diary, right here in front of this fireplace. Remembering is revering, my friend. It makes what's lost along the way not as lost. Gott willing, maybe you'll be here for that this June.

CHAPTER EIGHT

THE CRASH

On a Sunday afternoon, the eighteenth of June 1944, I remember the date because we had just celebrated Wilhelm's birthday without him on the twelfth. Mama was home. It was about four o'clock. She and Petra were having tea. Mama asked me to play a verboten piece, one of her favorites, Chopin's Nocturne in E Flat Major Op.9 No.2. She called it a cup of tea for the spirit. I was in the middle of it when we heard a plane approaching. Its engines sputtering. We ran to the porch. It was a British bomber! Trailing black smoke, and flying so low we could see the pilots. I waved. One of them waved back! We watched it float past and crash land in a large wheat field. Mama grabbed her medical bag and told us to stay inside. An hour later she returned and said the entire crew of seven survived. Colonel Blixt and the guards brought them to the Stalag.

The downed plane quickly became a local attraction. The entire town came out to see it and take pictures. There's Petra's photo of us on the far right.

I retrieved it.

Isn't Mama beautiful? And Petra, too.

The next day, after the SS made sure it had dropped it bombs and removed the ammunition, we climbed all over it. Just below the cockpit on the left side was a large, bright green four-leaf clover. Everyone wanted to sit in the pilots' seats. I waited my turn. What a feeling. It felt like Beethoven's Fifth. For the first time, I could imagine those young men Mama cared for climbing into those metal war machines, not knowing if they would live or die.

The SS interrogated the crew. Mama tended their wounds. From the beatings. Not the crash. They told her details about the Allied landing at Normandy. And the advance. The Allies were battling their way into France! It gave us all hope that the war might be over soon.

But soon did not come.

Mama reminded us of the Proverb, "The mind of man plans his way, but the Lord directs his steps." She believed that it applied to our plans as well as nations. She wrote it on a worn out, wooden cutting board and hung it in Petra's kitchen. We all hoped the proverb was true. But it seemed little comfort, especially to Papa. He worried for Wilhelm.

Mama was our steady cadence. She reminded Papa the Allies were on their way to Paris and went to the piano. She made up a song on the spot, "We're marching to Paris, marching to Paris" and a silly line about the Allies "crossing the Rhine raising a stein." By the second round, Petra and I joined her. Papa smiled but warned us to hold it down or we'd be marching to the Stalag.

In July, life played a very dark melodic theme, you might say. Early one morning we woke to sirens at the Stalag. Soldiers came to our door. Two prisoners had escaped. Guards searched the whole house and the barn. Asked if anything was missing. When they left Mama said something curious. That those two were "far away by now." Then corrected herself, 'probably' far away by now. She also feared for the other British POWs because there was always harsh retribution after escapes and attempts. I wondered how she knew they were British. The soldiers hadn't said that.

Retribution came swiftly.

Mama came home from her shift that night with terrible news. She tried to send me to my room. I argued I was fifteen and didn't have to be sheltered. She let me sit in the kitchen with Petra and listen.

The two escapees were indeed British pilots. The ones who crash-landed in the wheat field. The ones I waved to! They had not been caught. At noon, all the British prisoners were gathered in the muster yard. Several hundred. A doctor, Mama and another nurse were required to attend. Colonel Blixt announced the names of the escapees. The prisoners cheered. It subsided when guards brought out three chairs with tall backs and straps attached. Blixt ordered the crew of the escaped pilots to come forward. There were five. He paced in front of them while a guard collected their dog tags in a bag. Blixt turned it into a lottery. He ordered the commanding British officer to draw out two. The guards tied the unlucky airmen in the chairs. Bound their hands and feet. They were blindfolded and their heads strapped to the backs of the chairs. The third chair remained empty.

I wondered if that accounted for Aneska's reaction to my 'winning the lottery' reference when I arrived. I remembered she said, 'That all depends on the prize.'

Blixt announced he did not intend to kill the men. He was going to zähmen them, "tame" them he called it. He warned that for every escape or attempt, every insurrection, there would be a taming. He said if the two crewmen survived, they would never be the men they were. If they survived the war, they would be a burden on their families and a constant reminder of shame for their country. As he spoke, he opened an ornate wooden box and removed a very small pistol. He loaded three bullets. All the ranking British officers protested that this was against the Geneva Convention. Blixt silenced them. He said the first man who spoke again, or broke ranks would join the other two in the third chair.

Blixt held the pistol to one man's head. Moved the muzzle around as if selecting a certain spot and angle. He asked the man if he had any last words.

He spoke very loud. "Mum and dad, I love you. Hitler, burn in…"

Mama said a shot rang out before he finished. The airman's head jerked to the side then fell forward. A small red spot grew on his blindfold. Blixt walked over to the other man. Held the pistol to the side of his head. Mama said she started to cry. But something beautiful happened Herr Blixt didn't count on. He asked the prisoners if anyone would care to take the second man's place. Immediately, a drill command came from the ranking British officer, "Ten-Hut. Forward Front!" Every prisoner came to attention in unison and took a step forward! All the guards aimed their weapons at the prisoners.

Mama was close enough to see Blixt falter. He pressed the muzzle to the head of the second man. Mama thought the prisoners might rush the Colonel.

He pulled the pistol away and spoke. "Well played, lemmings. Take your man. I believe we understand each other."

The reprieved man's crewmates untied him. Mama helped get the injured airman to the infirmary and dress his wound. Blixt made the British stand in the hot sun for another half hour before the guards released them. Two chairs were left standing in the muster yard as a reminder.

The horror of it sank my soul. Like an anchor chained around my neck. I had to recalibrate the darkness a human heart can harbor. The black, maniacal, remorseless sin that deserves the eternal fires of a real hell. As usual, I took all that to the piano. I wanted to pound something dissonant and sharp-edged rhythmically. Beyond Bartok's rebellion. A lament beyond the prophet Jeremiah's. A righteous tirade like King David's to a God failing or waiting too late to intervene. Instead, I began to play Reflexion in A. And cried. Mama and Petra sat down on either side of me. We all cried.

Aneska's tears flowed freely as she spoke. It wasn't the first or last time the tissues rescued her. And me.

Mama said something I didn't want to hear. That the urge for vengeance in our own hearts was as black as the sin we hated in Colonel Blixt. It was a darkness Jesus died to save us all from. My spirit protested. But I wanted no part in becoming like Blixt. I acknowledged my own vengeful anger but letting it go was difficult. I didn't want to. I felt a right to it. And I clung to it.

Over the next few days, the music and what I call the Holy Spirit's velvet crowbar, helped me begin to release it. My friend, saying "Thy will be done, not mine" does not come easy in the crucible. But I said it. And whenever the rage resurfaced, I said it and let the rage go again. What eventually remained was a pure and righteous hatred of evil. And an iron will to stand against it.

That brave airman died a week later, in the night, while Mama was not on duty. The cause was recorded as "infection from battle wounds."

Aneska sighed deeply and peered into the fire.

To this day, evil makes me furious. Especially evil unchecked. Whenever I see that callous darkness brutalize the weak and innocent, or the shadow of it rise inside again in me, I picture those soldiers taking that step. Together. From that moment I wanted my music to motivate others to take that step like they did, without hesitation.

At first, I was relieved this cathartic story came at the end of one of our sessions. But when I returned to my quarters, a similar tension awaited me. I had wrestled grievances, anger and heartaches with the Almighty before. Haven't we all? Aneska's wrestling match with stony anger unearthed a dark knot in my own soul. Looking out over the nearly still water and sleeping pastures, I felt like a stubborn seed resisting Spring. But as Yeats observed, viewing and sitting beside Aneska's still water was drawing me, at the pace of the River Barrow, to a clearer, fiercer life, because of her quiet. Even if not wholeheartedly, I invited Spring to come. And for the velvet crowbar to have its way. Aneska was truly becoming part of my story. And we were only in the second movement.

CHAPTER NINE

THE DUET

The next morning as I set up the recorder in the study, I heard someone playing the piano in the front room. It sounded like the piece Aneska described as Reflection in A. I went to look. There she was at the piano. She slid to the left and patted the bench for me to sit beside her, all the while steadily arpeggiating the four-chord pattern with her left hand. My piano skills are less than rudimentary. I read the metal Latin sign directly in front of me: Dei magnum opus est amor, *and knew this would certainly not be my opus, magnum or otherwise. She encouraged me to dive in.*

Play whatever you want in the key of A with only your right hand. Or any grace notes you choose. As my jazz friends say, there are no bad notes, just clever recoveries.

Mentally, I reminded myself of the three sharps in the key of A major: C#, F#, G#. Intimidated by the magnitude of Aneska's gift, I timidly outlined a simple pattern of three notes.

Don't play what you think I would like to hear. Play the shape and colors of your soul right now.

Her gentleness relaxed me. It was easy to imagine her disarming manner was part of the attraction for her music students. After a bit, she played with both hands, embellishing and echoing whatever I played. It was like a dance. I lost track of time. After a while I felt her retard as if toward an ending. I followed her lead, just like she had done with Professor Nachtneder over seventy-five years earlier.

Nicely done. That was beautiful. Unrepeatable. And just between us and heaven.

In my mind I added "indelible." We moved to the study. She picked up her story where she left off.

After the taming, a part of the story I was not privy to came to light on Papa and Jakob's next visit. None of us could see it, but another theme Gott was playing in his duet with us had already begun.

Papa had amazing news, but thought it best if I went to my room. The less I knew, the better. Mama told him I was all in this now and we had a story for them, too. So, I stayed. And was amazed. But not completely surprised.

The two escaped British pilots "somehow" found their way to Papa's boat. That somehow was Mama. While tending to their wounds she just "happened" to mention Papa's boat, where it docked and that he made occasional "special delivery" trips to Sweden. The way Papa told the story, I could tell it thrilled him to play a part in the war effort. For the other side! But there was more to the story than that.

They launched on a moonless night with a slight tailwind. Less than an hour out, a German patrol boat hailed them and came alongside, shining a blinding spotlight. A sailor on the patrol boat manned a large machine gun on the bow. The British pilots hid in the fish hold behind a few boxes on ice. Papa always carried some fish to prove he was fishing.

A voice called out, "Identify your vessel, harbor, and prepare to be boarded." Papa said the voice sounded familiar but gruff. He relayed the boat's name and harbor.

"Fishing late? Only two of you manning that craft?," the officer shouted.

Papa yelled back, "The Navy needed my other crew members." He explained they were not trawling, only setting gill nets. That two of them could handle that.

The man barked orders to his own crew. Told them he would do the inspection himself. When he stepped on board, it was Wilhelm! They were Sprachlos! Dumfounded. Under the spotlight, they couldn't risk any emotion. Lieutenant Latva asked for their papers. Only he saw the Latva name on the manifest. Wilhelm ordered Jakob to remain on deck while he and Papa went below. Papa said it was the most difficult thing he ever did to remain quiet as they embraced each other. They spoke in whispers. Papa told him about the pilots and where they were. And their destination. Wilhelm informed Papa a U-Boat patrolled on the surface at night farther west in the Bay of Lübeck. That all patrols stop and turn off their engines for five minutes at the top and bottom of the hour to listen for engines. That's how Wilhelm located his boat. He sent Papa back up on deck and requested to interview Jakob down below. After a brief reunion, Wilhelm had to inspect the fish hold in sight of his own crew. Papa climbed down first. He let the pilots know what was happening. Wilhelm climbed down. He saluted the pilots and shook their hands, returned to the deck and gave his crew the 'all clear.'

Papa climbed up with a box of fish. "For the Lieutenant and his crew." Wilhelm removed the lid to take a look.

"Very generous. Thank you." He tossed the lid aside out of the spotlight. Papa realized why.

The lid was labeled, Latva Feiner Fisch, 'Latva Fine Fish.' It might have given them away. Instead of a Sieg Heil, they shook hands.

"Gutes Angeln, Kapitän Carl." Good fishing.

Wilhelm told Papa he would send out a radio report that his vessel had been inspected and cleared.

"Danke. Gott be with you and your men," Papa said to him.

Wilhelm responded like our family always did. "Und mit deinem Geist, Kapitän." And with your spirit, Captain.

The patrol boat turned south and west. Papa and Jakob and the pilots watched it disappear. They headed northeast, stopping every half hour to cut the engine. Just before daylight, the pilots were delivered safely to a network in Sweden.

Papa saved the best for last - letters from Mama's parents – one to her and one for me. Along with cheese and venison jerky, chocolate and wine, butter and jars of jam. That connected a lot of things in my head about Papa "trading" with other fishermen. Before I could voice my suspicions, Mama spoke up.

"Deit, don't you see? We made a plan, but the Lord is directing our steps. Aneska, we are not alone. Gott is always playing a duet with us."

Petra broke out some dishes, and we enjoyed the bounty and each other. I asked if I could pray. I admit I used the prayer to let Papa know I knew where he had been getting the special provisions. I prayed something like, "Thank you, Lord, for providing Oma and Opa to provide these treats for us - all these years." Mama and Jakob laughed. Papa smiled his big smile, raised his glass, and toasted Oma and Opa.

After dinner, Mama told them about the taming and the bravery of the British prisoners. How the wounded airman could only mumble and was blind in one eye. That his death a week later was suspicious. Papa seethed and struck the table. But didn't yell.

He only said, "This madness must end. Dear Gott in heaven, end this!"

Papa's plan had not worked out for us yet. I hoped Gott had a better one. We were not all together, and the war was not over. But everyone knew Germany was losing the war.

CHAPTER TEN

THE LESSONS

Papa and Jakob had to return to the boat. The fish would run the rest of the summer through the fall. They had to produce to keep their exemption from military service. Gill nets required longer days than trawling, but they caught more trout that way. Papa said the German officers took all the trout they didn't hide. The sheer presumption of that galled Papa. I don't know how he didn't explode and find himself in big trouble. But for many years, we all had plenty of practice in self-defusing in order to endure the daily tyranny.

To stay under the radar, I commented. She responded,

To color inside the lines.

It was my turn to volley. "To not rock the boat." Aneska didn't hesitate.

Here's an Irish one. To look as happy as Larry.

That tickled her. She began to laugh. So did I.

I love the Irish, she said.

I marveled. At her age, with all she had endured, and I still didn't know the half of it, her spirit and mind were nimble and playful. It was infectious. The wave of silliness passed, and she dove back into the stream.

Let's see. August '44. I still practiced nearly every day. Mama insisted on it. An idea came to me. I offered to help out a little by teaching piano lessons to some local children. She grabbed my face in both hands and said, "Who needs diamonds with you around?"

I told her I might have to "borrow" that to use in a song. Probably a Country song. She countered,

So, we're cowriting music now? My agent will contact you about the copyright portions.

We had another laugh. I told her we call that "splits".

Ah, ya. Well, the first one is on me. But that line is really Mama's. *She looked toward the table full of photos and continued.*

Mama found a young girl in town, age seven, who already played and wanted to learn more. Her mother paid me in eggs, flour and some vegetables from their garden. My dream of a music school became real. I already had the name - Beyond Words. I even made business cards by hand. After two weeks I had four students. We collected so many eggs we sold them at the farmer's market or traded for other things we needed.

There's a picture on the far end of me and my students. Petra took it.

I retrieved it. Her voice lit up as she talked about them. She remembered all their names.

My students each came twice a week for a forty-minute lesson. Only one showed enough proficiency to tackle Bach's Sonata in D Major, Lydia, my first student. She pointed Lydia out. I taught them basic skills and to improvise with Reflection in A. Sometimes one student played the left hand and another the right. Until they learned to play both. Their lessons were the high point of my week. They called me Maestra. I called them my Constellation of Shining Stars.

Ah, but Gunter.

She pointed to him and sighed. Something muted her joy.

Gunter changed our world. Well, not Gunter. I don't blame him. She set the picture on the table. After a few lessons, instead of his mother, his father brought him. He was an SS Lieutenant at the Stalag. Herr Schitli.

I couldn't suppress a laugh.

Ya, that was his name. And sad to say, it was appropriate.

Mama was at work. Petra invited him to wait on the front porch, but he declined. Just as I was relieved that we kept the verboten music out of sight, I saw the top of a Chopin folio visible under the edge of the couch. Petra saw it, too. She offered tea and directed him to the dining room while I got Gunter settled. I slid the folio out of sight with my foot.

Herr Schitli asked if I could play Mozart's Air in A-flat. Which I did. It's very brief. He asked if I knew by memory Beethoven's Bagatelle in A Minor, Op. 119, No. 9. These were simple pieces. We used them as warm-ups at Konservitory. I played a bit of it. He pulled the sheet music to both from his valise. I still have those folios here in the music room. He demanded that Gunter learn those two pieces. With typical Nazi disdain, he asked about the insipid piece Gunter was practicing at home. Why it was never the same twice. I told him it was merely an exercise to free the left hand from the right. He wanted to know why Gunter wasn't playing scales. I assured him that would come. But making some music early on would keep his interest and awaken his natural musicality and curiosity. That was my theory, which I use to this day. I already sensed Gunter was not top of the class in those areas. He would require more awakening. A lot more.

The Lieutenant then requested any of Mendelssohn's Scherzos. I didn't hesitate. I said Mendelssohn's music was on the verboten list. That pleased him.

He left Gunter and me alone with Beethoven on the music rack. We began side by side on the bench at half tempo. And slowed it down from there.

When Mama got home we told her about his visit. She was upset that he even set foot in the house. It worried her more than I understood. But her concern was soon justified.

The following week, Mama came home from work very quiet and burdened. At supper she told us Herr Schitli spoke to Colonel Blixt about Gunter's talented piano teacher. Blixt told, did not ask Mama, that I was to play for an officer dinner in the Town Hall. You can imagine my resistance. Let's just say I was not as happy as Larry about it. It was a good thing Papa was fishing. We might have all disappeared across the Baltic that night. Petra included. Mama did what she did so well under stress. She didn't panic. She prayed. Put it in the Lord's hands and said we would sleep on it.

Sleep did not come easy. I lay in bed, trying to imagine playing for that monster. How would I keep my hands steady or focus enough to remember the notes? Until that night, I don't think I understood what Jesus said about casting pearls before swine.

Breakfast was quiet. Petra left the table and retrieved her Bible. She hadn't slept much either. Before I said a word, she told me she understood how playing for the SS officers probably feels like, can you guess? Casting pearls before swine. She read us two passages.

Aneska knew them by heart.

"It is not the healthy who need a doctor, but the sick. But go and learn what this means: 'I desire mercy, not sacrifice.' For I have not come to call the righteous, but sinners to repentance."

Mark 2:17

I needed to hear the other one even more.

"When they hand you over, do not worry how or what you should speak;
For it shall be given you in that hour what you are to speak.
For it is not you who speak, but the Spirit of your Father which speaks through you."

Matthew 10:19 & 20

Mama took my hand. She looked me in the eye and said, "I will be there with you, mein Schatz. With Gott's help, you can do this."

A week later, on a Saturday night, Mama walked with me the fifteen minutes to the town hall. I don't remember what I wore. Mama looked nice. I remember that. She prayed some as we walked.

Upon arriving, Herr Schitli instructed me to play softly for fifteen minutes as the officers and their wives and dates arrived. While drinks were served. After dinner I was to play one solo selection as previously ordered, something by Mozart, the Commandant's favorite composer. Later that night at home, I heard Mama tell Petra the ladies were from not from Sandbostel. And most were not the wives of any officers.

I had prepared some music. Herr Schitli requested the list in advance. It was just what you might call the German Mount Rushmore of composers. Bach, Beethoven, Mozart and Brahms. Even for the pieces I knew well from memory, I carried folios. In case I faltered.

Gunter's father escorted us to a table where he introduced us to his wife. He seated Mama, but led me to the piano. Mama tried to follow but he insisted she keep his wife company. I felt like a lamb being led to slaughter. Herr Schitli gave me a cue to begin. People started to arrive.

As it turned out, no one listened to me. You can imagine, the room grew noisy with conversation and laughter of fifty or so people. Drinks flowed. I looked up a few times at Mama. Her smile gave me strength. I saw the Lieutenant introduce her to another officer. A fat man with a pencil moustache. Colonel Blixt. I lost my place momentarily but recovered. Probably only Mama noticed. Fifteen minutes went by. Herr Schitli motioned to keep playing. I defaulted of all things to the simplicity of Bach's Sonata in D Major. And had to concentrate to make it through that.

Schitli stepped to the microphone. He asked everyone to take their seats. Dinner was about to be served. He retrieved me from the piano. I walked behind him to a seat by Mama. The round tables seated eight. To my horror, Colonel Blixt and his escort sat down opposite us. My hands trembled. Mama gave me one of hers under the table and said, "Well done, mein Schatz." The entire table agreed. And for the first time, I heard the monster's voice.

I wondered what a monster would sound like. Someone who had no heart to speak from. I imagined it would be coarse from breathing fire all day. He raised a glass with the same hand that shot the airman. To my relief, he looked at Mama, not me, and spoke to her in a warm tone.

"Frau Pfieffer, Aneska has a gift. I understand she will treat us to some Mozart after dinner?"

The sound of my name in his mouth felt like a Requiem. His eyes stayed on Mama.

"Ya, Colonel, she has prepared…" Blixt cut her off.

"No, no, don't tell me." He leaned back, looked down his nose at me and said, "I want to be surprised." The grip of Mama's hand bridled the fear in my heart and my father's revulsion in my stomach. I couldn't even nod. At that moment, two waiters intervened and began filling the table with food from a cart. The entre: trout. With green beans and boiled potatoes. Before Colonel Blixt took a bite, he asked for another serving. Gott forgive me but I entertained myself with the thought of him choking on the bones from a fish my Papa caught.

I know there was small talk, but I don't remember any of it. Except Mama answering to someone that I studied at Hamburg Konservitory. I kept my eyes down.

The staff cleared the main course and brought dessert. Of course, Colonel Blixt had two servings. Herr Schitli went to the microphone and announced a short break. People mingled. Smoked. More drinks flowed. Blixt addressed Mama, "After the break I will say a few words and then Aneska will play."

When he took the stage, all the officers stood at attention and

Seig Heiled him. He returned it. They took their seats. I cannot begin to tell you the pomposity that followed. It was hundred proof pride.

I didn't interrupt her but made a note of that phrase for a Country song. 'Hundred Proof Pride.' We could negotiate later.

Mama and I knew the cruelty lurking behind his swagger. Blixt praised the Führer for his vision of a new order where those divinely destined to rule would indeed rule. I noticed he said, "one day rule." He lauded the officers for their parts in the Fuhrer's Master-Neuordnung. His master realignment. Which he defined by quoting Hitler in a loud voice, "Who rules Europe rules the world!"

But there was no applause. None. No unanimous shouts of agreement as in the early rallies. The audience sat quietly, drinking and smoking. Everyone in the room had to know the Allies had just liberated Paris. We knew it from the POWs. Mama told us how they celebrated. How all the Frenchmen cried. She feared the news was making the guards more cruel.

Besides quoting Hitler's doomed boast, I can only quote one thing Colonel Blixt said. It was so audacious. So haughty. I wrote it down when we got home. It was more memorable because a pigeon from the rafters startled him in the middle of it. He aimed his arrogance directly at me in an introduction that I didn't know was an introduction. He put his hands on his hips like the handles of a bloated trophy, looked down his nose at the crowd and declared,

"Meine Landsleute," My countrymen, "Most art is garnish, a side dish. Science is the entrée. Most art is window dressing, curtains. Science is the window." At this point the pigeon, apparently bored with the speech or its perch, decided to swoop down behind Blixt. By reflex the Colonel ducked. Mama squeezed my hand to prevent any reaction from me.

Blixt took a moment to regain his composure and continued. "But the greatest art, German art, reveals the heart and soul of the divine destiny of Aryan supremacy. I give you Herr Mozart." He didn't even say my name. He merely extended a hand toward me.

I was confused. Mama got up and walked me to the piano. She leaned down to kiss me and whispered, "It is not you who speak."

I took a deep breath. As I exhaled, I changed the plan. The list I gave Herr Schitli said Sonata No. 16 in C Major Allegro. Very famous, recognizable. It's very perky and positive. I was neither.

I didn't think twice. I let the room go quiet and began the somber opening of Mozart's Fantasia in D Minor KV397, Adagio. At a slow pace. It speaks the opposite of the bluster Blixt just spewed. It's full of shadows and grief mixed with cascading arabesques. Those are long runs of notes. It sounds like a search for light through worry and despair. Can you relate, my friend? The tension of chromatic notes speaks pain and insecurity. They are interspersed with the playfulness of hope and single hammered notes like fate vying for dominance. It ends with a very singable passage like an aria and finishes with fortissimo chords in triumph. You may notice I get a little intense about music. And the ones I love.

I agreed. Intense is a good thing. In both areas. I asked her why she switched to that piece.

Fantasia always made Mozart so human to me. That he felt the range of what we feel but can't express in the same remarkable way. I guess maybe in that setting, underneath it all, I wondered if there was anything human left in that audience, besides Mama. I didn't overthink it. I was just prompted to play it. It all happened in a moment. Looking back, I'm sure it was a Spirit thing. Gott's and my rebel spirit.

I'll ask Zuza to send you the recording I did of it over fifty years ago. An mp3. Aren't I modern? Listen to it walking the grounds and I think you'll see what I mean.

Getting back to that night, I struck the final chord with a full stop.

The room teetered in silence. Then applause erupted and everyone stood to their feet. I stood and bowed quickly. The ovation continued as I hurried back to my seat. Herr Schitli gave me a stern look, but his displeasure couldn't rival the affirmation of the crowd.

Even to this day, I hope Mozart's piece and my playing did not affirm the bombast of Blixt's comments. If it did, I hate to think there was not much human left in that room. But I prefer to think it testified, I believe is the right word, to the opposite. It does to me. Only the Lord knows what it spoke to each person that night.

I still take it as a good sign that afterward, it took a while for us to get out of the room. People were gracious and seemed genuinely moved by the music, especially the women. Even the cordiality of the officers, despite their intimidating black uniforms, made them seem too civilized to be part of such a ruthless force. I stood by Mama and thanked them all. Blixt was visibly under the influence. He made a comment to Mama that made us both cringe.

"Frau Pfieffer, truly, your daughter has a remarkable gift and is as lovely as you."

Mama and I walked home arm in arm. She compared Blixt to a defiant sparrow with his chest puffed out, oblivious to the storm that was about to blow him away. We were glad to be done with it.

But we were not done.

CHAPTER ELEVEN

THE OFFENSE

The unforeseen consequence of that event was a steady booking. "Gig" you call it, ya? I was requested, required, to play at least once a week at the officer dinners inside the Stalag. Petra came with us a few times to tune the good but neglected piano. Fortunately, I played before dinner during drinks, and we left before everyone got aufgesogen, Mama called it, soaked. What do you call being drunk?

Liquored up, I offered. Among other things.

The Irish, it won't surprise you, who enjoy tipping a glass, have many colorful descriptions of that condition - "stocious," which is one step above "gubbed" but not as drunk as my favorite, "blootered." What a colorful people. They argue with the Scots about who originated the terms, but it usually just ends in someone buying another round.

Mama noticed the more the German army retreated, the more the officers drank. I would play three selections and couldn't wait to leave. Colonel Blixt preferred lively music and required one of the three pieces to be Mozart.

We adjusted to the routine. Mama always accompanied me to the dinners. Sometimes Petra, too. Several weeks went by without incident. Then Mama had an idea. Petra and I thought it too risky. Why make waves? Papa would never have agreed to it.

Mama wanted to bring some beauty and comfort to the prisoners.

But couldn't reveal her true motive. She asked Herr Schitli if one evening a selection could be broadcast over the loudspeakers to the camp. It might help keep the prisoners calm if the music wasn't too rousing. She appealed to his national pride, saying it would show prisoners of many nations the obvious superiority of Aryan composers. And further subdue them. Of course, she believed the opposite. Mama was brilliant that way. It was truly enlightened propaganda. She even told him how good it would look next time the Red Cross visited. Schitli presented her proposal to Blixt as his own idea. The Commandant agreed but forbade the broadcast to the Soviet section. He had one other condition, which I never knew until after the war.

The next time I played, a microphone hung above the piano. Before my third piece, the dining room staff opened the large windows toward the camp side. Colonel Blixt took the mic and addressed the prisoners. His voice echoed across the camp. He was less bombastic than usual, but hubris dripped from his voice. He lectured about some people groups being destined to create culture and others marked to be the chaff of history. And how a superior culture and order were the only hope for the world, just as the prisoners' only hope in the camp was to maintain order. Most of it sounded borrowed from Mein Kampf, Hitler's manifesto, which was mandatory reading for us in school. Blixt wanted the prisoners to know they were about to hear one of the creators of culture, of the New World Order. I'll never forget the way he ended.

"I believe you will hear your unavoidable fate in it. And now I give you, Herr Mozart. Gern geschehen." 'You're welcome.'

Have you ever heard such psychotic drivel?

I told her we have another, but more course term for it.

Does it have something to do with a large farm animal and manure?

I confirmed that. And guessed she probably knew her cue to begin playing this time?

Oh, ya, and this time I was eager. Mama told me beforehand I would play to my largest audience ever. Thousands of POWs. But not to think about the thousands, just play to one prisoner. And without a word, the music would speak empathy for their pain and loss. It would comfort and assure them that the light will surely bring us out of the nightmare. From the first note, I knew I was smuggling hope right under the Nazi's noses. To the Lieutenant's chagrin, Blixt himself chose the Trojan Horse, Mozart's Fantasia, because he wanted to hear it again. Isn't that rich?

The following week, all the prisoners who came to the infirmary confirmed what Mama predicted. They were comforted and inspired. They reported that even the guards stopped and listened and seemed less aggressive, at least temporarily. The POWs wanted to know why it happened and when the music would play again.

Mama started what you might call a disinformation campaign. She told the prisoners to complain about the "depressing" music because the intention of the Commandant was to demoralize them. She was careful to give Herr Schitli all the credit to his face, but all the blame to the prisoners. I told you she was brilliant! It worked. The next week the deluded Nazi's broadcast Brahms' Intermezzo in A major Op. 118 no. 2. Its beauty is deeply emotional. The middle section drips with sorrow and pain, but it ends so gently and affirms that in spite of it all, everything is going to be alright.

I asked Mama how she knew her plan would work. Why Blixt would agree to broadcast the music.

"Mien Schatz," she said, "Tyrants have at least two giant blind spots. Their pride makes them presume to be more enlightened than they are. And they badly misread human nature, the divine spark in all of us. Even in themselves. And so, they become oblivious to the full range of what it means to be human." Mama simply played their blind spots against them.

I began to see Miriam's influence on Aneska's thinking. She continued about her mother's brilliance.

I have watched Mama's wisdom borne out. Not just on the world stage. I've seen those blind spots take a great toll on people I've known. Very human, God-given, outward-facing emotions, like tenderness and compassion become turned inward by narcissism into blind passion for a cause. Instead of compassion for people, a hypersensitivity breeds victimhood in the face of the slightest resistance to that cause and the person championing it. What emerges is a tyrant, who will bend logic, religion, history, language and law to achieve an end. At any cost. A bully who will lay blame on any scapegoat. Justify any action. Nearly my entire country transformed into ruthless domination. Hitler was like an abusive father, willing to sacrifice his own children and millions of others on the altar of his ravenous ego.

And if you think humanity has grown out of this, just look around, my friend. Tyranny is still everywhere.

But don't forget this irony, my friend. In a real sense, are we not born little tyrants, ya? It's all about me. For some, that metastasizes into a lifestyle. None of us, even with Christ's help, is immune from feeling more empathy for ourselves and our own plight than what others are going through. Especially when someone neglects or hurts us.

I marveled at her ability to articulate these insights in a language that was not her native tongue.

For Blixt and Schitli, in their ears the music reinforced the dark vision of their hardened hearts. Blixt could put a bullet in the head of a prisoner with no remorse. No revulsion. To him a prisoner was chaff. And Brahms was simply part of the soundtrack of his own glory.

I asked if she had recorded the Brahms piece herself.

Of course, ya. I will have Zuza send the mp3. You may have quite a new library by the time we're done.

I said if I complained about it would she make me listen to more? She got the joke.

Touché. Well played.

When the prisoners found out Mama's daughter was the one playing the piano, she became even more popular. That's why when she was suddenly assigned to the infirmary in the Soviet section no one was more upset and confused than me. It made no sense. She assured me and Petra it was temporary, but the hours were much longer, and she came home with horrific stories of the conditions. The Soviet POWs were emaciated, starving to death before her eyes. Hardly any of them spoke German. The need for an interpreter made everything slower and more difficult to give aid. The guards and other nurses there treated Mama badly. She didn't understand why.

I watched Mama's strength decline. She took on the suffering of the prisoners, like a weight. But always put a good face on, reminding me of our sure blessings in the middle of the uncertainty of war. She lived exhausted. That's when my emotions, and being my Papa's girl, landed me in very big trouble.

Playing one dinner a week turned into two. Petra convinced Mama to stay home one Friday evening to rest. Under the pretext of tuning the piano, Petra went with me. The sight of Blixt and his cronies laughing and drinking, oblivious to the torment and suffering they orchestrated, made me bullin' fierce, as the Irish say. Extremely angry. But I was also sad for Mama. I moved a Bach piece from third to second. If Blixt took the mic and announced Bach as the broadcast piece, I had another Bach composition ready. But what he said in his stiff English was simply, "Listen now, you vanquished, your only consolation is submission or the grave." I took it as a sign from heaven and launched into the soft arpeggiated intro of Consolation No.3 by verboten Hungarian composer Franz Liszt. It's a musical prayer, deep low notes and soaring delicate melodies, sometimes in octaves. It's meant to be played lento placido, very slow and placid. As I began, I felt heaven smile.

I played it as a wordless prayer for Mama and for all the prisoners, including the Soviets. With my fingers, I prayed for Papa and Jakob and Wilhelm. And I prayed no one would notice it was Liszt. Petra did. So did Herr Schitli. When I finished, he gave me a venomous look. But didn't say anything, perhaps fearing Blixt's wrath on himself.

Petra and I didn't tell Mama. To not worry her. Two days passed. We felt like it blew over. But on the morning of the third day, a Monday, Lieutenant Schitli came to our door. It was not the scheduled time for Gunter's lesson. Another soldier stood with him. He had paperwork informing me I had not served the required six months in the Reich Labor Service. I was being assigned to a munitions work camp, Lübberstedt, thirty-two kilometers west near Bremen! Just twenty miles - but a munitions factory! It was bound to be a target for Allied bombing. He took great pleasure in emphasizing the "consolation" was I was not a prisoner but a loyal citizen in service to Deutschland and the Führer. His reference to the Liszt piece was obvious. Petra and I both caught it.

He ordered me to pack one bag and a winter coat. This was the first week of October, 1944. Mama was at work. Papa and Jakob were fishing. Petra protested and argued that as a German citizen, Miriam was entitled to be informed and say goodbye. Schitli was aware of that. He planned to stop at the Stalag to give Mama the paperwork before I was driven to Lübberstedt. I was given twenty minutes to pack. Petra helped. The soldier followed us upstairs. I did not feel like a "loyal citizen." I felt like a prisoner.

Petra insisted on coming along, even though it meant walking back from the Stalag. Riding in the back seat of the military car holding Petra's hand, a rebellion beyond Bartok welled up in me. How could this be Gott directing our steps?

I won't describe the emotions of that goodbye with Mama. Because I can't. Even with a full orchestra. Schitli delivered the papers to her. Mama pointed out to Petra that they were signed by Colonel Blixt. She insisted on accompanying me to Lübberstedt. Not possible, the Lieutenant informed her. It was a military installation.

He gave us ten minutes alone. I cried and told her I blamed myself for playing Liszt. She held my face in her hands like she did ever since I was a little girl, and assured me it was not my fault. Petra said the same. In whispers, she let us know the infirmary patients told her the Allies were already on German soil, fighting in the city of Aachen. The war couldn't last much longer. And Lübberstedt was only thirty-five minutes by car. She and Papa would find a way to see me. She said calmly, as only Mama could under such stress, "Mein Schatz, Gott and the music will make a way for you." She quoted Joshua 1:9 to me.

> Be strong and courageous. Do not be afraid; do not be discouraged, for the Lord your God will be with you wherever you go.

Mama prayed. The three of us held each other. Schitli came back in the room. Besides 'I love you,' our parting words were what we said a thousand times at church.

Mama said, "Gott be with you, mein Schatz."

Und mit deinem Geist, Mama. And with your spirit.

Gunter's father led me away.

I waited, without speaking. If you're like me, I wanted to ask when she saw her mother again, but didn't want to know in case she never did. I decided not to ask. Better to let her tell the story.

CHAPTER TWELVE

THE CAMP

As you can imagine, the ride to Lübberstedt was miserable. I sat alone in the back seat. The Lieutenant and a driver in the front. It was a cloudy, dark day. But not raining. I watched the countryside glide by, taking me farther from Mama and Petra. My spirits sank lower and lower. My best student Lydia would show up for her lesson at 1:00 and I wouldn't be there. Herr Schitli made a comment to the driver about the clouds being a blessing, a protection from the Schweinebomber, the swine bombers. The word "blessing" in his mouth was like a canary caught in a snake's jaw.

He tried to make small talk about Gunter's playing. I wanted to lash out and tell him his son was as musical as a brick. But I wasn't mad at Gunter. Why hurt him? Mama always said in hurting someone else we always hurt ourselves, too. Instead, I suggested Bach's Prelude in C, "A Well-Tempered Clavier." It would be a pleasant way for Gunter to get his fingers moving. And the range of chords is good ear training. He thanked me. Took out a pocket notebook and wrote it down.

There were only two positive things about the ride. It gave me empathy for all the people from our neighborhood who I saw rounded up and loaded into trucks and cars, taken who knows where. I have never forgotten the feeling of being forcibly detained and leaving home and all the familiar world behind. I don't want that to happen to anyone. The only ones who should be forcibly detained are the tyrants who perpetrate that.

The other positive thing was the short ride, like Mama said. It seemed long, but after about thirty-five minutes we pulled up to the gate at Lübberstedt. The guards looked at our papers, made a call, gave crisp Sieg Heils to Lieutenant Schitli and opened the gate.

I remember brooding sarcastically about how pointless all the Sieg Heils were. You know it means 'Hail Victory'?

I did not.

Germany was about to be defeated. We all knew it. Cities were in ruins. Even Berlin was being bombed! And the Nazis were still Sieg Heiling! I wanted to blurt out something Papa started saying to himself when he had to fake a salute. "Christus ist der Sieg." Christ is the Victory. I held my tongue but spoke it in my heart. I was gloomier than the overcast sky. But saying it to myself steadied me some for whatever came next.

The car crept up to a long building. Two soldiers in black trench coats stood there like pallbearers to meet us. I felt like the third movement of Chopin's Funeral March, Sonata No. 2 in B-Flat Minor. I'm sure you know it. The major theme has been used in many cartoons for melodramatic effect. But this was no cartoon. And the drama was real. The driver opened my door. Schitli remained seated and handed the paperwork through the window to one of the guards, who asked him to wait for the commandant's signature. He disappeared into the building.

I fought back my funk. Somehow, probably for Mama's sake, I made a choice to be more civilized than Schitli. And I was not about to let him see me cry. I asked him if he would kindly tell my mother I arrived safely. He agreed to. I thanked him. And reminded him to encourage Gunter to play at least thirty minutes a day, twice on Monday and Wednesday. And no more. That might make him want to break the rule and play more. He nearly smiled and said he would. I felt like Mama would have been proud of me.

The guard returned with the paperwork. Without another word, Schitli rolled up his window, and the car drove away. The trenchcoats escorted me into the building.

It's funny what you remember. The unison clack of their boots down the long hallway matched the pounding of my heart.

They led me into a large office, the commandant's. The only one I had ever met was a monster. No one was there. A guard directed me to sit in the chair directly opposite the desk. One stood on either side of me. I don't know if twenty seconds or two minutes passed. Finally, someone entered the room and dismissed the guards. I heard the door close.

A warm voice behind said, "Thank you for your service to the Reich. Where's my apple pie?"

I turned around. It was Herr Hans Benedict! The kind manager of the Laeiszhalle! He stood beaming at me with his arms open wide. I burst into tears and ran to him like he was Jesus. In that moment he was Jesus. He was sent from God into my agony. I clung to him and couldn't stop crying. How could it be? How? Only a God so good could direct my steps here. And Herr Benedict's, too.

My first thought was how to let Mama know. To ease her worry, Herr Benedict said he would make that happen soon, but we must be careful. The air of suspicion everywhere made all communication delicate. In fact, our meeting had to be brief. He inquired about my family and gave me a quick overview of the munitions factory and my role in it.

About five hundred Hungarian women, most of them Jewish, had been transported from Auschwitz, which saved most of their lives. Many spoke a little German. They worked on a production line making ammunition for anti-aircraft guns, scatter bombs, naval mines and packed the parachutes to drop them. My quarters were separate from the forced laborers. There were eight other girls my age there, assigned like me, by the Reich Labor Service. There were no boys because all males sixteen to sixty had been called to active duty. The other girls didn't work on the assembly lines. They kept records of daily production and inventory. Herr Benedict assured me my job would be the same and my piano hands would never come near the machinery.

He lowered his voice to a whisper and let me know he doubted I would complete the six months. The Allies were already on German soil and Gott willing, we would all be home soon.

He saved the best news for last. There was a good piano in the officer dining room. He would find a way for me to play it as often as possible. But it needed a little tuning. Of course, I told him about Petra, where Mama lived, and wondered if they could both come for the tuning. He said that might be possible. Piano tuners were in short supply. Imagine the turn in my spirits. Chopin's Funeral March turned into Beethoven's "Ode to Joy!"

He called someone in to show me to my quarters. A woman. It was his wife, Brigitte.! She looked familiar, but I didn't know she was a nurse. Frau Benedict also oversaw the girls in the Labor Service. She knew who I was and told me she loved my recitals.

It was all overwhelming. I wondered how such good fortune found me.

The same way you found me, I offered. Providence.

Precisely, my friend.

Colonel Benedict impressed on me how crucial it was to keep our close connection confidential. He had to be careful not to show favoritism. Most of the guards and staff were not of the nastier Nazi version, and some were even kind to the prisoners. Most were ready for the war to be over. As long as production kept pace, the hardliners up the chain of command did not interfere.

Frau Benedict led me on a tour. First to my barracks. The other girls were working. She showed me a map of the facility. It was enormous - twenty-two production buildings and over one hundred bunkers for storing munitions. We went into one station where naval mine casings were prepared and filled with explosives. She put on a protective mask and showed me how to wear one. None of the workers wore masks. The key component was TNT powder, which was melted down and poured into bombs and mines. It was dangerous, toxic work. Detonators were attached at the end of the process, loosely to prevent accidental explosions. The munitions were loaded onto trolleys. Four women pushed and pulled them up to five kilometers to storage bunkers.

Brigitte. anticipated my question. The Allies hadn't blown up Lübberstedt yet because it was well hidden in the thick forest in the middle of nowhere. The roofs were painted tan and green. Some even had grass and plants growing on top. Bombs knocked out railway lines several times but had never fallen directly on the munitions camps scattered around the area. There were also bomb shelters for the SS and the prisoners. She took me down into the one assigned to me.

So far, I had asked very few questions, but I did here - if she ever visited Lübberstedt after the war.

Ya, in 1955. All that remained was one bomb shelter. The production facilities and bunkers were blown up near the end of the war by the Nazis.

Three of us Labor Service girls reunited there. We visited the cemetery where four Jewish women were buried and honored. Two died by beatings from a commandant prior to Herr Benedict. And two from supposed "illnesses." It was hard going back. Facing traumas can bring healing, but tears can open the scars again.

I thought for a composer who doesn't write lyrics, she certainly turns a phrase like a songwriter. I kept that to myself and asked if the rest of the workers survived.

No, I found out years later, of the five hundred, about three-hundred and eighty did. Some were evacuated by train to Bergen-Belsen. The Nazi's ruthlessness increased toward the end of the war, so nearly all of them at that camp died. Sixty died when their train was mistakenly attacked by the British, who thought it was full of retreating Nazis. The sad chaos of war.

I apologized for interrupting. She was gracious, as usual.

No bother, or 'toggy buggy' as the Irish say. Which literally means, "take it softly." Isn't that charming? I just love the Irish.

That never stopped being obvious.

It took several days for Herr Benedict to contact Mama. But he made it happen. It was a great relief to know she could let Papa know I was alright. Knowing him, he might have lost all restraint and made things far worse. I had to trust what I couldn't control. Don't you find that's one of the hardest things to do?

I certainly agreed. I told her that's why I like writing. At least I decide the next word on the page.

Ya, composing is similar. But sometimes don't you find ideas or phrases come to mind that you're pretty sure you didn't come up with? They just appear, like a kind of co-writing is happening.

Like a duet? I said. She chuckled.

Precisely. I tend to think my best pieces come more from a kind of listening than wrestling them out of the piano. At least the core sparks or themes. They're like jewels I place in a musical setting.

Can you understand why I hated for each fireside session to end? But I also needed a lot of time to label and archive the interviews and begin transcribing the epic mural of Aneska's life. I also had the luxury to spend hours walking the estate listening to her recordings of the compositions in her story. As she aptly put it, they spoke volumes – beyond words.

CHAPTER THIRTEEN

THE CAKE

The days at Lübberstedt began early. For the laborers at 5:00a.m. sharp. The girls in my barracks ate at six in the staff dining hall before the officers arrived an hour later. Frau Benedict escorted me to the laborer dining hall my first morning to meet the Kapos. They were prisoner managers in charge of each filling station. My job was to work with them, making daily tally sheets and cataloguing batch numbers. Their breakfast was a brownish broth that substituted for coffee and four slices of bread per day. In the final stages of the war supplies diminished. It was already down to two slices. Kapos ate a little better, getting scrambled eggs twice a week. Sometimes even a little sausage and fruit.

Frau Benedict ate with us every morning. Our food was much better. My first morning we had cheese omelets with apples sliced to look like ears and a smile, and eyebrows made of raisins. Helga, from Düsseldorf, that's farther west, said one of the cooks was quite handsome. The rest agreed. It was obvious they all had a crush on him.

Frau Benedict kept a close watch on the girls to make sure the SS officers and male staff kept their distance. There were many female guards as well. Most were fairly humane, but I could never tell if this was because they knew Germany was losing the war.

There was greater risk from male guards, of course. My roommates made sure I knew about the rotten apples in the SS, the ones who preyed secretly on the laborers. But even the wolves knew if just one infraction came to Colonel Benedict's desk, they were out the door to the western front. His official goal was maintaining the quotas of production, but Frau Benedict told me his real motive was the welfare of the women. His compassion didn't surprise me.

A dirty little financial secret kept the guards in line as well. Frau Benedict informed me the Luftwaffe paid the factory two marks a day for the laborers. Some of that went toward upkeep, food, medicine, etc., but the SS guards got a share of the money. So, it was in their best interest to meet the quotas. Injured workers made that more difficult to do.

Every morning the women walked in step a kilometer to the production buildings. They were forced to sing on the way. Lunch was thin soup with a slice of bread at the factory. They worked a ten-hour shift. Marched back to the barracks. Had roll call and a dinner of bread and quark. That's a cheap kind of cheese. And sometimes a little sausage. Other barracks worked the night shift.

The first morning in our barracks, I woke up with a tickle in my throat. Like I was coming down with something. Frau Benedict looked at my throat and checked my temperature. It was normal. She gave me aspirin before breakfast.

I wore my hair up in the required 'Gretchen' wreath of braids like all the other girls. And dressed in the standard uniform of the German League of Girls, a long dark blue skirt, white middy blouse with a sailor collar and a dark blue kerchief gathered at the front with an official swastika clasp. I hated that symbol. After I intentionally lost two, Frau Benedict let me use a simple leather one.

I had breakfast with all the girls and felt better. After eating, I walked over and tried out the baby grand piano. It was a Steinway! And not horribly out of tune. I was thankful to Gott for it. I don't know why but I began playing Brahms' Intermezzo 118 No. 2. It's the loveliest and most tender of his intermezzi. Very nostalgic. And romantic. Just the right amount of pain and hope. Frau Benedict and the girls gathered around the piano.

Not thirty seconds into it, the tickle in my throat made me cough. I paused then kept going, but coughed again harder and had to stop. I apologized. The girls' eyes were not on me. Out of nowhere, someone to my left offered a glass of water. It was the most handsome young man I had ever seen. Piercing blue eyes. Thick blonde hair and eyebrows. Dressed all in white. Like a chef. He bowed his head slightly as he handed me the glass, but never took his eyes from mine. My fingers brushed his as I took it.

All he said was, "Hallo."

I took a drink. Thanked him. And played the Intermezzo better than I ever had. When I finished, the girls applauded. From across the room the handsome young man in white did, too. Then disappeared into the kitchen.

Until that 'hello', I never fully understood Papa's story about meeting Mama. The moment he took her hand to help her onto the boat his heart was set on her. The only boy I ever liked, even a little, was Ben Blum at Konservitory. But he never knew it. And then he was gone. The girls told me the young man's name, Kristers Latva. I had so many questions. How old was he? Where was he from? Why was he there? And not off fighting somewhere?

I jotted down another song idea, "Until Hello" but didn't interrupt.

I couldn't stop thinking about him all day, hoping I would see him at dinner. Most of that day was spent learning my new job from a female guard and one of the Kapos. We had a very sparse lunch at one of the production buildings with the workers, but at a separate table. The women were almost all Hungarian, most of them Jewish.

On the outside and inside wall above the filling station door, was a phrase painted in large black letters. Laborers couldn't help but see it every day. Coming in and going out.

ARBEIT MACHT FREI

'Work will free you.' I didn't know then those words were a sadistic lie on the gates of death camps like Auschwitz and many others. I knew enough to know it was not work, but truth that sets us free. Lies enslave. This was a lie to lull prisoners into a false hope of freedom that would never come. Only the ovens or the grave freed millions of them.

A female Kapo must have seen me reading it. She chose her moment and leaned very close. She whispered, "Nur Jesus macht uns frei." 'Only Jesus can set us free.' Her risk took me by surprise. I smiled and whispered back, 'Amen. Are you not Jewish?"

"Catholic," she said.

"Lutheran," I responded.

She asked me to pray for the women. I promised to. Her name was Benca. Besides the Benedicts, she was my first friend at Lübberstedt.

The job wasn't difficult. Just very detailed with a strict process of counting, double-checking numbers, writing them in ledgers. To avert the threat of sabotage, only German guards checked the detonators to see if they were loosely attached. Every load had to be labeled with the date, ordinance count, and ID of the filling station and assembly line. In the event of an ordinance malfunction, laborers or even staff could be accused of sabotage and severely punished or even executed. Frau Benedict assured me that had never happened under her husband's command.

In the barracks before dinner, the girls teased me about Kristers. About the way he looked at me. They were sure he liked me. I tried to ignore them, but hoped they were right.

Dinner that night was a buffet. Bratwurst and some side dishes. Kristers stood behind the tray of Brats. The girls said he gave me two.

I don't remember. All I remember is he said, "I'm Kristers. Would you like more mustard?"

Aneska laughed. She stared into the fireplace with a faraway look. She was back there. Savoring every detail. I didn't rush the moment.

I stood there, speechless. He said it again, "Would you like more mustard, Aneska?" He knew my name! The way I answered 'Ya, Ya' you would have thought he asked me to marry him. Back at the table, the girls teased me. "Would you like more mustard, Aneska? Would you like a kiss with your brats, Aneska?"

If that wasn't enough fuel on the fire, for dessert Kristers delivered a beautiful Black Forest Cake with cherry preserves and whipped cream right to our table. As he cut slices and handed them out, he leaned in between me and the girl next to me. His face was closer to mine. He said, "This is for the beautiful music this morning." He wrapped up a generous slice and said, "For Herr Benedict. It's his favorite." And then told all of us, "No one tell. This cake was for the officers, but I'll bake them another one."

Aneska didn't sound like a woman in her eighties. She sounded like a young girl in love. Still in love.

That night after lights out, the teasing continued. The room finally settled down. Out of the quiet a girl said, "How many children would you like with that, Aneska?" Laughter broke out everywhere. When it subsided, I played along. "At least two. A girl and a boy," I said. The uproar started again. A female guard came in and spoke sternly to us.

There were strict rules about no lights at night because of the Allied bombers. But lying in my bunk, I pulled the thick curtain back just enough to see a slice of stars. I prayed for the Hungarian women. For Benca. I thanked Gott for her faith. And new friendship. For Hans and Brigitte.. I missed Mama and Papa and Petra. And my brothers. But new thoughts filled my mind. About Kristers. Brahms' Intermezzo played in my head. Though I wouldn't read Anne Frank's diary for a few more years, I felt what she wrote about doing just what I was doing. "When I look up at the sky, I somehow feel that everything will change for the better, that this cruelty too shall end, that peace and tranquility will return once more."

It was impressive she had committed some of Anne Frank's diary to memory. But in another sense, no wonder. Anne spoke what so many endured and hoped in the nightmare of that war.

But this was only October. 1944. The end that seemed near delayed. More carnage and cruelty raged against the sunrise of peace. But…

She picked up the little vase holding several delicate Snowdrops.

…even against enormous odds, beauty and hope can blossom.

I started to tell her several song ideas or lyric lines in all she just spoke. But an impulse said, 'honor the moment.' I jotted them down quickly, and waited, eager for her next verbal sonata.

CHAPTER FOURTEEN

THE CORNBREAD

The very next morning after breakfast, Frau Benedict took me to the Colonel's office. If they weren't my friends, it would have felt like the times a teacher escorted me to the headmaster for some infraction, usually verbal. But I was in no trouble. Herr Benedict had an offer for me.

He wanted to know if I would occasionally play a selection at the officer dinner. It would give me more piano time in preparation and performing. He could arrange my work hours around it.

First, that was remarkable because it wasn't an order, but an invitation I could accept or decline. What a difference, ya? I told him about playing for officer dinners for Commandant Blixt at the Stalag. He was fully aware of Blixt's arrogance and cruel reputation. He reminded me, even though it was so difficult to leave my mother, how Providence took me out of that… he searched for a word and lowered his voice when he found it… "that villain's reach."

Of course, I told him I would be glad to play and thanked him for the wonderful idea. That's when another remarkable thing happened. It was not the Colonel's idea. It was suggested to Frau Benedict by Kristers Latva, the chef! Can you imagine how my heart leapt? I was on Kristers' mind! My thoughts raced with the possibility of seeing him more. I didn't even know Kristers, but my heart knew more than my head.

There it was again. The low-hanging fruit of a song lyric, "my heart knew more than my head."

I tried to keep my composure and asked the Colonel if playing two times a week would be enough or if he preferred every evening. She laughed. Herr Benedict smiled and gave a knowing glance to his wife. Since it was already Wednesday, he suggested Friday at dinner for the first time and Tuesday and Friday of the next week. And then we would see.

On the way back to the barracks, I had a dozen questions I wanted to ask Frau Benedict about Kristers. I tried to 'play it cool.' Isn't that what you say in America?

Yes, but more recently we say, 'be chill.'

Oh, ya, well, then I tried to be chill. I asked her why Colonel Benedict called Kristers a chef and not a cook. It worked. She gave me a scéal, as the Irish say, his story. What she told me was the third remarkable thing in less than twenty minutes. You want more evidence of Providence? This is it, my friend. The Benedicts and Latvas both attended St. Martin Lutheran Church in Göttingen. Incredible, ya! That's a university town about two hundred and sixty kilometers south of Hamburg. They knew him as a boy. His parents were prominent bankers. Leading up to the war, they helped people move assets out of Germany under the radar of the Reich. Kristers' mother taught him to cook and bake. He graduated from secondary school at fourteen. A math genius. He was awarded a full scholarship to Göttingen University. Since he loved cooking, the summer before he started university he took a job at a fine restaurant. Who do you think convinced that restaurant to hire him? A phone call from the new manager at the famous Laeiszhalle in Hamburg - Hans Benedict. Two years later, Kristers was top of his class in applied mathematics and physics. His older brother and only sibling, Stéphan, was an aspiring pianist like me. He became a pilot and was killed early in the war in France. Apparently, he guided his damaged plane into a field instead of bailing out and letting it crash into a town. At sixteen, the Reich Labor Service sent Kristers a notice of his duty to serve Deutschland for six months. Herr Benedict stepped in. After being drafted, Hans was managing part of production at the U-Boat shipyard in Bremen. Because of his cooking skills, Herr Benedict managed to have him assigned to the officer kitchen. Six months later Kristers was drafted early. At the same time, Lieutenant Benedict was promoted to Colonel and made Commandant at Lübberstedt, so he brought him there.

I didn't even know him, but a portrait of Kristers began to emerge. A Lutheran. I knew that would please Papa and Mama. A scientific genius. Wonderful chef. A giver of cool water and baker of chocolate cake. He already knew the cost of war in a very personal way, which gave him a gravity behind his Adonis looks. I was already enthralled. But of all the things Herr Benedict told me, one thing set my heart on him. When he reported for duty in Bremen, Kristers felt comfortable enough with Herr Benedict to confide privately, "Lieutenant, if I may speak confidentially, I serve food and the Lord, but not the Führer." My heart was all in. This was a man after my Papa's own heart.

I had one more question. Kristers' age. Frau Benedict told me he had turned nineteen in July. Just three years and three months older than me. Perfect, I thought. Papa was nearly six years older than Mama. All I had to find out was if he had any feelings for me. The glass of water was sweet, but the cake gave me hope. Very sweet hope.

It was obvious she enjoyed revisiting those first encounters with Kristers. It only took one word to keep her on that trail. So...

So, I didn't have to wait long for clues. That Friday evening, I played for about twenty-five officers at dinner. Kristers cooked and helped serve the meal. When I sat down at the piano, there was a glass of water beside it on a stand. Next to the glass was a small vase holding a single red Marigold. I didn't want to assume he put the flower there, though I did. But it was also something Frau Benedict could have done. On my first night in the barracks, she placed a small vase next to my bed with a few of the last Marigolds of fall.

I played two selections after dinner while the officers drank and smoked. Their enthusiastic applause cheered my spirits. Colonel Benedict escorted me from the piano to the kitchen. He instructed Kristers to make a plate for me. The food was even better than what I ate with the girls.

I sat on a stool and ate at a counter while the kitchen staff served dessert. Kristers cleaned dishes and prepared a big pot of stew for the Reich Labor girls. He walked back and forth. Right by me. I had no idea what to say that wouldn't reveal I inquired about him. Do you ever rehearse several options in your head when you don't know what to say?

I responded 'ya,' which she enjoyed.

Kristers always spoke what was on his mind. Back then.

That seemed curious to me. "Back then?" But I didn't stop her to ask.

As he stirred the pot, he said, "So, the Colonel tells me you studied at the music Konservitory in Hamburg?"

All I could say was 'ya.' That's the only word he had heard me say. I think he could tell how shy I was, so he tried again.

"So, you're an artist. And I'm a cook."

I'm not sure why I blurted it out, but I said, "But I hear you're really a scientist."

He said, "So, the songbird does have a voice! I bet I know where you heard that."

And that's all it took. We chatted and laughed. He asked me to hand ingredients to him as he made maisbrot, cornbread. He was very precise with measurements. What you would expect of a mathematician. When the big trays came out of the oven, he cut two slices and we ate them with butter and honey. We stood side by side washing our hands in the big sink. He made a joke about me writing a song called sticky fingers and dedicating it to him. Even today, the smell of hot cornbread can make me cry.

In the barracks that night, the girls peppered me with questions. When Frau Benedict came in for lights out, I thanked her for the marigold by the piano. Can you guess what she said?

It wasn't her?

Ya! It had to be Kristers! In my bed, I looked up at the slice of stars and couldn't wait to tell Papa and Mama I had fallen in love with a man over a glass of water, chocolate cake and cornbread.

CHAPTER FIFTEEN

THE DEBATE

My new schedule of practicing in the officer dining hall, plus performing and eating there with the girls, meant I saw Kristers every day. At least twice a day. There was always a glass of water beside the piano. The kitchen staff were always there, too, so we were never alone together. Frau Benedict saw to that.

I loved Kristers' cooking. Everyone did. Some commodities were getting scarce, but he scoured local farms and markets, and even the forests to create more than the basics. He raised chickens for the eggs and meat. And grew an herb garden, with flowers around it to attract bees. Mostly marigolds. Window boxes lined the inside of the kitchen windowsills, where he planted seeds and bulbs.

Our talks in the kitchen were what I lived for. We covered the topics of our families and where we grew up. My mother and his father had roots in Sweden. We avoided talking about the war and Hitler or the Allied advance. A casual remark overheard by the wrong person could lead to trouble. We talked about our plans and dreams for after the war. How I wanted to be a concert pianist, travel the world playing with orchestras, compose my own concertos and someday open a classical music school. I assumed Kristers planned to return to his studies at Göttingen University. But he surprised me. He said something in Swedish his father told him. "Hemmet är där kärleken finns." Just the sound of it made me miss Mama. It means

'Home is where the love is.' He could study many places, but he would go wherever the love was. Can you believe a mathematician could be so romantic?

My dreams about music reminded him of his brother, Stéphan, who had planned to pursue a musical career after the war. I wanted to embrace Kristers out of consolation, but my motives felt very mixed.

Wherever Kristers studied after the war, he planned to pursue a doctorate and do research and development - to make the world a better place. I told him I wanted to make the world a better place through music. That's when our first friendly debate began.

Kristers claimed, with all due respect, that science improved conditions in the world far more than the arts. I told him Commandant Blixt's view, that art was only garnish, a side dish, but science was the entrée. Art was like curtains. Science was the window. That human beings are just the sum of our parts and science, not art, would discover all the parts, and someday be able to fix anything that broke, mend all injuries and heal diseases. I asked if he agreed with that. I was pretty pleased with myself and thought I painted him into a corner.

He pulled up a stool and sat directly in front of me. It was all I could do not to reach out and move his lovely hair from his forehead. He picked up a large sweet potato and started carving it. I finally said, "I'm waiting." He shaped the potato into a pipe, then took a couple of fake puffs on it before speaking. How charming is that? His answer was clever and diplomatic. He said the innovations of science make the world a more livable planet, but art reminds us we are more than the sum of our parts, and we need both. I couldn't argue with that. Truth be told, I wanted to kiss him. But I didn't, of course.

At the next meal, I left a note in the pocket of his apron hanging in the kitchen.

"Mien genialer koch, 'my genius chef', without art, man is a soulless machine."

He returned it under the glass of water at the piano. Below my words, he wrote:

"Without science, man is a wingless bird."

This went on for days.

I sent: "Without art - no culinary diversity." I thought that was impressive to use big words and his own cooking skills against him.

He simply wrote back: "Without science - no hot meals."

I asked Aneska if she still had any of the notes.

Only two. But I remember all of them and have them written down. I'll show you in a minute. At night I lay awake thinking how to stump him. I tried being philosophical.

I wrote, "Without art - time erases everything."

He responded: "Without science - no camera to capture time."

I knew he loved my playing so thought I could corner him with: "Without art – no music."

He came back perfectly: "Without science - no piano keys."

I thought I checkmated him with the simplicity of this one: "No art – no heart."

But he countered with the obvious: "No science – no mind."

A few days passed. The officers kept requesting me to play after dinner. So, I played, I think, four times that next week. The girls insisted I play for them, too. The practice and the affirmation made being away from Mama more bearable. I knew she would be proud and gratified that the music was making a way for me. After one of those dinners, Colonel Benedict told me the good news that Petra and Mama were coming that Sunday to tune the piano and it would be best if I told no one. The other girls would make a case to see their families. I understood, but it was like hiding an elephant to keep it to myself. Between Kristers and the news about Mama, it was difficult to sleep.

Kristers changed the note game on me. He delivered the next one. Let me show you our next two notes.

Aneska pointed to a fireproof box on a bottom shelf in a corner of the room.

The key is here. Zuza has another one.

She pulled a chain out of her blouse from around her neck, lifted it over her head, and handed it to me. I unlocked the box.

Bring me the green folder in the middle.

I grabbed a slender book with a green spine.

Not that one. That's one of my diaries.

This was the first I heard about any diary. She sensed my surprise.

Did you think Anne Frank was the only one who kept a diary back then? Every girl I knew kept a diary. More than one. Zuza and I translated mine into English. If they might be useful to you.

Of course, I said and asked how many survived the war.

Three. Why do you think I can remember so many details and names and how I felt during those years? You're a wordsmith. Don't you keep a journal?

It surprised her that I didn't. But I told her every ten years for perspective I jot down a few details about where I was every single month for the previous decade. So, if you ask me about any November, I can recall some things.

That's a good timeline, I suppose. But that's not a journal. It's a good thing Anne was more thorough, don't you agree?

Obviously, I agreed, took her gentle chiding, and found the green folder.

That's the one.

I retrieved the treasure and brought it to her. She talked as she sorted through the stack of papers. I sensed the green folder held a motherlode of treasured keepsakes. But kept my curiosity at bay for the moment, certain the folder would reappear.

I debated whether to tell Kristers about Mama's upcoming visit. These notes made that decision for me. By the way, Zuza photocopied of all these. Should anything happen to them, she can send those to you.

Finding the originals, she set the folder on the table between us. The notes were browning and fragile from age. She opened one and showed it to me. It was in German so I couldn't read it. She translated.

Kristers wrote, and this is so typical of a scientist and his brilliance,

"Life is like Pi, an infinitely unresolvable integer. In science, we can only know and be certain of what can be measured and observed."

I had to think about that one. That night I scribbled several responses and finally landed on this. I used one word in English because his was very good. Probably because of academia. I wrote back:

"Kristers, you are right. Life is like pie. Like my Mama's apple pie. A circle of wonderful flavors. We can only know and be certain of anything by tasting it or trusting those who have."

I didn't wait for another note from him. I sent this one.

"Life is a symphony with recurring themes. Two of them are love and suffering."

Kristers wrote back:

"Life is an equation with recurring certainties.
Ich bin mir sicher, dass ich dich liebe."
I am certain I love you.

She reached for a tissue. I did, too, but feigned cleaning my glasses with it. I jotted down another song idea: Equations of the Heart.

CHAPTER SIXTEEN

THE BLESSING

Sunday morning came. After breakfast I found a moment to tell
Kristers my mother was coming with my father's cousin to tune the
piano. But he already knew! Colonel Benedict asked him to prepare
a meal for them midafternoon while the dining hall was empty. Frau
Benedict planned a trip to a local market with the rest of the girls.
She explained to them my absence was to help a piano tuner. Once
again, the power of kindness overwhelmed me. We would have nearly
three uninterrupted hours.

Normally, factory workers were required to work seven days a
week. I don't think it will surprise you that Herr Benedict scheduled
a half shift on Sundays. As long as he met production quotas, no
higher-ups objected. On Sundays it was mostly maintenance,
cleaning and pushing trolleys loaded with munitions to the bunkers.
I had to be there to check counts and log batch numbers. I'm sure I
made errors that morning.

I hurried back to help Kristers in the kitchen. For the first time,
we were alone. The cornbread batter was already in the pans. I cut
carrots for a soup. He stood next to me cubing potatoes and salami.
Neither of us spoke. He held a slice of salami in front of my face. I
took it from his hand with my mouth. When I couldn't contain it in
any longer, I said it. "Kristers, I'm certain I love you, too." I wanted
him to take me in his arms and kiss me more than anything. I was

expecting it. But he didn't! He just smiled and kept cutting potatoes into a large pot of boiling water, then set a timer for eight minutes to add the carrots. He babbled on about the right sequence to add milk, celery and salami along with the butter, cream and garlic sautéing in a large iron skillet.

Just before I started to boil over, he turned to me and said the most beautiful words I had ever heard. "Aneska, meine Leibe, 'my love.'" He turned back to cutting onions and putting them in the iron skillet. I didn't know what to say. "Meine Leibe" was swimming in my head. The moment felt like a sweet musical rest but on an unresolved chord. I didn't know what was coming. But Kristers did. The next thing he said made it obvious he had been thinking a lot about us. I remember it all exactly. Why? Because I wrote it in my diary... *she said with playful emphasis.*

Tending the skillet, Kristers told me his mother taught him that making a good soup is like making a house of love. It takes good ingredients, good timing and the right heat. He said, "Aneska, meine Leibe, all we need is the timing. When I get your mother's blessing today, believe me, I will find the right time to kiss you."

Can you believe this man? He assumed Mama would give her blessing! I loved him even more. But my second response was panic. He planned to reveal our love to Mama in a matter of hours! We only confirmed it between the two of us minutes before! You must understand, Kristers always knew what he wanted, and he thought hiding that was no way to get it. Which presents a good question for any of us. What do we really want? And if we do, do we pursue it with all our heart?

She paused and gave me a direct look I had seen before.

My friend, if you don't mind me asking, what is it you really want? I hope your time here helps you answer that. And tell it to someone. Or at the least...write it down.

It was my turn to chuckle. But that question was to hound me like a hungry stray dog. Aneska threw me a bone.

I know you do that in your music and writing. I do it, too, in my music. But speaking your desires and visions out loud can give them good aim. The words can be like a key to open the door to them.

For instance, even as a young girl, I wanted to establish a music school. I wanted a loving, Godly husband, like my Papa. And a great love, like theirs. At least two children. I wanted to live in the country. I wanted to play with orchestras and write at least one great piano concerto and hear it performed by consummate musicians. I wanted to feel the smile of God on me. Of course, I wanted some things that didn't happen. Or haven't happened yet. But in matters of wanting and dreaming, isn't it always, 'God willing?' I've found his plans are better. And better for me. And often bigger than my own. Just look at this place! I didn't make this happen. But, as Mama said, it's a duet with God even when it comes to dreaming.

Her words made the stubborn seed in my heart begin to germinate.

To be sure, the cruelty of war and the never-ending struggle and heartache around the world make it clear. So many things are not God's plan, not his best. Because in the equation of life there is always what Kristers called the constant variable: humans. Broken, sin-captive, love-starved, messy, beautiful humans. And sometimes evil ones.

Alright, well, end of sermonette. Thank you for graciously letting me ramble on.

I didn't say it, but I thought, 'give me two tall Guinness and I'll show you rambling on.'

I left you hanging with Mama about to arrive at Lübberstedt. And I made myself hungry for potato soup and cornbread.

Well, as you can imagine, when Colonel Benedict walked into the dining hall with Mama and Petra, it was like Brahms, Chopin and Mozart all on the same piano at the same time. It had only been three weeks, but it felt like a reunion in heaven, except for the drab surroundings. Mama was thin and looked very tired. We both cried, of course. Petra, too.

Herr Benedict introduced Kristers. He removed his chef hat, toque blanche, he called it, and said how pleased he was to put faces with two of the people I talked so much about. He announced what would be served for lunch and excused himself to bring it out. Out of reflex I grabbed his arm, a thing I had never done, to ask if I could help. I immediately felt like everyone noticed. He insisted I spend as much time as possible with Mama and Petra and invited them to sit. He pulled Mama's chair out for her. Then Petra's and then mine. At every place setting was a white marigold. Herr Benedict reminded us we had about two and a half hours and excused himself as well.

When Kristers disappeared into the kitchen, Petra leaned in and whispered, "Well, I'll say it. That Kristers is some beautiful young man. Miriam, isn't Latva Swedish?" Mama just smiled and held my hands in hers, looking into my eyes. I diverted their attention to how I was playing for the officer dinners just like I did at the Stalag. And how kind the Benedict's were. I asked about Papa and my brothers.

Kristers brought out a large tureen of soup and a tray of piping hot cornbread. Butter and honey were already on the table. He filled our bowls. Mama invited him to eat with us. He didn't hesitate. He scooped another bowl and took a seat by Mama. Before I knew it, he asked her about Papa, Herr Pfieffer, Wilhelm and Jakob, by name. He even asked Petra about her husband, Herr Neumann. I didn't remember telling him their surname.

We ate and talked. The soup was delicious, of course. Mama was impressed and wanted the recipe. Kristers made a charming remark about when it comes to eating, being together is always the main course. When he took some dishes back to the kitchen Petra chimed in, "Cooks great and eloquent, too." She excused herself to tune the piano, which would take at least an hour. Kristers finished clearing the table and excused himself to the kitchen. I knew he did it to give Mama and me time together.

In half an hour or so, he came back out with dessert. A simple vanilla pound cake covered in a chocolate sauce with dried apricots on top. By the way, I have the recipe in one of my diaries. Petra stopped tuning to eat dessert. When she went back to the piano everything in me felt Kristers would make his move. If he did.

He looked at me and said, "Aneska, when Frau Neumann finishes tuning why don't you play that first piece when we all fell in love with you. When I fell in love with you."

Petra stopped. And looked our way. She smiled, and went back to sounding one note. Mama looked at me. Kristers was looking at me. I didn't know where to look.

Mama and Kristers spoke at the same time. He immediately deferred to her.

"In love, mein Schatz? Do you love this man?"

I looked at her. Then at Kristers. His face was calm. His gaze steady on me. I looked back at her and said, "Ya, Mama, with all my heart."

She addressed Kristers, calm as only Mama could have been in that moment, "If my daughter has told you the story of Deit and I, then you know we believe love can blossom very quickly." I had told him. She added, "But a wartime love can be desperate and fleeting. Aneska is only fifteen."

"Sixteen in April," I reminded her.

He assured her his intentions were not short term. "Lord willing."

That prompted her to ask about his faith.

I blurted out, "Lutheran, Mama, just like us!"

Kristers lowered his voice and repeated what he told Colonel Benedict, that he serves food for now, and the Lord, but not the

Führer. He made it clear we had not even held hands and certainly not kissed.

Mama asked Kristers his age. She and I knew she had no room to push back on that. She asked his plans after the war. He kept it brief. Göttingen University. Doctorate in Applied Math and Physics. She asked if he knew my plans and dreams. He did.

She laughed and said, "So, a scientist and an artist?"

I think he won her over with his response, "Frau Pfieffer, Gott ist beides." Gott is both.

She was very encouraged that the Benedicts had known him since he was a boy in Göttingen.

After a silence she said, "You know you will have to speak with her father."

He knew.

I took that as a very good sign. As well as what followed.

She asked him, "What do you have to say to me?"

The sound of the piano stopped. Petra turned to listen in.

Kristers asked Mama for her blessing to court me with the intention of marriage, in the Lord's timing. There it was. He knew what he wanted and spoke it out loud.

Do you remember, friend, and I know this is very personal, but that's usually what I do. Do you remember when someone revealed to you how much they loved and wanted you?

All I could do was nod, yes.

Think how many songs, arias, symphonies, novels, movies, poems, how much art has tried to capture that elation or the loss of it? I have been playing and trying to compose that kind of music all my life. Music filled with the hunger and searching for that love, found it and held it as long as Gott willed. I have prayed his Spirit would make me an instrument for people to know that love, the depth of it, a love that stays come what may, heals you in its embrace and carries you on hope. It's not a love that saves you, like Christ's love. No, romantic love isn't meant to save us. But it certainly helps carry us and flows from the love of God, "how rich and pure, how measureless and strong, it shall forevermore endure, the saints' and angels' song." And we've come full circle back to that lovely hymn, haven't we?

If she was "rambling" again, I didn't want her to stop. Her words hurt me in a good way. They touched a wound and blessing so profound it reminded me of the Roberta Flack song, "Killing Me Softly." I had known that elation. And that loss. More than once. If her upcoming piano concerto did to an audience what she just did to me, and sent them out with the kind of hope her life speaks, I couldn't wait to witness it. And let it hurt and heal me again.

There I go again. Maybe I'm subconsciously withholding what Mama said to him to build the tension, like I felt that day. Don't you writers do that?

I nodded. And marveled again at how keen her mind was.

Or maybe I just want to linger there because from beginning to end, Mama's visit was so rich. I think all my favorite composers do that. They fill the middle sections with tension and unresolved emotions and make you wait for the resolution. And see, I've done it again by explaining it.

Well, it works, I told her. I'm still here on the edge of my seat. She laughed.

Mama talked to both of us about how love goes through testing to reveal its strength. Kristers, ever the scientist, compared our love to an I-beam. He actually drew one on a napkin. He told Mama he and I were the flanges held together by the strength of the vertical piece, the Lord, which is like the strong three-fold cord in Ecclesiastes. I could tell Mama liked him. I loved him even more.

Our time was running out. Petra wanted me to play something to test the tuning. Mama was sitting between Kristers and me. She took one of my hands and one of Kristers. She put them together on the table with her hands on top. And gave her blessing. She called it a half blessing. Because Papa would have to give his. She advised Kristers that it wouldn't hurt his prospects if he cooked for Deit before talking to him. She asked me to play the first piece Kristers heard. The Brahms Intermezzo. The tuning was perfect. So was the moment. I had only finished the first beautiful movement when Colonel Benedict returned. It was time. I had to leave the Intermezzo unfinished.

Mama took my face in her hands and kissed me on both cheeks. She did the same to Kristers. My heart was too big for my chest.

She turned to Herr Benedict and said, "Maybe Christmas?"

I said something about how cold weather affects the tuning of a piano.

He laughed and said, "That may be possible."

I asked Petra to take care of Mama. I was worried about her. She assured me she would.

We all thanked Herr Benedict. Said our 'I love yous' and 'God be with you.' And they were gone.

I helped Kristers clear the dishes into the kitchen. Standing at the sink, I broke down. He held me. For the first time. I sobbed against his white shoulder. He took my face in both hands and gave me the softest, most tender kiss on the lips. My first. He didn't kiss me again till much later.

Just hearing her tell it, my heart was too big for my chest, too. I thought, 'This story is going to write itself. All I have to be is a good scribe.'

I suppose it would not surprise you what was for dinner that night? Aneska didn't hide from the cook what she wanted. And we all benefited. I even helped mix the cornbread batter and cut carrots for potato soup.

CHAPTER SEVENTEEN

THE DILEMMA

I set my hopes on Christmas and prayed there might even be a way for Papa and my brothers to visit. It gave me something to look forward to. It also eased my mind knowing Mama would tell Papa I was alright in Lübberstedt with the Benedicts. And of course, there was Kristers. We took care not to draw attention to ourselves, but girls being girls, my roommates knew there was something between us. How can you hide a love like that, ya?

I decided if this was my life, even till the war ended, I might as well pursue my mission, to make the world a better place through music. I approached Herr Benedict with the idea of playing occasionally for the workers over the loudspeakers, like Colonel Blixt permitted. It shocked him that a devil like Blixt would allow such a thing. I described Mama's reverse propaganda campaign. He had a good laugh at that. I told him how it encouraged the POWs, and the music even made the guards less aggressive. He agreed to try it two times on a Monday and Wednesday, but he wanted me to play in the morning during their breakfast before they walked to the filling buildings. That meant an earlier morning for me as well. He suggested something rousing, but left the choice up to me. Over the weekend I decided on Mozart's Rondo al Turco. It has such bright energy.

I practiced it on the officers at dinner Saturday evening and again for the girls on Sunday morning. Kristers loved it. He loved everything

I did. But in the kitchen, he made a comment, wondering if the lightness of it ignored the pathos of the workers' situation. After all, they were torn from their homes in Hungary and forced to make munitions to kill those trying to liberate them. I quipped back without thinking, 'What does a scientist know about pathos?' I meant it to be playful. But I could tell it hurt him deeply. I felt awful. He had spoken freely, with caring, and I backhanded him by being flippant. I took his hand in both of mine, apologized and begged him to forgive me. He did, so sweetly, and I assured him he could say anything in his heart to me.

That afternoon, it came to me. It was so obvious. The first piece I should play for the mostly Hungarian workers was Hungarian composer Franz Liszt, his famous Rhapsody No. 2 in C# minor. It has gravitas and energy, beauty and triumph. And it's Hungarian! But it was verboten music. Herr Benedict was not likely to object. But there was some risk.

That evening, I played just the first two and a half minutes for the girls, which was my plan for Monday morning. Kristers stood in the doorway of the kitchen. He beamed at me and applauded with the girls and kitchen staff. I told him about the composer and the risk. He said it was perfect and if there was any trouble, 'kerfuffle,' as the Irish say, he would claim Liszt was his idea. I loved him even more. If the kitchen staff were not there, I would have kissed him on the spot. It felt like our first duet. I never discounted his viewpoint again. Though we disagreed on some things. What lovers don't, ya?

I told her, ya, I'd heard that but never experienced it.

She laughed.

Where was I?

About to play Liszt.

Ya, danke. The next morning, I got up early to practice the Rhapsody one more time. Liszt is challenging. He was one of the most brilliant pianists in music history. The kitchen staff was there, including Kristers. A technician set up a microphone over the piano. As Kristers checked the table settings he paused near me and prayed quietly, "Lord, use this music and Aneska's fingers to send out your love this morning."

By this time, I knew what she was about to say. And it came right on cue.

I loved him even more.

The time came to broadcast. I knew Mama would be proud. I remembered what she said before the first time I broadcast at the Stalag. That the music would speak empathy and comfort and assurance. I couldn't see my audience that morning either, but I could picture them in my mind. I saw many of them throughout the week. They were so weary and worn and captives of a force they hated. Working with the TNT turned their skin yellow. Mama said don't think about the size of the audience, play to one person. So, I focused on the face of a young woman named Golda Szabó who brought me the batch counts to reconcile. Her German was broken but fair. She was from a small town called Visegrád just north of Budapest. Right on the Danube. It sounded like a lovely place.

I know this is jumping ahead to the third movement of my life, but I have to tell you. Besides writing about Golda in my diary, I remember her so well because her grandson plays cello today in the Budapest orchestra. As a boy, Golda told him about me playing for the workers at Lübberstedt and what it meant to them. At his request I helped arrange an exchange with the Hamburg orchestra because he wants to play in my piano concerto there in May! Isn't that incredible?

Her eyes filled with tears.

Only Gott can make that connection happen. I just play the music. Gott does the rest.

This remarkable vignette was just one portal into the panorama of Aneska's story. I was beginning to recognize the moments when her passion led to "rambling on" from her core. I knew enough to just let it happen. And it happened here again.

I'm sure in your writing you hope for that connection. You sit alone somewhere and speak to people you cannot see, will never see. And they will read your words in a solitary way, on a porch or a beach, maybe a crowded airplane. Maybe in a circumstance forced upon them. You will connect with them, one on one, and deliver something that makes them curious or hungry to turn the next page. You may make them laugh or cry, reflect or regret or hope. Maybe it's all about connecting, ya? Anne Frank certainly connected through her writing, didn't she?

Without a doubt, I answered. I told her this book, her story will connect with many people for whom she will never be able to play music live. And her story will connect with them, just like her recordings.

It's an awesome thing when you think about it. Gott himself connects with us through his words. Of course, he has an advantage. He can see his audience. We can't see him. But we can know him through his words, and, of course, the opus of the universe he made. Gott connects. He reconnected me with Herr Benedict for his purposes. With Kristers. He connected me with dear Brynn O'Cullen.

I was very curious to hear how that connection happened, but instinct told me again Aneska would get to that.

He connected me with you across an ocean. I got to know you some through your words and music before we even met. Gott knows something about connecting, ya?

She took a pause like a musical rest. I didn't have to nudge her about how the broadcast to the laborers went. She continued.

That morning, Colonel Benedict arrived in the dining hall. It came time to broadcast. The technician handed him the microphone. One of the Hungarian Kapos was there to translate. Herr Benedict's words were a world apart from the pomposity of Blixt. His tone was calm and steady. He sounded more like the captain of a cruise ship than a commandant. He reminded them to report to the infirmary with any ailments or injuries. And unlike Blixt, I had no doubt when to begin playing. He thanked the laborers for their fine work in meeting quotas the previous week and said, "As a special thank you, here is some music to start your work week from our own artist, Aneska Pfieffer." The honor of being called an "artist" for the first time, nearly in public, made me emotional. The technician placed the microphone back on the stand. I felt a special gratification knowing the music would need no translator. I pictured Benca and Golda, took a deep breath, exhaled and played to a nearly empty dining hall like it was Laeiszhalle in Hamburg.

She anticipated my next question.

Ya, I have recorded Liszt's Rhapsody. You simply must listen to it to picture that morning, and imagine the effect it had on the women listening in their dining halls and barracks facing another day of drudgery.

When I finished, enthusiastic applause came from the Colonel and kitchen staff. The Hungarian Kapo was in tears. The reports didn't take long to come in. All the workers were in tears. When I arrived on my shift, all forty women and Benca, the Kapo, applauded. Golda tried to explain what a gift I had given them. In her emotional state and broken German, she literally said I 'blew up' their hearts.

Aneska laughed and began to cry. She closed her eyes and leaned her head against the back of the chair. The tears flowed. I handed her a tissue.

Golda meant to say I filled up their hearts. I understood. But truly, my friend, I just played the notes. Gott blew up their hearts. Without a word. Honestly, I don't know how I'll make it through the concertos.

I had to sympathize. My heart was blowing up already. And she wasn't done.

On Wednesday morning I played just the first two minutes of Liszt's Rhapsody no. 6. It's based on Hungarian folk melodies and has a fiery temperament in forceful, two-handed chord strikes and cascading flourishes. The dramatic melodies use the minor three and flat six in the scale. Very distinctive to the folk melodies. I'll show you that later. There is no hint of defeat or surrender in it. Once again, the response was overwhelming.

But something happened no one saw coming. Thursday before dinner, Frau Benedict escorted me to the Colonel's office. I was fearful that someone complained about the music being verboten. But Herr Benedict met me with a big smile. He said even the guards loved the music and reported its effect on production. In the previous four days, spills, accidents and delays were down by sixty percent.

However, there was a dilemma. By Friday noon the weekly quota would be met, and the filling stations would be out of TNT. Resupplying would take till Sunday night. The Allied air superiority required supply trains to run almost entirely at night and only if tracks had not been destroyed. Herr Benedict saw no way around it but to give the workers half shifts on Friday and Saturday and the whole day off on Sunday. Rather than worried about it, he seemed very pleased. He went on and on about how my music lifted and motivated the whole camp. That I was a hero to the women.

Initially, I was pleased, of course. I'm sure you know that gratifying feeling when what you do makes a difference. But I had another dilemma. When I told Kristers about the meeting, he wondered what was troubling me. I was elated that the music lifted the spirits of the women, but it troubled me greatly that it motivated them to make bullets and bombs faster and more efficiently. I recoiled at the thought. I wanted no complicity in that. He tried to reassure me that it would all even out in Gott's math. He was always talking about Gott's math. He had an idea, but couldn't tell me yet.

I had one, too, but was uncertain about it in light of the circumstance. He looked at me with his 'you can tell me anything' eyes, so of course, I told him. My idea was to ask Herr Benedict if I could play one piece for the workers at lights out on Friday night. A gentle piece. But I was hesitant. I didn't want the unintended consequences of the music to motivate them to work better to help Germany kill more Allied airmen and soldiers. Especially when the end of the war seemed near.

Kristers was always so good with the right questions. He asked me what my mother would say and what would please the Lord. He advised me to take the night and pray about it.

The next morning, I woke up and I knew. And wasn't surprised. Mama would say, "Keep giving your gift." And I heard from the Lord, "and I'll take care of the rest." Kristers said that sounded like something they both would say, and the Lord had told him a similar thing when the Reich Labor Service made him quit university. Remember, that's when Lieutenant Benedict got him stationed to cook for the officers at Bremen.

Kristers called Herr Benedict the common denominator in Gott's equation for both of us. He used to say, "Gott is never solving for X. He already knows X, and Y and Z."

I asked Frau Benedict for a quick meeting with the Colonel. He loved the idea and wanted to precede the music with an announcement that the women's great work had earned them half Saturday off and all of Sunday. He didn't mention the supply chain problem, but Golda told me the women knew materials were depleted. They took it as a good sign that Germany was losing the war.

I was surprised to find out from Frau Benedict that Kristers had been to see the Colonel already that morning. Food supplies were running short for everyone, too. He reasoned that hungry, weary workers adversely affected production. And replacing sick or injured workers and training new ones slows output as well. If they could be incentivized by the music and a half shift on Saturday and Sunday for meeting quotas early, they would be more rested, do better work, and meet quotas consistently. In addition, if just a single, more robust meal was offered as a reward, say on Saturday evenings when they met the quota ahead of schedule, production would likely rise as well. The only random variables would be the supply chains of food and munitions materials.

Frau Benedict confided something that made me admire her husband even more. He was concerned not to overproduce. To exceed quotas. More munitions could extend the war and kill more people. I hoped that internal conflict was more widespread across Germany, especially since everyone knew the war was going badly. But it would be treason to voice it.

Kristers suggested to Herr Benedict ways to manage the pace of production to meet the quota by Friday noon. Then reward the workers with the half shifts. He also advised him not to tell the workers beforehand, let them be surprised by it, and make the connection themselves between work and benefits. Frau Benedict laughed and said Kristers even brought in charts and graphs, which included me playing three mornings a week and two lights out, Friday and Sunday. It was no wonder Herr Benedict agreed with my idea so quickly.

Later the Colonel said to me, "Someday I'll stop underestimating Kristers' brilliance."

Can you guess what followed this?

I loved him even more.

A hit song from the sixties came to mind. I asked if she ever heard, "I Love You More Today Than Yesterday" by the Spiral Starecase. She hadn't. I told her for a change I would send her an mp3. She thanked me sincerely. I asked her to please continue.

So, we put Kristers' plan in place. That first Friday night, I didn't tell anyone the piece I was going to play. Not even Kristers. I cannot remember a time when I felt more, um, anointed is the only word for it. Colonel Benedict made his announcement and introduced me. I took a moment to breathe and pictured Golda in her bunk. And Benca, the Catholic Kapo in hers. I played "Dear Lord Jesus, Take My Hand" to five hundred, mostly Hungarian Jewish women. I would never be able to pray for them in their own language, but I knew the Holy Spirit could. I just played the notes. And let Gott do the rest.

Only the Benedicts, Kristers, and the technician were in the dining hall. Beforehand, I requested no applause. To let silence be the Amen. As the final chord rang, I felt Gott's smile. I looked at Kristers. Tears were in his eyes. For a man of science, he was a real softy. Standing there with the three of them, he asked me what the "lovely" piece was, that it sounded like a prayer. I told them the title and they all laughed, Kristers most of all. The sweet irony was not lost on them - asking Jesus to hold the hands of those daughters of Abraham. Herr Benedict asked if it was a Lutheran hymn he hadn't heard. I told them it was one of my kritzeln, scribbles. Kristers said, "That's no kritzeln, mein Liebe. That's a Kronjuwel." A crown jewel.

I reminded her she promised to play it for me. She remembered and promised to.

When I put my head on the pillow that night, I knew Mama and Papa would be proud. I pictured Mama in her bed at Petra's. And Papa and Jakob rocking to sleep in the boat. Imagining Wilhelm was more difficult. He could be on patrol on the Baltic Sea or in a barracks of his own. But I knew we were all praying for each other. I prayed and had to trust what I couldn't control. I thanked Gott for the Benedicts and Kristers. And I felt the smile of Gott. I had played my part. It was a feeling like that American poet described. The one you quoted in your book, Emily. Help me with her last name.

Dickinson.

Ya, she wrote a poem about helping one fainting robin. Do you know the one?

I did. 'If I can stop one heart from breaking, I shall not live in vain. If I can ease one Life the Aching, Or cool one Pain, Or help one fainting Robin unto his Nest again, I shall not live in Vain.'

Ya, that's it. Beautiful. I must display that in the house somewhere and at the music academies. That's how I felt at the end of that day. I knew I eased some aching. Maybe even played one soul closer to heaven. And I wanted more of that feeling. Poor Anne. She never knew how many hearts she touched with her diary. Even so, she played her part and Gott took care of the rest.

I didn't want to rain on Aneska's revery and yet I had to think, did he? Yes, God amplified Anne's gift around the world, but he didn't rescue her. Or her sister Margot. Or Dietrich Bonhoeffer. Where was Providence for them and millions of other Annes and Dietrichs? I shouldn't have been surprised when Aneska interrupted herself with the same dilemma.

But why did Gott rescue Anne's diary and not Anne? I expect you wrestle with this as well, my friend. Why did I survive the war and not her? The gift is not more important than the soul that gives it, ya? Brynn and I spoke of this often. Her husband, Captain Sean O'Cullen, was killed by a sniper in Italy while dragging a wounded soldier to safety. But her son survived his bomber going down behind enemy lines and returned home.

I told her in that area, especially, God's math was beyond my understanding.

For me as well, my friend. Papa said high tide is better fishing, but we find more pretty shells at low tide. Grace is high tide. Mercy is low tide. Grace provides. Mercy reveals. The tides of grace and mercy rise and fall for everyone. I see that, but wrapping pain in pretty words doesn't answer why. Pain is pain. Trouble is trouble. And it comes to everyone. Even to Gott. Jesus wept, ya? Like Brynn, I've found no answers to why Gott allows such cruelty and agony, beyond free will and the brokenness of humans to wreak havoc like war.

But I know, I know Gott endured cruelty and agony and overcame it. And he gives strength and comfort for us to do the same without having the answers. From what I can tell, your experience with grief and loss has shown you that, too, ya?

I agreed and added that I gave up solving for X and just kept leaning on the One who knows X.

Amen, my friend. Amen.

That evening after supper, Aneska invited Zuza, Maja and I to the music room. Zuza lit some candles. Aneska played "Dear Lord Jesus, Take My Hand." Candlelight reflected off the metal sign bearing the Latin, 'Dei magnum opus est amor.' The music conjured images of what the women at Lübberstedt must have felt, lying in their bunks. How it must have touched their souls and soothed the aching for a few minutes. And perhaps reminded them of God's care and even carried them into his presence. As Aneska played, that's where it carried me. Kristers was right. The composition was a crown jewel. And I agreed with Zuza. Aneska should consider closing the concerto with it.

CHAPTER EIGHTEEN

THE KNOCK

November 20, 1944. It was a Sunday. Cold, raining and trying to turn to snow. The heavy cloud cover meant no air raids. I was secretly pining over Kristers by practicing Chopin's Raindrop Prelude opus 28 No.15 in D flat Major. I planned to broadcast it that evening at lights out.

Chopin wrote it in Mallorca, Spain, at a monastery. His doctor advised him to avoid another Paris winter for his health. His lover, Amantine Dupin, went with him. What a beautiful name, Amantine. It means 'lovable' or 'worthy to be loved.' Zuza's daughter is named Amantine Miriam Brynn. Her family picture is there in the front on the right. But leave it for now. That's part of the third movement.

Chopin and Amantine met at Franz Liszt's house in 1836. I find it fascinating how famous composer's lives overlap, like a good story. This will interest you. She was a writer. She chose the nom du plume, George Sand, to escape the prejudice against women authors back then. Publishers were not interested in female writers. Can you believe Jane Austen published anonymously? Back then, it was scandalous for a woman to write novels. That climate probably explains the absence of great female composers until more recently. It's silly how so many men can be intimidated by a gifted woman.

I made her laugh by apologizing on behalf of my entire gender.

Gifts are gifts, right? Are you familiar with Madeleine L'Engle's book "Walking on Water - Refections on Faith and Art?"

I was. And greatly admired it.

Her view is that God grants gifts and abilities as liberally as he does his grace. To believers and unbelievers. To anyone. Kristers was never intimidated by my musical abilities and aspirations. He celebrated them.

But let me get back to Chopin. The story goes, Amantine wrote in her journal that Chopin had a terrible dream he was drowning in a lake. That day during a rainstorm, she saw him at the piano wrestling to write the Raindrop Prelude. His repeating notes mimicked the steady rhythm of raindrops dripping just outside their quarters. It was his way of coming to terms with his dream. The Prelude clearly concludes the storm will pass and the light will return.

I'm sorry. I'm drifting again, I know, probably because the next part is so painful.

Midway through practicing the Prelude, Frau Benedict came into the dining hall. She took a seat across from me. I could tell something was not right. I stopped playing and asked her what was wrong.

She said four words that changed my world. "Wilhelm ist beim Herrn." 'Wilhelm is with the Lord.'

Aneska paused.

I know you have experienced sudden bad news like that, my friend. It's almost impossible to take in, isn't it? In wartime, the possibility hangs over you every day.

I did not see that coming, but the scarcity of Wilhelm's pictures on the table had telegraphed something unspoken. I could only express my empathy by reaching across to take her hand for a moment as she relived it.

Frau Benedict held me. She didn't have many details. There was an explosion on his boat. Colonel Benedict granted me three days of bereavement leave. He was waiting to drive me to Petra's. Papa and Jakob were on their way there, too. I quickly packed a few things and met Frau Benedict in the kitchen. She and Kristers were packing food for us. She gave me a minute with him. For the second time, he held me. It was not for the reason I wanted, but the empathy of feeling his arms around me and his heart close to mine was what I needed. He knew the pain of losing a brother to the war. He slipped a note into my pocket.

On the drive to Sandbostel, I watched the winter countryside glide by. My mind was numb, and my heart ached. The war had finally taken one of us, my protector and champion, Wilhelm. I pulled out the note from Kristers. "You do not have to be strong. The Lord, your family, the Benedicts and I are your I-beam. We will carry you." Below that, he wrote it out like a formula. The Lord plus family plus friends plus me equals your I-beam. I have it in the green folder.

I wanted to see it. But interrupting this memory was not the thing to do.

At Petra's, Mama and I fell into each other's arms. She was so thin. Herr Benedict brought in the food. Papa and Jakob arrived that evening. We wept together. Mama had more details.

That morning, there was a knock on the door at Petra's. Two soldiers gave her the news. Wilhelm's boat apparently strayed into a mined area at night. He ordered the crew into a life raft and steered the boat and leaking fuel away from them. Apparently, he hit another mine. The boat exploded and went down. The crew never found his body. They rowed to a nearby lighthouse. All of them survived.

The soldiers gave Mama an envelope from Wilhelm, a "just in case" letter all soldiers were required to write to their families in the event of their death. They also presented her a medal, the Iron Cross, for his bravery in saving his crew. And a thank you from a grateful Führer.

I thought Papa was going to explode. He clinched the medal in his fist then hurled it at the wall. He carried on about trading his son for a trinket from "that devil." And my brother being too good a sailor for it to be an accident. He was convinced Wilhelm deliberately sabotaged the boat. He went out on the porch alone.

When he came back in, he tossed an envelope on the table. It was addressed, "To My Family, Open if I do not return." It was still sealed. Wilhelm slipped it to Papa the night he boarded his boat. Papa put the first letter in the fireplace with the Iron Cross. Mama protested, but Wilhelm had told Papa about the official letter. It was nothing but lies monitored by the SS to convey loyalty to the Reich. Papa watched it burn.

We sat around the table looking at the second envelope. Papa finally opened it.

Aneska asked me to retrieve the green folder. She sorted through the stack of papers. Selected an envelope. She pulled the letter out with great care and read it.

My dearest family,

Should the Lord take me to himself in this madness, I want each of you to know something.

Papa, you are the man I always hoped to be. You taught me how to love the Lord, a wife, and the sea. What deserves a good cussing. And true faith is risking all for what the Lord values.

Mama, your steady faith steadies me now. From you I learned valor grows stronger in the face of my opponents, like my chemistry class, remember?

And now, as we face the fear and evil devouring Germany.

Jakob, my brother in blood and Christ, you taught me the blessing of a true friend.

Pulling full nets with you is how my heart feels when I think of you.

And my sweet music maker, Aneska. Your shiny soul poured joy and hope into mine. Mama is right, your music will make a way for you. You are meant to make the world a brighter place. Every time you played, I felt Gott's grandeur and tenderness.

You already know how much I love you all. Lord willing, I will be with you again when this darkness passes. If not, let's meet at the gates of heaven.

I hope to find any way to scuttle this evil. Pray my valor holds so I can say,

"I have fought the good fight, I have finished the race, I have kept the faith."

2 Timothy 4:7

My soul belongs to the Lord. My heart is with you…

Always, Wilhelm

Papa immediately latched onto the word "scuttle." For him, it was evidence enough that Wilhelm sabotaged the boat to take it and the crew out of service.

On the heels of Wilhelm's sweet and agonizing words, a terrible thought struck me. What if the naval mines Wilhelm hit were made in Lübberstedt? What if I counted the very batch that killed him? Even if not the actual mines, I was part of the war machine that was killing sailors and airmen. I blurted out my fear to all of them. And told them how my music was making the munition workers more productive.

Looking back, I know we were all hurting, and I piled more of my pain on them. But Mama held me. Papa knew how I felt. He described his own conflict. For years, he and Jakob and Wilhelm supplied food for the officers and soldiers who took part directly in the brutalities of the war. But he and the boys also smuggled endangered people to Sweden. That's the first time I heard him admit it to me out loud. He reminded me that as a nurse in Hamburg, Mama tended to wounded soldiers. She helped some of them simply survive, but made others well enough to go back into battle to kill or be killed. Herr Benedict didn't want to manage a munitions factory. Rolf didn't want to refuel machines of war.

Mama said, "We play our parts, mein Schatz. Gott knows our hearts. Whatever happened with Wilhelm, I know he played his part."

Papa's eyes filled with tears again. He said, "And with Gott's help, we will, too."

For another day, we clung to each other. Mama only had Monday off work. We baked a little. Petra cooked. Mostly, we sat with each other. It was too painful without Wilhelm to take any pictures and film was getting scarce. Papa and Mama were so tender with each other. Jakob thought we should all escape immediately to Sweden on the boat, but Papa said more of the German navy was in the Baltic to battle the British and Soviet navies. More patrols, submarines, and more areas were mined than ever. And besides, winter was already beginning. Papa thought between the winter and the Allied and Soviet advances, the war might end by summer. Best to keep steady on.

There was no church service. No memorial for Wilhelm. We lit candles the next evening at Petra's. Mama read some scriptures. Papa was silent. He asked me to play "Dear Lord Jesus, Take My Hand." I wasn't sure I could get through it. Mama sat beside me on the bench. We got through it. Jakob prayed.

Tuesday morning, Mama went back to work at the Stalag. Papa and Jakob drove the truck back to the boat to fish before big winter storms set in. That afternoon, the Benedicts arrived to carry me to Lübberstedt. I sat between them and leaned on Frau Benedict the whole way. I remember thinking this must be how Lazarus' sisters, Martha and Mary, felt when their brother died before Jesus showed up late to resurrect him. But there was no resurrecting Wilhelm. He was gone.

Christmas was just weeks ahead, but it seemed far away.

Everything and everyone seemed far away. We hoped to spend it at Petra's, Lord willing.

She handed me the handwritten letter from Wilhelm. I hesitated to touch it. It felt like a rare parchment, like the handwritten Mark Twain manuscripts my graduate school professor showed us in the inner sanctum of the library. He wore white gloves. We were not allowed to touch them as he passed them around. I remember the awe I felt having the same close view Twain did as the words poured from his storyteller mind through the ink onto the page. The passages we viewed had very few scratch outs, indicating a flow, an unhesitancy and clarity of mental vision.

Wilhelm's letter was similar. Only two edits. It was, of course, written in German, so Aneska translated. In the first line he scratched out 'Ruhm,' 'glory' and substituted 'selbst,' 'himself,' "Should the Lord take me to himself." I pointed out to Aneska the new word choice is much more specific than 'glory' and wondered if it implied Wilhelm's longing was to be with the Lord, not just in the realms of glory. She had noticed the change, too, and agreed that was very much Wilhelm's heart. The other word scratched through was 'besiegen,' 'defeat'. It was replaced by 'sinken,' meaning 'sink or scuttle' in the line, "I hope to find any way to scuttle this evil." I told her I had to agree with Deit. That could be a very strong clue to what Wilhelm eventually carried out.

Ya, very possible. In any case, I believe his valor held out. That's why my son's name is Deitrich Wilhelm Valor Latva, after my Papa and brother.

While the folder was out, I asked to see the note Kristers put in her pocket. His mathematic bent was evident in his language. It was precise. No edits at all. Even his penmanship resembled a printed font, like an architect's. But his great mind knew how to speak from the heart, even framed in a formula. "The Lord + family + friends + me = your I-Beam. We will carry you." I was familiar with that formula. I had been carried before. More than once.

Only one word in Kristers' note was underlined, 'not', in the first sentence. "You do <u>not</u> have to be strong." I wondered out loud to Aneska why Kristers emphasized that.

He was a man of faith, but math made him a realist. In solving anything, he used to say, all the factors have to be true, as accurate as possible to get a reliable answer or outcome. In baking a cake or in matters of the heart. I don't have to tell you, my friend, a false strength or denial of the pain delays healing. You don't pretend an amputation is an abrasion. You grieve the magnitude of the loss. But not like those who have no hope, as scripture reminds us. Kristers knew the dynamics of the heart and spirit.

I must tell you, he had these playful mathematical sayings, the Laws of Theodyanamics he called them. I wrote them down.

She pulled another paper out of the folder.

"Nothing equals love." "Hope multiplies courage." "Four-giveness is as high as God can count." Sounds like a children's book, ya? "Doubt divided by faith over time diminishes exponentially." "Only love renders entropy nil." And my favorite: "Pi times Infinity squared equals the circumference of Love." Back then his mind was his playground. Just like his canvases later.

I didn't tell Aneska then, but the song idea "Equations of the Heart" was nearly writing itself.

CHAPTER NINETEEN

THE SNOWDROP

Days trudged by. Nights brought more tears. Kristers was right. I was carried. I had no strength of my own to face Wilhelm's loss. He and the Benedicts nursed my heart. The Labor Service girls were so tender toward me. When they heard me crying in the night several would gather round my bunk, hold my hand, stroke my hair and pray. Most of them had brothers off to war as well. The laborers and even the guards treated me with such kindness.

After a few days, Kristers gently encouraged me to take my grief to the piano. Benca and Golda told me the women missed my playing. They hoped I would play again soon. Most of them had lost family members to the war. Golda's parents were sent to Auschwitz. I realized no one had a monopoly on loss.

It had been seven days since I played for them. Early Friday morning I went to the piano. The glass of water was there. In the vase beside it was a single snowdrop blossom. Its milky white head bowed. It looked so reverent. Kristers stood in the doorway of the kitchen, beside the Benedicts. Without any announcements or introduction, I played Liszt's Consolation No. 3. Remember? That's the one that made trouble for me at the Stalag. It was verboten there. But here, in that moment it took on a new dimension, like a healing prayer. It sounds like it was written for the day that breaks your heart.

There was another one. An obvious and tender song title. They poured from Aneska's soul like honey from the comb. I jotted it down and marked it like the others, with a quarter note beside it. "For the Day That Breaks Your Heart"

I didn't play just for the women. I played for my grieving family. For myself. And every torn heart around the world. Like Anne wrote, I felt the suffering of millions, because I felt my own suffering. And I knew Gott grieved, too. I played it lento placido, slow and calm as Liszt notated. His melodies and chord colors speak like someone who knew the pain that makes comfort so needed. Some think he wrote the piece grieving Chopin, who died the previous year. The Consolation ends in a sparkle of high notes, like sunlight on snow, then cascades slowly as if from heaven back down to earth, connecting both realms in simple pairs of thirds. It ends molto placido, very softly, on just two notes. Like a duet.

I was eager to listen to her recording of it as I walked the grounds later that day.

At breakfast, Kristers served pancakes with real maple syrup. Who knows how he got it or where? After we ate, some of us helped clean the kitchen. In two of the window boxes snowdrops bloomed in bright rows. They were so cheerful against the winter day outside. Kristers said a cold snap actually signals them to bloom. That they can grow in light shade like they do naturally under a forest canopy, but sunlight makes them stand a little taller and brings out their sweet scent. Kristers, the scientist remember, believed snowdrops were Gott telegraphing that winter will not overpower life. To hold on. Is it any wonder I loved him?

I held on. Or it's more accurate to say, they all held on to me. The sun kept coming up. And going down. I set my sights on Christmas and the possibility of the family together for even one day at Petra's. It seemed very unlikely. A travel ban was in place except for essentials, war materials and food. I hoped that meant Papa and Jakob could still deliver fish.

Quotas for anti-aircraft shells were raised. Everyone knew the increased Allied bombing was the reason. Kristers overheard officers talking about trains heading west every night filled with troops and the new Panther and Tiger tanks. He said it was no surprise the most lethal German tanks were named after alpha predators. I prayed for Petra's husband, Rolf, thinking he might be deployed to carry petrol for them.

We didn't realize Germany was launching a major offensive to regain the momentum of the war. Knowing would have crushed our hope that the end was near. No one had a crystal ball. We lived every day braced for bad news. The world had been at war for more than five years. A third of my life! Not counting the shadows that led up to it.

It would have been easy to think Gott had abandoned the planet. Kristers insisted if Gott was still growing flowers, it only followed, he couldn't be far away. He was always saying that. "It only follows."

While more and more of the so called "enlightened" in science and academia embraced a Gottless universe, Kristers keen mind continually led him toward Gott, not away. To him it just did not follow that, as he said, "nothing generated everything, matter urged itself into complex life, and randomness and chaos produced precision and order." To Kristers' mind, that took a lot more blind faith and flawed reasoning than following the evidence to a divine Designer.

While baking a cake he would talk about morality, art and love as proof of a divine imprint or image in human beings, beyond our physical, genetic makeup. "Take Gott out of the equation," he said, "a holy, loving, just, creator Gott, and it only follows, all manner of chaos, cruelty and perverse thinking will overtake the soul like a fungus or mold that thrives in the dark. Move the sextant one degree from true north and the most sophisticated ship will never find its harbor again. Take away light, what follows? Darkness. This holds for every person and any nation. It only follows."

She anticipated my question.

Ya, I wrote that down. It's in one of the diaries. Nearly every night I wrote in it. Can you see why I loved his heart, his mind and his soul?

I had stopped telling Aneska how many nuggets of song ideas I was panning from her stream. I jotted down "You Are My True North" and "It Only Follows" marked by quarter notes and kept listening.

I'm so sorry you didn't get to meet Kristers. We have videos of him. I'll show you when we get to the third movement.

That satisfied another curiosity. I imagined there had to be more than just photos of Kristers.

You see how the thought of him gets me off track? Let's see…

The week before Christmas, 1944, Colonel Benedict announced the news over the loudspeakers. "Under cover of foul weather, in a brilliant surprise offensive designed by the Führer himself, the superior Nazi military is at this very moment pushing back the Allied forces in the forests of Ardennes in Belgium and Luxembourg." In its wording, the old bravado was back, like all the fortissimo crowing in the streets of Hamburg at the beginning of the war. But Herr Benedict's delivery was far less than enthusiastic. He read it like a lunch menu. The news was not followed by a hearty 'Sieg Heil'. No one cheered. The Ardennes region was only four hours southwest of Lübberstedt! If the offensive failed the war might be over by spring. Maybe sooner.

I pestered Gott with prayers. Like I imagined Papa would. That the bullets the women made would misfire. That winter snow and ice would prove as great an adversary as it did in Germany's defeat in Russia. I prayed for the airmen and foot soldiers on both sides. Even though it meant death and destruction, I prayed the sky would clear so the Allied pilots could hit their marks. I even prayed Rolf's petrol truck would slide off the icy roads, but he would be spared. Anything to hamper the offensive. And, of course, I prayed against the odds for Christmas day together in Sandbostel.

The thought that thousands were dying in the new offensive overwhelmed me. All their loved ones would need more than Liszt's Consolation. They would need what I needed to grieve Wilhelm - the consolation of the Emmanuel of Christmas, bringing a hope beyond the grave. I understood clearer than ever what Isaiah wrote. "The people in darkness have seen a great light."

It was nearly Christmas and the world felt darker than ever. Still, in my sorrow the star of Bethlehem blossomed steady and defiant like a snowdrop in my heart. I thought I could never need Jesus more. I longed to write that hope into music. Maybe that's all I've been trying to do my whole life. In that bleak season I took a page of hope from the classical masters. Days before Christmas I broadcast to the camp Beethoven's "Ode to Joy," "Angels We Have Heard on High" by Mendelssohn and the chorus to Handel's "Messiah." To an audience almost entirely of Jewish women! *She laughed.* I felt the smile of God. And his strength flowed in my weakness.

Before Aneska could satisfy my curiosity about what happened that Christmas, Zuza came in to remind her of a meeting at the music academy just down the road in Carlow.

That afternoon I walked the estate listening to her recording of Consolation No.3, picturing the scenes she painted. Her loss of Wilhelm so fresh. The women listening across the camp. From what she already told me, a fourth of them did not survive the war. Passing Kristers' memorial, half a dozen lovely snowdrops blossomed around its base. Telegraphing life in the face of death. Aneska playing in my ears nearly wrecked me. It only followed.

CHAPTER TWENTY

THE SURPRISE

By this time, I had more questions than ever. The list kept growing. I checked them off as Aneska's story revealed answers. Interrupting her rhythm would be like standing up in the middle of a cocncerto to ask the pianist about a chord or melody choice and where all this was headed. I trusted her transparency. There was no reason to doubt that whatever she had not revealed yet, whether intentional or by nature of the eloquence of her heart, the missing pieces helped me experience her story as it unfolded, like she did living it, with only the revelations of the moment along the storyline but little foreknowledge of future outcomes.

Isn't that the way all our lives unfold? We ride the crest of the present, knowing what lies over our shoulder, driven by currents of good and evil with only our free will, wits and faith to navigate. We react to whatever comes, but we can also create a life by our choices, with truth and courage, or the lack of both, through a gauntlet of forces out of our control, forces munificent and malevolent, inside and outside of us. That's what Aneska and her family had done through one of the most turbulent episodes in human history. Like so many classical compositions, getting to the third movement of life seems like the prize.

It struck me, if my own life has three movements I was somewhere deep into the second. Dark forces cut Anne Frank's life short in her second movement. But the diary containing all her beautiful humanity and bright aspirations blossomed into her glorious third movement, albeit posthumously. And that movement eviscerated the darkness and dark actors that took her earthly life. Knowing Aneska's second movement surrendered to a brighter one gave me hope. And maybe that's why this story chose me. Maybe that's why it needed to be told. Just like her music needed to be heard.

I was hungry to know the whole story and experience her music, but could be content for a bit not knowing about Christmas 1944. I knew the first movement. Much of the second. I knew she and Kristers survived the war. Wilhelm did not. I knew the dark, second act was not over yet. And a third was coming. Many things were still unknown but there was plenty to occupy myself. Afternoons and evenings were spent archiving and transcribing the interviews and savoring the Irish countryside, and Magic Maja's menu.

More than a month had gone by since my arrival. I had seen Valor three times. He stopped by to introduce himself and his son, Vic, short for Victory, his middle name, Kristers. He bore a remarkable resemblance to his grandfather in the pictures in the study. Valor thanked me profusely for writing his mother's story. I told him it was practically writing itself. I still didn't know how he came to run the dairy down the lane. When I asked, he preferred to let his mother tell the story, saying she was the best keeper of the storyline. I couldn't argue with that. On the other two brief visits he delivered milk, cream, butter and cheese to the kitchen for Maja to work her magic. All the labels on the goods read simply, "The Dairy Down the Lane."

The next morning, my fireside session with Aneska began with Franzbrötchen, the famous cinnamon pastry of Hamburg. Maja brought them into the study as we began. Fresh from the oven. I was told the authentic recipe takes two days, letting two kinds of dough rest. The smell was magical. The taste heavenly. If someone set a plate of Loveless biscuits in front of me next to Franzbrötchen, high respect to the remarkable bakers at Loveless Café outside Nashville, but I'm reaching for the Hamburg confection first before they're all gone. The iconic pastry even played a part in her story.

I guess you see why we call her Magic. I asked Maja to make these two days ago not realizing where we would be in our conversation. This little pastry actually worked a miracle at Christmas 1944.

I was all ears because my mouth was full.

Two days before Christmas I went to the dining hall at Lübberstedt very early to practice. A light was on in the kitchen. Kristers stood at a counter kneading dough. I asked what he was making.

"A surprise," he said.

I looked at the ingredients on the counter - flour, milk, yeast, sugar, eggs, lots of butter and cinnamon. I helped Mama bake with those ingredients a hundred times in our kitchen.

"You're making Franzbrötchen, aren't you?" I said to him.

He tried to get rid of me. "What makes you think that? Don't you need to practice?"

I used his own words against him. "Look at these ingredients. It only follows." I was right, of course. But the miracle began the next day, Christmas eve.

Having worked in Hamburg, the Benedicts were big fans of Franzbrötchen, too. They discovered Kristers' surprise and set their own in motion. After dinner Christmas eve, Colonel Benedict announced that because increased quotas were met, Christmas day was a work holiday. I followed him with "Silent Night" to nearly five hundred Jewish women. I felt God chuckle. Herr Benedict asked me to play something Christmas morning as well. Like all the other Labor Service girls, I gave up on seeing my family. Lights out came. I cried myself to sleep.

Christmas morning, I thought about broadcasting part of the Nutcracker by Tchaikovsky, but felt playing a Russian composer might not be wise. Kristers agreed. I played Christmas Tree Suite No. 8 by

Liszt. It's light-hearted and delicate. And it's Hungarian. As usual, a glass of water and a single snowdrop in the vase accompanied me.

At breakfast, Kristers treated the kitchen staff and all the girls to Franzbrötchen and made them promise not to tell the officers. Frau Benedict told me to dress warm and meet her in the Colonel's office. Kristers was there, too. That was very puzzling. And delightful. The four of us bundled into the Colonel's car. He drove. Kristers sat in front with him. Brigitte. and I sat in the back.

Three minutes down the road I knew we were headed toward Sandbostel. The Benedicts thought we should deliver Franzbrötchen to Mama and Petra for Christmas! And since Kristers made them, he should bake them fresh in Petra's kitchen. The dough and ingredients were in the trunk, with other food items for a meal. We would be back by supper and hardly anyone would know we were gone. Oh, my heart! Their kindness eased the heartache and filled part of the cavern in my chest. The snow clouds hung low, but my spirit flew high ahead of us.

Mama and Petra had no idea we were coming. Communication was highly restricted. Herr Benedict said there was no way to let them know or get word to Papa and Jakob. This was purely spontaneous. If anyone questioned us, Kristers brought a few pastries to sweeten the way. We didn't even know if Mama had to work at the Stalag on Christmas day.

I raced to the door and knocked. It opened and Papa stood there! Neither of us could believe our eyes. His arms felt like the embrace of God himself come to say 'I see you. I hear you. I am Emmanuel. I am with you.' Mama even had Christmas day off work! The Hallelujah Chorus was not fortissimo enough to describe our reunion.

Do I need to tell you I was flying, too, hearing her tell it? I had the advantage of watching Aneska's face and hearing the colors in her voice.

How do you explain this, my friend? It's clearly a work of the

Spirit. Hearts so knit together can move without speaking. Without a phone or internet. There are bonds beyond words that synchronize lives and actions, like a musical score. Add divine choreography, and anything is possible. Move in the Spirit, and the Spirit moves, too.

Walk by faith, not sight, right?

Ya, precisely. You came here by faith, my friend. We came to Ireland by faith. And found hearts in the same rhythm as ours. Gott's ways are wondrous. And often unsearchable, too.

Being together was all the Christmas present I needed. Seeing Kristers in the kitchen with Mama, shaping and baking the Franzbrötchen and helping make the meal was nothing but a miracle. Even the aromas were healing. Even so, the cloud of Wilhelm's absence at the dinner table hung over us. Kristers could never take my brother's place, but his presence, as well as the Benedict's, gave us much to be grateful for.

I bet you're wondering how it went between Papa and Kristers, ya?

Ya, definitely.

Before we ate, Papa and the Benedicts went out on the front porch. That made me very anxious, but Mama reassured me. They weren't there long because it was very cold. We stayed busy in the kitchen. Kristers brought sugar, which was rationed and very hard to get. And cream, butter, olive oil and some herbs he grew - dill, rosemary, chives and garlic. He even brought Belgium chocolate to eat with the Franzbrötchen. Papa was impressed. Sweet smells filled the house.

At midday, we pulled two tables together and sat down to an impressive meal of trout, potatoes, red cabbage and pumperknickel rolls. Papa struggled through a beautiful prayer. His tears fell on the table. His were not the only ones.

There was no shortage of topics for conversation. The war, of course, and how soon it might end. Herr Benedict confided the new offensive was already stalling in the harsh winter and stubborn pushback of the

Allies. Just like I prayed. Papa said the Allies had a jaw like Joe Louis. "They can take a punch." We talked about shortages of staples and war material. News of old friends in Hamburg. Papa complimented Kristers on the way he flavored the trout, and in the same breath wished Hitler would choke on a bone from a fish he caught. Kristers "amen" made us all laugh and echo him.

Papa peppered Kristers with a series of questions. They all started the same way: "I understand you are from Göttingen? I understand you were a chef there.?" My anxiety rose again. "I understand you're really a mathematician? I understand you're indebted to our good friend, Herr Benedict, for your fortunate position away from the fighting?"

Kristers answered every question graciously. He asked some of his own, like, "Herr Pfieffer, I understand you and Frau Pfieffer both have Swedish roots? So do I."

They found other common ground when Kristers brought up his admiration for Deitrich Bonhoeffer and his book, "The Cost of Discipleship."

Papa said he regretted more German Christians and people of faith did not stand against Hitler early on. He said, "If so, we might not be in this terrible war." I knew what he would say next because I heard it a hundred times, "People who don't stand up will be forced to bow down."

As the meal wound down, I began to relax. But Papa silenced the room with this, and it was not a question. "Kristers, I understand you're in love with my daughter."

Mama took Papa's hand.

Kristers didn't flinch. He looked across the table at me, then at Papa and said, "Yes, sir. Wouldn't you be?" He looked back at me and said, "She's the most remarkable, beautiful person I've ever known."

No one said a word.

Finally, Papa responded. "I can't argue with that." He looked at me. "Aneska, mein Schatz, do you love this young man?"

I felt a surprising calm. I looked at Kristers and answered the same way I did when Mama asked me. "With all my heart, Papa."

For a Viking-sized, rough-hewn sea captain, Papa had the eloquence of speaking straight from the heart. I wonder if his early conversation with Mama's parents echoed in his mind.

He told Kristers, "Miriam and I fell in love quickly. We have prayed our children would find a love like ours, one that can weather stormy seas. The Benedict's tell me you have been a perfect gentleman. And I understand my wife gave her blessing for you to court Aneska. But that's only half the blessing you need."

Papa paused. We all waited like petitioners before a revered feudal Lord. I felt pulled between my compete trust of Papa and my love for Kristers. His next words implied he might not give his blessing. He talked about my age, that I didn't even turn sixteen until April and how Gott had given me an immense musical gift and dreams that must be nurtured and respected, as well as my faith in Gott. He talked about how the pressures and uncertainty of the war can make us all off kilter and desperate for something lovely and real. My heart sank. And then rose on one word.

"But" Papa said, "I trust Miriam's opinion and the Benedicts'. If you will respect these things and give Aneska a little time, I give my blessing to court her."

Electric joy went around the table. But Papa wasn't done.

"If the Lord brings the rest of us through this conflict, and your hearts' desire is to marry, come to me again. We will cross that bridge, and perhaps, I'll bring the fish." It was more than I hoped for. But Papa's face suddenly turned very stern, like a battle-worn lion staring down a younger one.

The electric joy turned to heat. "Young man, we know all too well tomorrow is not promised to any of us. But if you break my daughter's heart… I can keep you from seeing tomorrow."

No one breathed.

Kristers stood. He extended his hand to shake Papa's and said, "Of course, it only follows. I would want to die." Isn't that rich? And so dear. Papa laughed his big laugh. He stood and took Kristers' hand. The protective lion was won over.

After that, Franzbrötchen topped with shaved Belgium chocolate was never better. They tasted like the love that made them. Kristers wrote down for Papa how he flavored the trout. Papa asked me to play "Dear Lord Jesus, Take My Hand."

The time to go came far too soon. We stood in a circle in the living room to pray. Mama positioned me by Kristers to hold his hand. She held my other one. Papa prayed next to Kristers. He rarely prayed long, but this time he included protection for Mama working at the camp, Rolf's safe return, a blessing on the Benedicts and one for Kristers and me. The power of that blessing carried us every day. For the rest of our lives. Of course, Papa threw in the imminent demise of Hitler. And even prayed for the two British pilots he and Jakob smuggled to Sweden. He didn't mention Wilhelm. I don't think his heart could bear it. He paused and Mama took over. She thanked the Lord Wilhelm was safe in his presence. And asked Gott to watch over our broken hearts until we were reunited there one day. Last of all, she thanked Gott for her Magnum Opus, her family. Papa said "amen." We all did.

That parting was not sweet sorrow. It was agony. To leave such sweetness. Mama held my face in her hands, like always. Papa and Kristers embraced. There was embracing all around. And crying. And we said it again, "Gott be with you." "And with your spirit."

Every time I traveled the road from Sandbostel to Lübberstedt was an emotional ride. This time Kristers sat beside me in the back seat. He held my hand the entire way.

We arrived in time for dinner with the girls. Afterward, they asked me to play. I wanted to play something a little sad for Christmas, "O Come, O Come, Emmanuel." Frau Benedict requested "O Come All Ye Faithful." Even in the sadness, I felt joyful and triumphant about Papa's blessing. So, I played them both. What happened taught me a lesson I've never forgotten. I can explain it better if we go to the piano. We can have a little Christmas here in February.

I had no qualms with that. Any chance to hear Aneska play was a gift. We moved to the front music room.

"O Come, O Come, Emmanuel" is in a minor key and as I'm sure you know, it's about rejoicing in the midst of mourning and exile. As I played it I felt very blue, even though I had been so blessed that day. None of the girls spent Christmas day with their parents. Kristers hadn't heard from his in a month. So, my sadness was part pity party. You may remember the song ends on a Picardy third that lifts it from minor to major, from lament to hope. It pierced my heart.

She played it. Fluid and full of regal sorrow.

As the last major chord rang, I began "O, Come All Ye Faithful" slower than usual, and rubato, with only the melody line, pianissimo, very lightly in a high register. I brought in chords at "Come and behold him" cascading down to a long space after "born the King of angels." Then established a steady rhythm for the refrain. Like this.

She rewound to the final "Rejoice, rejoice" of the first song and transitioned to "Come All Ye Faithful" just as she described. At the ending, "Chri — ist, the Lord," she retarded and landed on the four chord over low bass octaves. In the high register she lightly played just the two notes of the melody of the first song, "Rejoice, Rejoice," twice, let it hang suspended, then rolled into the one chord. It rang warm and long.

Did you feel that? Something eases, settles in you, doesn't it?

I couldn't argue with that.

I already knew the power of music. But here's what I learned again that day. No matter how you feel – offer your gift. That's part of worship, to return the gift. And no matter what you've lost. Give thanks. Bring all of you, even what's left of you, to life and to the altar. And lay it down. Give it. Mama did that in her prayer about Wilhelm. His letter showed he was ready to, whatever the cost. Kristers did it with his cooking, and later his painting. Papa and Mama, Wilhelm and Jakob, the Benedicts, Petra, and later the O'Cullens, they all taught me this. Live all in.

Zuza was right in our first phone call. Aneska was more inspiring than I could imagine. Next to her I was living in half measures and muted colors. She wasn't done.

No one lived more all in than the Lord. He knew how to redeem more than sin. He redeemed loss and solitude and sorrow. He seized the moment instead being seized by circumstance. I wanted that. I needed it.

The Lord's frown on my pity party got my attention that day. In the span of two songs something was different in me. I took a deeper breath. And I can't say my determination had anything to do with it. It was more like a surrender. Then the freedom came. Like Mama, I surrendered Wilhelm. I've done a lot of surrendering since then. And the best of what followed was nothing I could make happen. Someday, my friend, I'll have to surrender this life, likely not many years from now. But if the Lord can be trusted, what's waiting is sweeter than Franzbrötchen and Mama's apple pie.

I said, It only follows. She laughed and played the refrain, "O come let us adore him. O come, let us adore him. O come, let us adore him, Christ, the Lord."

It was time for lunch. Maja's gift awaited.

CHAPTER TWENTY-ONE

THE POINT

Gott must have heard my prayer about making winter Germany's adversary. By new year's day 1945, the new offensive stalled. You may have heard of the Battle of the Bulge. The official German name for it was Autumn Mist. It had something to do with the element of surprise. I had to laugh. What happens to a mist in freezing weather? It turns to ice and falls to the ground. Besides, it sounded so passive, like something from a Goethe poem used to name a perfume.

The German army drove into the Allied lines, creating a spearhead, a bulge, hoping to cut them in half. But like Joe Louis, the scrappy GIs and Brits rallied. They delivered blow after blow. Frozen Autumn Mist proved no match for the Allied sledgehammer. On the Eastern front, the Soviets were doing the same. Wherever he was, I could hear Papa say Hitler was on the ropes. But we knew thousands of fathers and sons were dying on both sides. Civilians, too. And we still didn't know how many rounds till the knockout blow ended the carnage.

My days began with a repeat sign. Practice early. Help Kristers in the kitchen. Breakfast. Count and record the batches. Dinner. Play for the officers. Broadcast a piece three or four times a week. Write in my diary. Lights out. Through it all, snowdrops blossomed in the kitchen window boxes.

Mid-January, Kristers overheard the officers. The offensive failed and word spread fast. Kristers reacted by making cupcakes for the girls. Each one had a letter on top made of icing. Except mine. It had an Ausrufezeichen, an exclamation point. We couldn't eat them until we figured out the puzzle.

She wrote it down for me.

The letters were: L S I H E G I E He gave us a hint. It was two words. Any guesses?

I didn't know German, but it appeared fairly obvious. Sieg Heil? Hail victory?

Precisely! Most of the girls knew what he meant. Whose victory he was celebrating. For weeks they called me Kristers' Ausrufezeichen. I didn't mind. Especially when Kristers found out. Privately he began using it, too. "Good morning, mein Ausrufezeichen. Please, hand me the pepper, mein Ausrufezeichen."

Being so in love with Kristers made it possible to dream again, even in that place. I was ready for the coda of this movement. I thought about our future. I could see us living in Gottingen. While Kristers finished his degree, I would continue my music studies. Prepare to become a concert pianist. Start a music academy. I dreamed of composing, of hearing my work in the hands of skilled orchestras. Somewhere in there, Gott willing, we would have children. Make a family of our own. It's all in my diary from that time.

I knew what I wanted. But the war had killed the dreams of so many. There was every chance it could kill mine. Wanting and dreaming and believing only hold so much power. I surrendered them to Gott every night. But every morning when I saw Kristers, they were back.

One morning while watering the snowdrops, the words of Jesus about the lilies of the field came into my head. Mama used to remind me of them as I prepared for recitals confused about what to wear. "Gott takes care of the lilies. They don't toil or worry. He dresses them fairer than Solomon. So, do not be anxious about tomorrow."

"But Mama," I would say, "Gott knows I know that, and he knows I'm still anxious."

One day she told me something I later came to see was part of how she faced things with such steadiness and calm.

She said, "Aneska, you know how you practice every day to get better, stronger? There are ways to practice your faith, too. Scripture says, 'Cast your cares on Gott, for he cares for you.' Every time you feel anxious, cast it. That means speak it. Lay it in Gott's hands. Even if you have to do it every hour. Every minute."

Of course, I had another 'but Mama.' I had a lot of them.

"But Mama, doesn't Gott have better things to do than listen to the same thing over and over again from me?"

Mama laughed and told me, "Mein Schatz, heavens no. Caring for you is Gott's full-time job. Like mine, to be your Mama."

Looking at the delicate beauty of the snowdrops, it hit me new, like an Ausrufezeichen. Gott cares for me! I wasn't hidden from him in Lübberstedt like cloud cover from Allied bombers. He is Emmanuel, with me, and cares for me. Gott cares for you, my friend. He cares for us!

Right there in the kitchen, I thanked Gott for taking care of me. In Hamburg. Sandbostel and in Lübberstedt. I gave him my cares and fears and dreams and asked him to fulfill his dreams, his purpose in me, like he does with the snowdrops. Come what may. Live or die. Like Wilhelm. But I had so much to live for. I hoped Gott thought so, too. Apparently, he did. Here I am. I kept surrendering, casting my cares and dreams in his hands. I still do.

She turned somber.

But so many dear people from that awful time did not survive. People who also had a lot to live for. Did he not care as much for them? Of course not. Loving is Gott's nature. His full-time job, according to Mama. Surely, their deaths were not his best intention for their lives on earth. Like Anne Frank's. But great evil, not Gott, was to blame.

Like I said, so many of his ways are unsearchable. Which can sound like an excuse for Gott. Look at Job. All that suffering. The Devil caused it. But Gott allowed it. Sometimes life can seem like Gott's torture chamber, ya? But it's not. He created this life and called it 'good.' We are the main cause of the havoc. And he bore the brunt of it on the cross. To redeem the havoc and heartache. Maybe that's the point… of it all. More than anything, I want to be part of that redemption. I want my music to be part of that.

She seamlessly turned her thoughts to me, like a painter equally adept with a broad brush and a fine liner for details.

I know from your book you wrestled with Gott about these things. Someone you loved dearly died young, with so much to live for. Gone in an instant. She was barely into the second movement of her life, likely a beautiful movement. But we can't know what she would have faced, ya? I'm sure you cast that mystery and care on Gott for a long time. With no sufficient answers. I am so sorry that happened, but I'm glad you are still here. I'm glad your storyline includes loving again and your beautiful children. They must be such a joy, even in the current heartache. And whatever may come, they are certainly evidence of Gott's goodness. As mine are.

If Aneska's depth and tenderness shaped the music she was preparing, and I was certain it had to, the concerto promised to be a colossal experience. I had no doubt it would express the havoc, heartache, and beauty of her journey and celebrate triumph over darkness.

CHAPTER TWENTY-TWO

THE FLOOD

By February 1945, the German army was in retreat. News came Berlin had been bombed. Ferociously. Kristers' parents were assigned there at the central bank. They worked under duress, financing the war. There was no word about them.

Stress rose on the assembly lines. Supplies dwindled. Quotas were not met. A locomotive on a siding near us was bombed. We heard the planes and explosions. Some guards took out their anger about Berlin on the workers. But behind it was fear. Uncertainty and fear can bring out a person's true character. Others grew kinder. Kristers overheard two officers talking about how the captors might soon become the captives. That could explain some of the softer treatment. But most of the staff knew they were fortunate to be assigned away from the front lines, and simply did their jobs.

An early thaw brought rain instead of snow. Colonel Benedict informed us the muddy roads and rising rivers slowed the Allied and Soviet advances. My bomb shelter flooded. I imagined Papa welcomed the thaw to do more fishing. Talking in the kitchen with Kristers as the rain poured down, it felt like the whole world was crying. I prayed it would wash the war away and the river of blood that cried out from the land and sea would move Gott's mercy and justice to end the madness. Sooner than later. But darkness does not go quietly.

All of my previous surrendering was a prelude for what was coming.

Colonel Benedict called Kristers into his office one morning after breakfast. It was a Tuesday, February 6. His parents had been killed in the Berlin bombing that Saturday. There could be no burial. No memorial for now. It was my turn to be strong for him. I held him as sheets of rain pounded the metal roof. That evening, I broadcast Consolation No.3 with tears streaming down my face.

The deluge had just begun.

Two mornings later, Papa showed up in Herr Benedict's office. Mama was very sick. Papa used his status as an official food supplier to drive from Sandbostel. Once again, I went down the same road. But with a new heartache. Papa prayed and cussed as he drove. He begged Gott to spare Mama. He cursed the war. And the third Reich. He cursed the wicked leaders by name and aimed his hottest rage at Hitler. His fist pounded the metal dash til it bent.

We arrived at Petra's about 9:30 that morning. Jakob was there. Mama was very weak and frail. She had a high fever. It was typhus. It broke out in the Soviet section of the Stalag from the infestation. To fight it, Colonel Blixt even burned two barracks with sick Russian POWs still inside! Petra said Mama had been getting worse for two weeks. Papa arrived two days earlier delivering fish as a pretext to visit. He was shocked and angry Mama was working in the Soviet section. There was a new vaccine in limited supply to fight typhus, but the medical staff told Papa none was available. Petra said he came back from there enraged.

At that point, only Petra knew Blixt assigned Mama to the Soviet section. And why.

Aneska stared into the fire as she relived that horrible day.

Mama was dying. You think, 'This can't be happening. She just needs to rest, and she'll be fine.' But she wasn't fine.

As usual, she was calm. We sat with her all afternoon. Papa had ice blocks in the truck for fish. He fed her chips from it and applied cold cloth to her face. In the afternoon she asked us to move her to the couch in the front room where the piano was, so I could play for her. She requested one piece after another for half an hour, including the hymn, "It Is Well." I could hear her and Papa talking, mostly Papa, but not clear enough to know what they said.

In the middle of "Dear Jesus Take My Hand" Mama called my name. We gathered around her. Her breathing was fast and shallow. Like panting. It slowed enough for her to take a few deep breaths and speak. She tilted her head toward me. "That's my prayer, danka, mein Schatz," Then to Jakob, "mein Honigjunge." 'my honey boy.' That was her pet name for him. She called Petra, "mein süßer Freund." 'My sweet friend.' The short, rapid breaths returned. She gazed at Papa with such tenderness in her eyes. I was afraid she didn't have the strength to speak to him. But she said in Swedish, "Snälla Herr," 'Please, Lord.' Papa took her hand and cupped it against his face. Mama said in German, "That is my prayer, Mein Kapitän." She drew one last deep breath and said, "Lieber Jesus, halt ihre Hände." 'Dear Jesus, hold their hands.' The last word on her lips was, "Danke." Three times in short breaths. 'Thank you. Thank you, Thank you.' And then nothing. She stopped like a clock. We waited for another breath. But it didn't come.

Papa kissed Mama's hand and lay it across her chest. Jakob and I clung to him.

We sat in silence. The fire crackled. I suppose about a minute passed. It seemed much longer. I finally said all I could think to say. Thank you for allowing me into that. She nodded. After a bit she spoke again.

It was one of the most horrific and holy moments of my life. You have your own. You keep breathing… but you don't know how, ya? Color fades from the world. The heartache affects your whole body. Like a fever. You move in slow motion. Your timeline becomes marked before and after she died.

Those thoughts came much later, but in that moment, plans had to be made. The bodies of typhus victims were required to be burned or buried immediately. Papa had another plan: to bury Mama at sea. I fought him on that. It was all happening too fast. But he wanted no memorial in Sandbostel to return to. He brought her across the Baltic, he would return her there. And Wilhelm's body was in the Baltic as well. We kissed Mama's sweet face. Papa took the little gold cross from around her neck and gave it to me.

Aneska pulled it out of the neckline of her dress and showed it to me. She held it as she continued.

We pulled the two tables together from our Christmas dinner and laid Mama there. Petra and I washed and dressed her. I couldn't stop touching her hands. Those hands taught me how to hold a pencil. To write. And bake and play the piano. Tie a bow. They brushed my hair. They held my face thousands of times. We wrapped her in two sheets.

Aneska surprised me.

Give me your hands, my friend. Let me see your hands.

I put down my pen and notebook, leaned toward her, and extended my hands. She took them in her long hands and began to examine them.

You held your babies with these hands. You play guitar with them. I see you have those callouses on the tips like all string players. You paint with them. I bet you played catch with your kids. Held them up in the swimming pool. Carried them to bed at night. You've probably fixed a lot of things around the house. Built some things. I'm sure these two scars here on your thumb and first finger have stories behind them.

She squeezed my hands and released them. The gesture of her warm, human touch was one of the most endearing moments of our times together.

Our hands, my friend. What an awesome gift from God. With them we can bless or do great damage. Bake a pie…

Or Franzbrötchen I suggested.

Ya. Or make a bomb. We can lend a hand or throw a punch. Give a cup of water. Think about it. With our hands we can welcome life into the world, or take it, on the battlefield or even before the first breath.

Jesus said, "what the mouth speaks the heart is full of." Well, what's in the heart comes out the hands, too.

Did you know ten of Bach's children died in early childhood? All that heartache! And still the most beautiful music kept coming out of his hands. He signed many of his works Soli Deo Gloria. 'Glory to Gott alone.' That's what was in his heart. Gratitude, humility, and the desire to glorify Gott with his gift.

My Mama's hands did nothing but bless, care, give and heal. I was devastated by her death, but I knew where Mama went that day. Into Gott's hands. Kristers is there now, too.

I've done it again, haven't I?

If you mean speak from what your heart is full of? Yes. That's why I crossed an ocean. She chuckled and returned to the events of that day.

Touché, my friend.

Just after dark, Papa pulled the truck around to the back of the house. He and Jakob loaded Mama's body between the blocks of ice under a tarp and bags of fish. It was surreal. Like a movie I was watching. But also playing a part in.

I slept maybe an hour. I kept thinking of Mama cold and lying with the fish in the back of the truck. Even though I knew her spirit was with Gott and reunited with Wilhelm.

Early the next morning, there was good cloud cover from aircraft. Papa and Jakob drove me to Lübberstedt in the drizzling rain. It was raining harder inside my heart. I hated that road.

I scribbled down another song idea without interrupting her. "Raining On the Inside."

We said our goodbyes beside the truck with the Benedicts and Kristers. I wanted to go with Papa, but he said I would be safer there. They agreed. We all thought the war couldn't last much longer. He and Jakob would come back to get me. Papa lifted my chin in his big hand and told me I was as brave and beautiful as Mama. And that after this 'verdammt schwachsinnig kreig' damned moronic war, we would make a new life, "perhaps with this chef," he added. It sounded like another blessing. I took it as one. Papa shook Kristers' hand and embraced him. That lifted my spirit some.

I hugged Jakob. Papa wrapped me in his strong arms one more time. They got in the truck. Clinging to Papa's arm through the window I said, "Gott be with you, Papa and Honey boy."

"And with your spirit, mein Schatz."

And they disappeared down the road into the mist.

CHAPTER TWENTY-THREE

THE CODA

I didn't write in my diary for the next two weeks. There were no words. On February 16, my entry was just: 'Dresden bombed into rubble. O Gott, end this." Two of the Labor Service girls were from Dresden. We feared the worst.

Playing the piano was painful. In my limited practice time, I meandered over the keys, exploring formless, dissonant ramblings, like wordless diary entries. Some of that rambling found its way years later into the second movement of my concerto.

To honor Mama, I still broadcast several times a week to the women at the camp. Pieces she loved, like Chopin's Nocturne No. 20 in C-Sharp Minor. It always reminded her of the loveliness of her childhood in Sweden. In fact, besides Kristers, Chopin's nocturnes became my emotional comfort food, you might say. They are nostalgic and dreamy. The melodies became painfully sweet in grief. When Mama and Petra came to tune the piano, they brought me the folio of Chopin Nocturnes Herr Benedict gave me in Hamburg. It's in the front music room.

Sometimes, while Mama made dinner, she asked me to play his Nocturne in E-Flat Major, Op. 9, No. 2. It's probably his most recognizable. It closes in a coda that introduces a new third melody over more somber chords. And then returns to the main theme and ends light and simple, like a music box. Chopin was only twenty when he wrote it. The beauty and longing that came out of his hands poured into my aching heart.

That's one of the beautiful things about music. It can be like a blood transfusion for your spirit.

The pressures of the war intensified. The guards were on edge. Food rations for everyone were cut in half. Thanks to Kristers' chickens we still had eggs. Only the officers got to eat some of them. The Labor Service girls got chicken soup and cornbread. But it was Kristers' soup and cornbread. No one complained. Supplies for the assembly lines dwindled. Quotas could not be met. There were fewer batches to count and fewer munition trains to load from the storage bunkers. We heard the Allies were nearing the Rhine River.

On the inside, I moved in slow motion. Kristers was muted as well. He was an orphan. I was a half orphan. All around us things were happening fast. We talked some about where to go after the war. His parents' home in Göttingen might still be there. I didn't say it out loud, but I hoped Papa would become his father-in-law. Jakob his brother. That he would have family again.

After breakfast, it was Thursday March 8, I was helping dry the dishes. Why do you think I remember it so specifically?

I laughed. I got the point. You wrote it down that night in your diary.

Ya. Good. Though I don't think I would have forgotten it. Kristers pulled me into a pantry. He was very keyed up. I thought he was going to kiss me. Honestly, I was hoping he would. But he didn't. He told me not to tell anyone, to avoid getting hopes up and distracting everyone. He had big news. The day before, the Allies crossed the Rhine River at Remagan. That was still nearly four hundred kilometers southwest of us. But it was the beginning of the coda, the beginning of the end.

Aneska closed her eyes. I knew she was replaying the scene in her mind.

I couldn't help taking him in my arms. He wrapped his around me, too. I put my head against his chest and didn't want to let go. We just held each other.

She opened her eyes and looked into the fire.

It was the first time I felt a man's full body next to mine. For the sake of transparency, without being too indelicate, I felt a physical hunger for him. Like I couldn't get close enough to him. And I could tell, well, I won't say how but, he felt the same.

I chuckled and made a crack about passion in the pantry. And added that for a scientist, Kristers sounded very human. She chuckled.

O ya, Kristers was always very human. But nothing happened. He didn't even kiss me. That time.

With that she left me hanging. But not for long.

The next two weeks were disjointed and chaotic. Colonel Benedict insisted I broadcast music more often. Almost all the assembly lines shut down. Many munitions were left unfinished. There were very few batches to count. By the Colonel's order, some of those were never carted to storage bunkers. One night several explosions very close by disabled some rail cars on a siding. But we heard no planes. Kristers' chickens didn't lay for three days. Some of them paid the price in our soup.

March 24, on a Saturday at 10 a.m., Frau Benedict led me to the Colonel's office. Kristers was there, too. I thought we were in trouble. Instead, he informed us the pace of the Allied advance made it necessary for Lübberstedt to be evacuated! The next day! To Stalag X-B! Imagine how stunned we were. Kristers and I were to drive with the Benedicts to Petra's house. The other Labor Service girls were being escorted by female guards farther east for safety until they could be reunited with their families.

I asked about the Hungarian women. Most of them would walk the thirty-two kilometers. Twenty miles. In one day! The SS planned to load the weaker or sick women into munition cars on a train headed east. That sounded ominous. For years, rumors spread about the extermination camps. Fortunately, there were only two rail cars available. I found out later, Kristers helped Herr Benedict sabotage four others. That explained the explosions and no planes. And why some of the spooked chickens served the cause with their lives.

Kristers, the mathematician, scientist and chef, was a saboteur as well! There wasn't enough of me to hold the love I had for him.

I shook my head and jotted down another song idea. "Not Enough of Me"

We were to tell no one. To avoid panic, the Colonel would make the announcement very early the next morning after the workers' breakfast. As meager as it was, he wanted them to eat something before the long march. I insisted on walking with the women to Sandbostel. Herr Benedict sympathized but adamantly ordered that was not an option. It was far too risky, and he didn't want to face my Papa having put me in danger. I resolved somehow to let Benca and Golda know not to board the rail cars.

I couldn't even pack. That might create curiosity. But I didn't have much. Packing wouldn't take long.

I found Benca and Golda. I handed them both a note from Psalm 23. "Though I walk through the valley of the shadow of death I will fear no evil." I signed them, "Walk with the Lord. You must walk with the Lord, Gott be with you, Aneska." I underlined the word 'walk' three times. My hope was it would make sense when the announcement came.

That evening, Frau Benedict asked the girls to tidy up their areas. At lights out I broadcast "Dear Lord Jesus, Take My Hand." I prayed it would help the women get a good rest.

Getting to sleep myself was a challenge. I did something I had never done. I snuck down to the kitchen to get a glass of milk. Kristers showed me where he hid the key. It wasn't there. The door was unlocked. And a light was on.

There Kristers stood, his apron covered in flour. Three large trays of warm biscuits sat on a prep table. He was slicing salami and stuffing the biscuits with it.

"Manna for the exodus," he said. "There won't be time for the girls' breakfast in the morning."

I resisted every impulse to throw myself at him. For the next half hour, he sliced salami. I stuffed biscuits. We packed them in brown paper bags and cleaned up the mess. He asked me to put the flour and baking powder back in the pantry. He followed me in. This was the moment. I was sure of that, but I didn't know how to kiss. Kristers took my face in his hands, looked me in the eyes and said, "Come what may, Aneska, I'm yours. Tonight, and all my life."

Apparently Kristers was a mathematician, scientist, chef, saboteur and songwriter. I added to my list. "Tonight, and All My Life." If that wasn't a wedding song, I needed a drastic career change.

He leaned in and gave me the softest, sweetest kiss. I kissed him back. We heard footsteps. Someone called Kristers' name. It was Frau Benedict. He flipped the light off in the pantry, dashed into the kitchen, and responded. I stayed hidden. He explained his late-night mission to her. She thanked him for his thoughtfulness and helped set the bags along the cool windows to keep till morning. He said he would tidy up. She said goodnight. I heard her footsteps start for the door.

And then, "Gute nacht, Aneska. Danka for helping Kristers. You have two minutes to be back in your bunk."

We laughed quietly. "Ya, freundliche Frau." Ya, kind Frau. "Gute Nacht," I said. We heard her footsteps fade.

Kristers came toward the pantry, smiling like a lottery winner. I met him at the door and threw my arms around his neck. I kissed him like Mama kissed Papa every time he went to sea. The way I'd seen soldiers kiss their wives goodbye at the train station early in the war. I had no idea what I was doing. But it was a very good start.

To his credit, Kristers got us out of there quickly. As far as I could tell, no one else knew I was gone. But getting to sleep was even more challenging with the taste of his kisses still lingering.

Early in the morning, I arrived at the dining hall for one last broadcast, a coda of sorts, before bedlam broke out. The obvious choice was Hungarian Rhapsody. In my spirit I knew some of the women were headed to their deaths. The glass of water and snowdrop were in the usual place beside me. I played it as triumphantly as I knew how. Soli Deo Gloria. I would have played it in the back of a wagon beside the women all the way to Sandbostel if I could have.

As the last chord rang, Kristers shouted 'Bravo' from the kitchen door. He and Frau Benedict walked briskly toward me. Kristers held a basket filled with brown paper bags. For the girls. I grabbed the snowdrop to press in my diary, with half a dozen others filed there. As Frau Benedict escorted me to the barracks, Colonel Benedict's voice came over the loudspeakers. The news exploded across the camp.

Frau Benedict tried to calm the girls by telling them their service was completed. To use the bathroom. No shower. Dress warm. Take one bag. One blanket. One brown bag of biscuits. They were leaving. For a safe location farther east until they could rejoin their families. She gave us twenty minutes. We were ready in fifteen.

Frau Benedict led us out the front entrance. SS guards were carrying boxes of paperwork to a pile already burning in the courtyard. The sky was clear blue. There was no wind, but it was cold. She led us to a truck where she let the girls know I was not going with them but to my family close by. It was a tearful parting. Frau Benedict hugged them all, said she loved them and "Gott be with you, meine schönen." 'My beauties.'

The girls thanked me for the music. Helga, the one from Düsseldorf, hoped Kristers and I would find each other after the war.

And if I didn't, she said she would. We all laughed. They boarded and were gone. I think I mentioned, I saw some of them again at the reunion in 1955.

I marveled again at how much detail Aneska could recall. With or without diaries.

It took nearly three more hours for Colonel Benedict to be ready to go. He wanted to be the last to leave. The entire complex had to be emptied and inspected in case any laborers tried to hide to escape later.

I waited in his office. The Benedicts' luggage was there. Kristers things were stacked in a pile. He must have had a long, busy night. I couldn't help but snoop. There were boxes of spices and herbs. Flour. Corn meal. Some cooking utensils. A crate of egg cartons carefully packed in straw and newspaper. Envelopes of seeds, labeled in Kristers' handwriting. Half a dozen brown paper bags of salami biscuits. A metal trunk full of plucked chickens wrapped in butcher paper and packed in ice. There were a dozen small planting pots of blooming snowdrops and herbs in a wooden crate. Next to them sat a valise. Besides clothing, it contained a small box with a flip top. His recipes. The box is up on that shelf behind you. The recipes are in the firebox. Including his cornbread and Black Forest cake. Maja has photocopies. Part of her magic is Kristers'.

His clothes smelled like him. *She laughed.* I was literally smelling them when he walked in, but I pretended to be sniffing the snowdrops. He wasn't fooled. He left to bring the Colonel's car close to the front entrance. Together, we loaded everything into the trunk and the luggage rack on top. The eggs and snowdrops rode on one side of the back seat.

About half ten, we finally drove out of the gate. Down that road one more time. But this time, Kristers and I sat close, side by side. He steadied the eggs and box of planting pots with one hand. The other one was all mine under a blanket on our laps.

Not far down the road, we caught up with the column of women. Three abreast. They had been walking about two hours. Kristers estimated it would take them at least ten hours to get to Stalag X-B. Guards rode motorcycles up and down the line. Armed soldiers in open-bed trucks watched for stragglers or attempted escapes.

As we drove slowly up behind the column of women, I asked Herr Benedict if I could roll down my window. He permitted but asked me not to speak to them. It could bring trouble from the guards. I put my hands flat together in front of my lips and began throwing them kisses. Like prayer kisses. Mama used to do that as Papa and the boys pulled away from the dock.

She demonstrated.

Tears rolled down my face. I couldn't stop them. I probably can't stop them now. The women began calling my name and throwing kisses back to me.

Her eyes welled up. She stared into the fire. She was back there. On that road again.

The Colonel rolled down his window and spoke to the guards, to assure them all was well. Some of the women said, "Danke für die Musik." 'Thank you for the music.' Even a guard beside us on a motorcycle thanked me for the music. The women kept saying my name. The sound followed us like a wave for a two hundred meters. No tribute could ever mean more to me.

I spotted Benca. She was right next to me. My hand shot out to hers and I had to speak, "Gott be with you, Benca."

She smiled back and said, "I'm walking, Aneska. I'm walking with the Lord. Danka."

I kept looking for Golda but never found her. I worried for her.

But as I told you, she survived. Remember? Her grandson is the cello player. In his letter to me he wrote that his grandmother chose to go on the train to Bergen-Belsen that day to help the weaker and sick ones. Her train was the one bombed mistakenly by the British plane. By Gott's mysterious ways, she endured that and made it to Bergen-Belsen, one of the worst extermination camps. But it was liberated by the British three weeks later! Her grandson even knew about my note to Golda the day before the evacuation. Her story to him was that she "rode a train through the valley of death and walked out the other side with the Lord." Praise Gott. But it was many years before I knew all that.

My friend, Gott is watching over so many things out of our sight and beyond our reach.

I could only say 'amen' to that.

Ya, Amen, indeed.

The drive that day wasn't anything like the first time. Obviously. The world was different. Mama was gone. The end of the war felt very near. Kristers, the love of my life was by my side. His entire immediate family was gone. It was like a page you have to turn, knowing the rest of the story will be different for the rest of your life. And still, uncertainty hung over the next chapter, too.

Petra had no way to know we were coming. When her house came into view, Papa's truck was out front. I was overjoyed, of course. I ran to the door with Kristers right behind me. The Benedicts followed. I waited till we were all on the porch to knock. Petra opened the door. Before we could say "surprise" she burst into tears and wrapped me in her arms. We went into the front room. Petra couldn't speak. She covered her face with her apron and sobbed. Jakob came in from the kitchen. The look of pain on his face sent chills through me.

I said, "Where's Papa?"

CHAPTER TWENTY-FOUR

THE LIGHTHOUSE

Jakob said it straight out. Papa rammed a German submarine. A U-boat. And sank it. His boat went down, too. He was gone.

The instant reversal of joy to agony took my legs out from under me. Kristers kept me from dropping to the floor. Jakob broke down. He sobbed, saying over and over there was nothing he could do. It happened too fast. Petra and Kristers and I surrounded him as he wept. It felt like we were standing on a boat in giant swells.

Three quarters of a century after the event, I was blindsided, too. It made sense now why there were no photos on the long table of Captain Carl after the war or in Ireland. It was equally stunning how much the soul sitting in front of me had endured and yet radiated such vitality of spirit, in spite of it all. I wanted that.

When the first wave of anguish eased, we moved to the kitchen table. I was never as steady as Mama. She was as constant as the sunrise. I didn't feel steady or constant, and certainly not as brave as her, like Papa said the last time I saw him. The shock paralyzed me. Petra and Frau Benedict moved around us, making tea and setting out the salami biscuits. Herr Benedict came in and out like a spirit, bringing in the luggage and perishables. Kristers never left my side.

Through bouts of tears, Jakob told us what happened.

Six weeks earlier, after they left that night with Mama's body, Papa had a plan. The moon would be darkest February 12 and 13. Papa always tracked the phases of the moon, like a good fisherman and sailor. And people smuggler. Depending on the weather, one of those nights he planned to hug the coast to the western shore of Lübeck Bay, near the spot where Wilhelm went down. He knew to stay inside the band of mines protecting the harbor from Soviet and British submarines. In case a patrol caught them they were just fishing. They often dropped gill nets along that coast, and they had their papers.

February 12, the sea was calm. No wind. Scattered clouds blocked most of the starlight. They set out following Wilhelm's tip, stopping the engine for five minutes at the top and bottom of the hour to listen for other boats.

Jakob described how angry Papa was on the way. "You know how he got, Aneska. 'Damn this war! Damn that devil Hitler! You build a life. Have a family. Try to serve Gott. And all it takes is one delusional madman to send your sons and brothers to be slaughtered for his evil mania. Because no one stood up and took him down before he addicted enough degenerate parrots to power, and they stripped us of our rights and courage.'"

That sounded just like Papa.

About two hundred meters from shore, they cut the engine near Dahmeshöved lighthouse. Its beacon was not lit to avoid giving bombers a landmark to navigate.

They prepared to bury Mama. Jakob wept as he described how Papa talked to Mama and Wilhelm and prayed over her body. As they stood on both sides of her, about to slide her body overboard, a submarine surfaced less than a hundred meters to the east. It cut its engine. They lay Mama on the deck and didn't breathe. Papa made Jakob put a lifejacket on in case anything happened. They clearly heard the sailors speaking German on the tower. They seemed to be arguing. One of them raised his voice, saying they would never surrender for the "glory of the Fatherland and the Führer." Papa retrieved a flare gun in case they needed to make it obvious they were just a fishing boat. But the lookouts never spotted Papa's boat against the dark profile of the coast.

When the sailors went below to submerge, Papa suddenly shoved Jakob overboard and told him to swim to the light house. He would meet him there. If not, get to the truck, go to Petra's and find me. The last thing he said was, "You and Kristers take care of Aneska. Ich liebe dich mein Sohn." 'I love you, my son.'

Papa started the engine. Jakob watched, helpless, as Papa's last boat, Against the Wind, moved away. He heard the engine whine to full throttle. The boat heaved up onto the sub and crashed into the tower. It must have ruptured a diesel saddle tank along the side. A flare ignited the fuel on the water. Jakob saw Papa's silhouette shoot three more flares. He kept shouting for Papa to jump, but a huge explosion rocked the sub. Then two more. The flames engulfed the sub and Papa's boat. In less than ten minutes, only floating debris and fire remained. Jakob shouted again and again for Papa. But there was no answer. And no way to search through the burning oil and diesel for him or his body.

"He went down with Mama," Jakob said. He didn't believe Papa planned it. There was no way. It just happened.

No one spoke. What could be said? It was too sad, and unreal, and too soon for theories and reasons. It was something that happened to someone else, in a book of tragic and heroic stories. But not in your own life.

Dahmeshöved lighthouse was unmanned. It had provisions stored for mishaps at sea. Jakob hid there for two days. He knew the explosions had to be visible from shore. A search and rescue patrol boat crisscrossed the area the next day and night. On the second day, it was gone.

It took Jakob three weeks walking by night and hiding by day to get around the bay and through Lübeck, back to the truck at the dock near Wismar. Papa built a secret compartment in the truck to hide money and valuables. The keys never went to sea with them. Jakob slept in a small shed on the dock. He fished to eat. After two weeks of that, he bought ice and some fish at another dock to get through the checkpoints. The guards knew him and Papa well. He told them Kapitän Carl stayed with the boat. He arrived at Petra's just a few days before we did. I was so proud of him. It had to be the loneliest journey.

Somehow, in the fog of it all, Frau Benedict and Petra got dinner ready. Kristers tried to make me eat something. Petra prepared beds. I spent the night in her room. Mostly sleepless.

I could see the moon out the window. It was almost full. I wondered how it could be so calm and steady, like Mama, watching over such agony down here. I got up once to use the bathroom and tripped over someone on the floor just outside the bedroom door. It was Kristers. He wanted to be there in case I woke up traumatized.

All night, I wrestled with Gott on and off. He had to know where the U-boat was. When and where it would surface. He watched the two boats moving toward each other. Did Papa plan his way that night, but Gott directed his boat? Gott knew Papa's thoughts, that he didn't want to kill all those young men. I prayed he wouldn't judge Papa harshly.

For some unknown reason, the thought of the German ocean liner, the Wilhelm Gustloff, came to mind. Papa took us to its christening in Hamburg shipyard, the first time we saw 'the devil,' Hitler. That was Spring of 1937. I remember we teased Wilhelm that they named it after him.

More recently, in late January, news came that a Soviet submarine sank the Gustloff with over ten thousand civilians and German troops on board! They were escaping the advancing Russians from the Baltic states. Over nine thousand souls went down! I tried to picture that in my mind. All those lives and storylines cut short. And Gott watched it all happen. Just like my Papa going down with thirty-five crewmen trapped and drowning in that exploded U-boat.

All this was beyond my math, as Kristers often said, and it could have led me to see Gott as uncaring, even calloused. A lot of people do that math and become cynical and bitter for the rest of the journey. Gott has the power to intervene, but doesn't. There are endless senseless tragedies and suffering, so they reason it only follows – Gott is heartless because he's outside our pain. But we know better, ya, my friend? He walked this brutal road. And conquered even death. He said we would, too. Not our bodies. We will all die physically. But our spirits will live, eternally. Our hope in him gives our lives meaning. Gives our suffering meaning. And purpose, his purposes, as hidden as they may often be to us. But I have to be honest, our future glory and the agony of the present moment often collide. The catastrophes of life can make coming fully alive again seem impossible, as you well know, my friend.

Again, I sensed Aneska aim the force of her spirit directly at me. She was discerning enough to see that for me, the jury was still out on living fully again. Her own vitality, despite great tragedies, was compelling evidence for her case.

All these thoughts led me to this. What if Papa saved lives by sinking that submarine? He heard them say they would never surrender. We believed the end of the war was near. Papa thought so. But what if Germany rallied? What if peace delayed? What if Papa was Gott's instrument to save the lives that submarine crew could have taken? And how many? We will never know. Not in this life. Asking why is often futile. But we ask anyway, ya?

At breakfast Kristers said maybe Papa reached the tensile strength of his heart. His breaking point under all the pressure and grief. Doesn't that sound like a scientist? The tensile strength of his heart.

I agreed sorrow had to be part of it, but told him I believed Papa acted out of the true strength of his heart. Like a righteous arrow held back until the right moment. Papa finally said, "No more!"

Jakob gave me one of the best compliments of my life. "Aneska, you sound just like Papa."

I still believe that. For Papa, there was no more hiding in the dark, holding your breath, hoping evil overlooked you and your loved ones, and passed you by. I don't think that U-boat was just a symbol to him. It was the physical extension of Hitler's monstrous evil. And Papa said, "Enough." No more dodging. No more watching others sacrifice to stem the tide. The moment came to strike. It only followed. I believe that's what Papa did. In time of peace, you take careful aim with your vote. In time of war, you aim your boat.

Whatever the reasons for Papa's actions, for us the question quickly became 'what now?' The Benedicts had no choice. They reported to the Stalag to oversee the treatment of the Lübberstedt workers. Kristers could be shot as a deserter if he didn't go, too. So, he reported as Colonel Benedict's attaché. We all agreed Jakob had only one option: hide Papa's truck in the barn and stay out of sight at Petra's.

We heard exciting news the Allies were pressing east past the Rhine River. But it was alarming to the officers and guards at the Stalag. Surely, it was only a matter of a few weeks til they reached us. We just had to hold on a little longer.

Kristers and I were both orphans now. That made the bond between us even stronger. Like Papa, Kristers had a plan.

The second morning at Petra's, he asked me to do two things while he was at work. Read Psalm 23 sitting at the piano. And play Reflection in A, no matter how I felt. Even for just a few minutes. I got angry with him. How could he ask me to play at a time like that? He understood, but asked me gently to at least read the Psalm and then choose whether or not to play.

I avoided the front room til nearly noon. Petra asked me to get some plates from a cupboard in there. Mama's Bible was on the music rack of the piano. I went back in, sat down and opened to Psalm 23. A note fell out. From Kristers.

Before I could even wonder if she still had it, Aneska asked me to retrieve the green folder. She sifted through the treasured papers and handed his note to me. She spoke it in German. And then translated.

Halt durch, meine Liebe.
Hold on, my love.

Das Licht wird zum Leuchtturm zurückkehren.
The light will return to the lighthouse.

Stets, Always, Kristers

CHAPTER TWENTY-FIVE

THE LOOK

What happened next may sound rash, but you must understand, the emotional extremes in wartime do one of two things to a person. It can add layer upon layer of self-protection to armor you from more hurt until you don't feel much at all. Or it strips you down to your naked soul. Where you feel everything intensely, with no filter. Either way, the only defense or lifeline is what lives at your core, who you are, what you believe, about Gott, human nature, about the meaning and value of life itself. If that core erodes, you will not make it. You will not find your way again. Back to life.

The first condition was everywhere. The hollow people, I called them. During the war, and after. People haunted by the traumas they witnessed and endured. They survived. But never revived. I have no judgement of them. Everyone has a load to bear. My sadness for them was mixed with anger at those who brutalized them. I knew I didn't want to live hollowed out. I held on to what Mama said about my opus. And how it was part of a greater Magnum Opus. But grief laid my soul bare.

I wondered if Aneska could see my hollow part. And if that's why this story chose me. Why I drew the lottery ticket to sit near her vitality and fullness. I asked if she was familiar with Viktor Frankl's book, "Man's Search for Meaning."

Ya, in fact, I met him. On my trip back to Lübberstedt. He was speaking in Hamburg about his story and Logotherapy, his clinical approach with patients. I had read his book. It came out only a year after the war. You know he survived three years, in several camps, including Auschwitz? The Nazis forced his wife to have an abortion and later gassed her at Auschwitz. They killed his parents and brother as well. He came out of the war with those horrible wounds. It was astonishing that he was not hollowed out. In fact, just two years after the war, he remarried! Anne's father, Otto Frank did, too. Seven years after the war, in spite of all he suffered and lost.

How does a heart go on from that kind of trauma, ya? To love again. To enjoy life again. You've been through your own version of that, my friend. I'm so sorry you're facing those questions again.

Aneska's empathy was deeply touching. It was part of her nature. From the moment I arrived for the purpose of telling her story, she peppered me with questions about my own.

I'm sure you would agree, Herr Frankl's work confirms so much of what we've experienced.

I did.

I was honored to talk with him briefly that night in Hamburg. He asked me a remarkable question. "What intentional acts during the war gave your life meaning?" I told him about playing piano for the POWs and the Hungarian women. He was the first person to urge me to write down my story. We even corresponded twice.

She had his letters in the firebox. I wanted to see them, of course, but was more eager to know what happened next. She was not done with Frankl.

Herr Frankl was all about how our choices create meaning in our lives. But even more crucial, the source of our choices is what gives them meaning. In his view, if Gott is not that source, people can still choose purposeful paths. They can do philanthropic or creative work and find value and meaning in that, but any other source than Gott will not provide the power to keep going in the face of suffering. In concentration camps, the primal incentives of power and pleasure were gone. Frankl discovered that the psychological drives of Freud's concepts, the ego, id and super-ego, will not sustain meaning or life in great trauma. To survive but also to thrive, takes a connection to a source, a fountainhead of meaning outside the self. There must be a crucial connection which cannot be severed, even by the fear of your own death, or the suffering and death of those you love.

Dr. Frankl was so brilliant and compassionate. He reminded me of Kristers. Kristers called Gott, the operator in the equation. An operator transforms one thing into another, like a multiplication or division sign. Only Gott can transform suffering into perseverance, character, and hope. And even into gratitude, not for the suffering, but for Gott himself, the Eternal operator, who is present in our suffering and transformed his own agonies into hope for the whole world.

Aneska had obviously taken deep dives into Frankl's views and the psychology of human nature. I had a feeling it was leading up to what happened next. Besides, I had heard so much wisdom and insight from the musings of her heart, I didn't want to rush past a single nugget. Once again, I didn't interrupt the flow.

I wrote Herr Frankl, asking him if he thought Freud's own ego stripped himself of that essential Gott connection. He agreed. And wrote that Freud explained Gott away as an illusion to absolve ourselves of guilt and shame. Nothing more than mere "wish fulfillment" to comfort ourselves with a belief in a loving father. Not an actual spiritual reality, a presence.

That reminds me, Kristers coined a term for what happened to so many of our countrymen who committed atrocities without remorse. He called it a scham-ektomie. A shame-ectomy. If wrong is no longer wrong, guilt and shame are useless, like an appendix in the psyche. I can hear him say it, "If morality no longer suits your purpose, amputate morality, and shame goes with it." He and Frankl would have hit it off.

Frankl called Gott the "partner of our intimate soliloquies." Isn't that beautiful? Gott is that near. And cares for us in all our conflicted nature. Gott even gives meaning to our suffering. And provides the strength to face the worst of life with courage and dignity. Like Jesus did. I saw that courage and dignity with my own eyes, in Mama. And Papa. Wilhelm. And many of the women at Lübberstedt.

In my lifetime, I've also seen the Gott-denying psychosis up close. I call it a psychosis because it's a break from reality, the ultimate reality of God. I've watched it spread. And wreak havoc and agony in every generation. Look around. There are hollow people everywhere, masking it with anger or hedonism. Power or drugs. Or even with causes and creativity. Without Gott humanity is, what did Rumi the poet say? "Like a hollow reed cut from the earth, always making a crying sound." He wrote, "Anyone pulled from a source longs to go back." But so many souls have cut themselves off from the source. From Gott. They are like so many spinning tops running to the next self-help fad for momentum and balance. Without Gott there is only the limited power source of self-reliance, and no balance. Truth becomes malleable. Without truth, meanings and values shift. When that happens, unspeakable acts can be justified. Kristers said even back then the Nazis were the worst version of hollow - a deadly mixture of narcissism and tyranny. That kind of hollowness still breaks out in the world today. That's why for Frankl, choices, actions, tell the tale about a person, from Hitler to Mother Teresa.

Once again, I was stunned at my good fortune to be sitting with her. For a person who preferred to let music do her talking, Aneska's verbal "ramblings" were as elegant and powerful as any concerto.

You probably noticed the Latin motto over the front door, "Spectemur Agendo." Let us be judged by our acts. Brynn O'Cullen,

Gott bless her soul, was very keen on that. So was Jesus. He said, "You will know them by their fruit." Good tree - good fruit. Bad tree - bad fruit.

Which reminds me, are you ready for tea? I can smell Maja's scones, and I'm sure there are fruit preserves.

I could smell the scones, too, but whenever Aneska dove deep, I was eager for her to continue.

Well, she'll serve them soon. I see I've gone all around the world to get to what happened next.

You could say what followed that terrible blow was one of my most intentional choices ever. And it gave meaning to the rest of my life.

Just three days after hearing about Papa, on Wednesday March 28, Kristers took me out to Petra's front porch. He knelt on one knee and asked me to marry him! The following Wednesday, on my sixteenth birthday, I did!

Aneska laughed like the telling of it made it happen again. I'm sure in her mind it did.

Kristers' previous plan was to give some time for things to sort out and marry me after the war. But with Mama and Papa and Wilhelm gone, and the future so uncertain, he talked it over with Jakob and Petra, and the Benedicts. The ending of the war would likely not end the chaos. We could be scattered who knows where. Kristers knew what he wanted and spoke it out loud. They gave their blessing.

His proposal wasn't the only surprise. He had another one. The ring. This ring.

It was still on her finger. She extended her hand to show me.

It was Mama's. Papa removed it from her hand and left it in the truck. I can't imagine how difficult that was for him. He put this on her finger twenty-two years earlier. Then to take it off her lifeless hand? What an agony. But a treasure, too. Jakob said Papa planned to give it to me. I didn't have a ring for Kristers, but Jakob had Papa's ring, too, though it was too big. He never took it to sea for fear of losing it. Even before casting off that last time, he hid it in the truck with Mama's ring, some money and the truck keys.

We only had a week to prepare for a wedding. Herr Benedict convinced the old Lutheran pastor to perform the ceremony in the little church in Sandbostel. The Pastor was also the mayor, so he provided the marriage license and even the suit Kristers wore. We agreed, no uniform! I had no intention of marrying a soldier of the Third Reich. Petra altered one of Mama's dresses for me. A soft yellow mid-calf with a pleated bodice, slightly puffed at the shoulders. She wore it to my recitals or out to dinner with Papa.

I looked, but didn't see a picture from the wedding on the long table. But again, chose not to interrupt her.

So, Wednesday, April 4, 1945, at 1:00 p.m., as the Allies pushed the ragged German army east toward us, and the Soviets pushed them west, Herr Benedict stood as Kristers' best man. Frau Benedict was my matron of honor. Jakob stood beside me at the back of the small church.

As she often did while recounting moments from that time, Aneska peered into the fire, like it became a portal.

Petra began Mendelssohn's wedding march on the church piano. The look on Kristers' face was, it was beyond words. Like he had discovered a new element. If I could choose only one moment of my life to relive, it would be that one. That look. Fortunately, it wasn't the only time he looked at me that way.

Jakob walked me down the aisle. The song ended. Petra took her place beside Frau Benedict. When the Pastor asked, "Who gives this woman to this man?" Jakob said, "With the blessing of our father and mother, I do." He placed my hand in Kristers' and stood beside Herr Benedict. In the traditional words, we chose. For better or worse, for richer or poorer, in sickness and in health, til death parts us. I can still hear his words before he put this ring on my finger. He used the Swedish saying his father taught him, "Hemmet är där kärleken finns." Home is where the love is. He added in German, "Aneksa, Auf dieser Seite des Himmels bist du mein Zuhause." This side of heaven you are my home.

Almost involuntarily I harvested another song idea: She's Home.

I can close my eyes and picture Kristers moving near my face, his eyes closing, about to kiss me.

And how natural and miraculous it felt. He kissed me softly. I kissed him back. I became Frau Aneska Latva, with snowdrops woven in my hair. And Kristers became my husband, my forever love and muse.

The joy in my heart for the beauty of their love story shared company with an ache for my own less than forever loves. Like Aneska, music was the way I processed life, both joy and heartache. So, as usual, another song idea dropped out of her words like low-hanging fruit. I jotted down "Forever Love." And later what might be the opening lines to an Al Green, Motown kind of groove. "Everybody wants a love that lasts forever. That's what I was lookin' for when I found you."

I wish I could describe the look of pure joy on her face as she relived the profound beauty and pathos of that event amid the grief and devastation of war.

There was no rehearsal dinner. No reception after. There wasn't even any film left for Petra's camera. So, no pictures.

That explained the absence of any among the gallery on the table.

Our honeymoon was only two nights. Again, the pastor proved resourceful. One of his parishioners gone to war owned a hunting cottage three kilometers into the forest beside a spring-fed pond. It had a wood-burning stove and a fireplace. Kristers actually brought his Luger, which I rarely saw him carry. He said he was mein Beschützer, my protector now. But it was mostly in case of rats.

We spent our first two days and nights there. Mama taught me about sex when I turned thirteen. Kristers and I were both virgins, but not ignorant. All I will tell you is we discovered a rare element - the intimacy of two hearts and bodies never given to another. I don't say that with judgement of anyone else. Gott can mend and bless, but only to say, how do I put this? We experienced the astounding depth and joy Gott built into his design for that union. I loved Kristers' soul so much it made holding his body such a holy thing. But a very human as well, I assure you.

She paused, leaned toward me, and lowered her voice.

I've never told this to anyone. In the cottage he scratched a variation of Einstein's relativity formula on the wooden wall by the bed. He called it Einstein's Theory of Proximity:

$$E = me^2 / u \quad \text{Energy equals me square over you.}$$

She covered her mouth with her hands and giggled and blushed like a schoolgirl.

That may be too risqué for publication, but that's how Kristers was. You must understand, a mind that immense and a spirit that nimble was always full of surprises.

I just shook my head, laughed and didn't say what I was thinking. Which was, if that equation were included in this story, it would likely wind up on a T-shirt and might make more money than the book. Per publication, I argued it would reveal such a delightful aspect in Kristers' legacy. As you can see, she consented.

Our second morning in the cabin, I woke to find him gone. He left one of the white lilies that were blossoming around the pond and a sweet note saying he noticed mushrooms and ginseng in the woods. He went to gather some. In about an hour he returned with heaps of them, and a bag of truffles, wild Rapunzel lettuce and onions to make a salad.

Before we returned to Sandbostel that day, he wrote something else on the wall beside the door: "Siegfried and Brunhilde were here." They are the mythical lovers in Wagner's operas. Until then, I didn't know he was familiar with Wagner. Kristers said he felt sorry for them because they were only fictional characters. He much preferred our real-world love over a mythological romance. One he could actually hold and touch and kiss.

She lowered her voice again and confessed.

I wrapped him in my arms and made love to him again before we left. Again, I apologize if that's too intimate. But that's how my marriage began with my scientist, genius, mathematician, chef and lover. Always full of surprises.

I assured her there was no need for an apology. Often the power of a story is in the details. She poured us more tea and composed herself.

As you can see, my friend, it clearly was an extreme time. Ten days after finding out Papa was killed, I married the forever love of my life and made love to him in a cabin in the woods. We were so young and the world so fractured, but I knew we could go the distance with a love so strong and tender and true.

There it was. Another line for the song "Forever Love." I added it to the treasure trove. "We could go the distance with a love so strong and tender and true."

I can't put into words the clash of emotions we all went through. I think that's why Gott gave me music. Nothing else expresses the lowest lows and highest highs of being human, at least for me. There were more lows and highs to come. And for reasons known only to Gott, we didn't have to wait long for them.

CHAPTER TWENTY-SIX

THE ORDERS

I was hoping the Allies would reach us before Colonel Blixt found out I was back in Sandbostel. But word of my return got round to the POWs. They inquired if I would play for them. As a result, the day after our honeymoon, Herr Benedict and Kristers showed up at Petra's with, of all people, Lieutenant Schitli. He strode into the house as condescending as ever. There was no mention of Mama. No condolences. I tried to ignore his disdain by asking how Gunter's playing was coming along. I confess it was not a gracious impulse. Pride gripped me. Isn't it odd how feeling superior can be a subtle thing, ya? I had no time for a twinge of conviction before he gave me even more reason to pity Gunter.

He told me, "Music is not Gunter's gifting. He has higher callings in science and leadership."

What can you say to that? Our silence spoke for us. He got to the point of his visit.

Colonel Blixt not only knew I was back, Schitli was there with orders from him. I was to play at a dinner for the International Red Cross. They were doing an inspection on April 13. And that wasn't the only order: three selections, two before dinner, one piece after. Mozart, Bach or Beethoven only. They would broadcast all the music to the entire camp, including the Soviet section and the barracks where the Lübberstedt women were held. A list of compositions must be submitted two days prior. But the information that shocked us most was about the meal. Herr Benedict had told Colonel Blixt that Kristers was an excellent chef. Blixt put Kristers in charge of the meal for the inspectors and ranking officers, twelve people altogether.

Something inside me rose up. I stunned Schitli and everyone else. Including myself. I told him to tell, propose, to the Colonel I would be honored to play one Mozart and three other selections, all of my own choosing, since the POWs had inquired about me playing again. He cocked his head slowly. Gave me a stern look. I was prepared to inquire if the Red Cross inspectors were aware of the taming, but there was no subtle way to do that. And I knew it would put us in danger. I waited. A chill came over the room.

The Lieutenant agreed. He would take my proposal to Colonel Blixt. He addressed Kristers, ordered him to come to his office in an hour to discuss the menu. With a click of his heels, he turned to leave. I always hated that sound. It felt especially spiteful at that moment. Standing in the doorway he paused and surprised us all.

With some effort, he said almost as an afterthought, "My condolences about your mother. She was a strong woman and a caring nurse." He gave a quick nod of his head and suddenly added, "That's a beautiful ring."

I extended my hand and stepped toward him to shield his view of Kristers' ring.

I managed a polite response, "Thank you. It was my mother's. Papa wanted me to have it."

Without another word he turned and left, without a "Seig Heil." That spoke volumes. Perhaps even Schitli knew a German victory was impossible. Why pretend anymore? I had to give him some credit for the crumb of humanity he mustered. But only for Gunter's sake. When he left, I was shaking. Kristers held me. He said, "Remind me never to play poker with you."

From that point, we wore our rings around our necks on chains.

My instincts proved correct. According to Herr Benedict, Blixt was putting on a show for the Red Cross about how well the POWs were treated. It behooved him to cater some to the prisoners. The inspection was likely the last one before the Allies came knocking. Hans believed the dinner was a cynical attempt by Blixt to cast himself in a good light to avoid indictment for war crimes. Even Blixt knew the end was near.

The only good thing about the whole situation was watching the Nazi haughtiness wither in the face of certain defeat. Perhaps I enjoyed it too much. But I don't think so. The cost of their pride and savagery was immeasurable. How many families like ours suffered losses we carried for the rest of our lives? Losses on both sides.

Even back then I believed, liked Papa, if the world does not learn to stand up to tyrants swiftly and decisively, there is no excuse. Tyranny will break out again and again. And as you can see, my friend, sadly, the world has not learned. Appeasement, detente, negotiation, endless summits and all the ink spent on treaties do not work, without the strength and resolve to meet a threat head on. There will always be the kind of aggressor whose hubris leads to brutality and subjugation.

As I said before, a petty tyrant lives in all of us. Left unbridled and unredeemed the results are control addicts. "Control freaks," I think you call them. From domestic abusers and ragers to the engineers of holocaust and genocide. Even democratic processes can be hijacked by a tyranny of the majority or a minority willing to embrace violence or deceit for their cause.

Aneska was well into one of her soliloquies that appeared to flow out of many years of observation and rumination, gathering under volcanic pressure. I just happened to be fortunate to be near when it erupted. This time, it flowed hot and steady.

As an American, you may not see it clearly, but the rest of the world, whether or not we admit it, we admire your protection of individual rights. We envy the brilliant checks and balances your visionary founders crafted to keep tyranny at bay. A tyrant may arise in your country for a season, but a free people can go to the ballot box and spit in King George's eye. Again and again, if necessary. I watch your country's struggle between the sly, hate-driven bullies and the guardians of freedom. I lived through the slaughter of freedom lovers who did not stand guard. Too few did, like Bonhoeffer, and it cost them their lives.

I assure you, most of us outside America are watching to see if a government of the people will prevail over the elite, self-anointed dominators. Look at the waves of people risking everything to get into your country. They flock from places of oppression and limitation to taste your freedom. Your land of opportunity. How sad if they and their children wind up under the same oppression they sought to escape. I tell you, my friend, we are hoping freedom wins. The whole world needs freedom to win.

She took a deep breath and a long pause. There was at least one giant song in her impassioned eloquence, more likely a symphony, but I just let the power of it roll over me. When she spoke again, there was a sadness in her voice.

That's the frame of mind I was in after Schitli's visit. I have always been my Papa's daughter. The war was about to end, and like Papa, I had had enough. I've thought about it a lot over the years. And I know that's what led to the trouble.

CHAPTER TWENTY-SEVEN

THE GAMBLE

That was April 7, 1945. We had less than a week before the dinner. I felt too overwhelmed to prepare any new music. I was a newlywed, grieving my father. My husband was sleeping in a barracks at the Stalag with the guards. Playing for Blixt was the last thing I wanted to do.

As usual, Kristers put his finger on the heart of the matter. The camp population had grown to more than twenty thousand from all the evacuees. He described the horrendous conditions. Typhus and starvation were everywhere. Rations were reduced, activity rooms and libraries cleared to make room for new prisoners. It was more like a concentration camp than a POW prison.

Kristers assured me I was not playing for Blixt. The prisoners would be my largest audience ever. Many of them were dying. It would be their last taste of beauty. I could touch and comfort more souls than ever. He didn't know how much he sounded like Mama. He put new fire in me.

The next day, Herr Benedict brought word that Colonel Blixt accepted my proposal, but a list must still be provided two days ahead of the dinner. Tensions were high among the officers and guards. As well as the prisoners. Everyone knew it was only a matter of weeks before the Allies arrived.

Herr Benedict spent the next week preparing the camp for the

Red Cross inspection. The American and British inspectors were to be taken on a very limited, specified route. They were allowed to talk only to prisoners who looked well and had been briefed beforehand, threatened actually. The overcrowding would make it difficult to hide the suffering and deprivation. Typhus quarantine signs were posted in many sections to keep the Red Cross out. Of course, the two taming chairs in the muster yard went away. To ensure the threat of compliance, Blixt would attend the meeting between the British senior officers and the inspectors. There would be plenty of time after they left for retributions in case of infractions. Once again, no inspections of the Soviet section or recent civilian detainees were allowed because neither were protected by the Geneva Convention.

To this day it staggers my mind and infuriates me how detestably people can treat others. And it's still happening today. All over the world!

I anticipated another soliloquy just under the surface, but Aneska paused. She took a sip of tea and put any commentary on a back burner.

I won't go there now. But not promising I won't at some point.

I told her that was fair enough, and I was riding her train wherever it took us. She reached out, took my hand and locked her bright blue eyes on mine.

Oh, friend, I'm so grateful you've come here. Remind me to tell you that more often.

I agreed to. She continued.

For the next few days, Kristers gathered ingredients from the woods and local farms. I prayed and played and thought about what music to perform. Prisoners from many countries were packed in the Stalag - Poles, French, Russians, Hungarians, Americans, British. I couldn't play compositions from all their countries. But I knew, like Mama said, music arises from a culture, and reaches beyond cultures, to our common humanity. I was confident my selections would speak to every soul. When I played there before, the music had even touched many of the guards. I remembered one of the scriptures Petra read to us before the first dinner in front of Blixt and all the officers.

It shall be given you in that hour what you are to speak.
For it is not you who speak, but the Spirit of your Father
which speaks through you.

With Gott's help, I chose to begin with Mozart's Air in A. It's very innocent. Unconflicted. And short. Only about a minute. Mozart wrote it when he was seven years old. The next year, he wrote his first symphony! Isn't that astounding? My second selection was verboten - by Chopin. He was born in Poland to a Frenchman. The Poles and French both claim and revere him. As a boy, he dreamed of living in Paris, so he did. I chose his Nocturne in E Flat Major Op.9 No.2. The melody is one of his most beautiful and recognizable. And I was very familiar with it already. It's very playful and nostalgic. I hoped it would reassure the prisoners there is still beauty in the world, not just behind us in our memories, but ahead of us, too.

Those two pieces take less than six minutes to play. Kristers wanted to know. To time the meal. I told you he was very precise.

After dinner, for the Russians, I chose Tchaikovsky's "Swan Lake." Its melody is one of the most elegant ever composed, and very famous. Mama gave her life caring for the Soviet prisoners. So, it was a tribute to her as well. You may know Tchaikovsky composed it as a ballet. In the story Siegfried's undying love transforms Odette from her captivity as a swan back into the real woman he loves. The melody starts so simply but rises in more dramatic bursts, like a swan struggling to take flight. It ends with two low, deep Bb minor chords in the serenity of two lovers in each other's arms. I was certain every

Russian in the camp knew the legend. I prayed it would give some the strength to hang on till freedom arrived.

And for the finale, because the Hungarian women would be listening, I chose, ya, a third verboten piece, Rhapsody No.2 in C# minor by Liszt. Just the first movement, about four minutes long. It's gentle, playful, bold and defiant, but concludes pianissimo, very soft and consoling, in C-sharp major. I imagined the women's faces, their tears. I felt the smile of Gott on my plan.

I showed Kristers the playlist. It troubled him. I could see it on his face. He asked me to do "the emotional math." He cautioned my selections could send Blixt into a rage. The slight to Mozart itself would be enough, but three verboten composers? I could appear to be using the music to rub the Commandant's nose in the imminent defeat of Germany. Honestly, I had not consciously thought of that until Kristers pointed it out. But for that very reason, I liked the selections even more. I was my father's daughter. Kristers understood but reminded me we would have to face the Colonel after the inspectors left. Until the Allies were physically inside the camp Blixt was a dangerous man. It was a gamble with real risk.

Imagine that! Beautiful music being too risky to play. I don't want to live in the kind of world that can censor or cancel whatever it deems offensive based on race, religion or ethnicity. Who would?

I agreed. And resisted bringing up the same societal cancer growing in my own country. A discussion for another time.

I took Kristers' input seriously. He was very discerning. I said I would pray about it.

The next morning, I was more confident than ever in my selections. But I took his advice about Mozart. At the top of the list, I added the first composition Mozart wrote when he was only five, "Minuet and Trio in G major." I learned it very early on as an exercise.

And a ploy like my mother's came to mind.

Two days before the dinner I would send a message to Schitli with the playlist telling him this would impress the inspectors. It would show the Commandant cared enough for the prisoners to ease their confinement with familiar music. I had never spoken before I played, but offered to announce that myself before beginning, giving Colonel Blixt all the credit. And emphasize how the two examples of Mozart's genius at an early age affirm his revered status as a German composer. I counted on Schitli to sell my propaganda to Blixt. Knowing most Germans love precision, Blixt in particular, I also requested that Petra and I be permitted to tune the piano the day before to insure the finest experience possible.

As an added persuasion, I asked Kristers to write out his menu to be delivered at the same time. Blixt loved to eat. His obesity gave that away. Remember? I witnessed his greedy appetite at the very first dinner at the town hall. I suggested to Kristers he might plan on an extra serving for the corpulent Colonel. Korpulent. We have that same word in German.

Kristers menu made my mouth water.

She remembered every detail.

Chicken ginseng soup with brötchen, bread rolls. A salad of Rapunzel lettuce, wild onions and goat cheese drizzled with oil and vinegar. For the entrée, roast chicken with a mushroom and truffle cream sauce, and, of course, the staple of every German meal, boiled potatoes. The wine, a Reisling from an old farmer's private stock, buried in his barn. Slightly chilled. For dessert, Franzbrötchen with cream and fresh strawberries Kristers found growing on an abandoned farm. It was all too good for a monster like Blixt. I told Kristers the only thing missing was an ample serving of hemlock in the Commandant's mushroom sauce. We gave each other a "why not?" look and laughed hard, which led to, shall I say, an affectionate interlude.

She chuckled.

You don't blush easily, do you, my friend?

"Nein," I responded in German. She laughed again.

Kristers admired the strategy. He had his qualms, but he thought it would work. I knew the Americans and British, who loved my mother, would see through the setup. So would the Hungarians. The majority of prisoners most likely did not speak English or German, but I new they would relish the music. I not only felt Gott's smile. I felt Papa and Mama and Wilhelm's, too.

Forty-eight hours before the event, Herr Benedict delivered Kristers' menu and my list to Schitli.

The day before the dinner, first thing in the morning, Herr Benedict drove Petra and I to the Stalag to tune the piano. We were grateful for his escort. Entering the front gate again past the central guard tower brought heavy memories of Mama. She made that trip nearly every day for over a year and a half. The guards in the tower manning machine guns looked younger than me. Many guards were older men. They leered at us from weary, dead eyes. The row upon row of wooden barracks lining the broad main street looked shabbier than ever.

We were ordered not to look at or interact with the prisoners in any way, and were ushered quickly toward the officer dining hall, across an open space. The stench was overpowering. Behind the barbed fences just across the main road, hundreds of ragged men stood or sat in the dirt. I could see them out of the corner of my eye. One of them shouted in English, "It's Aneska!" They began to stand at attention. It had been over five months since I played for them! Yet they remembered my name. I'm sure they remembered Mama. One soldier began clapping in a slow, steady cadence. The rest joined in. I was so moved. All I could do was bow my head, look straight ahead, and keep walking. I placed a hand over my heart, hoping that would convey my gratitude and acknowledgement. The clapping grew louder as we entered the dining hall. Schitli met us. He did not look pleased, but there was nothing he could do. Come to think of it, I never saw his pleased look. Poor man.

We spent about an hour and a half tuning and playing the piano. I remember it was still in remarkably good shape. A guard stood watch the entire time. Kristers was in the kitchen making dough for Franzbrötchen. He glanced out a few times, kneading a ball of dough in his hands. We had to be careful. He gave me the look. In response I played a few bars of Gymnopedie No.1 by Erik Satie. It was already part of our love language, you might say.

He brought us both a glass of water as an excuse to say he might not be able to leave the Stalag that evening. Too much preparation to do. I understood but struck a dissonant chord on the piano. When Petra and I were satisfied with the tuning, a guard led us out by another way to Herr Benedict's car.

I spent the rest of the day playing through the five pieces. I wanted them to be second nature under my fingers. The atmosphere at the dinner would be tense. "Tension is the enemy on your instrument," Herr Nachtneder used to say, as he made you tense by the snarl in his voice hovering over your shoulder. Maybe that training would pay off playing in front of Blixt again. I said a prayer for my old teacher. Wherever he was.

Sleep did not come easy. So many things were not right in the world. Kristers absent from my bed was one of them. The miracle of finding each other in the upheaval of the war made any separation feel like a theft. Petra made us some tea from Chamomile blossoms Kristers collected in the forest. Of course, he would think of that. But drinking tea made from his thoughtfulness was a long way from wrapping myself around him.

She suddenly caught herself and apologized.

I'm so sorry, my friend. I just realized recalling my intimacies with Kristers may touch a nerve of the losses you endure. The human touch of someone we love is one of the rarest gifts. Without it, whatever the circumstance, lonely nights are lonely nights. Please forgive me if my recollections thoughtlessly hurt you in any way.

I told her there was nothing to forgive. I admitted their deep love made me envious and sometimes sad by the contrast to my own situation. But it also helped me recall my own seasons of being a willing captive to the gravitational pull of the loves I'd known. And at my core, were thankful for. I thanked her for being sensitive to my 'love history nerve' but hoped that wouldn't keep her from the unvarnished version of her story. The one I came to hear.

I appreciate that so much. Let me just say, before we move on, I know you have loved and lost and loved again. That is a triumph of the heart. And testimony that maybe love can always find us down another road, ya?

I answered in a way that always amused her, 'Ya,' adding an 'amen.' And jotted down yet another song idea: Down Another Road.

CHAPTER TWENTY-EIGHT

THE TRAP

The day of the dinner came. It was Friday the thirteenth, but our family paid no heed to superstitions. Whatever you've heard about the luck of the Irish, Gott's providence never takes a day off to let luck have a play day.

I wore Mama's dress that Petra altered for our wedding. Out of habit, she started to braid my hair. But I wasn't a schoolgirl anymore. I was a married woman. She parted it on the left side, swept it back from my face and pinned it with a yellow clip of Mama's. On the audience side. My natural waves fell past my shoulders. I felt a little vain, but Jakob said I looked twenty years old and more like Mama than ever.

Herr Benedict arrived to escort me. We stood in Petra's front room with her and Jakob and joined hands. Herr Benedict said a beautiful prayer, then led us in the Lord's prayer.

Our course was set. By choice and by Providence.

We arrived thirty minutes early so I could warm up. The dining hall was bustling with kitchen and serving staff. I looked toward the kitchen but didn't see Kristers. One long table stood perpendicular to the stage. A chair at each end. Five on each side for the Red Cross inspectors and Senior SS officers. There were name cards at each place setting. I did not expect to be seated for dinner. I preferred not to be. The setting at the head chair was Blixt's, of course. I walked the length of the table toward the piano. Five names in a row were not German sounding. The Red Cross inspectors, I assumed. The name on the setting at the other end of the table stopped time. "Frau Aneska Latva." Herr Benedict read the shock on my face. He looked at the card. At the same instant Kristers came out of the kitchen door in his all white and tall chef hat and hurried toward me.

He threw his arms around me and kissed me full on the lips. He said, "Hallo, meine Liebe!" Hello, my love. "Isn't it wonderful? We're having a wedding reception after all!"

I was completely rattled. If Herr Benedict was, he hid it well. I thought Kristers had to be drinking. But he wasn't. He was keyed up, but not rattled. And he was wearing his wedding ring! With a piece of tape around the back to make it fit tighter. He kept a jovial look on his face and fiddled with the table settings.

He spoke in varying soft and louder tones. **"You look so beautiful, mein Schatz.** It was Schitli. He got to the mayor and found us out. Let's go with it. Lean into it. Centripetal force. I'll explain that later. **Colonel, I trust Frau Benedict is well?** The more conspicuous we are the less likely Blixt can cause us trouble. **Yes, what a fine spring day for this.** I told Schitli we would be honored if Colonel Blixt would make our announcement and propose a toast when he introduces you. Maybe say how remarkable it is that love can blossom even in the most challenging times. **You're going to love the entrée.** If I know Blixt he will milk it for PR with the inspectors. **My darling, I need to make sure der brötchen goes in the oven at the right time. You warm up.** Gott is with us."

He kissed me quickly and hurried to the kitchen.

Herr Benedict managed a reassuring look. He tried to calm me by saying Kristers was required to get permission to marry from his commanding officer. That shouldn't be an issue because his own name was on the marriage certificate. He noticed his seat was on the corner next to mine.

"Look, I'll be right here with you," he said.

I read my place card again. "Frau Aneska Latva." It was the first time I saw my new name in writing. The beauty of it settled my nerves. A bit. That and the sheer energy of Kristers seizing the situation. I was only beginning to learn what a force he was. On the wave of his momentum, I took a deep breath and went to the piano. Something Mama quoted to me came to mind, like she whispered it to me. Does that ever happen to you? Inner whispers?

> Be strong and courageous. Do not be afraid;
> do not be discouraged, for the Lord your God
> will be with you wherever you go.

Can you guess what greeted me at the piano? A glass of water and a single snowdrop blossom. I loved my new husband even more.

Sitting down at the piano calmed my anxiety. It was a place I had spent thousands of hours. The black and white keys in front of me always presented an ordered, reliable world, but one of endless combinations. It was a language I understood. Music spoke to my soul. Helped me speak my own. And discover what I carried deep within, out of sight from anyone but Gott, the "partner of my soliloquies." What does scripture say? The Spirit intercedes for us through wortloses stöhnen, 'wordless groans.' The piano took me inside the wordless groans, the deepest agonies and highest reveries of the famous composers across time. Every time I placed my hands on the keys, I entered that world. To listen and to speak the language.

I warmed up for about fifteen minutes. And did what Mama told me to do. I imagined Benca somewhere out in the camp. I hoped the four remaining airmen from the crash the summer before would be listening. And thousands more clinging to life and hope. I felt focused. Called to the moment. And ready.

Kristers brought a tray of something out of the kitchen. He set whatever it was around the table. Pausing in front of me, he prayed softly, "Lord, make Aneska an instrument of your peace." He gave me the look and returned to the kitchen.

As I left the piano, Schitli entered the dining hall. He came directly to me. He instructed me not to speak at all. To say nothing before any of the selections. And the big shock, Blixt would begin with a toast to Kristers and me for our marriage. After that I would go to the piano to play. Schitli himself would say a few words on the microphone. After that I was to begin playing. All I had time to say as he turned away was, "Javole, Danke." I noticed there was no 'Sieg Heil' or clicking of his heels. But I didn't have long to enjoy that.

A moment later, Blixt strode into the dining hall with the SS officers and Red Cross inspectors. My anxiety rose again. A man not in a uniform was speaking to him, an inspector, I assumed. As usual, Blixt's nose was in the air, hands behind his back like we often saw Hitler in the war films. Servers met them with trays of full wine glasses. Schitli guided them to the table. They found their places and took their seats. Herr Benedict, Gott bless him, escorted me to my chair and sat down beside me.

Blixt remained standing behind his chair. He began with a few comments about what a long, productive day it had been, how it was his honor to offer the Red Cross the finest German hospitality, food and music. He called for the chef to be introduced. Kristers came out of the kitchen holding his hat in his hands. He walked directly to my end of the table as if choreographed.

"Gentlemen, the cuisine you are about to enjoy has been chosen and prepared by Corporal Kristers Latva from Göttingen. The music you are about to hear will be presented by his new bride of nine days, Frau Aneska Latva. I propose a toast." Everyone stood. He asked me to stand next to Kristers.

Glasses were raised. Wonder of wonders, Kristers script came out of Blixt's mouth. "To love blossoming even in challenging times." Everyone drank and sat down. Kristers headed back to the kitchen.

If I didn't know the real Blixt, I might have been fooled. But I knew the black heart behind the immaculate uniform and silver tongue. Blixt turned it over to Schitli and sat down. That was my cue. I went to the piano. Schitli walked to a microphone in front of the stage. The moment he spoke, I knew my propaganda hit the mark.

He announced that, owing to the largess of Colonel Blixt, all my selections would be broadcast to the entire camp. That it was the Commandant's aim to ease the prisoner's confinement from time to time with beautiful music familiar to them.

Like most tyrants, they were so accustomed to lying another farce came easy.

I didn't interrupt to say it, but that hit close to home. Too many of our politicians, bureaucrats and media fit the same profile. Another discussion for another time.

Schitli had swallowed my bait whole to stroke Blixt's ego. And probably to secure his own. Freud was right about some things. The ego is a fickle master, hungry for affirmation and control. If it holds the reins inside a person - feed the ego - steer the horse.

Kristers stood in the kitchen door with his arms crossed. He gave me a tender look and made a quick victory sign with one hand against his arm.

Schitli went on say I would begin with two "pure" and "innocent" Mozart selections. He emphasized Mozart's age when he composed each piece. And drew the conclusion for everyone that Mozart's early genius clearly illustrated the pre-eminence of German composers. He did not mention the other composers by name. That was no surprise.

As he followed my script, I nearly felt like the director of a play. It taught me a lesson I have never forgotten. Even the supposed "adults" in the room can be gullible, willing pawns under the right pressures and need for self-glorification. Any of us can. That's why our core identity must be built on the solid rock. I'm sure you know that hymn, my friend.

All I had to say was, "all other ground is sinking sand."

Precisely.

Schitli turned toward me and said in a pleasant enough tone "Frau Latva." But if looks could maim, his would have. And if my ego had been my only defense, his look would have hit its mark. But it bounced off. I can't take credit for that. I knew Kristers was praying in the kitchen door. And Herr Benedict in the front chair, smiling that same smile since the day we met. Frau Benedict and Petra's prayers carried me, too. And I felt the invisible support of a heavenly audience.

I took a deep breath, pictured Benca again in my mind, and entered five-year old Mozart's uncluttered world with his Minuet and Trio in G major. After the second piece, his Air in A, I intended to launch directly into Chopin's Nocturne. But Blixt stood and applauded. The SS officers followed his lead. Blixt raised his glass and toasted Mozart. I paused just long enough for them to take their seats and launched into Chopin's lovely homage to the eternal resilience of beauty. I felt again like the first time I broadcast to the POWs. Like I was smuggling hope right under Blixt's arrogant nose. This time from a verboten source. I let the final C-sharp major chord ring very long. As I put my hands in my lap, applause erupted from one side of the table. The inspectors gave me a standing ovation. Behind it in the distance, I heard the prisoners join them. Blixt and the SS officers remained seated. I didn't need the applause or approval from any of them. Gott and heaven's smile were enough.

Kristers applauded longer than anyone. That made me a little nervous. But he was my new husband. Who wouldn't understand that?

I stood and bowed slightly and returned to the table. Herr Benedict pulled my chair out and seated me. I was relieved the chicken ginseng soup and warm brötchen arrived immediately. Blixt's loud voice dominated the conversation. No surprise.

I enjoyed the luxury of a bit of conversation with Herr Benedict and the British inspector to my left. He asked me about my training and plans, and lowered his voice to add, "after the war." I told him perhaps more music study while Kristers pursued his doctorate in applied mathematics. That my dreams were to become a concert pianist playing with orchestras around the world, to someday compose piano concertos and start a classical music school.

As Kristers placed a salad in front of the Commandant, Blixt startled me. He addressed me by name. His question was clearly meant as a trap.

"Frau Latva, you have played compositions from many cultures. Whose music would you say rises to the top, against which all others must be measured?" All eyes turned toward me. Kristers took a few steps back. He gave me a reassuring look and placed one hand on his heart. I felt like Jesus in a snare set by the Pharisees. But the Lord was wisdom itself and there was no coin I could use to answer a tax question. I looked down at my salad. Miraculously, an answer came.

"Sir, I may be too naive to judge such a thing. I can only say, some compositions are meant like a soup. They whet the appetite. Others are cool and light like a salad. There are short, sweet ones like a dessert. And then there are the entrées, the opus of a symphony or opera. It takes all of them to make a feast."

The inspectors laughed and raised their wine glasses. Blixt was not amused.

"Very clever, Frau Latva. Much like your mother."

The reference to Mama through his cordial sneer touched off a burning anger in me. I kept it at bay, but only with great effort. If I could have rammed Blixt with one of Papa's fishing boats, I would have.

The salad course pleased everyone. But the entrée brought raves. True to form, Blixt had a second serving. Kristers truly was a gifted chef. The inspectors insisted he take a bow. More wine flowed and coffee was served. That was my cue to move to the piano.

With no introduction, I began Tchaikovsky's Swan Lake. I could only imagine the Russian prisoners. How the first notes sang in their astonished ears and poured into their spirits. They were all captive swans, forbidden to fly, except for some by death into the arms of Gott.

I rarely cried when I played, but after the climactic four octave cascade, all my anger, grief and my love for Kristers combined in the defiant and triumphant finale. Tears ran down my face. The keys blurred during the fortissimo melody in octaves which repeats pianissimo. As the last warm chord rang out, Herr Benedict brought me a serviette.

In the silence, a distant sound like approaching rain came from across the camp. It was applause and cheering. Blixt stood and started to speak, but the inspectors stood and applauded. I think the SS officers thought Blixt was giving me a standing ovation, so they stood and applauded, too. Blixt told Schitli to tell the kitchen staff to bring dessert. But they were applauding, too.

As the ovation subsided, Herr Benedict, that blessed man, turned to Blixt and said, "Pardon me, sir. But Frau Latva has one more number. It was a favorite of the Lübberstedt women under my watch who are here now."

The inspectors insisted on one more. Blixt couldn't go against the tide without revealing his hideous side. And that would shatter the veneer of Schitli's praise of the Commandant, of his concern for the prisoners' confinement. He was trapped.

Blixt stood as tall as a fat man with a dead soul can, looked down his nose at Herr Benedict, and said in a graciousness as counterfeit as his concern, "Very well. One more. For their service to the Reich." He called for Corporal Kristers, who was standing not far away. "Corporal, after this, do not serve dessert cold to our guests. Understood?"

Kristers responded immediately, "Jawohl, Kommandant."

The room quieted. I closed my eyes and took a few deep breaths. I waited til Benca's face came to mind. And Mama's. And then I gave everything in me to Liszt's Hungarian Rhapsody, to an audience I would never have again. And will never forget. I finished to more applause. But the smile of Gott and Kristers' look from the back of the room rang louder in my heart. I returned to my seat. Dessert was served. The Franzbrötchen created sounds of delight and compliments. The event seemed be a success.

Just when I was beginning to relax, looking forward to being with Kristers later in the evening at Petra's, Blixt pressed his earlier question.

"Now, Frau Latva, all cleverness aside, tell us, which composer's entrées must all others be measured against?"

Tension grew around the table.

I knew the answer he wanted. And that any other answer could go very badly. Sitting there, with all eyes on me again, I trusted what to say would be given to me. I opened my mouth, and something like this came out. In the best English I could muster.

"Sir, as you see by my age, I am short on history. So, I will leave it to history to place that crown. But I will say what someone much wiser than me said about that."

I looked Blixt straight in the eye. "My mother taught me that great music rises from many cultures. But it reaches beyond culture to our common humanity. I believe we heard that earlier in Mozart and Chopin. And just now in Tchaikovsy and Liszt. I would only add that it seems to me composers who feed the human soul care more about that and less about who wears a crown. In fact, Beethoven and Handel, just two of our revered German composers, signed many of their works, Soli Deo Gloria, glory to Gott alone. They believed only Gott wears the crown. Sir, I'm sure you know that about them, but perhaps our guests did not."

Silence followed.

Finally, one of the American inspectors, Gott bless him, stood and proposed a toast. We all stood with him. I will never forget his kind face. He looked at me, scanned the stern faces of the SS officers, raised his glass, and said to Blixt in perfect German, "An unsere gemeinsame Menschlichkeit. To our common humanity. und Soli Deo Gloria. and to God alone be the glory.'

I was elated and anxious. I couldn't be sure if he helped or hurt the situation. Blixt raised his glass, but didn't drink. That was not a good sign.

Both the British and American inspectors extended gracious invitations to me to visit their countries. Herr Benedict found an appropriate moment to escort me out. At the door, Kristers embraced me. He said, "Bravissimo, mein Leibe."

I asked him quietly if we had anything to worry about.

He answered, "Did Odette in Swan Lake?" He whispered something more intimate and romantic in my ear. I will only say, it was closely related to Einstein's theory of relativity. My friend, you invited me not to withhold delicate matters, did you not?

All I could do was nod and chuckle.

Kristers told us he might be another hour because the kitchen must be put right. Herr Benedict would return for him.

On the short ride to Petra's, my anxiety grew. I couldn't fight the thought: Odette's happy ending was a legend. This was real life.

CHAPTER TWENTY-NINE

THE UNTHINKABLE

Two days went by. We braced ourselves for trouble. Kristers could only leave the Stalag to find food for the officer dining hall with Herr Benedict. Or by his permission. He stretched those trips into the evening so we could have a few hours together. One afternoon, I met him at the hunting cabin. I will only say what a wonderful sanctuary Gott provided in the love between a man and a woman spalten, cleaving, to one another, body and soul. The whole world can be falling apart, but the cathedral of that bond stands amid the rubble.

Aneska looked at me. I knew what was coming.

My friend, I'm sorry your sanctuary collapsed from within. That's part of your agony. But it's only a part of your story. Gott, the author and finisher of our faith, and our stories, is not done writing yours, or mine.

The fact that her tenderness survived and deepened, in spite of all she had endured, gave Aneska's words gravity and good aim. They touched me like the skilled hands of a surgeon. I crossed an ocean to hear her story. But she remained aware of mine. Her gaze returned to the fire.

There's a story being written in every heart. It will either be a story of redemption and freedom or one of decay and captivity. Too often in this world, what matters is only who prevails. Less and less remains sacred. More than ever, we need a Savior. But, my friend, as one of your songs says, many still prefer a hero. A story with a hero is inspiring. A story with a Savior is transforming. Back then I already had a Savior. And the heroes were on their way.

Aneska was clearly becoming one of my heroes.

On April 15, Herr Benedict heard Bergen-Belsen camp was liberated. That was less than two hours southeast of us. The British were already reaching beyond us. We felt liberation could come any day.

April 18 news came that hundreds of thousands of German soldiers surrendered in the Ruhr valley. That was only three hours west of us!

Under the pressure of the Allied arrival, Blixt went on a rampage, like a cornered animal. Hundreds died daily from forced starvation, especially in the Soviet section. When the wind blew from the Stalag, the stench reached us. Herr Benedict watched over the Lübberstedt women the best he could, but many of them were abused. Some disappeared.

Tensions were high. Blixt put the two taming chairs out in the courtyard again as a deterrent. No one doubted he would use them. One night, we heard the noise of trucks passing through Sandbostel. It was German troop carriers headed east, not west, staying off the main roads. Herr Benedict assumed they were headed to defend Berlin.

A few nights after that, on April 19, during an air-raid alarm, gunfire from the Stalag woke us up. An hour later, several hundred prisoners marched past Petra's house under heavy guard. Apparently, a large group had stormed a kitchen for food. Rumor went round they were executed out in the countryside somewhere. After the liberation, that was confirmed, and a mass grave discovered.

April 20 was Hitler's birthday. For many years, there were celebrations all over Germany. This one came and went without so much as an announcement. Guards were too busy burning records and piling bodies for mass burial. They couldn't bury them fast enough. Several barracks full of bodies were set on fire. The black smoke had a smell I will never forget. Like a grease fire, part charcoal aroma, but pungent and metallic.

Aneska paused for a long time. She asked me to bring her a picture. The one from the surprise Christmas of 1944. Petra had taken it. Noticeably absent was Wilhelm. Aneska kissed her fingers and touched them to the picture before setting it on the table between us. She hesitated to go on. This was a pattern. Whenever the next thing was painful, she grew quiet, collecting herself to relive it. I knew enough to wait, that I was about to enter more holy ground of her suffering. She sighed deeply. Looked into the fire and continued.

Four more days went by without incident.

April 25, 1945, the unthinkable happened. It was after midnight. Herr Benedict had given Kristers leave to spend a night with me at Petra's. After all, our marriage was not a secret anymore. He was beside me in bed. We were asleep. And naked.

We woke to a loud knocking. A male voice argued with Petra downstairs. We heard heavy footsteps stomping through the house. Fortunately, Jakob had begun sleeping in the barn, in case we had surprise visitors. The boots started up the stairs. Kristers pulled his pants on. He grabbed his Luger and pointed it at the bedroom door as it burst open. We couldn't see the face of the dark figure in the doorway, but when he spoke, I knew instantly it was Lieutenant Schitli. The serpent sneer in his voice would have been enough, but no one else would have said what he said to me.

"Aneska Latva, ihre coda ist endlich da." 'Your coda has finally come.' "Korporal, treten Sie zurück." 'Stand down.' Kristers lowered his weapon but stood between him and me. Schitli barked at both of us to get dressed. "Jetzt! Mach Schnell!" 'Now! Make it quick!' He ordered Kristers to surrender the pistol. As he turned to leave, my furious husband demanded to know what this was about. Schitli ignored him. He stationed two soldiers at our door and went downstairs. Kristers pulled rank on the soldiers. He ordered them to turn their backs while I dressed.

Going out the bedroom door, I looked both guards in the eye. Like Mama taught me. I didn't have time to process what was happening. But at that moment, I knew firsthand what millions knew. What Anne Frank experienced. The malevolent, stony face of tyranny. The hatred behind its eyes, like demons possessing young men who only a few years earlier were blue-eyed, laughing school boys kicking a soccer ball. Boys with dreams traded for a maniac's vendetta. Relinquishing all humane impulses. Willing to drag people from their beds, their families, destroy their businesses, burn their churches. And with morbid pleasure, even take their lives, end their stories, seduced by the age-old tyrant's delusion of a "greater cause."

I felt anger rise in my own chest, and a dread at what was coming.

Downstairs I was able to hug Petra for only a moment before we were rushed into the back of a troop truck behind Schitli's car. I had seen this many times on our streets in Hamburg. But now it was us. Instead of driving toward the Stalag, they headed the opposite direction. After just a few minutes the truck stopped. The guards pushed us through the back door of a building, our own Sandbostel town hall. We heard single, sparce piano notes.

Colonel Blixt sat at the piano, picking out a random string of notes. In no particular key. As the guards brought us toward him, he addressed me in his smug tone.

"Frau Latva. Ironic isn't it? This is where we met." He talked about how clever, beautiful and sly my mother was. And how much I was like her. I thanked him for the compliment. His tone remained calm and menacing.

"You will soon not thank me. Tonight, you will not glibly escape your duplicity."

Kristers demanded to know on what charge we were being detained as German citizens. Schitli read an official sounding arrest document accusing me of giving aid and comfort to the enemies of the Third Reich and flagrant insubordination by playing verboten composers and compositions.

Two guards brought out a highbacked chair with straps on it. Kristers had to be restrained. He protested vehemently that the British would arrive any day now. That this was a war crime and Blixt and everyone present would pay dearly. I had never heard him raise his voice like that. Guards handcuffed him standing to a post facing the chair. The look we gave each other was far from the one in the church just three weeks earlier.

Blixt blathered on like all megalomaniacs do - about the only crime being the world would not yet be ruled by the only ones who deserve to rule. He spouted more insane nonsense. At some point in his prattle, he asked me if I would like to play one last composition before sentence was imposed. Anything of my choosing. Even a verboten piece.

At first, I didn't hear his offer. I couldn't take my eyes off Kristers. You know that sensation when your eyes lock open, and you lose your train of thought? Like your brain slips out of gear until you blink and re-engage? When I blinked, it hit me. My bliss and gift, my opus, and most likely my life, were all about to be taken away by that monster.

Blixt asked me again which last composition would I like to play? I could tell he relished the drama of it. Like a fiend whose own black heart drove him to eradicate from the world any happiness or beauty that mocked him in his own misery. It was diabolically cruel.

How could I possibly play at a moment like that? My only thought was that playing something would at least delay Blixt's plan. Anything might happen. I imagined Jakob crashing into the room in Papa's truck or the sound of British tanks and trucks rolling up. Neither came.

Kristers spoke, "Play me something, my darling." The look he gave me, and the tenderness in his voice, surrounded me like a barrier against the evil in the room. I don't know how my legs moved, but I walked slowly to the piano where Blixt still sat. I looked him in the eye and paused, as if to say, "get out of my way." He did, and sat in a chair where he could watch both of us.

I sat on the bench facing Kristers. Titles scrolled through my head. I nearly began Satie's Gymnopedie No.1, that playful signal of passion between us. But I didn't. Brahms' Intermezzo in A major came to mind. The one he told Mama I played when he fell in love with me. But I hesitated. Looking at Kristers, a calm came over me, like a presence. I can only describe it as if Jesus sat down beside me on the bench. The reminder came to mind, "it shall be given you in that hour what you are to speak." I could see Mama sitting at the table at that first dinner, the steady, unintimidated look on her face, surrounded by those pseudo-civilized officers, most of their hearts blacker than their uniforms. And it came to me. I took a long, deep breath. Exhaled. And began "Dear Lord Jesus, Take My Hand." Lento placido. Very soft and slow.

Every note was a plea to Gott. And a farewell to Kristers.

As the last chord rang out, Kristers spoke before Blixt could. "I understand you asked the British prisoners if anyone would like to take the place of the airman that day."

Blixt stood and answered him. "Das ist wahr. That is true. Are you volunteering to take Frau Latva's sentence?"

"I am," Kristers said.

I cried out, of course. That was NOT going to happen! I was the one charged!

For the first time, Blixt raised his voice. "Silence! Or I will have you both shot here and now!"

He paced back and forth, his hands behind his back, his nose in the air. I locked eyes with Kristers and shook my head back and forth, mouthing silently, "No. No!"

"This is delicious," Blixt said. "If only Wagner were alive to write this into an opera."

"Maybe he already did," Kristers responded. I had no idea where Kristers was headed, but he was obviously crossing swords with Blixt. And the reason became plain.

"How so, Korporal?"

Kristers appealed to Blixt's pompous vanity saying the Colonel was like Wagner's Valkyrie, holding the power to choose the slain who are worthy – deciding who deserves the most severe and honorable death.

Kristers stretched it a bit. The Valkyries didn't choose the manner of death. In the legend, they only chose the honorably slain and carried them to Valhalla, paradise, in the afterlife. But I saw where he was going and begged him to stop. Blixt wanted to hear him out.

"Which is the higher drama, Colonel? The deeper pathos? To aim your wrath at Brunhilde or Siegfreid? Slay the disobedient one, or the object of her greatest affection? Wouldn't a modern Wagner, like yourself, do what Wagner did, let the songbird live but without a triumphant song to sing?"

"Very compelling," Blixt said. He rubbed his fat hands together in front of his fat face, reveling in Kristers' proposal.

I knew in the opera Seigfreid dies first and later Brunhilde rides into the flames of his funeral pyre. Kristers was trying to convince Blixt to do the same with us, counting on his maniacal ego to hurt me to the core by putting Kristers in the chair. I didn't know at the time that the miscreant was also exacting revenge on me for my mother's rebuff of his advances. The more I protested, the more Blixt warmed to Kristers' argument. I watched him swallow it whole.

True to form, the villain who killed far more people by intentional neglect than any soldier on the front lines, tried to mitigate his malevolent nature by saying he had no intention of executing either one of us. He prattled on about a "fascinating" case of a railroad worker in the U.S. who blasted an iron rod through the front of his brain while tamping explosives. He wasn't even knocked unconscious. The man lost one eye but survived. "Granted," Blixt lectured us, "he had limited intellectual capacities, and spontaneously uttered profanities. But he lived another eleven years." The monster maintained survival is "in Gott's hands." But Blixt only believed in Gott like Satan does, all defiance and no allegiance.

I have to admit, at that moment I would have put an iron rod or a bullet through his head without hesitating, just like my Papa rammed his boat into that submarine.

Blixt paced back and forth, his nose in the air, looking up at the rafters. He turned to Kristers and said, "As you wish, Korporal. I salute your valor and ingenuity, as I suppose your Gott will." He aimed his cold, dead eyes at me and said, "But I am sure your bride will bear the weight of your valor every day of her life and in every note she plays."

He ordered the guards to place Kristers in the taming chair. This time it was me who had to be restrained. They shackled my hands in front of me around the post, where I could watch.

She paused to collect herself. It was obvious the pain of it all was resurfacing.

Like you, dear reader, though I knew Kristers survived the war, I wondered if this dire scenario begs the same questions in you as it did in me. Would I take that chair for someone? And for whom? Certainly, for my children. No question. On the other hand, how would I respond to such a sacrifice for me? If it meant a lifetime of caring and serving and bearing the load of surviving physically, but dying to a future forever marred, stolen and altered. And what if it put my own dreams on hold? Would I sacrifice them for the daily care of another? Given a love with the depth of theirs, I believe I would. Love bears all things, right? Love doesn't just declare. Love acts. And catastrophe proves its mettle, its tensile strength.

As I waited for Aneska to resume, a flashflood of emotion washed over me, I suppose from the cumulative effect of their story and the anticipation of the pain ahead. Now it was my eyes that filled. I had to close my eyes and lean my head back on the chair. Aneska's empathy didn't surprise me. She asked,

Do you need a minute?

I thanked her and told her, no, that my old paster used to say, "Lean into it. If you don't now, you'll have to later."

A wise man. This is the part where I have to do that. Lean into it. And I have never gone into this much detail, even with my children.

Aneska took a sip of water. To my surprise, she did the last thing I expected. She asked me to pray and extended a hand. I took it. I thanked God for sparing Aneska and Kristers' lives through this ordeal, for redeeming their pain, and to use their loss and story for his purposes.

Before I said 'amen' she surprised me again. She prayed for me. For nearly the same things. For the Lord to redeem my pain through forgiveness, adding my children and Ex as well. She asked God for a new season and story in my heart. She said 'Amen.' Thanked me. I thanked her. I wondered if there had ever been a Saint Aneska. There was in my world. She took a deep breath and leaned into it.

I watched the guards strap Kristers into the chair, just as Mama described from that day with the airmen. Blixt opened an ornate wooden box. He removed a very small pistol and loaded one bullet. I remember screaming and begging, "Gott, No! Gott, please!" and sliding down to my knees. Blixt admonished me in his sickening, calm tone about having some respect for my husband's valor.

He said, "Careful, Frau Latva. How do you want Kristers to remember you? If he does."

Kristers eyes never left mine.

Blixt circled us both. He went into a maddening description of the pistol. An Austrian made, Kolibri, which is German for 'hummingbird.' The word can still sometimes ambush me when those beautiful birds visit our gardens. He boasted about the low muzzle velocity for this application and the precision of the small bullets. He had them specially made with a coating of nickel.

He said to Kristers, "Do you know why that is important, Korporal? I'll tell you why. The bullet will not fragment and biodegrade over time like lead and copper."

He looked at me and spoke slowly, like a surgeon reassuring me of an outcome. "Your husband could carry it the rest of his life without the ill effects of metal poisoning. At least that's the theory."

It was all meant to torture us. And it worked.

Before they blindfolded him, Blixt asked Kristers if he had any final words for me.

Kristers gave me the look. We gazed into each other eyes, trying to freeze the moment. To stop time. We were fully alive to each other, standing on the brink of losing that and our entire future. Inside, I was still screaming. I wanted to topple the post like Samson and bring the whole building down on us. But Kristers' gaze held me steady. He finally spoke, as calmly as if he were boarding a train for a day trip and would be back for supper. He had the same steadiness as Mama.

He said, "Aneska, the Ausrufezeichen of my life, 'the exclamation point of my life.' Our love is stronger than death. God will prevail. It only follows. I love you, my snowdrop, always."

At this point Aneska needed another minute. I did, too. The power of their love swept over me in a tidal wave of awe and loss.

As I revealed earlier, I was unchosen by someone who decided to opt out of "for better or worse," the mother of my children, which happens all too often. Sadly. Like so many couples, we said the same vows as Aneska and Kristers. We promised "til death do us part." But forever came and went. To be circumspect, (if that's even fully possible), perhaps my truant bride had longings like my own that I didn't meet in her as well. But whatever the reasons for the change of season in her heart, listening to Aneska's love story, the central question became this: aside from the obvious sacrificial love of Christ, is there a love in this world stronger than death? Able to endure come what may? A love that demonstrates, as a dear friend put it, the "expressed spirit of God through us." Is there a glory in human love that reflects the glory of God's?

Aneska and Kristers' story was assuring me there is. I already knew I wanted my children to find that kind of love, in spite of their parents' failure.

Once again, Aneska's honesty and vulnerability unleashed the velvet crowbar of the Holy Spirit to open my own heart to the hope of that kind of love in my own story. I even had a new thought. "Maybe even for my Ex in hers." That was more charitable than many thoughts I'd harbored toward her. Afterall, that longing is core to who we are as humans. Who wouldn't want Aneska and Kristers' kind of love? In any season of life?

I'm sorry, my friend.

No apology necessary.

These are the moments I avoid revisiting most. But they also set in motion the most remarkable means for Gott to prevail, as Kristers said.

Remarkable was sitting in front of me. Again, aside from the crucifixion of Christ, how could the worst possible thing in one's life set the stage for the remarkable and miraculous? Their scenario tested the tensile strength of the scripture, "In all things God works for the good of those who love Him, who have been called according to His purpose." In ALL things? Like most of us, I wrestle with this on a personal and global level. Is it possible evil can rage and God remain sovereign? And good? I already knew Saint Aneska's answer to that.

Kristers' words helped carry me across the decades. They provided motivation not merely to go on, but to create the music academies, celebrate blessings, face adversity, and why the concerto must be completed. But let me get back to the horrific events of that day.

Blixt proved he was incapable of feeling any humane impulse. If a light of any kind ever lived in him, it flickered and died a long time ago. After Kristers' beautiful words to me, that completely hollow deviant uttered one word, in a dismissive tone, "Touching." With a flip of his hand, he signaled the guards to blindfold Kristers. They strapped his head stationary to the back of the chair.

Blixt walked around Kristers, taunting him, lecturing about the marvels of the brain like a medical scientist. He advised Kristers it was very important to remain perfectly still. Once he determined an entry point and angle, the slightest motion could take away his sight, taste, speech, or hearing.

Out of sheer cruelty he said to him, "Imagine never hearing Frau Latva play again or taste the fine dishes you cook. One twitch and your ability to walk could disappear. Or cherished memories of your loved ones be completely erased. Along with your recipes."

It truly was a living nightmare. I begged Blixt to tame me instead. In the panic, I tried to use his own words to make him relent and punish me. After all, I argued, if art was just garnish, Kristers, the mathematical genius would be of far more worth to the world and the new Germany. But it backfired.

Blixt concluded that was all the more reason to tame Kristers. He flattered himself with the pathos. He said, "Imagine one genius casting another into the crucible in the sight of Gott Almighty. Like a clash of Titans!"

He actually said that! As if he were any match for Kristers or Gott Almighty. Later, it struck me this wasn't just a vendetta against me or my mother. Blixt's cruelty was an assault on Gott himself. If only I'd had the faith of Elijah to call down fire from heaven, I would have burned him to a pile of ashes on the floor.

But no fire came down.

Blixt commanded me to be silent, or he would shoot Kristers in the back of the head near the spine. A spot he assured me would kill him instantly. He continued circling, the muzzle directed at half a dozen spots around Kristers' head. With the air of a university lecturer, he described the faculties that would likely be affected at each spot. This made me wonder how many times he had done this.

I tried another argument, if only to delay him. I told Blixt his expertise must have come from a lot of this kind of research. That those records would damn him in court after the war. I heard Kristers chuckle. How was that possible? But he did.

That only heated Blixt's rage. He strode over to me, bent down and put his nose nearly against mine. I could feel the heat from his face. His calm tone made him even more menacing. He affirmed he had indeed done extensive research on subjects whose sacrifices advanced the cause of science. And that all evidence and records of his groundbreaking work had already been destroyed. The essential knowledge remained only in his head to be built upon after the war.

He added two new threats. If I didn't keep quiet, he would cut off all my fingers except the kleine, my pinky fingers. I would be relegated to playing Chopsticks for the rest of my life. He assured me my father and remaining brother would be sacrificed for science as well.

So, he didn't know about Papa. But Jakob could be at risk, especially if liberation delayed.

Kristers spoke from behind his blindfold, "My darling, you know how I love your hands."

The fight went out of me. I was down for the count. Where was Joe Lewis when we needed him?

Blixt walked back over to Kristers. He turned to me and gloated, "Maybe after the war I will write your story and enlist a great German composer to score it."

I was too in shock to react anymore. The weight on my soul,

heavier than I ever felt, made it hard to stand. But I did. I had to. I would not let Blixt beat us.

He circled Kristers. Reminded him to remain perfectly still. There would be no countdown. The muzzle remained poised half an inch from my true love's head. He paused behind Kristers. I thought the shot would come. But the maniac pontificated more about the possible damage to that area. Paralysis. Blindness. Impotence.

A guard sneezed. Someone said, "Gesundheit." It was Kristers! I couldn't believe it. The love of my life actually wished the soldier 'good health.' I feared it was the last word I would ever hear him speak.

The guard apologized to the Colonel. Blixt dismissed him to wait outside, and continued to circle.

There wasn't much time. I spoke to Kristers, "Remember my voice, my love. Remember me."

He answered like only he would, "Always. I don't need my brain for that, my love."

"Silence!" Blixt shouted. Our affection irritated him. He stopped on Kristers' left side, holding the muzzle nearly against his head, just above his ear. The fiend looked at me once. I stood as tall as I could. Blixt turned the angle up and down a bit, as though searching for the right spot. Finding it, he said, "Have a good sleep, brave Seigfreid."

As Blixt uttered the name Seigfreid, the unimaginable happened. A pigeon launched from a rafter at him, just like it did at the first dinner! Simultaneously, a shot rang out. Kristers head jerked violently to the right. And then fell forward. Blixt turned his fury on the bird. He aimed at it all around the room as it circled. He kept clicking the trigger before realizing he had no bullets. My eyes went back to Kristers. Blood seeped into the blindfold on the left side of his head. There were a few drops on his leg. The next time I looked at Blixt he had a Luger in his hand. I feared the worst. He scanned for the pigeon, but it had escaped somehow.

The spirit of my mother must have come over me. I looked Blixt in the eye and in a voice I barely recognized as my own I said, "Sir, please let me tend to my husband and return us quickly to Frau Neumann's."

The demon composed himself. Holstered the Luger. He never broke character. He replaced the small pistol in the ornate box, turned to me, and said, "As you wish, Brunhilde."

A guard released me. I tore off part of my skirt and held it against Kristers' wound. They loaded us up. Ten minutes later we carried him into Petra's front room and lay him on the sofa.

He was breathing. The bleeding had stopped. The battle for his life and the war had not.

We took a break. We both needed it. But only until the afternoon. I convinced Aneska I couldn't wait till the next day and try to sleep, not knowing what happened next.

CHAPTER THIRTY

THE LIBERATION

I told you Kristers was brilliant. He used it to sacrifice himself for me.

On one level, that was infuriating, but I didn't have time for that. We were too busy trying to save his life. He was unconscious. Mama wasn't there to help. We propped him up a little, thinking that might prevent more bleeding. Jakob put ice packs around his head to keep swelling and fever down. Petra had some sulfa powder on hand to prevent infection. But the entry wound was no bigger than a pea. Sulfa couldn't reach the depth of it. We knew he could be unconscious for days. If he woke up at all.

Petra knew he had to have fluids. She risked her life by walking to the Stalag near daybreak. She tried to find Herr Benedict but he was overseeing the Lübberstedt women. A guard who owed her a favor happened to be at the gate. She had given him one of Rolf's winter coats and a pair of gloves. She lied and told him I was very sick with fever; the medical supplies were for me. That Colonel Benedict requisitioned them. The guard loved my music and Mama. She nursed him once in the infirmary when he was sick. He secured the IV bags, tubes, and needles. Mama's kindness and the music made a way, with a little help from Herr Benedict's borrowed authority.

At noon that day, Kristers was still alive. He looked peaceful, sometimes almost smug about what he had done. I know that was just me painting him with my frustration. He was beyond my reach, but I held his hand and spoke to him.

We felt so helpless. So we prayed. What else could we do? We read scripture to him. I whispered in his ear, "Fight, my darling. Come back to me." And kept touching him to let him know he was not alone.

That afternoon the Benedicts came to the house with another nurse from the medical team at Lübberstedt. They heard I was sick. You can imagine their shock and outrage. I never saw Herr Benedict in such a state. He watched Kristers grow up. Become a remarkable man. Hans and Brigitte had no children. Kristers was like a son to him. He swore Blixt would pay.

The nurse and Brigitte. commended us for all we were doing. But Kristers had a fever. He needed penicillin and there was none to be had. We continued keeping him cool, with his head and shoulders elevated. And prayed.

On the second day, his breathing became shallow. German troops streamed east through town. In retreat.

On the third day, April 29, 1945 British troops rolled through Sandbostel and liberated the Stalag. Our prayers were answered. They not only freed us. They saved Kristers. Their medics had penicillin. Clean bandages. And more hydration pouches. They gave us everything we needed to tend his wound.

Prayer and penicillin turned the tide. All Kristers needed was time and care. But the kindest British doctor, an Irishman, couldn't give us a very positive outlook. He had seen far too many head wounds from battle. He said if Kristers lived, there was no predicting what he would be like. But very likely not my same Kristers. Ever again. He likened the effects to a stroke. Potential loss of speech, hearing, taste, smell, memory and even mobility. The military had a few mobile neurosurgical units equipped with X-ray machines, but none in the area. He encouraged us not to rush it. Be patient. He told us, "The amazing human brain, your love and le cúnamh Dé, wonders are possible." That's the first time I heard the Gaelic language. Le cúnamh Dé means "with the help of Gott." At least Kristers was alive. Gott had done that much. My handsome, brave husband was still alive.

The doctor, Dr. Deegan, wanted to know the cause of Kristers' head wound. We told him all about Colonel Blixt and the taming of the British airman, and Blixt's own words about the similar brain "research" he had done on others. Though we had only Blixt's word about that. He told us to expect an attaché of the British general to come round for our statement.

April 30, in the evening, Kristers' fever went down. We thanked Gott. The first sense of relief was followed by startling news. The old pastor who married us came to the door late in the afternoon. He was euphoric.

Hitler had killed himself! The war was over. Or would be in a few days.

My first reaction was anger. Why didn't the devil do it a week earlier? Why didn't the British arrive earlier? Blixt's vengeance might have been averted. But none of that outcry undid reality. Kristers still lay in bed with a hole in his head.

It makes you wonder, ya? Is God good when his timing seems terrible? Lazarus died while Jesus delayed getting there. But Lazarus lived again. Kristers' life hung in the balance, and without a miracle, he could be gone or severely damaged. My friend, I know you've wrestled with this kind of thing. Gott's timing or seeming lack of it. I'm sorry if that brings up painful memories.

No worries, I told her. Of course, I questioned God's timing and lack of intervention. I wondered if an angel missed an assignment. I told Aneska that years later, my daughter put it in a providential perspective. Driving down the road one day, she was curious about that time in my life when I loved someone before her mother. She understood I couldn't be glad about the painful tragedy, but asked if I was glad to have her and her brothers. Of course! Yes! No question. God wrote another story. Full of rich blessings.

Ya, he did. He does. But in the crucible of trauma, faith becomes hardest. When the loss is excruciating. That's where we were with Kristers. In the crucible.

Jesus didn't show up late and instantly restore him. He still hung between earth and heaven. Sometimes I sat just watching him breathe, as if I could will him to take the next breath. But like so many other things, that was out of my hands. Blixt was right about one thing. Kristers' survival was in Gott's hands. It was a long time before we realized the Lord showed up on time in other ways. But I'll get to that.

I also wished Papa was alive to celebrate Hitler's suicide. I imagined him raising a stein and shouting, "Der Teufel von Deutschland ist tot!" The Devil of Deutchland is dead! "Durch seine eigene feige Hand!" By his own cowardly hand.

There was other news. Colonel Blixt greeted the British at the gate like a concierge. He offered his full cooperation. Against his protests, he was arrested and housed in the shoddy barracks with other guards and the Wehrmacht SS, to await trial. The captors became the captive.

Jakob wanted to volunteer to help bury the dead before most of the locals were pressed into that gruesome service. But Herr Benedict thought he should lie low. The British might wonder why he wasn't in uniform and take him for questioning. Hans said the conditions were horrifying. The dead and dying were scattered everywhere in the slime of human waste. Hundreds were still dying from starvation, typhus and other diseases. The smoke from burning barracks reached us in town. Some were burned to prevent a typhus epidemic.

Gott forgive me, all those poor souls mattered to the Lord and their loved ones, but one soul mattered to me more at the time.

Just before sunrise on the morning of May first, I was sleeping beside Kristers. Holding his hand. Something twitched. It woke me up. At first I thought it was just me. You know how you can suddenly jerk in your sleep? I listened for his breathing. It was steady and clear. I closed my eyes again. The twitch happened again. I looked at our hands and waited. His finger tapped against mine! I looked over at him. His eyes were open. And he blinked! Slowly, several times, like a man in a heap. That's Irish for a hangover.

Six days after that terrible night, Kristers woke up!

I called out for Petra and Jakob.

I held Kristers' face in my hands. His eyes closed again. I asked him, "Can you hear me, my love? Blink if you can."

He opened his eyes, blinked once and closed them again. He could hear!

I asked Petra to light a candle. She held it in front of his face. When his eyes opened, he squinted from the light and followed the flame back and forth. He could see! I wanted to find out if he had feeling in his legs and feet, but Petra reminded me the doctor said take it slow. Kristers was alive, semi-awake. He could hear and see. It was enough miracle for that day. He breathed a deep sigh, like a wind from heaven and fell back to sleep. Petra and I went to the kitchen to make chicken broth for him. We held each other and wept for joy. My love was alive! He could hear my voice. And see my face.

Aneska's tears flowed freely. I shed a few myself.

Other miracles were to come, but they would take a while.

I thanked her for what it must have taken to revisit the most painful episodes of her life. In her humble way, she said the advantage of hindsight, knowing the outcomes, made the telling much less painful than living through it. She "rambled" some about that.

Don't you find the fear of uncertainty magnifies pain and potential loss? Not knowing how things will turn out. That's why my mother's calm under stress always made me hope for a faith like hers. It still does. The confidence in believing "If God is for us, who can be against us" can turn to thin bravado in the crucible. Mama's faith and courage steadied her in crisis.

Zuza could not have understated it more in our first phone call. Aneska was more inspiring than I could have imagined. Against the panorama of her story and her stature, I began to see that tyrants play a minor role compared to those who triumph in spite of them. And those who overcome pass into the human pantheon of heroes, not for their own sake, but to embolden the next generations to face their own Goliaths. I was sitting with one of those heroes.

It was half two, as the Irish say. Nearly teatime. We broke for the day. I told Aneska I needed to let the magnitude of her story sink in, and pray I wouldn't get in the way writing it down. She leaned toward me, took both my hands in hers, and looked me in the eye, like her mother taught her.

My friend, you were meant to be here. You were chosen for this. Just as I was chosen for my story, and why I'm driven to complete my concerto. The story, together with the music, ensures Papa and Mama, Wilhelm and Jakob, Benca and Golda, beautiful Kristers and countless others will never be de-storied. Together we will make it clear again, those tyrants didn't win. And perhaps, by Gott's mercy and the united might of the resolute, current and future tyrants will meet their just end sooner than later.

I told her she sounded like Churchill. We embraced. She turned down the corridor toward the front entrance. As I headed the other way to my quarters, I heard the now familiar arpeggios of Reflection in A coming from the music room, followed by the delicate, sparse melody in her right hand. She was communing. The same Spirit drew me to do the same, sitting in silence by the still waters and dreaming pastures.

As the river glided by, Aneska's words struck another chord. Deeply personal. Not global. I had my own tyrants. Not as lethal, but able to de-

story me. She was living proof tyrants only win if we succumb. Look them in the eye, stand, walk on, and though they inflict real pain they become only cameo bullies in a storyline of restoration. I couldn't help but think Aneska knew this all along — why she was interested in my story - and glad to be part of it. I resolved to tell her this revelation at the proper moment: the British liberated her from tyrants. She was liberating me from mine.

When I returned to my room from the chilly air, someone had delivered a tray of warm cornbread, butter, honey, and a pot of hot tea. The aroma smelled like victory.

CHAPTER THIRTY-ONE

THE NERVES

Kristers improved daily. His waking minutes were few, but enough to give us hope. And he had feeling in all his extremities! Another miracle.

I slept beside him. Every time I woke to hear his breathing, my anxiety eased. When he opened his eyes, I thrilled to it, even though he didn't recognize me.

I counted our blessings and miracles. Kristers was still alive. He was awake. The helpful guard Petra knew at the gate. The IV supplies. The penicillin. The kindness of Dr. Deegan. All providential. I even wondered if Gott cued the pigeon and, in that split second, redirected the bullet to a less damaging pathway. There was so much we couldn't know. But with Gott, all things are possible, ya?

Ya. of course, I said. Or He couldn't be God.

Precisely!

Since that day, I've carried a fondness for pigeons. They mate for life, you know. And they are reliable messengers because they can find their way home. Gott's design is remarkable. When I walk the estate, I carry seeds for them.

I would never look at a pigeon the same way again.

From the porch we watched British soldiers pass down our road. We cheered them on and thanked them for liberating us. They were so kind, even weary from battle. Some of them were no older than

Kristers. I couldn't imagine the horrors they had seen. The losses. And yet they greeted us with smiles and freely shared their provisions. Even chocolate! There is no antidote to our difficulties, like kindness. And chocolate.

I agreed.

Even this was like the hand of Gott. Scripture says it's his kindness that leads us to repentance.

My protector, Jakob, was cautious for me about the British. He warned me not to get too friendly. They were men. Lonely men a long way from home. Sure enough, standing by the road with Petra, one of them kissed me on the cheek. His buddies dragged him away. They apologized sincerely. I wasn't angry. It just seemed like exuberance.

I goaded her a little, saying, sure, just innocent exuberance. It couldn't be that she was the most beautiful thing they had seen in a long time. She laughed.

Ok. You're slagging me. I get it.

My Irish vocabulary grew again. She explained 'slagging' meant good-natured teasing.

Maybe I was a little naive. But no harm done, except it made me wonder when Kristers would kiss me again. Or if he ever could.

As usual, her truest feelings were right at the surface. And she didn't hesitate to reveal them. I envied her that. Historically, my truest feelings and desires tended to live a few levels down, guarded and privy only to a trusted few. Like most of us, I suppose. I've regretted more than a few times when I should have spoken my heart.

She paused and took a drink of water. We spoke at the same time. She insisted I go ahead. I apologized for touching a nerve.

My friend, isn't that why you're here? Feel free to touch any nerve you like. Do I have permission to do the same for you?

We both laughed. Yes, of course, I told her. Aneska had an irresistible way of drawing you out. I'm sure she did that for everyone she met. From our first meeting, she became one of my trusted few.

Two mornings later a British officer, a Lieutenant Camden, the attaché from the British general, came to the house to take our statement about Blixt. His secretary came with him. The tribunal was in three days. The General was determined to maintain order to prevent retribution breaking out. One Nazi officer had been beaten to death by other SS officers for trying to disguise himself as a private.

The demand from the POWs for justice was loud. But the British had no intention of behaving like the Nazis. In the General's view, justice must prevail. There was no lack of witnesses to Blixt's barbarism, but they needed evidence. None of us had been present at the taming of the airman, but we described in detail what the maniac did to me and Kristers. Including his threats to Jakob. When we mentioned Schitli, Lieutenant Camden told us that was the officer who was beaten to death.

At first, I felt some empathy for Gunter, to go through life without his father, as I had to. Then, Gott forgive me, I wondered if in his case it was a mercy to him.

Lieutenant Camden predicted Blixt and his staff would likely go to prison, but not for as long as their crimes warranted. The General had field authority to order executions, but not without clear evidence of crimes. Without it, the process could go on for years.

After the war, that proved to be the case. Thousands of brutal camp guards escaped conviction and returned to civilian life. Many of them as police officers! Shocking. How did they live with themselves? Carrying around all those memories of who they became and what they were capable of. Perhaps in many cases, only a shame-ectomy kept their sins at bay.

Just a week after liberation, in all the chaos, getting a clear picture of the culprits was difficult. Nearly every German at the camp bore guilt on some level. Certainly not the Benedicts. Of that, I was confident. Hans and Brigitte could have fled with some others, but they remained to watch over the Hungarian women. The testimonies to the kindness and care of the Benedicts helped win their acquittal and release.

During our interview, the secretary typed our statements. We signed them. The Lieutenant wished Kristers Gott's speed in recovering and sincerely thanked us for letting them intrude.

I had nearly forgotten what courtesy and caring looked like. So many of my countrymen had abandoned compassion and civility. We had lived many years under the constant threat of accusation and authoritarian bullying. The British were a bright contrast. Even their accent sounded pleasing in my ears. Of course, I love the German language. It's my native tongue and can be beautiful and strong. But its harsh sounds became like weapons of war in the angry mouths of the Third Reich, especially Hitler. He spewed hate like a machine gun. That's probably why the British, including the Irish and Scottish, sounded so cheery to me. We were ready for some cheer.

I think that's what led me to the idea of playing for them.

Herr Benedict came round that afternoon to check on us. It was odd to see him out of uniform. But refreshing. He sat with Kristers. Stroked his hair like a father would a son. Kristers rewarded him by opening his eyes and looking right at Hans. It was a calm, but blank gaze, just a few seconds before sighing and resting again.

Back in the front room I told Herr Benedict my idea. I wanted to thank and honor the British for liberating us by broadcasting a piece to them. He thought the idea wonderful. But asked if I was ready to walk into the Stalag again. Talk about touching nerves. I knew it would. But I already pictured in my mind the good it could do.

He asked what I would like to play. I knew, but wanted it to be a surprise. After he left, I practiced the piece by memory until I got it just right. At a somber pace, for the gravity of the setting.

I didn't expect to hear from Herr Benedict till the next morning.

But about half six he returned. The British general gave an enthusiastic thumbs up and requested I play the very next morning. For the entire camp! And he didn't even want to know what I was going to play! Artistic freedom had returned. Hans urged me to have a second piece ready. There was sure to be a demand for an encore.

I knew Mama and Papa and Wilhelm would be proud. And if Kristers could speak, he would encourage me to take my heart to the piano.

CHAPTER THIRTY-TWO

THE GOTCHA

That same evening, about half seven, I was at the piano. Jakob was in the barn working on Papa's truck. Petra was in the kitchen warming chicken broth for Kristers. Dr. Deegan instructed us to feed him a little, "if" he wakes, the doctor said at first. Then corrected himself. "When" he wakes. Once again, his gentleness and caring blessed us.

A sound from Kristers' room startled me. I knocked over the piano bench, rushing to get to him. Petra was right behind me. His eyes were shut tight. His hands seized on the bed cover. His whole body was taut and shaking.

Dr. Deegan said seizures were likely and told us what to do in that event. Kristers' teeth were clenched. He was breathing rapidly, struggling for air. We wrestled his mouth open. In her haste, Petra had carried the wooden spoon from the broth. We got it between his teeth. I gripped his shoulders firmly. Talked in his ear. Petra pulled the IV needle from his arm so that wouldn't harm him. The whole thing probably lasted less than a minute, but it seemed like ten. Thank Gott it was over before the fright caught up with me.

We watched over him together. He didn't open his eyes. His breathing became relaxed and steady. I wet a towel and cooled his face. Petra replaced the IV in his arm. He flinched. We took that as a good sign. Petra smelled the broth burning. The wooden spoon remained by the bed, just in case. I stroked Kristers hair and kept talking close to his ear, telling him "I'm here, my darling. It's alright. Just sleep."

Petra called from the front room. Her tone was urgent.

She stood by the overturned piano bench.

"Was ist es?," I said. What is it? We bent down together. She pointed to something underneath the corner skirt of the bench. Something heavily covered in black tape. Jakob came in the back door and saw us. He bent down and looked, too. He tried to pull it free but had to cut it loose with his pocketknife. Whatever it was, the tape encased it completely. We forgot all about telling him Kristers had a seizure. He carried the square blob to the kitchen table. Jakob pulled and tugged and cut the tape away. He set two objects on the table.

"Those are my film cannisters," Petra said. Her initials, 'PN', were on the top of both. And there was writing on the sides. One was labeled "Red Cross." The other, "Erwischt."

Literally, that means 'caught.' But the idea is 'gotcha.'

I said it first. It had to be Mama!

That made sense to Petra. She taught me and Mama how to use her camera. A Leica. It was her prized possession. She left it to me in her will. Gott bless her brave heart. It's right over there and still works beautifully. German engineering, you know. You should take some pictures with it while you're here. To keep us in mind while you finish the book. Zuza can load the film and show you how it works.

Aneska's generosity was as boundless as her soul. If Miriam Pfieffer was the one who used that film, it was surreal to think of holding the camera. To place my hands like hers. Look through the viewfinder like she did. And imagine what she saw. It reminded me of touching a faucet lever in Anne Frank's hiding place, standing where she stood to wash her face and brush her teeth. Most famous history exhibits strictly forbid touching anything. Aneska offered me full access to her history. I would not need photos to keep all of them in mind. But I thanked her and accepted the offer.

We had watched Petra develop photos in the lab at the back of the pharmacy. Some photos on that table came from there. Petra realized that's why there was no film left for my wedding. Mama used the last of it.

From what I've told you about her, you probably won't be surprised that Petra didn't hesitate. She wanted to go immediately to the pharmacy to develop the film. She still had keys to both doors. But it wouldn't be dark for another hour. There were strict curfews. If she got caught, who knows what would happen to her, and the film. We prevailed on her to wait til after dark. Jakob advised if she got caught to drop the film. We would retrieve it later. She could tell the British sentries she worked at the pharmacy and was only out to get something to ease her sister-in-law's headache. She had the keys, so that sounded plausible.

Depending on how many exposures were used, probably thirty-six per roll, Petra estimated it could take two hours, maybe more. At about ten o'clock, she sneaked through the woods to the back of the pharmacy.

I changed Kristers' IV pouch and laid down beside him. Thank Gott, he was sleeping peacefully.

By midnight, we hadn't heard anything. At half twelve, Jakob wanted to check on her. I insisted we wait. What good would it do if he got caught? So, we waited.

At nearly half one, Jakob and I were sitting at the kitchen table. The back door opened. Petra stepped in with a satchel under her arm. I'll never forget what she said, "Gott bless your beautiful Mama, the spy."

Petra said it took so long because nearly all the frames were exposed. And she took the time to make about twenty-five enlargements. She laid out the photos from the cannister marked "Red Cross" first. They depicted horrific images of the conditions in the camp, exclusively from the Soviet section. Mama took care to include some of the Russian signage. The perspectives were all over the place, like they were shot hastily in secret, from a low angle. There were piles of naked, emaciated bodies. One photo showed two Nazi guards with pistols drawn and aimed, apparently making sure no victims remained alive. In one photo, a guard appeared to be laughing. Two enlargements showed prisoners dragging bodies to massive pits.

It was clear. Somehow, Mama smuggled the camera in and out of the Stalag. She risked her life to take these photos. She wanted the Red Cross, which was forbidden to inspect the Soviet section, to see what was going on. The backgrounds in the photos would also help locate the mass graves.

Petra carefully stacked the first batch of photos and put them back in the satchel. Before showing us the photos from the "Gotcha" cannister, Petra took both of us by the hand and said the most beautiful thing, "There is a Gott of mercy and justice. Your dear mother was an instrument of both."

She laid out the photos. They were steady and deliberate, taken mostly at night, without a flash. Petra said that took skill from Mama to know the proper shutter speeds. The first one was a barracks at a distance between two others in the foreground. Two more photos showed exterior shots of a long barracks, from two sides. The next few were panoramic in sequence of the interior of a barracks, taken in what Petra said was the light of a flashlight. Black fabric covered the windows. By the next sequence, you could tell Mama walked through taking shots of several charts on the wall. Charts of the human brain. A skull was perched on a pole. There was writing all over it, labeled with the location of certain faculties, hearing, speech, sight, etc. Three closeups of it made it clear Mama walked around it. More shocking, shelves along one wall held about fifty skulls, labeled with at least one brain function. Each had a small hole in a different location. It was the stuff of horror films. A high-backed chair with straps attached sat in the middle of the room. A taming chair, identical to the one Blixt used on Kristers.

If you're like me, you're probably curious to know where those photographs were now. I wanted to interrupt and ask the same thing. But had learned to wait.

The most horrifying thing of all was the bunks in the back of the barracks. Four had bodies in them, with IV bags hung beside each. Two men and two women. All the victims' heads were bandaged. They each had a toe tag bearing only a number: 317 to 320. They looked deceased, but I'm sure Mama checked. She was not only a nurse, but a compassionate Christian. These things must have broken her heart.

It was obvious. This was Blixt's laboratory. Jacob asked if anything tied him directly to it.

Petra saved the best for last. Mama took a picture of a wooden filing cabinet and closeups of five research reports and observations. She took the time to pull them out of the files. Blixt's ego doomed him. He dated and signed every report. Several other signatures appeared as "assisted by" with other signatures. One label read, "Subject 317 – Female. Polish."

Gott, forgive me. I was relieved the file did not read "Hungarian." Petra said it confirmed the rumors that Blixt abused the Polish women who arrived in the fall of '44. I doubted he was the only one guilty of such crimes.

Hearing all this, the thought of holding the camera became even more surreal. To actually take pictures with it, hear the shutter snap open and closed, promised to be a portal as monumental and sacred as any I had walked through. But at that moment, I was more interested in what happened with Frau Pfieffer's photos.

Early the next morning, a British officer was coming round to drive Petra and me to the Stalag to play for the camp. Jakob would stay with Kristers. We filled him in on the seizures and what to do.

Petra sewed a hidden compartment in the satchel for the photos in case the British soldiers at the gate searched us. Jakob advised us not to reveal them to Herr Benedict yet. To deliver them directly to the British general. In the presence of his attaché. This kind of explosive information could be too easily leaked. We all agreed.

It was late, but we were so keyed up.

Petra had one more thing she wanted to tell us. She had been waiting for the right time. We had no idea what it might be. She laid it straight out. Blixt had assigned Mama to the Soviet section because she refused his sexual advances. Jakob jumped up and let fly a stream of profanities that made Papa's seem tame. I could only bury my face in my hands and mutter, "Mama. Oh, Mama."

So much started to make sense. That's why she got so worn out and thin. It explained why the medical staff in that section treated her so badly. That's where Mama contracted typhus. And why she died. Blixt's intent was retribution. My righteous and unrighteous anger outmatched Jakob's tirade.

Petra apologized for not telling us sooner. But we assured her this was the right time to find out, especially now that we already had the deviant in the crosshairs.

When we calmed down, we did what Mama would have done. We prayed. I thanked Gott for Mama's courage in the face of such risk. For standing up against that filthy Goliath. Jakob thanked Gott for putting the stone in our hands to bring him down.

Sweet Petra asked me to play something to soothe our spirits. I practiced the second piece if there were calls for an encore. I hoped there would be. After considering half a dozen, I chose a sonata with the diverse audience in mind. The Hungarian women, of course, the liberated prison population, our liberators, and the now captive Germans. Especially Blixt.

Very late in the night, I laid down beside Kristers. I remember listening to his steady breathing. Next thing I knew, Petra was shaking me to wake up.

CHAPTER THIRTY-THREE

THE DELIVERY

Driving up to the Stalag gate brought a flood of memories. Mama accompanied me whenever I played at the officer dinners. Schitli drove me through the gate that day to say goodbye to her before delivering me to Lübberstedt. Only weeks earlier, I passed through to play for the Red Cross dinner.

A new image emerged, too, of my courageous Mama walking through that gate smuggling a camera. If discovered, it would have meant certain execution by Blixt, probably in the same barracks laboratory in a taming chair.

Whenever I didn't write in my diary, it was easy to lose track of the days. But not this day. It was Sunday, May 8. And what a difference entering the gate. The British guards were expecting us. They were courteous and yet official. There was no search. The stench had eased but still hung in the air. It was a pungent reminder of the horror we were waking up from.

Another wave of emotion washed over me walking into the dining hall. I could picture Kristers beaming at me from the kitchen door at the Red Cross event. I was surprised to see Herr Benedict coming across the room. His story about me garnered such favor with the British they let him be present to help make me comfortable. I will never forget their kindness.

A microphone hung above the piano. Another one stood on a

stand in front of it. I contained my emotions until the three of us walked up to the piano. Do I have to tell you what was on a stool beside the bench? A glass of water and a small vase holding a single snowdrop. I felt my lower lip quiver. I looked at Petra. She pointed to Herr Benedict. I buried my face in his shoulder and let go. He didn't say a word. Just handed me his kerchief and let me cry a bit.

"Kristers would be so proud of you," he said. "We are, too. Brigitte sends her love."

We only had about thirty minutes before the broadcast. As Petra listened to the tuning, I played Reflection in A, but in several keys. Petra's excellent ear picked out only two notes she wanted to adjust. She did, and I played a little again. It was in tune. And so were our hearts, but so heavy amid all the celebrating.

The commanding General arrived with his entourage. We stood in front of the piano to meet him. He walked right up to me. His attaché, Lt. Camden, introduced us. The General shook my hand and thanked me for all the comfort and beauty my music would bring to his troops. He talked about his men like they were his sons, and all they had been through to get to this day.

I thanked him as well for liberating us. For the great sacrifices they made. For trusting me to choose the music. I told him how under the Reich we lost even that freedom. And I started crying again. The General put his arm around me. I'd never been hugged by a General. The world truly had changed. Petra touched my arm and prompted me with a simple, "und", 'and.'

I lowered my voice and told them we had something for just the two of them. "In the way of evidence," I said to Lt. Camden. I explained we would like to deliver it in private after I played. They agreed. I remember Herr Benedict looked puzzled.

It came time for the broadcast. The General walked to the standing microphone. Herr Benedict stood beside him to translate.

The General wanted the Nazi prisoners to understand. He addressed his troops first, expressing his pride for their courage. Herr Benedict translated after each sentence. Later, I wrote down some of it. He said, "We will never forget those who have fallen beside us for the sake of freedom." I thought of Papa and Mama and Wilhelm, of course. They played their parts. He went on.

"In their honor we will preserve the peace so our children, Gott willing, may not be required to die for it again." And then his words turned to the Nazi soldiers imprisoned in the barracks. "But if called to," he said, "every tyrant should know, the people of Britain and the free world, will again secure that freedom, even at such a cost." His eloquence and delivery made it no wonder he was a General.

He asked Gott to satisfy the souls of the fallen with their heavenly reward and directed a moment of silence to honor them.

One more statement set him and the liberators apart from the inhumane brutality of the Nazis. He gave his word the defeated German soldier, though a former enemy, would be treated with dignity. But those convicted of war crimes would, in his words, "meet swift justice." I took a particular pleasure picturing Blixt scoff at that, still believing the core of what could damn him had been destroyed.

The General's introduction of me was gracious and kind. For the second time in my life, I was called an artist. He said "Our thanks today to the fine artist, Frau Aneska Latva. May the sounds of war give way to songs of peace and healing."

I paused. Thousands would be listening.

By the way, after the war, I saw the British report. There were twenty-three thousand held in Stalag X-B when the British arrived. They called it "Little Belsen" because of the horrors they found.

In that invisible sea of humanity, I pictured two faces. Dr. Deegan and Colonel Blixt. I was playing to thank the first one. And torment the other. The thought of that monster hearing my name over the loudspeakers, I have to admit, felt deeply satisfying. And then to play not just a verboten piece, but the victory song of his captors, was triumph mixed with righteous vindication. I took a deep breath. Exhaled. And at a slow, reverent cadence played "God Save the Queen." At the opening phrase, everyone stood. The first time through I played very simple, sparce. The second with more embellishment and deep walking arpeggios in the left hand. I landed the ending gently, reverently, befitting a state funeral for the fallen.

The distant sound of rain happened like before. A steady torrent of applause and cheering from across the camp. The General clapped enthusiastically and strode to the microphone. He said, "Anyone besides me like to hear one more?" The rain started again.

He said, "Aneska, honor us again, please."

As I said, I wrestled with what to play if this moment came. When I pictured Blixt listening and fuming in a barrack, I wanted to pound Bartok. But honestly, my chops, as you probably say, were not in any shape to attempt Bartok. I suspected Kristers would think it too rich a moment to waste on a personal tantrum aimed at that fiend. Best to keep the others in mind. Those still suffering. And dying. The weary British soldiers, relieved but grieving their losses. I wondered what music Mama would suggest. Or Wilhelm like to hear. Or Papa, if they were listening in from heaven. The night before, when I prayed and asked what the Lord would speak to all of them, the choice became clear. Though it might speak different things to different hearts.

I let my hands lightly kiss the keys. Pictured Benca in my mind. And the young British soldier who kissed me on the cheek. I took a deep breath. Exhaled. And began the gentle opening to Consolation No.3 by Liszt. The one that caused Schitli to send me to Lübberstedt. What he meant for evil, Gott meant for good. Because of his vindictiveness, I met Kristers and was reunited with the Benedicts.

Schitli was beyond consolation now. Blixt too. Probably pacing in a dingy barracks, smug and impervious to the wordless prayer I was playing. But I knew the compassion that poured out of Liszt was pouring through my hands to Benca and all the Hungarian women in their own musical tongue. And flowing with no need for translation to the rest of the liberated prisoners, especially to the ones who would not see another sunrise. And to all those young British soldiers, traumatized from battle.

What I did not expect was the consolation of the Savior washing over my heart as well. Near the end, where the pairs of thirds rise and then fall to the simple ending in a duet, tears began running down my face. The final notes rang, followed by a long silence. I sat with my eyes closed until I heard footsteps. The General went to the microphone and simply said, "Amen. Thank you, Aneska. Gott bless you." The sound like rain came again from across the camp.

I wanted to get back to Kristers immediately, but the attaché's approach reminded me of the other matter. After introducing me to a half dozen other officers, he led me and Petra into the kitchen. We prevailed on him to permit Hans into the meeting. He posted a guard at the door. The General was waiting there for us. He thanked me again for the service I had done to his men and the entire camp. He asked the title of composition. When I told him, and that it had been on the verboten list, he laughed. He said he doubted if it provided much consolation for Commandant Blixt and the other Nazis, now prisoners in their own hell hole. He turned to the matter at hand.

It took a few minutes to describe Mama and her role as a nurse at the camp. How we found the film cannisters. Why Blixt assigned her to the Soviet section. About her typhus and death. They extended their sincere condolences.

Petra set her satchel on a metal prep table. She showed them the concealed compartment and asked for a kitchen knife to cut the stitches. Her ingenuity impressed them. She laid out first the photos intended for the Red Cross. Revolted by them, the General assured us the RC would be notified. As appalling as the first batch was, the Gotcha pictures horrified and infuriated them. Hans was shocked and exuberant. The General and Lt. Camden were astonished by Mama's courage. We were not. Just like Papa and Wilhelm, it was who she was.

They thanked us profusely. The photos would make the case against Blixt and his accomplices airtight. The camp tribunal was in two days. Lt. Camden said we would be called as witnesses. He swore us to confidentiality until then. I relished the chance to see the look on Blixt's face when he presented the evidence.

They expressed their condolences again. The General thanked Hans for his part in making the music happen. He was allowed to accompany us back home. The same courteous officer drove us.

Jakob was ecstatic. He expressed it in colorful language. He wanted to attend the tribunal. We apologized to Herr Benedict for not telling him until delivering the evidence. He understood and reveled in the thought of Blixt paying for his atrocities. He had to sit down. I remember his voice became shaky as he praised Mama and her courageous heart. What a dear man. You can imagine we were all very emotional. Years of struggle and darkness were lifting. But new struggles remained.

Kristers seemed much improved and stable. He ate some broth. Just after three o'clock the old pastor burst in to deliver the news. Churchill had just announced victory in Europe! We wept.

If not for Kristers' injury, the color would have returned to the world. That would take more time. I celebrated by feeding my love more broth.

CHAPTER THIRTY-FOUR

THE RECKONING

Just before noon the following day, Lt. Camden came round with a photographer and a written request for Petra and me to attend the tribunal as witnesses. They were sensitive to Kristers' condition, but needed photos for the trial. Dr. Deegan would also testify. The photographer didn't take long. Kristers even opened his eyes for one shot. Petra offered to develop the film, but the army had their own mobile lab.

Lt. Camden, the lawyer for the prosecution, detailed how the proceeding would go. We asked if Jakob could attend. Since he was a material witness, that was allowed. Other witnesses to the taming of the airman would testify before us. And Herr Benedict, too, as a character witness to our integrity. We were glad to hear that. It could take a while before we testified. We would be sworn in. I asked if I could bring Mama's Bible to do that. He thought that very appropriate. Counsel for the defense would cross-examine us, which was a surprise. He explained in the British judicial system, the accused is presumed innocent until proven guilty. As in your American system. This was entirely upside down for us. Under the iron hand of the Third Reich, we became accustomed to being presumed guilty unless one could prove their own innocence or purity of bloodline.

I was curious about what the defense might ask. "Not to worry," the Lt. said. It would likely be simply to confirm our signatures on our written testimony, just a formality for the record. The only defense strategy would be to question the jurisdiction of the court and assert it had no authority to try crimes against humanity. That would be a matter for the international tribunal, which was bound to come. And it could delay justice for a long time. But Blixt and his accomplices were being tried for our kidnapping, the torture of the tamings, including Kristers, and the murder of hundreds of prisoners of war. If it went the way Lt. Camden predicted, a war crimes charge would not be an issue. I didn't understand all of that at the time. He made it clear, if Blixt and his cronies were found guilty, they could be executed the same afternoon.

Lt. Camden tried to prepare us for one more thing. Colonel Blixt and three other accused would be just across the room, shackled and under heavy guard. At any point, we could request a break. If the defendants caused any disturbance, they would be removed from the courtroom. We understood. We were determined to see it through.

I admired the Lt. very much. He was extremely bright, highly-skilled, patient and caring. All things that I admired in Kristers. And for that matter, in you, my friend.

That wasn't the first time she demonstrated how few words it takes to fill a person's tank. I thanked her and quipped that I would probably edit out flattery.

Don't you dare! That's not flattery. That's a genuine compliment. And you are now part of me telling my story. We're in this together.

As you can see, dear reader, in order for Aneska's grace and radiance to spill over on you, she won that round.

That night to help us sleep, Petra brewed tea from dried Chamomile blossoms Kristers had collected from the countryside. Lying beside him, I squeezed his hand. For the first time, he squeezed back! I called Petra and Jakob in to see it. But he didn't do it again. For me, it was like his first tiny step back to life. Between the excitement of that and the tribunal looming, I was surprised we slept at all.

At eight o'clock the next morning, Frau Benedict came to stay with Kristers. At nine o'clock, the tribunal began at the Stalag. Petra, Jakob and I waited outside with a few other witnesses, British POWs, for nearly an hour and a half. They remembered Mama and my playing kindly. Each of them went in to testify before us. Herr Benedict arrived, escorted by a British soldier, and went directly in. He came out as we were called.

Aneska asked for a sheet of paper from my notebook. She sketched a diagram of the courtroom as she spoke.

The General and two other high-ranking officers were seated on a raised platform behind a long table at the head of the room. I assumed the empty chair to the left was the witness stand. A British flag hung on a pole behind it. I remember its colors being such a relief from so many years of the trademark black and red of the Nazis. The General nodded slightly to me. Without smiling. That fit the solemn tone of the room. A soldier led us to chairs on the left behind a desk where Lt. Camden and another officer sat. The defense counsel sat alone at a table to their right. Colonel Blixt and three other accused were seated and shackled on the right side of the room behind a three-sided railing. One of them was female. A nurse. I knew it was likely she had mistreated Mama. Four armed soldiers stood behind them. I glanced at Blixt only long enough so see his head cocked to one side, his nose in the air as usual, trying to look down on me and everyone in the room. His shackled hands rested on his huge belly.

Referring to her rough sketch she said,

Obviously, Kristers was the fine artist between us. But I'll sign this masterpiece if you like.

I wondered if her touch of humor was a brief delay in recounting the heaviness of the trial. But I was wrong.

This part of the story, my friend, is gratifying after all these years. It gives me hope that Goliaths can still be defeated.

Facing Blixt was, of course, extremely painful on one level. But I was my Mama and Papa's daughter. In that moment, her steadiness settled on me. His righteous passion flowed in my veins. I felt the power of that great hymn, "Mine eyes have seen the glory of the coming of the Lord. He is trampling out the vintage where the grapes of wrath are stored. He has loosed the fateful lightning of his terrible swift sword. His truth is marching on." That courtroom was the beginning of the coda of the second movement of my life.

I'll try to be brief because by now you must be eager to know the outcome.

I assured her, I wanted to hear as much as she wanted to tell. I turned her own words on her. 'We're in this together' remember? She smiled and put her hand on my arm.

Jakob was called to the witness chair first. He broke down once describing Mama. I don't know how he controlled his anger. At one point he spoke directly to Blixt. Very calmly. He told him if our Papa was alive, he would cut him in a dozen places, float him on a line and let the sharks tear him to bits. But given the chance, Jakob himself would just gut him like a fish. Blixt stared straight ahead like he was made of stone. I was surprised the judges let Jakob go on like that. Lt. Camden advised us the day before we would each be given a chance after the verdict to make a statement directly to Blixt. Jakob decided to unload beforehand. That's another reason sleep didn't come easy the night before. I kept thinking about what I would say.

The defense attorney only asked Jakob to verify his signature on his written statement. That's the only question he asked each of us.

Petra went next. Prompted by Lt. Camden, she detailed the things Mama told her about Blixt, the taming of the airman, to corroborate the stories of the prior eyewitnesses. And why Blixt assigned her to the Soviet section, where she contracted the typhus that took her beautiful life. She described the night Lieutenant Schitli kidnapped Aneska and Kristers. And brought Kristers back with a head wound from the taming in the town hall.

As planned, Petra's camera was introduced as an exhibit. The defense attorney didn't object because he was made aware of the evidence beforehand. 'Disclosure,' or maybe 'discovery' I think they called it. For the first time, Blixt took note. He leaned forward and objected. A soldier pulled him back in his chair. The lead judge ordered him not to speak.

Lt. Camden asked Petra how proficient Nurse Miriam Pfeiffer was with the camera. I liked hearing Mama's name. I liked Blixt hearing it. And that she was a nurse, who cared for people. Unlike the heartless monster sitting in the accused box. Lt. Camden referred to Mama many times as Nurse Pfeiffer. I wondered if that was intentional, to emphasize her caring role and nature. Whatever the case it made me admire her even more. And miss her.

Petra described how good Mama was with the camera. That's the only time Petra looked at Blixt. As if to say, "You're about to find out."

I was so proud of her. There was never a truer, dearer friend to Mama.

The defense asked his one question to Petra.

It was my turn.

The hardest part came next. Lt. Camden asked me to describe the night at the town hall. To take my time. He acknowledged how painful it could be. And it was. For the first time I described the nightmare in detail, very much as I told it to you. It almost took on an aspect of reporting, like something that happened to someone else. I was surprised my emotions remained so in check. Like Mama. Not in denial, but in control. Beforehand, I decided not to give Blixt the satisfaction of a breakdown or outburst of rage. But wondered if I could manage that. Thank Gott. And Mama. I did.

When I came to the part where Blixt droned on about the pistol and the special bullets, Lt. Camden introduced the fancy box and pistol as an exhibit. He opened the box. Showed it to me and asked if it was the pistol. In his arrogance Blixt had not even hidden or disposed of it. Neither the defense nor Blixt objected. How could they? The Colonel's name was etched in a brass plate on top of the box.

I paused before getting to the actual taming.

Aneska peered into the fire.

Lt. Camden brought me a glass of water. You know who that made me think of. I pictured Kristers. That strengthened my resolve. It also helped that another exhibit was introduced - a photo of Kristers in bed from the day before. Lt. Camden referred to the medical report from Dr. Deegan's testimony. When he said the extent of the damage and long-term effects done to Kristers remained to be seen, I saw Blixt shift in his chair. He realized Kristers was still alive and out of his reach.

After describing the torture and taming, I was ready for the reckoning.

Lt. Camden graciously allowed me the next volley. He asked me to explain what we were about to see. I looked Blixt straight in the eye and began.

"My courageous mother smuggled Petra's camera into the Soviet section of the camp to inform the Red Cross about the horrific conditions and abuse there."

On that cue, two soldiers carried a large bulletin board into the courtroom. They set it on a stand between the judges and the accused. It was covered with photos from the first roll of film. Two other soldiers distributed some copies to the judges. The General had already seen them.

The defense attorney scored his only win by objecting that this was a matter for a war crimes tribunal. Lt. Camden agreed to withdraw them from the proceeding but be retained in the record. The judges agreed. He turned to me and asked, just like we prepared, "Frau Latva, did your mother, Nurse Pfeiffer, at great personal risk, take any more photos?"

Again, I looked directly at Blixt. He lowered his head and leered at me.

I didn't flinch. I felt like the shepherd boy David ready to sling the fatal blow. And I aimed it right between his eyes. First in German, "Ya, das hat sie." Then in English, "Yes, she did."

The board was turned around to reveal photos of the taming barracks. The three other accused took one look and hung their heads. Not Blixt. But as he watched Lt. Camden describe the torture chamber called a "laboratory," his face and body shrank, like the air leaking out of a tire. Everything he thought was destroyed by fire and unmarked graves, the photos resurrected. Lt. Camden was thorough, down to the files signed by Blixt and the other three. He even brought out a skull exhumed just the day before. It had the telltale bullet hole. By the time he finished Blixt's nose was back in the air, perhaps out of habit, but he had the look of man who knew he had only hours to live.

As I walked back to my seat, I heard soft clapping. It was Blixt. I stopped and turned to face him. A diva to the end, he bowed his head slightly and said, "Bravo, Brunhilde." My restraint had to be heaven sent. I stared at him calmly for a moment, said nothing, then returned to my seat.

Court went into recess for the judges to deliberate the verdict and sentence. We were led outside to wait, and get ready to make a final statement. I hoped it wouldn't take long, though I knew Kristers was in good hands with Brigitte. She was a nurse. Remember?

It was nearly noon. The British offered us tea, of course, and cheese with small corned beef sandwiches. Cut into triangles, I remember. I thought that was so civilized. It was something Kristers would have done.

We talked about our statements. Jakob deferred to me saying he already spoke his mind to Blixt. Petra preferred to let her testimony speak for itself. A herd of things had been running through my head since the night before. I knew I had to speak and speak boldly. I was hoping what I wanted to say would be given when it came time. But that didn't keep me from mentally gathering a long list of vicious accusations to gut Blixt.

We hadn't finished eating when court was called back in session. After only about twenty-five minutes. I remembered the General's word about swift justice. He was keeping it.

A court clerk read the charges. There were too many to name. The most general ones sounded so like the British, 'torture and inhuman and degrading treatment.' What an understatement. The counts included our kidnapping, physical and mental torture, Kristers' maiming, and based on the toe tags and files, three-hundred and fifty-six counts of systematic torture, assault and murder, as well as abuse of corpses. The verdict was no surprise. All four guilty on all counts. None of them blinked an eye. There were no defiant 'Sieg Heils'. In fact, I think the last 'Sieg Heil' I heard was the hasty one from the guard Blixt dismissed for sneezing during his blather about brain functions. I hoped to never hear another one.

The sentence was handed down. By the General. Death. To be carried out immediately. One of the accused men sobbed softly. The other two sank in their chairs. Blixt sat stoic, staring toward the ceiling.

The lead judge asked if any of us had a statement to make to the condemned.

The jumble of things prowling my mind since the night before cued up in my head. How they all had brought shame on their family names forever. And on their country. How they blasphemed Gott by disregarding the souls made in his image and treating them worse than lab rats, like expendable tissue, useful only for science. Instead of unique individuals nurtured and loved by a mother and father and family. And now missed forever. Like I missed Mama.

But I wanted to single out Blixt in a blistering tirade. Berate him for having no shame. For the shame-ectomy that amputated his soul. For choosing a wicked, detestable road by extinguishing the last spark of light inside himself. And turning that darkness on the world, on my world, my family, my blessed, brave husband! But I didn't say any of that.

I stood, clutching Mama's Bible. It's right over there. First shelf. Could you?

I retrieved it. The power of holding Miriam Pfeiffer's personal Bible was even stronger than touching Petra's camera. Aneska kissed it, then turned the pages until she found a passage.

I walked to a small podium beside Lt. Camden's desk.

The single word 'wicked' in my head triggered something. I opened this very Bible to Psalm 73. And read this.

> Pride is their necklace; they clothe themselves with violence.
> From their callous hearts comes iniquity;
> their evil imaginations have no limits.
> They scoff and speak with malice;
> with arrogance they threaten oppression.
>
> Surely, Lord, you place them on slippery ground;
> you cast down the wicked to ruin.
> How suddenly are they destroyed,
> completely swept away by terrors!
> They are like a dream when one awakes;
> when you arise, Lord,
> you will despise them as fantasies.

I tried to imagine Blixt and the other three condemned hearing those damning words. Surely, even the steeliest, soulless heart could not withstand them.

I closed the Bible. The three accomplices hung their heads, resigned to their fate. But not Blixt. I looked him in the eye and said, "My Papa taught us, evil will not, cannot win." Oddly enough, looking at four condemned souls, staring the blackest heart in the face, I felt most of my malice fade. Maybe righteous justice has that effect. It satisfies a grievance, a wrong, without darkening and damaging your own soul. Unlike vengeance.

I started to turn and sit down. But another whisper came. I didn't want to hear it. Much later, upon reflection, I realized it spoke to the remaining shrapnel of rage deep in my heart. It was as clear as Mama's voice in my head. 'We forgive. God absolves.' My malice resisted, justifying itself as the righteous banner of the wounded party. Though only a small seed, I knew it was as poisonous as the evil that ruled Blixt's entire heart. I froze. Even though inside I was hurrying back to my seat. Ever have that feeling? Your mind is in overdrive but your feet in neutral?

The lead judge asked me, "Is that all, Frau Latva?"

I finally said, "No, sir. Just one more thing."

I couldn't believe my mouth formed the words. I looked Blixt in the eye again and said, "I forgive you."

I could have left it there, but didn't. I told him my forgiveness didn't absolve him of his heinous acts. Only the Lord could do that. "But I forgive you."

And I tell you, my friend, I returned to my seat between Jakob and Petra, free. Free of him. Free to move forward without dragging the heavy weight of malice, bitterness and hurt for the rest of my life. Did it try to return? Of course. Many times. But I learned to meet it with a measure of sorrow. And it couldn't stay. Its power to drag me down was gone.

Aneska, had no idea how deep her words, and her mother's words, spoke to me. Or maybe she did. I didn't interrupt to tell her. That was for another time.

It was time for sentencing. The General commended us as witnesses. He called my offer of forgiveness extraordinary and undeserved. He praised Mama's courage and sacrifice and hoped it would inspire others to stand against tyranny of any kind. I especially loved that.

I knew, again, why Aneska's story had to be told. But chose me for other reasons as well.

The General ordered the convicted to stand. He borrowed some of my words, Mama's words really.

He said, "This court does not absolve you of your unspeakable crimes. I don't know why our heavenly Advocate would. But that is out of our jurisdiction."

He sentenced them to death by hanging at 2:00 p.m. It was nearly half one. Swift justice indeed.

Looking back, it's so clear what I said before. There's a story being written and told in every heart. It will either be a story of redemption and freedom or one of decay and captivity. Both stories need a Savior. The four accused had only half an hour to change their storyline.

Defense counsel asked permission to speak. The condemned had two requests: time to write a last letter to their families and execution by firing squad instead of hanging. Death by bullets would likely be much quicker.

No one in the room would ever forget the General's answer.

He asked if their victims were given a chance to write a last letter. Or did they choose their manner of death? His decision was final. "Denied."

Even Blixt was visibly distressed. I took no gratification in it. Maybe that was an inward sign of my newfound freedom.

The General did offer them one choice - to meet with a Chaplain. I heard later only Blixt declined.

Court was adjourned. Blixt and I exchanged one look as the soldiers led him out. I half expected him to click his heels and put his nose in the air. But he only dipped his head slightly.

Lt. Camden invited us to witness the executions. As much as I believed Blixt and the others deserved it, something in me, the Holy Spirit or another whisper from Mama, made me decline. I realize now more than then, having the images of their agonizing final moments in my mind would have unearthed dark rage again and again, and pulled my soul backward toward vengeance. And it might have given Blixt a chance to have the last word.

Petra and I walked home. Jakob chose to attend. He regretted it, for the same reasons I declined. Over the years, other memories have returned to bring pain. Some still do, though with less power. But not that one. Vengeance is sinking sand, my friend. Justice is solid rock.

Third Movement – Beyond Words

CHAPTER THIRTY-FIVE

THE BABÓG

Liberation and VE day didn't end the chaos and suffering. Hundreds still died every day at the Stalag and camps all over Germany and beyond. Millions of displaced people faced the challenge of sheer survival. Like me, they had the choice of making their way back home to find there was no home or resettle elsewhere. For the time being, we were safe at Petra's. Hans and Brigitte moved in with us.

The waiting began. To see who would return from war and who wouldn't. There was so little communication in all the turmoil.

About ten days after VE day, Rolf walked up to the door. He hitched rides and walked with thousands of other soldiers. Nearly three hundred kilometers! It was a joy to see Petra so happy. I told him about my prayers for his petrol truck to slide off the snowy roads to slow down the German offensive. He said that happened three times! And to many other trucks as well. We had a big laugh. Sure enough, winter wreaked havoc on the supply lines, like we all hoped.

I believed the same Gott who could do that could mend my Kristers. We already had the miracle he was still alive. I wanted more. Don't we always?

In the weeks following the tribunal, Kristers made good progress. He was awake more. Even propping up to be fed. He could chew scrambled eggs and pastries. Another seizure came. About the same severity as the first. There would be more. We still didn't know the extent of the damage. Especially how much he would remember. Or if he would speak or recognize anyone.

Dr. Deegan came round often. He was surprised and hopeful about Kristers' progress. Every visit, he tested his reflexes and responses. The hearing in his left ear was not as good as his right. Likely a result of the gunshot happening so close to it. Physically, my darling seemed remarkably whole. The doctor described a condition common to head injuries, post-traumatic amnesia. It could last weeks or months. Or be permanent in some areas. Depending on where the bullet traveled and lodged, any number of faculties could be affected.

A new field hospital was set up outside the Stalag. Not the neurosurgical kind. But it did have an X-ray machine to help surgeons see where bullets and shrapnel lodged in a body. It saved a lot of lives. As Dr. Deegan put it, "Sometimes believing brings healing. Sometimes seeing does as well." He promised to authorize some X-rays. Brain surgery was not an option yet but might be some day in a better facility with a surgeon skilled in that area. With Lt. Camden's help, he even gave me a bullet from Blixt's gun case. It could help determine the proper approach to treat Kristers. In the meantime, he assured me he would do everything he could for stór mo chroí - the treasure of my heart.

Dr. Deegan, Lt. Camden and others like them gave me hope for mankind.

One morning as he examined Kristers, I was making scrambled eggs. He came into the kitchen and asked for a glass of water. I remember it so clearly, for two reasons. He said he was so thirsty he could 'suck the sweat from a tinker's sock.' I didn't know what a tinker was, but it struck me so funny. I hadn't laughed in so long. My love for the Irish began with Dr. Deegan. Five minutes later I became so nauseous from the smell of the eggs I 'puked me ring' as the Irish say. He insisted on examining me, and asked a few questions. He smiled and said, "Congratulations, Aneska. You and Kristers are going to have a honeymoon Babóg, a baby." We'd only been married seven weeks!

I had to ask. Third movement?

Ya, the third movement of my life began that day in Petra's kitchen with nausea and sweet news. But happiness was mixed with such sadness and anxiety. It was impossible to share the joy with Kristers. We couldn't be sure he would ever understand he was a father. Underneath that, it made me miss Mama even more. The blessing brought all my losses to the surface. The Benedicts welcomed the news and understood my mixed feelings.

The theme I've written to begin the third movement reflects that tension.

I made another note to listen for that as well. My eagerness to attend the concerto grew daily. I wondered if perhaps I'd heard that theme through the door the first day I arrived. But again, interrupting seemed imprudent.

Morning sickness became part of my daily routine well into the summer. Between Brigitte and Petra, they knew a lot about herbs and what could help with the nausea from the pharmacy. The only thing they requested of me was for the baby to call them Tante, 'Auntie'.

The summer of '45, the world began to come alive again. A new life was growing inside me. We worked in the garden a lot. Got more chickens. The farmers market reopened. Driving by the town hall in Papa's truck was painful. Two of my piano students took up lessons again. The Stalag became a prison for suspected war criminals and civilian Nazi collaborators. Talk about a world turned upside down - the British officers invited me to play for them occasionally. I even broadcast a few times to the German prisoners. Would it surprise you I almost always chose verboten music?

It didn't in the slightest.

Kristers got stronger as I grew bigger. Except for some hearing loss in his left ear, all of his senses and motor skills seemed intact. The first time he walked out of the bedroom with his arm around my shoulders, my heart played Mozart's Rondo Al Turco. Dr. Deegan was there for that. As part of his therapy, we took walks. Very short at first. I held his hand and chatted away. He could hear me, but I couldn't tell how much he understood. He couldn't speak. Or make any sound at all. That was agonizing. But the worst of it was when he looked at me. There was no spark of recognition. Sometimes I let him walk ahead of me to see if he would respond. I'd say, "Stop!" or "I love you." Or "We're having a baby!" Sometimes I'd just say his name. He would turn toward me. But the look was not there. I couldn't be sure it ever would be again.

He sat in the front room while I played for him. One day, I chose Mozart's first composition. The very short one. His Air in A. I turned around. Kristers was looking out the window. For the first time, there was a very pleasant expression on his face and the sweetest hint of a smile. I cried, of course. A week later, it was raining. He sat in his spot where Papa used to sit, looking out the window. I played "Dear Lord, Jesus, Take My Hand." From the dining room, Petra got my attention and pointed to him. His eyes were glistening, and a tear ran down his cheek. Kristers was in there. And he was awakening.

Will you indulge me one intimate detail?

I had to smile. Of course.

One morning, I was giving Kristers a sponge bath. He got, well, as the Irish say, randy. Let's just say I discovered another bodily function that was intact.

I must have blushed a little or shifted in my chair.

No need to get scarlet. Don't tell me you haven't wondered. As you know, we had more than one child. But I'm getting ahead of the story.

I quipped, 'Well, thank you for sharing.'

You're quite welcome.

We chuckled. Which I always enjoyed. She continued.

Dr. Deegan arranged for X-rays. He showed us how the bullet had not spiraled or flattened, which minimized the damage. It missed any major blood vessels. The placement itself was a miracle. I thanked the Lord and the pigeon out loud.

He responded, "Begorrah! His ways are fierce good." I learned two more Irish terms. 'Begorrah' means 'by God' but more casual, like 'by golly.' 'Fierce' is just a colorful way of saying 'very'.

I interjected, You were fierce blessed to have Dr. Deegan.

That's it! You've got it. Doesn't that feel good in the gob? 'Gob' means 'mouth'.

The next time Maja made cornbread I had my new compliment ready.

The good doctor pointed out in the X-rays a few small bone fragments nearer the surface that could be more easily removed than the bullet. But only a neurologist could assess Kristers fully and determine a course of treatment. He was stable, except for the seizures, which came nearly once a week at first and then once a month or so, but not as severe. Kristers' eyes would roll back, and his body stiffen for thirty seconds or so. After each seizure he began to lay his head on my shoulder and hold me. And fall asleep. That was the first physical sweetness that returned between us.

The look on Aneska's face made it clear the memory was still fierce good in her heart.

That summer slid by. Kristers liked the chickens. He helped me gather eggs. And without breaking them. We took that as a good sign as well.

In August, news came about the atomic bombs. Japan surrendered.

Shortly after, Hans and Brigitte called a meeting. They were in contact with their old friends in Göttingen. Most of the city was untouched by the Allied bombing. The Latva house was still there. It had been closed up since his parents moved to Berlin. Besides being a university city, it was a renowned medical center. Brigitte could easily get a job. Thousands of wounded soldiers needed her skills. Hans was offered a management position at the Aula, the Great Hall of the University, the main event center. I could study music. Kristers could receive skilled care. Hans would help settle the Latva estate for us.

If we were open to it, there was plenty of room for all of us to live in the house, including Jakob. It was only three hours south of Sandbostel. We had Papa's truck and the Benedict's car. For food, I had helped Petra can a large stock of garden vegetables, fruit and berries. We had more eggs that we could carry. We often boiled them. Rolf's smoked chickens could travel well. Fuel could be the biggest challenge. But Jakob surprised us. He had been hiding cans of gas and food in the garage for months. He said that's what Papa would have done. I was so proud of him.

Rolf had family near Sandbostel. He and Petra would stay. But there was one hurdle. Thousands of German soldiers were assigned to reconstruction details all over the country. Rolf could be conscripted for that. Herr Benedict came through again. Because food was scarce, Hans arranged an exemption as a registered farmer. Just like Papa and the boys had done for fishing. He could stay home with Petra. Except for leaving them, the plan sounded perfect.

I must stop using that word. I've lived long enough to know 'perfect' is not possible this side of heaven. Fierce good and fierce blessed, ya. But not perfect. We prayed together about it, of course. And slept on the decision.

The next morning, we were all in agreement. If Dr. Deegan approved Kristers for travel, we would leave for Göttingen in September, well before winter set in.

Dr. Deegan did approve. He was leaving soon as well. Headed home to Ireland to mend wounded soldiers in Dublin. He had his own stór mo chroí, treasure of his heart there. A wife and two children. And let me tell you about Gott's fierce good ways. Imagine this, my friend, Dr. Deegan lived and worked in Dublin, but was born and raised in a place called Carlow, a kilometer from where we're sitting.

I saw my move and took it. With just one word, 'Begorrah!' We had a good laugh.

Precisely. And by Gott's grace, our paths would cross again.

In all the preparations to move, there was one thing I had to do. Jakob drove Kristers and me as near as a dirt road would take us to the hunting cabin. The one where we spent our first two nights. I led Kristers by the hand the rest of the way through the woods. It was as lovely as ever. The lilies around the pond were blooming. So were the snowdrops on the forest floor. We sat in the cabin. I watched him. He looked briefly at the names by the side of the door, Siegfried and Brunhilde. I ran his fingers over the formula he scratched on the wall beside the bed. The child we conceived there was beginning to show. I put his hand on my belly. Then on the formula again. And back to my belly. I held Mama's ring on my finger beside the one on his. I wanted to believe there was a glimmer of recognition. It was more hope than reality. As we left, I picked a lily and handed it to him. After just a few steps, Kristers got down on both knees like a little boy. He looked a long time at a snowdrop blossom. Then picked it so gently. He held it up to give to me. Maybe it was just a mimicking act. But you can understand how I took it as much more.

Sometimes believing brings healing. Sometimes seeing does as well. Ya?

CHAPTER THIRTY-SIX

THE SHAMROCK

You may recall, my friend, the Communist Soviets seized control of eastern Germany as part of peace negotiations. We were not fully aware then, but another vicious tyrant, Stalin, would gobble up all of Eastern Europe as spoils of war. Fortunately, Göttingen fell in the British zone, or we would have moved into the shadows again. This time under Communism. We were done with tyrants.

Sadly, the world has not stopped producing them, has it? Or negotiating with them until the cost is so high they have their way. For a season. The Soviet brand took seventy years to collapse, ya? And still the strong suppress the weak there and bully its neighbors. Even worse they hold an atomic threat over the rest of the world. But that's for another discussion, over a pint perhaps?

I agreed with 'amen, and 'sláinte.'

It took us a day and a half to drive the three hours to Göttingen. There were check points and streams of people walking the roads, pushing carts, headed who knows where. Fortunately, Herr Benedict was a master at paperwork and red tape. All our papers were in order and sometimes a jar of jam sweetened the negotiations. We camped the night in a field under the stars between the vehicles. I curled up in Kristers' arms. Jakob kept watch. There was such poverty, even good people resorted to stealing. We gave a little girl a jar of corn. She lit up like it was gold nuggets.

The Latva home stunned us. It was a mansion on several acres. The Benedicts used to go there often, but Jakob and I were in awe. Kristers' father must have been a fierce successful banker.

I watched Kristers as we went through the place. He paused many times, like an old man who forgot what he came into a room for.

In the enormous front room, obviously meant for entertaining guests, there was a covered piano. A nine-foot Steinway! Jakob made another discovery. He led us to a large room at the rear of the house. A seven-foot Bösendorfer was there! Can you imagine? A Steinway and Bösendorfer in the same home! I seated Kristers on the bench and sat to his left. "Ode to Joy" came to mind, so I played the first verse and chorus. He watched my hands like a child and his head began to rock back and forth slightly with the cadence. When I finished, he reached his right hand toward the keys and with one finger played a single note. Several times. The second A above middle C. My entire heart was an ode to joy! That's when I determined to use Refection in A as part of his therapy. But that came later.

Out of musical curiosity, I asked what the difference in sound is between the two pianos. She elaborated several minutes about the round, mellow tone of the Steinway compared to Bösendorfer's heavier bass but lighter treble range. She explained the rim of the latter is thinner than the Steinway, and some faster players prefer the action of the Bösendorfer. Like a car running out of gas, she trailed off as the memory pulled her back to the Latva mansion.

Others prefer the volume and evenness of the Steinway.

She sighed, like changing gears.

Sitting there, I realized the Bösendorfer must have been Stefan Latva's practice piano. Kristers probably heard him play it nearly every day. I somehow felt Stefan's legacy, his dream, blend into mine. If that makes sense.

It made perfect sense.

At my piano concerto Stefan's name will appear in the program on the dedication page.

That made perfect sense as well.

Behind the house, across an overgrown garden area, was a guest house. And another structure built to look like a country schoolhouse. In fact, that's what it was. Hans told us the Latva's specifically designed it for schooling Stefan and Kristers. They didn't leave their sons' education in the hands of the public schools, especially once the Third Reich began the indoctrination. Bookshelves lined two walls, with rolling ladders to reach the top. Models of airplanes and painted birds made of paper hung on fishing line from the vaulted ceiling. Formulas and a few quotes covered a giant chalkboard on a third wall, mostly in what appeared to be Kristers' handwriting. A statement across the top of the blackboard read: "Frei denken ist gleich freiheit." 'Thinking freely equals freedom.' The handwriting was different. One of the pull-down screens had maps of the world and a chart of the elements. What is that called?

A periodic table.

Ya. Thank you.

A desk on one side bore Stefan's name on a brass plate. Another one on the right was Kristers'. A smaller desk at the front of the room had no name. Hans said it was for various teachers the Latvas employed, some of them professors from the university. Projects covered several long tables, models of bridges and buildings, a microscope. There was a telescope on a tripod in one corner. Dozens of pencil and ink sketches and canvases filled shelves next to a drafting table. There were detailed drawings of bridges and skylines of cities, but also of flowers and bugs and birds. An easel stood next to the drafting table, still holding an unfinished painting. In the upper left, silhouettes of four small birds were flying away from what looked like a dark storm on the right. Most of the drawings and paintings were signed KRL. A few by SAL. Stefan's middle name was their Papa's, Azzo. It means 'noble at birth.'

I looked through many of the drawings and canvases with Kristers. He seemed interested. But showed no signs of recognition. Some of them are in his studio here. I've been waiting to show that to you. Third movement things. You understand by now, ya?

'Oh, ya, mein freund.' I answered. She laughed. I had wondered where Kristers painted. But assumed Aneska would get to that in time.

Your German is coming along nicely.

I thanked her. In German. Danke schön.

We settled into the Latva mansion. As you can imagine, there was much to do. Including securing our title to it. Herr Benedict, Gott bless him. Management and finances for him were like fishing to my Papa. He handled the transfer of the estate to Kristers and me. Kristers couldn't sign anything. And I wasn't old enough legally, so I gladly assigned the power of attorney to Herr Benedict. What is more, Hans discovered Azzo Latva transferred most of their financial wealth before the war to a bank in Switzerland. Nearly half a million dollars! Back then, that was like eight million! Imagine the difficulty of trying to reclaim that money after the war. Hans took a train to Zurich. He found favor with the Swiss bankers. They remembered and admired Herr Latva's courage and resourcefulness before the war to help so many secure their holdings from the Nazis.

Everything began to fall into place. Brigitte found work immediately. Herr Benedict took the position at the University Great Hall. He arranged an interview and audition for me with the music department. Within two weeks, I was admitted with a full scholarship.

All in the same year, we went from prisoners, poverty and homeless to wealthy, employed and official homeowners and residents of Göttingen. And it was barely October. This was going to be our new life. And a home to our child.

But it was not to be.

Kristers could not get the care he needed. The hospitals were overwhelmed with wounded soldiers. Thousands more critical than him. His stable condition worked against us. We put his name on half a dozen waiting lists. But it could take a year!

So, what did we do? What Mama would have done. We prayed.

Remember her reminder from Proverbs? We make a plan, but the Lord directs our steps.

Jakob went to visit Rolf and Petra to help them with their harvest. The Lord prompted me to send them fifty-thousand dollars with Jakob. That may have been another whisper from Mama. She was always so generous, even when we had so little. It seemed only fitting after how much Petra had done for us. Besides, she was family. Jakob hid the money in the secret compartment in Papa's truck along with the papers, proving it was his. He was searched at three check points, but they never found the money. My only regret was not seeing the look on their faces when Jakob delivered it.

While he was there, a letter came via a British military post. Can you guess who it was from?

I took a stab. Dr. Deegan?

Ya! You're sound as a pound, the Irish say.

I said how much I enjoyed the Irish wit. She pointed to her head and said,

Ya, here's an even better one. Your cabbage is savage.

I had a fierce good laugh at that.

Dr. Deegan was all that and a heart big as the sky. Gott bless him and save the Queen. He told Kristers' story to a doctor in Dublin, none other than the father of neurology in Ireland, a Dr. McConnull. The letter said a team trained by him offered to assess and perform surgery on Kristers! As a gift of good will to the German people!

Aneska's eyes misted. I waited.

Gott is so good. And people can be, too.

I couldn't imagine how such a trip could happen in the shape the world was in. But between Herr Benedict and Dr. Deegan, there were few obstacles they couldn't overcome. And that's not all. Dr. Deegan arranged a place for Kristers to recover and receive personal care. Would you like to guess where? Need a hint? It rhymes with Snowdrop Manor. And has paintings of them all over the place.

Question answered. That's how they came to Ireland. But why did they stay?

Turns out, hospitals in Göttingen were sending patients to England for treatment. The British flew regular routes to evacuate their own wounded servicemen.

October 10, 1945, Herr Benedict drove us to the airport. We watched a military plane land. A DC-3, I think. As it rolled to a stop, we saw something just below the cockpit - a bright green shamrock. Just like the one on the plane that crashed-landed in Sandbostel. A pilot in uniform came down the boarding steps and headed straight for us. He was smiling from ear to ear.

Jakob immediately blurted out, "It's him! It has to be."

"Who?" I said.

The name tag on his jacket read, 'Capt. O'Cullen.' He greeted Jakob with a firm handshake and they embraced like old friends.

He said to Jakob, "Begorrah and by St. Patrick, I never thought I'd ever get to thank you properly."

I was so confused. Jacob introduced me.

My legs nearly gave way when he said, "Aneska, what a great honor. I'm Darby O'Cullen. Your father and brother smuggled me and another pilot to Sweden. We owe them our lives."

Some things, my friend, you just know, it has to be Gott. There is no other explanation.

Capt. O'Cullen remembered Mama's kindness in tending him and his crew.

My friend, are you getting this? This man met Mama! He met Papa! And Wilhelm briefly on the boat that night! He remembered a girl waving to him just before they crash-landed in a wheat field. Until that moment, he had no idea that girl was me!

We were all gobsmacked. Dumbfounded. And beyond elated. You can imagine. It was a lot to take in. Dr. Deegan was a lifelong friend of the O'Cullens, and also their family doctor in Carlow. He knew Darby was flying runs to Germany and back. So, he contacted him about Kristers' case. When Dr. Deegan told him our story, the name Pfieffer and the town Sandbostel put it all together in Darby's head. His mother, dear Brynn, had arranged a place in Dublin for us to stay while Kristers received treatment.

In a symphony, this would be the first full flourish building toward the triumph.

I could see that and made a note to listen for it in the third movement of her concerto. She continued.

There would be plenty of time to continue chatting later. We boarded along with about fifteen patients on stretchers. In about three hours the plane made one stop in London for an hour to unload nearly all of them. Two hours later, we landed in Dublin. A journey of about six hours for us took the Allies nearly a year and hundreds of thousands of lives to make.

Before the trip, Jakob and I had every intention of returning to Göttingen. But Ireland had other plans.

She paused and refilled my teacup.

Friend, are you getting all this? Not just the details. But the magnitude of what Gott can do?

She looked me in the eye and took on the tender tone I had come to love. Against the magnitude of her own story she pivoted to mine.

My friend, Gott can do that in your story. Beyond what you can ask or imagine. That's what I hope you're getting.

She leaned toward me and took my hand in both of hers.

Let me pray for you.

I looked down at her talented hands. They could reach into the passion of the great composers of three centuries and express the range of agony and ecstasy of being human. They made apple pies with her mother – washed and dressed her lifeless body. Her hand still bore the ring Kristers placed there. Those hands played that awful night in the face of losing everything – pressed against the wound on Kristers' head to stop the bleeding – tended to him like a baby. How in God's name did my hand come to be in those hands? And so near to the heart behind them?

I was getting it. The magnitude. How could anyone miss it? As Aneska prayed, Emily Dickinson's poem about hope, the 'thing with feathers that perches in the soul' came to mind. Of late silent in my soul, it cleared its throat. If nothing else, that was worth the whole trip and perhaps another reason this story chose me.

CHAPTER THIRTY-SEVEN

THE CHOICE

October 1945, I was sixteen and six months pregnant. In a new country. A new city. Jakob and Kristers and I were welcomed into a lovely flat just south of the River Liffy, not far from St. Patrick's Cathedral. Kristers' examinations began at the hospital. My new heroes were his team of doctors.

You must understand, my friend, try to picture this. We lived many years under the dark shadows and brutality of the most perverse, mass evil the modern world had ever known. An evil that reduced the value of some human lives to less than the barnacles my Papa and brothers scraped from the hulls of the boats. The worldwide outbreak of tyranny had just been defeated. At great cost. Including to my own family. Millions of people stood against it. They came from the other side of the world and laid down their lives. They had their own stories cut short in horrific ways to free those they would never meet. For Jakob and the Benedicts. Petra and Rolf. For Benca and Golda. For me and Kristers. And for generations not yet born. Like my child. And you, my friend. The only way to repay that is to live well and free. And stand resolute against the shadows wherever they reappear.

I told her she sounded like Winston Churchill again. At that moment, I would have voted Aneska prime minister of the world. Or at least the global musical ambassador.

I'm certain the doctors could not fathom how shiny they were in my eyes. Who were we to them? And yet, Kristers' story united them to give their goodness and great skill to my darling. To us. To our story. Just one of millions of stories. Again, it had to be Gott. It had to be.

On our second day in Dublin, Darby's extraordinary mother, Brynn O'Cullen came from Carlow to see us.

Her eyes moved to the painting of Brynn. The look on Aneska's face reflected the tender regard she held for her.

She greeted us in Gaelic, "Míle fáilte," which means 'a thousand welcomes.' She wanted us to know she would provide anything we needed. We knew about Darby's father being killed in the war. Our bond was immediate in the fellowship of grieving, which in those days touched nearly everyone around the entire world. But we also connected like mother and daughter. It was only natural. I missed Mama so much. And she never had daughter.

When I wasn't at hospital, I sometimes walked over to St. Patrick's Cathedral to pray under the magnificent, vaulted ceiling. But more often in a small alcove behind the main altar. A book was there on a brass podium to write prayer requests. Every visit, I wrote a request for Kristers. The prayer book is still there today. Next time I go to the Royal Academy in Dublin, let's visit and write in it. I have a particular prayer for you.

I was eager to do that, of course, and curious about her prayer for me. But I had another goal in mind. Aneska spoke it before I did.

And maybe while I'm at my meetings you can tour the Guinness brewery.

Perfect, begorrah.

I also discovered the prayer labyrinth in the courtyard of Christ's Church Cathedral. A vicar showed me how to start on the outer circle. He said the twists and turns are like the struggles of life and our journey toward Gott, our true home. We talked and walked.

Before I knew it, we were at the center. Isn't that just like Gott to send someone to share the journey?

She reached out and took my hand. Those moments were like a transfusion. Something flowed into me from Aneska, wordlessly feeding the feathered thing with laryngitis perched in my soul.

Standing together in the middle of the labyrinth, the kind vicar prayed for Kristers. And for me and our unborn child. We visited several other times as well. Such kindness helped heal me. Slow but sure.

One day at the center of the labyrinth, I realized that praying sincerely, 'Thy will be done' does not come easy in the crucible. I prayed it. And prayed it every time I reached the center of the maze.

There were always pigeons around the labyrinth. I thought about how our souls are like homing pigeons. Drawn to the center of it all. Or we can choose to fly away from it.

Sometimes I wrote my weekly letter to the Benedicts at one of the cathedrals. Communication with Göttingen was best through the military transports. Darby O'Cullen made sure they got there. Yet another great kindness.

On a morning walk, I happened to discover the Royal Irish Academy of Music near Trinity College. By sheer impulse I went in, hoping to find a piano. I hadn't played in more than a month. The place seemed empty except for the sound of someone practicing violin down a long hall. Someone very talented. I followed the sound. It led me to a small concert or recital hall. Since there was no one to ask permission, I sat down at a beautiful Steinway grand. But I couldn't decide what to play. The beautiful room seemed like a space completely removed from the catastrophic world events of the last decade. Sitting there in the quiet, listening to the distant violin, I began to cry. And play Reflexion in A, pianissimo. Very softly. Meandering through a flood of feelings. It turned into full improvisation, moving back and forth between a major and minor key. It later became a piece I titled 'Snowdrop Air in G'.

I heard the sound of someone taking a seat. I paused and looked up. A man said, "No, please don't stop." I continued a short while and then retarded to an ending. Letting it ring full out.

"Thank you. I needed that," the man said.

I tried to apologize for intruding and presuming, but he wouldn't have it.

Turns out he was the principal of the Academy. A Mr. Daggs. We had a lovely talk. He reminded me of Herr Benedict. I didn't know then it was the beginning of a long relationship. I went looking for a piano and found a new friend.

You see, even in our impulses we are searching, feeling for the next thing. The next heart connection. Should we always trust our impulses? No. But we can trust them to our heavenly guide. As one of St. Patrick's prayers says, 'May God's strength pilot us.' He piloted me that morning. As he does you and me now.

It had not been lost on me how Aneska was taking on the role of a life coach. Moving me from melancholy to possibility. Because I trusted her, there was no reason to suspect any particular end game. Still, her prayer request planned for St. Patrick's cathedral made me curious. And curiosity felt like a healthy sign of life.

Well, another rabbit trail, forgive me.

I told her I trusted her narrative impulse. She chucked her delightful laugh. Then continued.

Kristers underwent three weeks of cognitive and physical tests as well as more X-rays. All the attention confused him. He had no memory of what had happened to him. After a week, the team of doctors called me and Jakob in. Their findings were mixed.

The path and location of the bullet were a blessing and a challenge. The bullet entered the thinnest part of the skull. So, it held its shape and didn't fragment. But the impact sent some bone fragments into Kristers' brain close to the surface. These could easily be removed. That was the first of the surgeries. The doctors marveled that the bullet missed a main artery and lodged just below the auditory cortex, or Kristers would have lost his hearing. But it partially damaged a place called the hippocampus, a section they theorized is related to memory.

You must remember, this was 1945. So much about brain function has been discovered since WW2.

The bullet was relatively low velocity, so it stopped short of a ventricle, a space filled with fluid that cushions the brain. This explained why his brain didn't swell very much. Certainly, another miracle. It came to rest next to a thing called the amygdala. There was some research that it processed emotions related to response to fear. It helped trigger adrenaline. That might partially account for Kristers' docile nature. In one test, the doctors tried surprising Kristers by letting a rat run across the room. He didn't flinch. The doctors said he could live with that damage, but he might not respond quickly to threats or danger. I never knew Kristers to be very spooked about danger or sudden surprises, so the rat test and others like it seemed of small consequence to me.

I lost count of the miracles. Kristers was coordinated, all motor skills intact, except speech. The doctors said it was like his larynx had been unplugged. He responded to simple commands and had feeling all over his body. He could taste sour and sweet and spicy, hot and cold. His digestive tract worked fine, though over that summer he had to be potty trained again like a two-year-old. Diapers and all. He never seemed embarrassed by that. In fact, like a toddler, he sometimes ran around the house and into the yard in the nip, as the Irish say. Completely naked.

There were also hard losses. His memory was greatly impaired, and he couldn't speak. Next to the look of love in his eyes, I missed his voice the most.

She paused.

And I never heard it again. A few years later a remarkable therapist spent months retraining him to whisper the shapes and sounds of letters and vowels. But his limited language comprehension and generation complicated that. Even so, he got better at communicating in simple terms. He could hold a pencil but only write scribbly lines and a repeated meandering spiral, like a coiled spring. Overall, the doctors were optimistic about his chances of living many years. They reassured us the brain held possibilities of mending itself and rerouting functions, simple responses and even higher faculties. Like perception, learning, imagination, desire, decision-making and emotion. Only time and good therapy would tell. And of course, prayer.

My friend, we truly are fearfully and wonderfully made. The most mundane actions are a choreography of immense complexity.

She picked up the teapot and refreshed my cup.

Watch. Simply pouring a cup of tea, dropping in a sugar cube, adding cream, stirring, bringing it to the lips, testing its temperature, swallowing, savoring and replacing the cup in the saucer is a physical, chemical and volitional symphony. Kristers was alive and still capable of all that. But remembering how your friend likes their tea, that's another level of composition, if you will. My thoughtful, eloquent, hilarious, compassionate genius and chef was altered, muted and buried deep within my beautiful husband. Likely gone forever. By his own choice. For my sake.

Emotion welled up in Aneska. She leaned her head against the back of the chair.

I've felt that loss every day. But the gratitude that his life was spared, and the magnitude of his sacrifice for me, has fed my soul even more. It still does. How could it not? It pours into me and through me. Into the music. Into the way I see and value every soul. Every act of kindness and love.

Beyond that, I know when I crossover to the other side, all will be restored. An even better version of Kristers will greet me. He is home now. All is well with him. I can't say all is always well with my soul, like the hymn, but it will be. On the other side, certainly.

The wave washed over me as well. And even then, I couldn't help it. As I collected myself, I jotted down another song idea, 'When I Cross Over."

Well, looks like I fast forwarded from 1945 to future glory. She chuckled.

Let's see, oh, yes, the doctors told us the main challenge was the risk of removing the bullet. The procedure could do more damage than it relieved. Because of the small caliber and nickel coating, they advised leaving it in place. If it shifted position, migrated, they called it, they would reconsider removal. Meanwhile, seizures could be managed some by medication.

Five weeks after landing in Dublin, Kristers was ready to travel. Darby could arrange to fly us back to Göttingen.

We made plans to return. But Brynn O'Cullen came to see us again. Out of gratitude to my father and Jakob for saving her son, she invited us to live here, at her magnificent estate. Within easy reach of the doctors and therapists, for as long as we liked. There was plenty of room. She was so sincere and fierce persuasive. She argued it was already November. Winter had begun. I was seven months pregnant. Our friends in Germany would understand the danger. The world in Europe was still in chaos. After all we had been through, she predicted the beauty of the Irish countryside alone would help heal our spirits. And, besides, she had a seven-foot Steinway in her front room. She implored us to let her thank us this way, acknowledging, "Of course, everyone finds their own pot of gold where love it bound to lead."

No, I didn't miss that song idea. Three blind mice could have seen it.

"Where Love Is Bound to Lead" went immediately into my notebook. Thank you, Brynn O'Cullen.

I never pictured our baby not being born in Germany. But I guess by now you put it together.

We stayed. That was over seventy years ago. Looking back at our journey, for us, Ireland was where love was bound to lead. It only followed.

CHAPTER THIRTY-EIGHT

THE PUB

Near my fourth week with Aneska she announced I needed a break. Her prescription: a classic Irish experience. An evening at a local pub where people gather regularly for laughter, live music, and what she called Guinness "therapy." In her view, music best expresses the heart and soul of the Irish people. If I was to capture that in my writing, nothing would help better than playing with a few local musicians, except perhaps falling in love with an Irish woman. I told her I already had. She countered in a perfect Irish accent, "Aye, lad, but I'm only an adopted Irisher. And besides, tá mo chroí tógtha, my heart is taken."

I couldn't imagine how the abundant harvest of song ideas that poured out of her could possibly turn into songs, but I added "Taken" to the list.

I didn't bring a guitar from the states, but Aneska had that "sorted." One of the local musicians would bring an extra, a fine Lowden, made in Ireland. Her musician friends were eager to play with a songwriter from Nashville, so I best be prepared to play a few of my own tunes. She herself would be playing a squeeze box, a concertina. She advised me to prepare for a very late night.

That Saturday evening was cool and clear. Maja's magic had the night off. She and Zuza and Aneska and I drove to The Ferry Inn. The core of the building was older than the United States. Classic pub décor. Hand-hewn, age-darkened beams overhead. Bookshelves and wrought iron candle holders on white stucco stone walls. Dark oak floors scuffed by the feet of countless patrons, some of them famous, including perhaps the English General, the Duke of Wellington who defeated Napoleon at Waterloo in 1815. Apparently, Wellington met his own Waterloo in the vicinity. Some years after his famous victory, he built a home just outside Carlow for his local mistress, with whom he fathered a child. I wondered about the odds of any patrons in the crowd being Wellington's descendants. I stored that thought away for perhaps a toast between songs, but decided against it. I wasn't sure it might touch a sensitive nerve in Irish - English relations.

Except for the glow of TV screens to watch soccer matches, crossing the threshold of the pub was a kind of time travel. Many a pleasant evening had passed there. For nearly three hundred years! Under the warm hum of conversations, a fire crackled in a hearth. The place was a hive of comaraderie and good cheer.

Everyone greeted Aneska. Everyone knew everyone. Introductions over a first round of Guinness worked up an appetite. The music would not begin til about 9:00 p.m. So, we visited over a second round. Aneska fielded questions about the progress of her concerto debut. A couple of young men buzzed around Maja and her two attractive friends. The girls' Gaelic names, Eimear (pronounced Eemer) and Caoimhe (Kweeva), added to the sense of immersion into the storied land that is Ireland. Their names also piqued my curiosity about how much the person was drinking who first spelled Gaelic names.

It didn't take long for the natural hilarity of the Irish to erupt. An older man known to everyone entered. He hailed the bartender for a pint saying, "Make it quick. I'm drier than Ghandi's sandal." Brian O'Kelly was his name. He sat down with us and introduced himself as a retired pastor and town poet. His wife had passed in the last few years. I offered my condolences.

Brian excused himself to visit a woman across the room who he claimed had been hitting on him for twenty years. Knowing he was a pastor, I asked if he took her advances seriously. He said he did until he met Maja. More laughter, especially from Maja. She was at least forty years his junior. When he returned, Pastor O'Kelly leaned toward me and confided he had never been a pastor. For fun, he occasionally introduced himself as a reverend to see how people treated him. I felt like I'd landed in a sitcom, that all this was well-scripted and choreographed. But it was pure Irish reality. And vitality.

Brian had some of his poetry with him in a satchel. Naturally, he was, after all, the town poet. His buddies did not have to egg him on to read one. The pseudo-reverend Brian sorted through a few papers and selected one. The font appeared to be from an actual typewriter. Aneska shot me a broad smile and a nod. She seemed to know what was coming. The first two lines brought approvals and laughter.

Brian began, "I remember the first time I did it / I was only a lad of sixteen." The poem described the intimate event in country terms, including a barn and the aroma of clover and new mown hay. And details like his shyness and her warm body.

The circle of listeners leaned in expectantly. Pints went still for the climax. Pun intended. Brian had them under his spell. Me included. The final quatrain did not disappoint,

> I remember that wonderful evening,
> as if it were happening now,
> the first time I sat on a three-legged stool,
> and attempted to milk our brown cow.

The place erupted like George Bernard Shaw was in the room! Pints clinked.

In order not to forget such indelible moments, I took a not-so-subtle cue from Aneska. Much, much later that evening through a

Guinness haze I scribbled down what I could remember of the poem, while it was fresh. Sláinte! to Brian, a master of pastoral poetry.

For dinner Maja and Zuza ordered classic Irish fare - fish and chips. So, of course, I did, too.

Just as our third round and food arrived, so did Valor, accompanied by a beautiful, willowy woman. Though younger than him, I assumed she might be his wife. Probably a second wife. Brian and another lad (listen to me wax Irish) vacated their seats. I stood. Aneska introduced me to her namesake, Saoirse (pronounced Sur-shuh) Aneska Murphy. Valor's daughter! Ah, Aneska's granddaughter. Mystery solved. It dawned on me. I had seen her face in some of the pictures in the study. I felt a mixture of two things: curiosity related to the book, she being directly related to Kristers and Aneska. And a twinge of what I will call - typical male intrigue. I admit, not necessarily in that order.

Aneska said to her grandaughter, "Sit here, my Bluebell." Saoirse sat between us. Valor ordered a Guinness and Connemara single malt whisky for them both. On the rocks. Saoirse's long auburn hair reflected hints of red in the candlelight. It cascaded around her face, past her shoulders, just like Aneska and Zuza's tresses. Her eyes were blue as sapphires glowing under dark eyebrows. Her complexion creamy with a hint of freckles and crow's feet around eyes wisened by life and time. An Irish beauty, for sure. Her age was hard to guess. I knew Valor was born shortly after WW2 and married young. Whatever the case, her beauty was timeless.

I only observed in such detail mind you because, that's what I do. As a writer, you understand. And I noticed another thing. As Aneska took both of Saoirse's hands in hers on the tabletop, I saw she wore two rings. On her left ring finger, a wide combination of overlapping bands, each studded with small diamonds all around. Fierce shiny. Fierce dear, as the Irish say. Very expensive looking. On her right ring finger, a simple, silver Claddagh. I knew something about the famous

Irish ring because on my previous trip to Ireland I bought one in Galway, where the ring originated. A present for my daughter's birthday. The jeweler said it could be worn as a wedding ring on the left hand with the heart facing inward. Outward meant engaged. Worn on the right hand with the heart facing inward indicated single but in a relationship. Worn heart facing outward meant single. Unattached. The heart on Saoirse's right ring finger faced outward. Do I have to tell you my curiosity grew? As Aneska was fond of pointing out, everyone has a story.

But the rings weren't the only revelation. Saoirse and Aneska's hands looked remarkably alike. Obviously, one pair younger than the other, but mirror images in shape, nails, and length. In recent years, I noticed the back of my hand on the steering wheel began to mirror my Dad's on the wheel. Though he's been gone some years, the similarity is a tender, visceral connection with him. I remarked about the similarity of their hands.

Saoirse affirmed it, saying she inherited her Mimi's long hands but not her piano skills, though she took seven years of lessons from her. Aneska insisted Saoirse's playing was lovely and from the heart. That she played "Dear Lord Jesus, Take My Hand" better than her Mimi. She also pointed out her granddaughter's less visible inheritance - a gift for numbers.

Saoirse asked me, "Any guesses where that came from?"

Her grandfather, Kristers, of course. Grasping for anything else to say, I asked, "Why Bluebell?" And immediately bungled pronouncing her name. Fortunately, she laughed. She pronounced her name for me slowly a couple of times. "Like inertia. Saoirse." When she did, her lips formed into a pucker, a kissing shape. Sur-shuh. Sur-shuh. I told you. I notice things. As for the source of her nickname, she was born in April, when bluebells bloom and her eyes were fierce blue. Yes, I had noticed that, too.

All I could muster was, "That's beautiful." I composed myself and proposed a toast. Glasses raised. "To Kristers and his living legacy. Sláinte."

It promised to be a fierce good evening.

Saoirse thanked me for writing her grandmother's story. I told her the book was really writing itself. I was just glad to be the scribe. She disputed that, saying she read my book her Mimi gave her, and that I was a 'fierce' good wordsmith. I attempted a joke, saying that was fierce kind of her. It worked. Aneska seemed amused by our interaction.

I wanted to know more about Saoirse's story and especially her recollections of Kristers. But all that would have to wait. A few more musicians arrived. More introductions. Instruments came out. We tuned and arranged ourselves in a circle, just like some songwriter nights in Nashville.

There were four acoustic guitarists, including me, a bass player with a small amp, Aneska on concertina, and a singer, the wife of a guitarist. Most of the players had chart folders, with chords and lyrics to hundreds of songs. Except Aneska, she played by ear and memory.

I seated myself facing our table, beside a guitarist, James O'Meara. I was more intimidated to play with Aneska, a world-class pianist, than the Irish musicians. And just between us, Saoirse made me a little nervous as well.

The next hours were some of the best I've ever spent. I knew time was passing, but it felt like it was passing us by. That's a part of music I marvel at. And crave. The time signature of great music is timeless moments. It happens in other things, too, writing, painting, enjoying a great meal, making love, playing with your kids, worshipping - anything that feeds your soul and connects you with who or what really matters.

We played Irish tunes like "Tipperary on My Mind" and "Galway Girl," not the Ed Sheeran one, but the traditional Irish version. Many patrons sang along. The ballad "Black is the Color" poured out the exquisite beauty of the Irish heart in love, rich and deep like the Guinness that flowed. We played international hits, too. Gordon Lightfoots' "If You Could Read My Mind"; "Back Home Again" by John Denver; "Will the Cirlce Be Unbroken" and a couple of songs by the Eagles. I experienced the connection between the Irish soul and Amercian Country music and Blue Grass on a new level.

A few of my own tunes were well received, especially a new one called, "One of These Days," a bit of a swampy, country thing that starts, "I must be livin' in the wrong time zone / Most nights I wake up in the pale moonlight." It's about love lost and some dreams turning out to be out of reach, but still believing something good's gonna come - one of these days. After that song a waitress brought over a glass of something on the rocks. Connemara whiskey. She pointed to Valor as the sender. We raised our glasses to each other.

One guitarist and his wife sang a sad and sweet duet in Gaelic, a capella. It sounded centuries old. When they finished I asked what the song was about. It told of a poor young man forced to go on a fierse long sea voyage to make a living for his young bride. After a great while he returns with a bag over his shoulder to find a whiskered man sleeping in his bed. The husband grabs an ax to kill the intruder, but his wife stops him. The man in the bed is his grown son! The sailor had been gone that long! He takes out the only bounty from his bag, a cake, to discover someone baked gold coins inside it. So, he didn't have to go back to sea. The song would never be not top forty fare, but as Aneska pointed out, it was very telling about the Irish view of the hardships and hidden treasures of life. It was clear to me why she resonated with that.

It also helped explain why the Irishers reacted strongly to "One of These Days." The bridge says, "Life is hard, gotta play your cards, even when you get a raw deal / The way I figure, Somebody bigger / bound to have a hand on the wheel."

About 11:15p.m. Aneska, Zuza, and Maja excused themselves. Maja had an early morning to cook breakfast. Valor decided to catch a ride with them. Saoirse wanted to stay for more music. James, the guitarist, and his wife Olive offered to give me a lift. But so did Saoirce. James smiled and deferred to her. Valor kissed his daughter on the cheek and told her not to keep me out all night.

"After all," he said "like one of his songs says, he's livin' in the wrong time zone."

That impressed me in two ways. Valor precisely remembered some of the song, and he trusted me with his beautiful daughter.

We played music two more hours. My pint never ran dry. My thirsty soul drank even deeper. For a man still fairly numb around the heart, I hadn't felt that alive in a while. The alchemy of music, humor, stories and conviviality was life-giving. It was a kind of church. A revival.

Packing up, the Lowden guitar owner suggested I keep it in during my stay. I declined his gracious offer. Having a guitar around, especially one that fine, would gobble songwriting hours from my mission with Aneska. Two other musicians offered places to stay if I ever needed it. One, a second home on the west coast near Galway. The other the vacant house of James' mother-in-law recently passed. Their generosity was exceeded only by their capacity for laughter and Guinness.

As we packed up I learned all the musicians had their own stories of struggles and challenges: a contentious divorce, a past drug battle, an autistic son. James himself had beaten cancer a few years back. The joy of the evening took on deeper colors. The enchanted Emerald Isle was not immune to heartache and catastrophe. And yet. It was infused with robust signs of life and abundance of spirit.

And the night was not over.

On the ride back to the manor, I learned some of Saoirse's story. Her name, a stiff challenge to an outlander in a Gaelic spelling bee, was chosen by Valor because she was born April 29, the day the

British liberated Stalag X-B. Saoirse is Gaelic for 'freedom.' She owned a fierce successful real estate brokerage in Dublin, lived in a brownstone there during the week, but most weekends returned to a nineteenth century cottage three kilometers south of Snowdrop Manor on the River Barrow. Leukemia took her husband nearly three years earlier. No children. She had wonderful memories of her remarkable grandfather and would be glad to share them if it helped tell her Mimi's story.

I let her know that would be greatly appreciated. She hoped I enjoyed my baptism into Irish pub life. I called it a much-needed dose of music, laughter and Guinness therapy.

She said, "That sounds like something my Mimi would say."

I confessed. "It is. I stole it from her."

She drove away in the pale moonlight.

Aneska was right. I needed a break. But Irish "church" at the pub, communing over the elements - Guinness, Irish whiskey and fish and chips - was more than a break, it was a breakthrough. Just one of a series from the collateral benefit of being pulled along by Aneska's ineluctable gravity.

By the time I wrote down some details from the soul feast of the evening, it was after three in the morning. Even then, sleep did not come easy. I wrapped in a quilt and stood outside in the brisk air. The River Barrow flowed imperceptible and silent as time. A song lyric from earlier came to mind: I must be livin' in the wrong time zone / most nights I wake up in the pale moonlight.

CHAPTER THIRTY-NINE

THE LILY

The first time we pulled into the O'Cullen estate, I'm sure was like your experience, my friend. It was like a storybook. Snowdrops at the entrance and all around the grounds. As Brynn used to say, the tiny blossoms laughed at the Goliath of winter. Remember I told you, I always dreamed of living in the country? It came true here. And nothing I did made it happen. It would have been a good story if me or my music had anything to do with it. Brynn O'Cullen knew I was a pianist, but nothing about my dreams. So, instead of a good story, I got a testimony. Of Gott's making. Just like Mama always reminded us, we make a plan, but Gott directs our steps.

Kristers and I slept in the same room, in the same bed, so I could be near in case he had a seizure or other trauma. But also because we were husband and wife. He had clearly lost a sense of that, but he enjoyed me holding him and stroking his hair or arm as he went to sleep.

Brynn treated us like family. She took over where Mama left off. She busied herself making preparations for the baby. We spent many hours sitting in this very spot, a cozy fire on the hearth. She taught me to knit and crochet. She read to me, from the scriptures and many of these books. Kristers often joined us and listened. Once Brynn heard me play, we often sat in the music room. I hoped music would somehow help mend Kristers' mind and memory. And I relished the thought that our baby was already hearing wonderful music and feeling the rhythm inside my body. When the baby moved, I put Kristers' hand on my belly so he could feel it. His curiosity gave me great joy.

Christmas 1945, I was as pregnant as Mary with Jesus. The season heightened our losses, our mourning, but also our blessings. Because of Capt. O'Cullen's duty in the war, that was Brynn's third Christmas without her husband. She told me Ireland was officially neutral in the war, but thousands of Irish-born men and women joined the British armed forces and gave their lives in the cause. Imagine that. Capt. O'Cullen and his son Darby did not have to join the fight. But they did. I was struck again with admiration and gratitude for all who stood and those who fell.

Sean O'Cullen flew home on leave in the Spring of '44 before the D-Day invasion. That's the last time Brynn saw him. This was her first Christmas, and Darby's, mourning his death. Even so, they decorated the house beautifully. Darby and Jakob cut a magnificent Douglas fir from the property. They even built a manger to put next to the tree. "In case the baby comes," Darby said. The lovely meals and aromas from the kitchen filled the air with goodness. And our bellies.

I'm not sure why, but I prayed our baby would not be born on Christmas. Like so many things, that was out of my hands. Brynn invited neighbors and staff and their families for a sing-along, the afternoon of Christmas eve. It was one of her traditions. Everyone brought a dessert. I played all the traditional songs. One neighbor asked Brynn if I would consider teaching piano lessons to their daughter, once the baby was born and settled. That felt providential but made me miss my students in Sandbostel. And Petra. And everyone.

Christmas came and went. No baby. December 31st about 8:00 in the evening, I was sitting at the piano, just noodling on the keys. My water broke. About twelve hours later, January first, 1946, our honeymoon baby was born. I had Zuza's name in mind since the day

Kristers and I last visited the hunting shack before moving to Göttingen. Zuza may have told you; it means "lily" in Hebrew. I thought Kristers would like that. He took to her immediately. There's a picture over there of him holding her.

I retrieved the photo. Aneska looked at it as she continued.

The look on his face says it all. See how they're staring at each other? That look is very much like the one I told you about at our wedding. The one he gave me so much. At first it pierced my heart. But Brynn put it in a better light. She said it proved that sacred place in Kristers was alive and well. The more I thought about that, the more it comforted me. In fact, it rallied my spirit. For all Blixt's intent to torture and rob me of Kristers, his malevolence missed its mark. The wonder and awe on Kristers' face was undeniable. What is love, my friend, if not wonder and awe for another? And tender caring? We taught Kristers to take care of Zuza. To feed and dress her. Change her diaper. He relished it, though we had no way to gauge if he completely understood Zuza was his daughter. Our daughter.

We had just celebrated the birth of the little Christmas child and our new year began with new new life.

There was another one. I added "Little Christmas Child" to the growing litany of songs to be mined from Aneska's mother lode.

We lost so many precious lives to the war. Zuza was not only Gott's declaration of hope and renewal to us. She was his measuring stick of what mattered in the world. What mattered to Gott. Life. Every life. The crucifixion and resurrection declare it, certainly. "For Gott so loved the world he gave his son." But the baby Emmanuel's birth declared Gott's heart as well - for the weakest and most vulnerable. Imagine entrusting the hope of the world to a little baby. To a young carpenter and teenage girl in a hostile and hazardous world.

The comparison was obvious to Brynn. She said Gott made a way for Zuza through a world at war, from the brink of death. Gott delivered Jesus from the villainy of Herod. He delivered Zuza from the villainy of Blixt. That terrible night in the Town Hall, I had no idea I was already pregnant. But Gott did. That was not lost on Zuza. As she learned the story, she knew her daddy saved her, too. And Gott brought us to a safe and beautiful place, surrounded by people who loved us, delivered by his Almighty hand.

Brynn and I agreed on something else. Zuza was a repudiation of any power that diminished, devalued, harmed, or destroyed any life because every life bears his divine spark, and is destined for a sacred journey, even before birth. You have a song by that name, don't you? "The Sacred Journey?"

Yes. That was one I had already written. But I had to confess to Aneska I appropriated the title and inspiration from a book by the same title by Frederick Buechner, one of my favorite writers. She pointed to several of his books on a high shelf. His "Sacred Journey" was one of them. Why was I not surprised?

In a couple of days, when I was able to get to the piano, Kristers sat on the sofa holding Zuza. The first song I played was what my heart was singing, Beethoven's "Ode to Joy." I'm sure you know that wonderful line. "Hearts unfold like flowers before Thee." Thanks to Gott, he planted us here in this Irish garden and we were blooming again.

Zuza appeared at the door. Lunch was ready. Aneska's segue sparkled.

Ah, and here's my lily blossom now.

CHAPTER FORTY

THE INVITATION

My friend, in case you're feeling any apprehension that the third movement of my life will take as long to tell as the first two, let me ease your mind. Measured in years, of course, my third movement has lasted many decades. I'm still living it. Though the time since Kristers' death feels like an epilogue. Once it became clear Ireland would be our new home, the years glided by like the River Barrow. We found a new stride, with some challenges along the way. So, don't worry that I'll talk till Spring arrives.

That prospect was a long way from a worry. But I already sensed the energy of her third movement growing toward a finale. At some point. For the first time, my apprehension, besides capturing her story well on the page, was that at some point the finale would come and this rich time would be over. Oddly enough, except for missing my children, I hadn't spent a moment thinking about returning to the States. I chalked that up to Aneska's magnetic pull and the lure of Snowdrop Manor and the Emerald Isle. Maja's cooking cast its own spell. There was also the prospect of playing at the pub more. And I could certainly write anywhere. Mixed in all that was a seed of intrigue about Saoirse. Mostly about her close history with Kristers. Mostly.

I told Aneska as far as I was concerned, she could talk into summer if she liked.

I'm enjoying our time too, my friend. But I've got a concerto to present, and you've got a book that will need a period at the end. But our friendship and our stories will go on. Lord willing, some of our music and words will even outlive us. That happened to Anne Frank. Of course, not in the way she hoped. But it happened.

I sensed a quote coming on. It was uncanny how many nuggets of Anne's diary she could pull out of thin air. Sure enough…

Anne wrote, "I want to go on living after my death! And so, I am grateful to God for giving me this gift…of expressing all that is in me." I can't tell you how that stirred my heart when I read it just after the war. It still does!

I hoped to be half as passionate at her age.

Don't we want that, too, my friend? Something to live on. Especially in the ones we love and who love us. My Papa and Mama's love is as alive and real as ever. Even if the music doesn't last, that love lives on.

And that's just another example of why I could listen to her into the summer. All I could do was agree and thank her for another song idea, "Love Lives On." She laughed.

You're welcome.

Now, as I was saying, the third movement of my life has been a long one. But musically, a composer typically covers a lot of ground quickly after the dark struggles of the middle section of most symphonies. And brings the conclusion to triumph, or a mixed resolution of victory in the face of loss or struggle. Some end with an accepted tension between the two. Mahler's first symphony, though it has four movements, is a good example. It runs about an hour. The final movement is less than ten minutes of the entire symphony.

By the way, I have a surprise invitation. Another break for you. As providence would have it, the National Symphony Orchestra is performing Mahler's Symphony No. 1 next week at the National Concert Hall in Dublin. The same hall hosting the premier of my concerto. I took the liberty and got us tickets. And since Saoirse lives in Dublin, I invited her to join us. As the Irish say. Would you be on for it? We can make a day of it. Visit St. Patrick's and write in the prayer book. I need to meet briefly with the conductor of the symphony. You can tour the Guinness brewery. We'll meet Saoirse for dinner before the concert. How do you feel about driving on the correct side of the road?

That all sounded fierce good. I had driven around Ireland many years ago, so that should come back to me. And I wondered when I might see Saoirse again. But I didn't say that to Aneska. Something told me I didn't have to.

As you listen to his symphony, you'll find it hard to believe Mahler wrote it when he was only twenty-seven. Obviously, his soul was much older. I'm excited to experience it again.

Her word choice struck me. She didn't say "hear" the symphony. She said, "experience" it. Music was clearly not a spectator sport for Aneska.

This symphony, as well as works by other composers, mentored my concerto. The opening, the first two movements in Mahler's case, celebrates the vitality of youth and the joy and beauty of life. In the middle section, even into the final movement, you can hear the struggle to overcome a great darkness. For a moment, the angst of possible defeat arises. But courage and beauty rally to fight on.

It was obvious why Aneska resonated with Mahler's symphony. It sounded very much like the dynamic of her own story.

Mahler described the beginning of the fourth movement as the "outcry of a wounded heart." Isn't that the condition of every heart, my friend? Everyone is wounded. Maybe that's why we go to concerts. Why we compose and play and listen to music. We want to celebrate something but also hear empathy for our own struggles and the possibility of being mended. Boiled down, we want to be more alive.

My revival in the pub was still vivid testimony to that.

I hope the opening of my third and final movement will sound like the bittersweet lament and triumph of a wounded but mending heart. Isn't that the hope of every soul? Blixt and his ilk excepted.

Brynn believed, perhaps even deep within the frozen core of the stone-hearted, walking dead like him, an ember of that longing still flickers, waiting to catch fire. Only Gott knows. But Brynn's capacity for grace was greater than mine.

From what I'd observed already about Aneska, I had reason to doubt that.

At the risk of giving too much away, Mahler's last nine minutes build to an explosion of triumph. When the orchestra is at peak volume, he instructed the entire brass section to stand for the final minute and fill the hall with the victorious theme. Witnessed live, it's a heart-pounding passage of unrestrained jubilation and freedom. A few years after we arrived in Ireland, Brynn took me to a performance of it in London. During the long standing ovation, I turned to her and said, "I think I just got born again, again." Some years later, I took Kristers to it in Dublin. Several times and during the ovation, tears streamed down his face. The minute we got home, he wanted to make love. He kept the ticket his whole life. But I'm getting way ahead of myself.

Aneska and Kristers' intimate detail and the news about attending a symphony with her and Saoirse felt like a brass section standing up and belting it. I resisted pursuing either topic, but with great effort. Instead, I debated whether to listen to Mahler's first before the concert. I decided against it. Aneska more than whetted my appetite, and I wanted my first hearing to be fresh. It seemed like a 'you-had-to-be-there' experience.

I made a note to listen for the dynamic pattern she described when I returned to attend her concerto in late April, two and half months ahead. Having been privy to so much of Aneska's epic story, I wasn't sure how only one hour of music could adequately convey it. That is, if the movie, the soundtrack in this case, would be as good as the book. But I had no doubt I would hear, or rather, experience, her soul in every note.

CHAPTER FORTY-ONE

THE ANGEL

In early April of that year, 1946, an angel came to our door. Not a celestial being, but a real person. Her name was Katie O'Grady. Brynn met her on a trip to Dublin. I knew the reason for her trip was to attend a ceremony honoring Capt. O'Cullen and meet with a representative of the British army about his military benefits. But I was not aware of her two other missions. She arranged an audition for me at the Royal Irish Academy of Music with the principal, Mr. Daggs. Remember him? Her other purpose was to meet with Katie O'Grady.

Brynn escorted her into the front music room while I was practicing. They stood behind me, listening until I noticed them.

Our meeting was indelible. Katie looked like she walked out of a Van Gogh painting. There's a picture on the table of her with Brynn and Kristers and me.

Per our routine, I retrieved it. A black-and-white photo. Aneska held it and reminisced.

Talk about beautiful, like a pleasantly plump Maureen O'Hara. That first meeting, her red hair was piled loose on her head like a haystack. Three long feathers for hairpins stuck out of it. Her bright blue eyes smiled behind round, wire-rim glasses above her rosy cheeks. She was wearing a deep blue jacket over a rust-colored peasant skirt that draped to her ankles. She lit up the room. Brynn introduced us. Katie complimented my playing in a cheerful voice. Called me a 'finger ballerina.' And herself a 'helpless melophile'. That was a new word to me. It means…

An ardent music lover, I interjected.

Yes, of course. Why am I not surprised you would know that?

Brynn explained Katie was there for me to interview her to work with Kristers. Like Brynn, her husband died in the war. Early on. When Katie handed me her card, I knew she was sent from Gott. It read:

Katie O'Grady

Art Therapist – Speech Pathologist

Penny Whistler - Miracle Magnet

"I can't promise miracles," she declared. "But miracles have been known to find me." She moved that very day into the guest house where Jakob had been staying.

The penny whistle mounted on the wall in the guest house made sense. Aneska confirmed it belonged to Kristers. It was the one Katie gave him. Gracious as always, Aneska encouraged me to play it. I resisted. But she insisted, saying an instrument should be played. Like every soul, she believed, an instrument has music in it that needs to be released. Breathed out.

Oh, I should tell you, during that time Jakob took a job on a fishing trawler out of Dublin. He felt the sea calling him. I think it made him feel closer to Papa and Wilhelm. But it was more than the lure of the sea. The daughter of the fishing boat's captain caught his eye. He moved to Dublin to help prepare the boat for the Spring fishing season.

Back to our angel. Katie was the jolliest person I ever met, though she shed tears easily, too. Her warmth and charm were disarming. The first time she met Kristers, she took his face in both hands, looked him in the eyes and said, "Hello, Kristers Latva. My name is Katie O'Grady. It rhymes. Katie O'Grady. Hello in there, Kristers. Can you come out and play?" He beamed at her.

Their first session together she played the penny whistle for him. He was captivated. She took out another one and showed him where to put his fingers. Turns out the penny whistle was Katie's way of improving Kristers' breath control.

At her direction, we set up an art therapy studio. We filled it with paints and canvases, crayons and colored pencils, drawing pads, popsicle sticks and glue. And objects of all kinds. Colorful maps and prints of animals, bridges, and buildings on the walls. It looked like a first-grade classroom. High on one wall, I hung a sign in German and English, "Thinking freely equals freedom." One day, I peeked in while she and Kristers were blowing balloons and feathers into the air.

To develop his speaking skills, Katie taught Kristers to make the sounds of letters, using only his breath. I watched her hold his hand near her mouth to feel the 'ha' of the letter H. Then put his hand over his own mouth to feel the air and direct the sound back to his own ears. Two weeks after her arrival, she invited Brynn and me into the studio for a demonstration. Kristers had learned his first word. He stood in front of me, put one hand up just below his mouth and whispered a very breathy, "Ha – n neth – k k kah." And then a second time with more confidence, "Ha - neth - kah." I broke.

Her eyes welled with tears. She had to pause.

That first miracle led to others. Kristers' vocabulary increased. He often mixed German and English in the same sentence. He began to color and paint and draw. For the first two months only splashes of random shapes and scribbly pencil lines.

One June afternoon, Katie called us into the studio. Kristers had a present for me. A tablecloth covered a small desktop easel. Katie positioned Brynn and I in front of it for an unveiling. She and Kristers stood on either side of the easel. Katie nodded to him. Kristers lifted the tablecloth.

Both my hands went directly over my mouth. I knew immediately what it was. On a white piece of ordinary typing paper was a pencil sketch. A single line rose and curved gently over and down to the right in a graceful arch. The line was perfectly smooth, not shaky at all. Made in one sweeping motion. Two narrow, oblong shapes branched out from the base of the upward line. One on each side. The tips pointed up. Their green hue was the only color on the drawing, and the green extended outside the lines a bit. Suspended from the short end of the curved line were three petals of different sizes. It was unmistakably a sketch of a snowdrop blossom.

She needed another tissue.

My heart celebrated like it did when Kristers first told me he loved me. Like the first time he kissed me. I threw my arms around him and kissed him full on the mouth. He gave me a confused but pleasant look. I had been very restrained about showing him romantic affection.

Katie and Brynn enjoyed the reveal nearly as much as I did. Katie showed us a pile of dozens of sketches that led up to this one. She truly was a miracle magnet.

There was no way to tell if any lines in Kristers' brain had been redrawn. If he reconnected with our relationship before his injury. But something shifted between us. That night, I threw caution to the wind. I undressed in front of him and removed his clothes. We made love. More than once.

The next day…

Aneska chuckled.

…he gave me another drawing.

We both had a good laugh.

As Mama used to say, 'Einmal Mann, immer Junge.' Once a man, always a boy.

I resonated personally with that, but didn't say so. Instead, I wanted to know where the sketch was. She pointed to the firebox. At her instruction, I retrieved a worn red folder from the firebox. She cautioned me to be careful. The sketch was preserved between two pieces of glass. Aneska pulled it out as deliberately as a museum curator. The drawing was exactly as she described. Smooth lines. The faint green of the two leaves still visible.

Thanks to Katie, Kristers made steady progress. In his whisper talk. And in his art and music. She enlisted me for his music therapy. He explored Reflection in A beside me, whispering the names of the notes. I transposed it to the key of D for Katie to play along on her penny whistle. Kristers played his, too. His favorite song was "Amazing Grace." He became quite good at it. The three of us laughed a lot. Kristers' voiceless laughter became music to my ears.

Katie O'Grady, the miracle magnate, stayed with us through the summer.

That September, I resumed my music studies three times a month in Dublin at the Academy.

March 9 the next year, 1947, nine months after Kristers first snowdrop drawing, Valor was born. Kristers watched my second pregnancy with more interest than the first. He adored Valor. And Zuza. His understanding grew that they were our children. The breathy way he spoke their names was adorable. The letter 'R' was difficult for him to enunciate. So, Valor often sounded more like "Valoh."

I put my music studies on hold for the rest of that year. Brynn argued there was plenty of help for the children and Kristers, that I could continue my trips to the Academy. But I wanted our little family together. Kristers' seizures had not completely disappeared. And besides, practicing the piano with two little ones around and nursing the baby was quite a balancing act.

The pause in my studies wasn't the first one. And wouldn't be the last. But it led to something else I always wanted. A family. And another dream. We make our plans, right?

I finished her thought – but God directs our steps.

Ya, my friend, so you have been listening.

CHAPTER FORTY-TWO

THE DREAM

While my babies grew that year, Brynn recruited several of the neighbors' children who wanted to learn piano. I taught a few lessons a week. It was quite fulfilling, though it sometimes brought memories of my students and the difficult times in Sandbostel. But it put my foot on the road to another dream.

Since you're as glic as comes down the pike, my friend, can you guess where the lessons led?

I had no idea what 'glic' meant, but it sounded like a compliment. I hazarded a guess. The music school in Carlow?

You are fierce glic. Once again, your cabbage is savage. Ya, precisely. But it took time. Dreams may come at night, but most don't come true overnight. And many hands on the clay shape all our dreams.

That summer of '47, we had visitors. Petra and Rolf came for two weeks. The Benedicts arrived three days before they left and stayed a month. They doted on Zuza and Valor. Hans fished with Kristers in the River Barrow. Petra tuned the piano. Just like old times. Darby was still in active service but managed a few days leave from duty. It got so crowded he stayed at the cottage down river that Saoirse owns now. What a reunion we had! You can imagine the stories and laughter. And the tears, especially when I played "Dear Lord Jesus, Take My Hand." Katie O'Grady made a short visit to work with Kristers. Of course, they all fell in love with her. We had a full house of full hearts.

There was only one heartache. Kristers met our visitors courteously enough, even whispered 'hello' and a few words, which thrilled them all. But there was no sign of recognition. Still, we hoped interacting with Petra and the Benedicts might switch some lights on in him.

Unknown to me, Brynn spoke to Hans and Brigitte. about my idea of someday opening an academy of music in Carlow in association with the RIAM in Dublin. On the pretext of a sightseeing trip to Dublin, Hans met with Mr. Daggs about it. Brynn toured them around Carlow to scout possible buildings to house it. I found out all this later. Can you believe how good people can be?

I could. The evidence was all around and right in front of me.

During the Benedict's visit, something else flew into my head, one of those ideas that rises in your mind like a beautiful bird. Does that make any sense?

I had to quip, Yes, maybe hope is not the only thing with feathers? Aneska laughed.

You are fierce glic, my friend. Ya, at first the beauty of an idea catches your eye, but when it sings, you understand. This bird encouraged me to transfer the title of the Latva estate to the Benedicts. Not simply for their kindness over the many years, but as a clear sign - there was no going back to Germany. Ireland would be our forever home.

I told Brynn. The idea lit her up. We decided to surprise them. She instructed her lawyer to draw up the papers. He found a way for me to avoid traveling back to Germany in person to make the transfer. Though years later I returned for a visit. But that can wait.

One evening after dinner, we gathered with the Benedicts in the front music room. I asked Hans to listen to a piece of music I was working on. I handed him what he thought was a music folio. My handwritten title on the outside read, Willkommen Zuhause, Welcome Home. I went to the piano as if to play it. Hans opened the folder. A confused look came over his face. When he realized what it was, he held it toward Brigitte to see. She cried. So did I. The three of us embraced. Rivers of suffering and deliverance we lived through together came pouring out. Kristers wasn't sure what to do. He walked over and tried to put his arms around all of us. Brynn handed out handkerchiefs. When we regained our composure Hans began to laugh.

I spoke to him in German, "Was ist das?" 'What is this?'

Brynn said, "Aneska, we have a surprise for you as well."

Hans handed me a folder. On the outside, it was labeled "Für Deinen Traum." For Your Dream.

Inside was a letter from Mr. Daggs committing the RIAM to affiliate and help develop a music academy in Carlow. And there were two checks. One in pounds. One in Reichsmarks. From Brynn and the Benedicts. Together it was the equivalent of $20,000 US!

And, of course, the note was in the fire box. She read it.

Dearest Aneska,

This is for a location, pianos, sheet music, whatever you need.
Your mother said your music would make a way for you.
Beyond Words Academy will make a way for many others.

It was signed by Brynn, Hans and Brigitte. There was a P.S.

When you are ready, we will ship the Steinway to you for recitals.

Aneska sighed and gazed into the fire. I said, "People can be so good, ya?"

Ya my friend, that was the best Christmas I ever had in July. But there was another surprise. A dream of another kind.

Several days later, at dinner, Kristers was unusually quiet. And pensive. Just after we began eating, his fork stopped halfway to his mouth. He froze with his eyes locked on Hans sitting directly across the table. I looked at Katie. We braced ourselves for a seizure. In my lap, I rolled up my napkin to force between his teeth. It got quiet.

Kristers made a 'K' sound. He never took his eyes off Hans. We watched him whisper twice "K-ake. K-ake." A moment later he distinctly whispered to Hans, "You like k kake." He repeated it. "You like cake." And smiled at Hans.

That little connection between them burst into the room like the Holy Spirit on Pentecost. We all knew immediately. The glimmer of a memory broke through.

Hans, the kindest man who ever lived, smiled back at Kristers and said, "That's right, Kristers. You remembered. My favorite is your Black Forest Cake with cherry preserves and whipped cream."

I wanted to wrap Kristers in my arms. Instead, I took his hand under the table. He began eating again. We all did. And the world was not the same.

The next day, I got his recipe out of that very box over there. Brynn called all the neighbors to find some cherry preserves. We whipped and chilled some cream. And the two of us laughed and baked a Black Forest Cake.

CHAPTER FORTY-THREE

THE TOAST

The day came to attend the symphony with Aneska and her granddaughter. Since this is Aneska's story, not Mahler's, I won't spill too much ink about his symphony. At least that was my intention before experiencing it. But can I assume you might be as curious as I was to watch Aneska experience Mahler's Symphony No. 1? In the same magnificent hall in which her concerto would shortly debut? Especially after her description of it. I was also curious, all right, eager, to glean what I could from Saoirse's relationship to Aneska and her intimate view of the family saga. At least that was my intention — my main intention. But for those who read well between the lines or understand "once a man, always a boy," you know the last few sentences more than verge on gobshite. Saoirse's Mimi would be the first to say so. (You probably can make a close guess what 'gobshite' is Irish for.)

Back to Aneska's story.

For our trip to Dublin, I was at the wheel. Sitting on the wrong side of the car. Right out of the long gravel drive, I turned onto the wrong side of the road, into the oncoming lane. The second time it happened, Aneska said something about surviving WW2, disco, the Cold War and wanting to live long enough to attend her own concerto. For both our sakes, I got the hang of it.

We dined at a restaurant within walking distance of the National Concert Hall. Aneska and I arrived first and were seated. When Saoirse walked in the front door, Aneska said, "Isn't she stunning?"

Not missing a chance to banter with Aneska, I said, 'I hadn't noticed.'
Her return volley was immediate.

"Ya, just like I didn't notice Kristers when he handed me that first glass of water. She gets her beauty from him and her mother. And me, of course." I was laughing with her as Saoirse arrived at the table.

"Did I miss a good joke?" Saoirse said. *Aneska took the banter to a new level. At my expense.*

"No, someone was just trying to deny noticing how beautiful you are." *Her granddaughter deftly flipped it to give me some cover.*

"Mimi, don't hide it. You can tell me I'm beautiful anytime."

At this point, do I have to say how my intrigue graduated to adulation?

Saoirse wanted to know how the book was coming. And the concerto preparations. I wanted to hear about her and her world, but she peppered me with questions about my children and what I thought of Ireland. Dinner came. Aneska asked about her granddaughter's business, bragged about her a while, and then it was time to get to the concert. Saoirse insisted on picking up the tab, saying I could get the drinks after the concert. I liked the sound of that.

I had been to a few symphonies. But could not have predicted how heart-expanding the next two hours would be.

Aneska walked arm in arm between us, up the steps into the National Concert Hall, between giant stone columns topped with scroll capitals. The true giant walked beside me. Her arm in mine. Knowing Aneska's story in such detail, how it led to this place, this moment in time, was surreal. I sensed this was only a hint of the magnitude ahead of us on the evening of April 29 when we entered this hall for her long-awaited masterpiece.

Beyond the front lobby, another giant amplified the grandeur of the evening. A two-story sparkling chandelier hung from the second-floor ceiling through an elegant opening to the main floor. Standing beneath it, concert goers came over to greet Aneska, excited about her upcoming performance. Most knew Saoirse as well. More than a few men vied for conversion with her. Aneska introduced me as her dear friend, author and fellow musician from the States. It was just like her to put me on a par with herself.

The hall manager came over. Aneska thanked him for the tickets. That solved the mystery of how she captured them only a week in advance. Our seats were on the front row of the balcony, dead center of the hall. Aneska preferred the sound there and a clear view of all the musicians playing and moving in sync. The balcony narrowed into long arms on each side approaching the stage.

By the time we were seated, nearly all the orchestra members were in place, tuning and adjusting music stands. There must have been at least seventy-five players. No piano, which would not be the case for her concerto.

Aneska sat between us. Stealing glances at their profiles, the resemblance was clear. It was easy to imagine Saoirse as an echo of a younger Aneska. The entire hall radiated with a golden glow. So did their faces.

A towering pipe organ directly behind the stage stood like a sentinel of something momentous and sacred about to happen. The description of Mahler's symphony in the program included this: Mahler wrote his first symphony attempting to reflect the powerful story in Jean Paul Richter's novel, "Titan." In it, the main character strives to lead a passionate, noble and heroic life against great odds. *No mystery there why it resonated with Aneska.*

The buzz of muted conversations died out as the house lights dimmed. A faceless voice made the standard welcome and announcement forbidding recording devices and flash photography. Ten or so seconds of silence followed. From a stage door to our left, the conductor entered, without an introduction. Apparently, he didn't need one. The audience erupted in applause. As he took his bow, Aneska leaned toward me and said, "He's my conductor as well. Beyond marvelous." The hall quieted. The Maestro mounted the rostrum. Aneska grasped my hand and one of Saoirse's, like we were about to ride a rollercoaster. And we were.

At this point I will not attempt the impossible, to translate into words what only music can speak. I suggest you find a recording of "Titan," and unless you are comfortable showing unfiltered emotions on a commuter train, plane or a restaurant surrounded by strangers, I urge you to experience it, in a quiet, private, beautiful place, where tears and verbal elation can flow easily. If you are willing, even if like me, classical music is not a mainstay in your musical diet, I wager his symphony will morph into the soundtrack of your own story, of struggling against the odds to realize your core desire to live a more passionate, heroic, perhaps even a redeemed life.

To say I got caught up in the music is an understatement. The beauty, agony and struggle became the soundtrack to my own experiences. In many passages, Aneska closed her eyes, sometimes tears rolling down her face. Saoirse did the same. At one point she handed her Mimi a tissue. I could imagine how the music was touching Aneska's soul, rewinding the agonies and moving toward mending and triumph. As much as I knew of Saoirse's recent journey it wasn't difficult to imagine the resonances in her as well. At times, they both looked like worshippers, abandoned in the presence of God himself. It was beyond beautiful. And beyond words. Aneska was right. Mahler's soul was much older than twenty-seven when he wrote it.

As I said, I was caught up in the ebb and flow as well, drawn into the struggle Mahler painted, and carried along toward the anticipated triumph. In the last minute of the symphony, when the brass section stood, everything in me wanted to stand with them. After making the entire hall reverberate, the fortissimo finale came to a dramatic full stop. Applause erupted. It went on and on. No one remained in their seats. Each section of the orchestra was recognized and honored. The Maestro exited and returned twice for more bows and adulation.

I understood why Aneska had told Brynn during the standing ovation she felt born again, again. And why Mahler's musical passion and climactic finale made Kristers so alive he wanted to make love to her afterward. The music worked its magic. I was more alive. A little more mended. And the music forged stronger bonds between the three of us. Our common humanity, pain, faith and hope spilled over and into each other.

None of us having anyone to make love to, we poured out of the hall with the vibrant throng into the beautiful, cool night air of Dublin. Saoirse led us to a pub she liked nearby. We savored our experience over a communion of Guinness, whiskey and appetizers. In our heightened state, it all tasted better than ever.

We tried to do the impossible, put into words the power and depth of Mahler's music. I asked Aneska if a world-class work like that, proven over time, was intimidating or inspiring for her. Her answer, as usual, came from a soul tested and tempered by the same challenges, agonies and elations experienced by Mahler. Or any of us for that matter. Her words carried the characteristic aroma of her grace and humility. I soon regretted not having my recorder or a notepad to capture verbatim what tumbled out of her. Later, with her help, I was able to capture it.

"Did the Beatles intimidate you, my friend? I imagine at first, certainly. How could you write songs that good, that creative, timeless and widely acclaimed, ya? Clearly, my friend, at some point you found your own voice. At some point you outgrew childish comparisons and regret that you were not born Paul McCartney. Gott already made a Paul McCartney. A Mozart. A Mahler. And so, you get on with the essential pursuit of your own purpose, your own gifting, and find your own voice. We are influenced, inspired by the greats, certainly. We model or mimic them to learn. But at some point, you write the unexpected, discover something fresh, that can come only from your own well. Your pen. And then let it find its audience, however narrow or wide. As one of your own songs says, "though the world is not impressed, the ones who knew you best will stand" and revere you. For you. For your contribution to the pantheon of music, or whatever your profession. But far above that, you hope to be honored and remembered for the love and care you gave along the way, in spite of the resistance, sin and heartache that made your own mending necessary."

Saoirse and I looked at each other. There were no words. I was trying to take it all in, including the fact that she quoted one of my songs to me. Saoirse leaned over and kissed Aneska on the cheek. Her Mimi wasn't quite done. Aneska looked at me and added,

"My friend, what did Paul write? Not the Apostle. The Beatle. "In the end the love you take is equal to the love you make."

It was getting late. We still had to drop Saoirse at her place, then an hour or more back to the manor, in the dark, with me at the wheel. Aneska proposed we each make a toast. We raised our glasses. She went first,

'Here's to the mending.' Glasses clinked.

I waited for Saoirse, but she nodded to me. Something came to mind that rhymed. I meant it sincerely in reference to Mahler's symphony and Aneska's life. But as it came out of my mouth, I felt a twinge of anxiety that the rhyming might come off too clever, especially to Saoirse. I suppose a boy's insecurity and desire to impress is never quite crucified. It was too late to edit.

"Here's to redemptive endings."

They both said at the same time, "Amen." Glasses clinked.

Saoirse capped it off. She looked at Aneska. Then at me. As soon as she spoke the tumblers in the vault of my heart moved.

"Here's to new beginnings."

Aneska laughed and repeated all three toasts, "To the mending, redemptive endings and new beginnings."

We all chimed in, "Sláinte!" *Glasses clinked.*

Irish whiskey was the libation. But we drank hope.

CHAPTER FORTY-FOUR

THE ASHES

The third movement of my life was going beautifully. We had survived the war. Our great losses made every day and our dear ones more dear. Kristers was getting the care he needed. Brynn made her lovely home ours, too. We had two beautiful babies. The dream of a music academy was on the near horizon. Jakob fell in love and married the daughter of that fisherman in Dublin. Once Zuza and Valor were both toddlers, I found time to increase my practicing and studied in Dublin several times a month.

Kristers made steady progress. His sketches and paintings became more refined and even dimensional, though, as you have seen, his subject matter most often centered on snowdrop blossoms. His language skills and vocabulary grew like a first grader's. But always whispered.

Katie returned for a couple of months the next year and worked wonders with him, including his handwriting. His ability to understand what he heard continued to be greater than his ability to generate language.

Most remarkable of all, his memory began to reassemble. But unpredictable. In pieces. Like a jigsaw puzzle. It was fierce slow, but you can imagine how surprising and encouraging that was. Often his bits of recollections related to food. One day, he blurted out something about Papa's sea trout. Not just trout. But sea trout. During a dinner he whispered something that sounded like Fan-bo-chin. We finally understood he meant the pastry, Franzbrötchen. Maja enlisted his help to make a batch. After that, he spent more time in the kitchen helping her cook and bake. He was even becoming quite good on the penny whistle.

And how shall I put this? His physical passion for me grew more affectionate and tender. The looks he gave me weren't always tinged with sexual desire. At least I read them that way. I hoped the great love he bore me in the beginning was rekindling. Still, if I gazed at him lovingly, even from across a room, he would take my hand and lead me to our bedroom to make love, no matter what else was going on or who was around. One thing hadn't changed. He knew what he wanted and pursued it.

Well, love doesn't have to be subtle, I offered.

Ya, no, it doesn't. Wanting is part of loving. I hope you get the chance to take your own advice.

The only response I could come up with was 'well played.'

I was grateful for Kristers' new tenderness, of course. But among other things, I missed his playful eloquence. I had given up on him ever fully returning to his former self, but little by little my hope grew that he was returning to us.

September 1950, Beyond Words Academy in Carlow was scheduled to open. We rented and renovated an old school. Through a series of auditions, we had twelve students, including four internationals. And three teachers committed to commute from the RIAM in Dublin, for violin, viola, cello and string bass. I was the piano teacher. We planned to add more instruments as we grew. The Steinway from the Benedicts sat in the recital hall like a solitaire gemstone.

One beautiful August morning, two weeks before opening day, I left Kristers asleep and took my weekly prayer walk with Brynn. For an hour or so. Sometimes longer. In her endearing way, she described the cloudless sky as a clean blue canvas. She thanked Gott for it and prayed that whatever Gott painted on it, we trusted his goodness would prevail.

Returning to the house, we were alarmed to see Dr. Deegan's car in the drive. After the war, he returned to his practice in Carlow. The cook had called him. She said Kristers missed breakfast, which he never did, and they found him unconscious in our bed. His vital signs were good, but he appeared to be in a coma. An ambulance took him to Dublin. I rode along by his side. It reminded me of the terrible trips between Sandbostel and Lübberstedt. Kristers remained unconscious, but I talked to him the whole way.

Needless to say, the clean blue canvas turned dark and ominous.

By late afternoon, the same team of doctors discovered the bullet had migrated. It was creating pressure on new areas and might breach a ventricle. They recommended immediate surgery to remove it. But there were unpredictable risks, including brain damage, and it was always possible Kristers might not survive the procedure.

Overnight, the rich days of summer turned into an early winter.

Anyone who has ever spent time in a hospital waiting room knows the razor edge of those hours. As you know, my friend, any minute life can take a drastic turn. Just the look of the staff person who comes out to give an update can capsize your world.

Understand, this was 1950. The medical team operated without all the new high-tech wizardry. Even X-ray imaging came with risks to the patients and technicians. The lead doctor informed me they were using some new radiology method as well, to map the area around the bullet, encephalo-something. Again, I had to trust what I couldn't control.

The surgery lasted seven hours. We got three updates from nurses. The first two began with, "Not to worry." Kristers was doing fine. The third brought good news. "The doctors have successfully removed the bullet." An odd impulse rose in me. I requested the bullet. Finally, the head surgeon himself appeared. He had a grave look on his face. Crossing the room, he extended his hands to me and managed a smile. What I read as sombre news was just weariness. All had gone well. Very well. Minimal bleeding. The ventricle was not ruptured. Kristers was strong and out of danger.

Aneska took up her broad brush like I had seen many times.

But are we ever totally out of danger, my friend? Every day is on a razor edge, ya? The number of our days is in Gott's book, but hidden to us. Most days are normal, beautiful, boring, or challenging. Not catastrophic or lethal. The day that takes us to glory is only painful for the ones who remain behind, but glorious for the one who is rescued from the deep. Did I borrow that from Melville or one of your songs?

I wasn't sure I didn't borrow it from Melville, but I credited him to Aneska.

I had prepared my heart many times for Kristers to crossover. That awful night in Sandbostel. The days following. Every seizure. And yet he remained. Gott granted us many beautiful and challenging days together.

In that waiting room, I prepared my heart again to release him. I prayed, 'Thank you, Lord, for making beauty from ashes again and again. Thank you for our beating hearts, for knowing you are near and for all the days you give us together, stormy or clear."

She couldn't help herself. Did you think I let that worship song idea slip by? Even though songs about thanking the Lord have been written thousands of times.

But Gott knew I wanted something else. I wanted more. So, I asked him for more. Out of his mercy and goodness, he granted it.

But what if the doctor had come out with the worst news? That Kristers was gone? Did that mean Gott was not merciful or good?

Aneska looked over at Brynn's portrait.

As Brynn used to say, Gott's goodness is the well we draw from in the desert of affliction.

It might have been merciful and good to call Kristers home that day. Excruciating to me, but in time I would have been glad for Kristers. For his release. Just as I am now. My Kristers is home. More whole and alive than ever. And I'll see him soon enough.

She gazed into the glowing embers.

Where was I? Oh, ya. After all the explanations, the doctor reached into his breast pocket and pulled out the bullet in a little plastic bag. He placed it in my hand. The last one to touch it, before the doctor, was Blixt. Six years later, there it was lying in my hand. I rarely thought of Blixt. The bullet connected us again. But more pressing thoughts of Kristers pushed his memory aside.

I wondered what happened to the bullet, but again, assumed Aneska would get to that detail in time.

The doctor told us there were many unknowns about the long-term outcome, that the human brain is a highly complex creation. Countless connections and impulses follow pathways, and in theory can make new pathways. Kristers' brain would likely experience a 'reset' he called it, but it could take quite some time.

He was right. The months after the surgery were almost like starting over. Katie O'Grady Quinn, now remarried, returned with her new husband, Finnegan. Like her, he was a delight, and a calmer, perfect balance to Katie. He was a writer, like you, my friend.

The academy launched without me. Good, good people stepped in to make that happen, including Hans Benedict. He came and stayed through Christmas. Brigitte joined us for the holidays. Hans and Kristers spent hours together. Hans read a lot to him.

We watched Kristers' strength grow as his hair grew back. Like Samson, Brynn claimed.

Through Katie's creative touch, in less time than before, Kristers' speaking ability rebooted, I guess you could say. Though still not his voice. His letter 'r' improved, but he often pronounced the letters 's', 'z' and soft 'c' like a 'th.' It was endearing and sometimes made him sound Spanish. His penny whistle stayed in his back pocket. We hid it sometimes just to get a break. Zuza and Valor played and scribbled artwork with him. He and Maja started baking again. And we noticed new things. Longer sentences. He asked more questions. About the people in these pictures. And the scar on his head.

I showed Kristers the bullet for the first time and told him the story. The choice he made for me. He got very quiet. I couldn't tell how much he understood or remembered. He just sat, looking at the bullet between his fingers. Finally, all he whispered was, "Bad man." Katie and the doctors took that as a very good sign that Kristers understood bad and good. The bullet never came up again. And our bond deepened. He reached for my hand more and would stroke my hair at night.

As the holidays approached, I had an idea for a Christmas gift for Kristers. I had mixed emotions about it, but found a local jeweler to melt down the bullet. He molded it into a small bird flying upward, the size of a charm on a bracelet. I didn't expect Kristers to understand, but for me it was a tribute to the pigeon, God's providence, really. It obviously affected the bullet's path, and likely contributed to his survival. For me, the bird also symbolized Kristers' spirit rising from the trauma. I mounted it on a chain. On Christmas morning, he unwrapped it. I put it around his neck, but Zuza loved it so much he took it off and gave it to her. She wore it every day for over a year until I explained where it came from. After that, she couldn't bring herself to wear it. I'm not sure where it is now.

I realized I didn't need it around. Symbols can be good, but I had Kristers right in front of me. Grief and hope can make you do curious things.

As we sipped tea and gazed into the fire, I told her during my grief many years ago, out of my love for whales, I built a giant humpback whale tail in my garage, thirteen feet wide and six feet tall, fastened together out of scrap wood. Sometimes I worked on it all night because I couldn't sleep. It was some kind of symbolic act. Maybe a Jonah reference of feeling captive and carried deep under the sea. In fact, I named it "Deep". It was meant to stand in my backyard to look like a whale lived there, but I didn't finish it. When we moved from that house, I broke it into pieces and hauled it to the junkyard with a lot of other stuff.

Birds and whales. Powerful symbols, my friend. I'm glad you returned from the deep. And know it's possible.

There it was again, Aneska's depth and compassion. And her hand reaching for mine.

In late November, in the middle of the day, it was snowing. I found Kristers in the music room by himself staring at a music folio, Satie's Gymnopedie No.1. I told you about it before. The one Professor Nachtneder called 'unangemessen,' inappropriate. Kristers handed it to me. I went to the piano. He walked to one of the large front windows and stood looking out at the snow. I began to play it. The piece is only about three and a half minutes. Very gentle, spacious. It's a bittersweet dance between major and minor chords. Kristers stood with his back to me the whole time. Framed in the beautiful arched window against the falling snow, it was easy to imagine Kristers as I first met him.

As the final minor chord rang out, he turned and looked at me. It was as close to the look as I had seen since that night, just before the taming. His chin and lower lip quivered, and his eyes teared up. He walked to me, took my hand and led me to our bedroom. We hadn't been intimate since before the surgery. I felt our soul connection being restored. Silently. Mysteriously. Beyond words.

That's when Satie's folio on top of the stack became a signal that he wanted me physically. And the tenderness of those interludes grew.

It would be sheer denial to say I heard this sine invidia, without envy. Their connection, even muted and diminished by the damage done, awakened want in me. Pause here and put on Satie's Gymnopedie No.1 and you will get a flavor of that hunger.

Miracles kept finding Katie O'Grady. Kristers' painting and drawing went to a new level. He painted this one over the fireplace a couple of weeks before Katie and Finn departed. I still love to say their names. Katie O'Grady and Finnigan Quinn.

I threw in, Sounds like their hearts rhymed, too.

Ya, precisely. How lovely. Two hearts that rhyme in a dissonant world is a beautiful thing, my friend. One of the most beautiful.

She took a sip of tea and added,

I may as well tell you. I'm praying you find a rhyming heart. As you know, the Lord is fond of duets.

Before I could think of a response she pointed at Kristers' painting above the mantel and continued.

This painting is dated February 1951. We all gathered in the studio for its unveiling. Kristers pulled the cover away. We applauded and cheered wildly. It was his largest canvas ever. So simple, understated, but powerful. The string of barbed wire surprised me the most. We assumed it surfaced from somewhere in his memory, which was another remarkable good sign.

After the unveiling, Katie announced Kristers had something to say. He took my hand. What came out of his mouth thrilled us more than the painting.

My darling looked me in the eye and whispered. "Anethka, you are my thnowdrop."

I burst into tears and fell into his arms. We held on to each other. As you can imagine, the moment was seismic. But Katie said there was more. Kristers held me at arm's-length. He took a deep breath and sighed. With an intense look on his face, he repeated "Anethka, you are my thnowdrop." Then added, "But I will never drop you in the thnow." And grinned.

It was a joke! His first joke! Everyone burst out laughing! He seemed very pleased with himself. Zuza still remembers that. She was, let's see, six. She repeated his joke for years. On top of all that, Maja had made a cake for the occasion. She brought it in decorated with a snowdrop blossom made of icing.

I didn't need a doctor to tell me Kristers' joke was a remarkable sign of a sophisticated cognitive process.

Aneska made a brief editorial comment, which I always enjoyed.

Humor, by the way, my friend, is just one aspect of human nature that disproves Darwin's theory of evolution. How does humor and laughter insure the survival of the fittest?

I told her it was about the only way a skinny boy like me survived the bullies at school.

Point taken. But I'm sure you can see, in just a simple wordplay, my charming Kristers resurrected a bit that day. Once again, the Lord made beauty from ashes. My friend, that's just what he does.

The next morning, I woke to see Kristers looking at me from his pillow. He whispered three words that filled my being, "Good morning, thnowdrop." He whispered them to me nearly every morning for the rest of his life. I suspect that's what he'll say to me when I cross over. Either that or "It only follows, my love." Whatever he says, I'll finally hear it in his sweet voice. More than anything, Kristers' growing affection proved what he said the last time I heard his voice. He really didn't need his brain to remember or love me.

CHAPTER FORTY-FIVE

THE CRESCENDO

Time is a funny thing, my friend. In life and in music. A favorite song begins, draws you along, and when it ends, you realize you didn't notice the passing of time for the beauty of the music. But you are farther downstream. Those early years in Ireland flew by like sonatas. They felt like months. The decades became symphonies. More than half a century carried us into this new millenium.

I blinked, and Zuza and Valor were taller than me. The academy flourished. With Brynn's help, Kristers and I became dual citizens of Ireland and Germany. The new version of Kristers became as endearing as the original, even in the absence of his voice, verbal eloquence and full mental and memory capacity. Painting, drawing, cooking, and playing with the kids became his main pursuits. Besides me.

Her chuckle was like a drum sting after a punch line.

Zuza married Darby's son, Sean Carl O'Cullen, named after his father and mine. They grew up together. Blending our families brought Brynn great joy. Valor, I think I mentioned, married the daughter of the dairyman down the lane. They both married young. How could I protest that? Thank Gott they found rhyming hearts and lived locally. So many families scatter and drift apart. My children began having children. We became a blended Irish-German clan. The years danced along like an Irish folk song in 6/8 time.

As you know yourself, the world at large battled new bouts of tyranny, communism, the threat of nuclear annihilation and civil unrest. But heartache gave us a personal respite for a long, blessed season in County Carlow. The third movement, even with the scare of Kristers' surgery, filled us to the brim with new life and vitality.

Like a well-poured Guinness, I interjected. On my tour of the famous brewery in Dublin, I learned the proper way to pour one.

Precisely. You're thinking more like an Irishman every day. Shall we take this tale to the pub for one?

We did. It was midafternoon. Only a few people were there. We sat near the fireplace. Aneska continued over a Guinness.

After my return trip to Lübberstedt in 1955, I began composing my piano concerto, though I told no one. It's possibly the longest gestation of any musical piece in history. Something about walking around Lübberstedt and Hamburg again, especially standing in the Laeiszhalle, awakened my desire to compose. Anyone who visits their childhood places understands how much it can bring to the surface. For many years, I explored bits and pieces, themes and melodies. But Kristers, our children and Darby's, and the academy, were more important and pressing than composing. And then came enkelkinder, grandchildren! It was a glorious season.

But seasons are seasonal, ya? Heartache can only take a Guinness break for so long.

I raised a glass to her wit with a 'Sláinte' and flipped her comment into a line for a country song, "even heartache takes a beer break now and then." Aneska's laugh was like the frothy head on a Guinness.

Heartache eventually remembered our address. There's a picture in the study of the whole clan. Nearly all of us. It was taken at Brynn's eightieth birthday, 1981. We were blessed that Jakob and Brynn both lived to see all the grandchildren born.

Brynn adored all the children. And they adored her. They called her 'Kweenana'. As a toddler, Zuza gave her the title Queen Nana.

But Valor slurred it into into Kweenana. And the name stuck. Two years after that picture was taken, in March 1983, she joined her husband Sean in glory. One morning in the study, she just bowed her head and slipped away, in the same chair I sit in for our conversations. The evening before she crossed over, we were all together playing music in the front room. In fact, Saoirse played "Dear Lord Jesus, Take My Hand." She would have been fourteen, no, ya, about to turn fifteen.

I marveled again at how keenly Aneska could hold and grasp so much detail and dates. The same way I marvel that every note in a symphony can come from one mind. I asked her how she remembered so much, so well.

I think that may be because over the years I began to see the people in my life like an orchestra. They all play their part. Each enters at a certain point. Some are soloists. Some form ensembles. But every person contributes to the symphony. And I play a part in their life symphonies as well.

Her answer didn't surprise me. And neither did her summation.

And the co-writer and conductor of them all is Gott himself.

Dear Brynn played such a key role in all our lives. In the lives of so many. At her memorial, the Cathedral of the Assumption here in Carlow couldn't hold all the guests for her homegoing, as you call it. I like that term very much.

Jakob is not in that picture. But his widow Charlotte and their sons are, Liam and Carl. I haven't told you, in 1975 Jakob was lost at sea in a storm saving another man on his crew. I guess heroism runs in the Pfieffer men.

And the O'Cullens, I added. Captain O'Cullen.

Ya, brilliant. Brilliant recall on your part, I should say.

Jakob has two memorial stones. One is in a cemetery for fishermen and sailors near the docks in Dublin. And another one you may have seen here in the family cemetery, not far from Kristers' marker. It bears the scripture from Revelation about what will happen when the Lord wraps things up, "And the sea gave up the dead that were in it."

I visited the family cemetery only once when I first arrived, at first curious and thinking it would help piece timelines together. But I decided not to discover too much ahead of Aneska's sequence of events. I found her trail was more interesting to follow if I didn't know too much of what was ahead. Knowing the future could take the intrigue out of the present. I'm not sure why at this point I connected that same sense of mystery to Aneska's prayer for me to find a rhyming heart, but I did. What I didn't know felt like hope. That, in itself, was a welcome reset in my soul.

The beauty and losses of those years shaped my composing, as I hope you will hear in the concerto. Joy and sorrow live hand in hand, ya? In a dance. Like a duet between a penny whistle and cello. Or a bowed string bass and uilleann pipe.

I had the feeling Aneska was tipping her hand about elements of her concerto. Come April 29 I would know. Similar to what remained of her story, I didn't want to know too much til then.

Especially miraculous through all those years was Kristers' steady transformation. He became more animated. And curious. Whispering all the way. He cooked with some of his old flair. We planted herbs and flowers together. I kept a journal of the flashes of memory that blurted from his mouth. His understanding of our story grew little by little and so did his skill on the pennywhistle. The first time he joined me and the local musicians at the pub, the lads raved about him. But it was a challenge to convince him not every song needed a pennywhistle. The cure came from one of the musicians. He gave Kristers lessons on the bodhrán, the Irish hand drum. It has a wooden beater.

I was familiar with it. Like a lot of tourists, I bought one on my first trip to Ireland, and learned the hard way how much skill it took to play one well. Having a more than fairly good sense of rhythm, I never mastered it. It became a souvenir hanging on a wall.

Kristers played it nonstop for a month. Even at the dinner table. Drove us crazy. But he truly had a knack for it. The pub gang carved out breaks for bodhrán solos. He could make your heart rate go up. My favorite part was the joy on his face.

He also got funnier. One winter after a blizzard, he chased me outside, carried me to a snowdrift, and fell backwards into it. Lying there, face to face, he whispered, "Thee, I did not drop you." We rolled around in the snow like school kids while Brynn, Zuza and Valor laughed behind the front windows. The kids joined us for a snowball fight. Til the day she left us, Brynn said it was one of her favorite memories. That we looked like a happy family in a snow globe.

There was no Lutheran church near us, so we split our Sundays between the Cathedral of the Assumption, Brynn's home church, and the Anglican church in Staplestown, just fifteen minutes from us. Brynn bridged the divide between Catholic and Protestant with such grace. Ireland could have benefited from her example.

Easter Sunday, 1964, after church at Staplestown, Kristers witnessed a baptism, a full immersion in a nearby pond. The next day at breakfast, he announced he wanted to be baptized in the River Barrow by the pastor from Staplestown. I knew he was baptized in Göttingen when he was twelve. It was recorded in the Latva family Bible. But like so many things, Kristers didn't remember that.

He started asking questions about heaven after the JFK assassination the November before. I wondered if he should watch it. The news reels disturbed him. Disturbed all of us, of course. We watched the funeral procession and cried for his wife and children. Brynn had a picture of JFK in the front room, like so many Irish Catholic homes. It's still there. I didn't understand why it hit Kristers so hard until one day, he stood staring at the picture of JKF. He whispered, "Thot in the head. Like me."

It was a mixed blessing Kristers understood some of what happened to him. But it sank under the weight of wondering how much loss of his former self he could even process. I think it weighed me down more than him. Because I remembered how much he lost. At the same time, I cherished how much remained.

After seeing the baptism at Easter, Kristers was adamant. He needed to be baptized. Brynn warned him the River Barrow would be fierce cold.

Kristers told her, "The Lord fathed the croth. I can fathe the cold."

How dear is that? His response assured me of two things. The passionate Kristers I fell in love with in Lübberstedt was still alive. And it showed all of us he had a depth of mental and spiritual comprehension. We had wonderful talks about it all. He understood who Christ is and what the resurrection meant for his soul. He understood sin and the need for a Savior, for "thalvation." And heaven. He wanted to go there someday to be with Jesus and see his parents, my family members, and JFK!

But the crowning moment came when the pastor asked him why he wanted to be baptized.

Kristers answer filled my soul. He said, "My thin, hith forgiveneth, and heaven. Pathtor, it only followth." That's the first time I had heard that phrase from him in nineteen years.

So, the arrangements were made. On a cool, clear day, April 4, on my birthday and our wedding anniversary, Kristers was baptized in the River Barrow. I remember we had chicken soup, hot cornbread and tea after to warm everyone up. We wrote it down in the O'Cullen family Bible and in Mama's.

After his baptism, Kristers began to volunteer to say grace over our meals. It was usually a short list of things. His whisper gave it such reverence. "Thank you, Lord, for the day, for food, for family, for your grathe." One morning he surprised us all, me especially. He began his usual list of things. At the end he paused and added, "and thekth with Anethka thith morning. amen." We all opened our eyes at the same time. Kristers was grinning. There was a moment of silence before the laughter exploded. He and I had been intimate early that morning.

I couldn't help laughing either.

But our joy had to dance with sorrow. In 1965 Petra lost Rolf. He had a heart attack plowing their field. A year later she remarried, to the son of the old mayor of Sandbostel. A week before her wedding Brigitte Benedict died. I attended both services. I never wanted to return to Sandbostel, but Kristers traveled with me. I thought the sights might jumpstart some memories.

The town hall was gone. Replaced by shops. Petra's wedding was in the little church where we were married. Kristers walked me down the aisle. We stood with Petra. He was very quiet. There was a funny, dear moment. When the paster said, "you may kiss the bride," Kristers kissed me. Remnants of Stalag X-B were there as a war memorial, but we didn't go. The hunting cabin was falling down. I pried a wall board loose where he scratched the formula. It's under our bed. I can show it to you.

I was eager to see it.

In Göttingen, Kristers lit up when he saw Hans. At his childhood house, he stared a long time at a small painting by his brother Stephan. Hans insisted we take it to Ireland. With Brigitte gone, Hans boarded music students from the University. He visited us once more. He died five years after her. Zuza and Valor went with me to his memorial. I gave a eulogy and played one piece. Can you guess what that was?

Dear Lord Jesus, Take My Hand?

Precisely. Hans, blessed Hans. In his will, he bequeathed the estate to the university.

Petra outlived her second husband, too. I invited her to come live with us. She sold the farm. What a joy to have her around. Between she and Brynn, they lavished the children and grandchildren with love. She took some of the wonderful pictures around the house. When she was dying, Petra asked to be buried in the O'Cullen family cemetery. She said the most endearing thing, that going to heaven from Ireland would be a much shorter trip. You'll see what she requested on her marker. Below her name are just two words, 'Miriam's friend.'

Aneska gazed into the fireplace, ruminating, gathering her thoughts.

Even with the sorrows, what a beautiful life Gott gave us. Like a very long crescendo. The Academy thrived. Our children and grandchildren thrived along with the O'Cullens. Kristers and I did, too. When I carved out a little time, the beauty and energy of our life flowed through my fingers, filling page after page of sheet music.

One day at the piano, I set Kristers original sketch of a snowdrop blossom on the music stand. Without even thinking, I immediately described it in a delicate, seven-note pattern that rose and fell and hung there begging for the next phrase. I knew after this motif was introduced in the second movement, it would reappear throughout, like a sweet, recurring memory.

She sang it to me. Dah-dah-daaah-dee-daaah-dah-daah. D E F♯ A G F♯ F♯ I couldn't get it out of my head. Still can't.

Once the major themes and dynamics spilled out on the pages, I spent two years studying the orchestrations of my favorite composers. The Royal Academy in Dublin brought in a guest instructor in orchestration recommended by Hans Benedict. He was from, of all places, Göttingen University. A Professor Johann Dichter. Are you ready for a divine chess move? He was the nephew of Herr Nachtneder, my piano professor from Hamburg! Ya, and if that wasn't divine choreography enough, his family were acquaintances of the Latva family as a boy in Göttingen! You can imagine how we connected. He told me his uncle passed peacefully about ten years after the war and often spoke fondly of me. Of the many wonders in my life, I had the privilege to study under Nachtneder's nephew for six months. By the way, Dichter is German for 'poet.' And he was. My concerto would not be the same without his touch.

Do you see it again, my friend? We plan. Gott directs.

I explained to Herr Dichter that my concerto, like our journey, was linear, direct, no frills, influenced by classical and Irish music, with emotional outbursts of agony and elation peppered with Mama's steady quarter note constitution. The first time I played him the major themes from each movement, he understood completely.

Without getting too technical, Herr Dichter helped me interpret the character of our family saga, our love story, and Kristers' valiant journey, into orchestral expression. Where best to use octaves; voicings on a wide variety of chords, like diminished sevenths; surprising chromatic melody lines and chord transitions; rapidly cascading and ascending arabesques, runs; and the art of contrast, pianissimo to fortissimo, feathery soft to fierce loud. He guided me in placing recapitulations and variations of themes in their proper places. And suggested fresh combinations of instruments. I intuitively leaned away from decorative baroque frills and trills on the piano, except sparsely, to paint the feeling of the beauty of nature and blossoming sections. He was very enthusiastic about my desire to integrate traditional Irish instruments. Through it all, Professor Dichter never wrote a single note, but his touch is on the entire concerto. Does that remind you of anyone, my friend?

I knew she meant God but to slag her I said, 'Ya, the government.' Aneska laughed loud. And made a toast with the last of our Guinness.

To the hand of Gott on our lives and loves.

CHAPTER FORTY-SIX

THE TICKET

During the many years of composing the concerto, besides Professor Dichter, the only person I played pieces of it for was Kristers. I'm not sure he understood the pieces were part of a larger work. But he loved it. And I suspect because of his experience at Mahler's symphony, he was fond of giving me a standing ovation.

Periodically, I caught Zuza and Brynn, and later Saoirse, listening at the door. I told them as little as possible and some wee fairy tales about creating passages, exercises really, for the students at the Academy. Brynn wasn't fooled. She knew my dream and was my biggest supporter and patron. Upon her death, I found out she set aside funds in her will to help bring it to the concert hall.

I have to take something back. I played some of the concerto for Hans Benedict on my visit to Göttingen for Brigitte's memorial service. It thrilled him to hear my dream taking shape. After that, he always mentioned it in his letters. He assumed I would debut it at the Laeiszhalle in Hamburg. But I told him my spirit said Dublin was the place for the premier, to honor all Ireland had given us, as well as its musical influence. I hoped for a follow-up in Hamburg. Besides, I joked, I wasn't sure many of us would be alive by the time I finished it, including me. Sadly, so many are not.

Finally, with the help of the Royal Academy, the conductor of the National Symphony Orchestra agreed to review my manuscript and hear portions of it. To my relief, he raved. He paced around the room and begged me to let him conduct it. He thought it sensational to have an original work "by one of Ireland's own." I wish Brynn could have heard him call me that. More than anyone else, she made me Irish.

The Royal Academy began at once to create momentum. Word spread. Over the next two years there was fundraising and promoting. Specialty players to audition. Guests to invite. Polishing and music folios to copy. Rehearsals to schedule. Every aspect was coming together, like the finale of a long journey. A date in the symphony calendar was about to be set.

And then in winter, Kristers fell ill. It started with abdominal pain, nausea. That led to weight loss and fatigue. By the time it was diagnosed, it was too late. Pancreatic cancer. The doctor gave him six months. Barring a miracle, it would be our last Spring together.

That kind of reality is always so jarring. More so I think because Kristers was always so healthy. Physically. We both were. He was spryer than me. On our long walks, it was an effort to keep up with him. So, it was strange when he needed to lean on me just to walk down the drive and back for the mail. He didn't have the breath to play the penny whistle anymore. He managed a few paintings. But even as he declined, his spirit remained pleasant, even buoyant.

Standing at the river one day, he asked what we both knew. In his whisper it sounded like a secret just between the two of us. "I'm getting my ticket to heaven before you, aren't I, Anethka?"

I told him, "Ya, my Siegfried will probably see Jesus before his Brünnhilde." He didn't understand and asked who that was. I told him they were names from a very old, very beautiful love story.

He asked me, "And they were together again?"

"Ya. stet." Always.

He didn't have six months.

Aneska paused. A long time. I wondered if she was tracing their days through that Spring, deciding how much to tell. Whatever her thoughts, she sketched it simply, like Kristers' paintings.

Saoirse and I played for him. Zuza and Valor and their children, and Jakob and Darby's all visited. Some read to him. Near the end, they came by to feel a squeeze from his hand and kiss his cheek.

In his last hours, he and I didn't talk much. We didn't need to. The look was back. The last words I spoke to him were, "I will see you on the other side, my love."

He whispered, "Thnowdrop, it only followth."

He closed his eyes. His breathing wound down like a clock. And stopped. Just like Mama.

She paused.

I thought mine would, too. But it didn't. And here I am. Still here. With you, my friend.

I took her hand for a moment.

Blixt was right. He said I would carry the weight of Kristers' decision every day. In every note I played. But like all evil, he misjudged what he could never understand. I carried the weight of the glory of Kristers' act of love. And the shining light of it. Every day. Like snowdrops bear the glory of hope in winter. I carried that glory in every note, every touch and kiss, through the many years Gott gifted us. What was meant to harm me, blessed me, and countless others, through three generations, and counting.

I know Kristers would agree, and hope like I do, that every day remaining and every note in my concerto speaks Soli Deo Gloria.

CHAPTER FORTY-SEVEN

THE CAESURA

After more than six weeks at Snowdrop Manor it was time to return to the States until the concerto. As the Irish say, I was bleedin' sad to leave. Aneska used that term to me a few days before my departure. Naturally, I wanted to see my children. And besides, between the recordings, my notes and Aneska's translated diaries, I needed time to put the manuscript in order, up to the point of the big event. Besides, Aneska's time for the next two months would be jammed with preparations. I was scheduled to return a week before April 29, then three weeks later travel with Aneska's entourage to Hamburg for what was sure to be another crowning performance in Laeiszhalle.

In the last two sessions before my departure, she showed me a collage of videos beginning in the late 1950s taken on early 8mm movie cameras. Zuza had digitized all the formats from over the years. Watching everyone grow and change through the decades felt as close to time travel as one can get. Like the omniscient view God has of everyone throughout history. In a few hours, I saw Aneska and Kristers, so young and vibrant, grow old. The graceful Brynn O'Cullen and her handsome son, the pilot, Darby, too. I watched the Carlow Academy expand, and the Latva and O'Cullen children change from babies to adults.

The day before my flight, Aneska slagged me by saying she hoped it wouldn't make me too mad if Saoirse drove me to the airport. She had volunteered to take me. Let's just say I was as happy as Larry.

The most pleasant thing about the ride was how much we laughed. Saoirse's wit peppered Aneska's stories of Kristers' quick mind and humor. Combined with her beauty and Irish accent, 'charming' could only hint at how delightful she was. I mangled some Irish slang just to amuse her and told her I saw the family videos, had practically watched her grow up.

She slagged me in a faux American Southern accent.

"And here Ah ayum, the full-growed human bean before you." She apologized for the "hahdship" it must have been for me to eat fish and chips without cream gravy and grits.

But she also pivoted easily to more serious matters. She asked what my children were like, and how they were handling the divorce. Her shift from humor to empathy and vulnerability was seamless. She said her marriage was not blessed with children, which was difficult with babies being born all around. The grief she must have borne for her late husband expressed itself only in several very honoring mentions of him, followed by, "Of course, we had our struggles. Like most marriages."

We arrived at the airport too soon. Sitting in her car, she made a comment that Aneska and Ireland must now hold a permanent place in me, in her words, "like a tattoo on my soul." This led to a discussion about tattoos. I showed her the only one I had on my right upper arm near the shoulder: the tail of a humpback whale diving into waves over the words "Deep calls to Deep" from Psalm 42, with three birds flying overhead to represent my children. My son, Will, asked me to draw it for him, and then talked me into getting similar tattoos the same day in Nashville. Saoirse took off her right shoe and winter sock to reveal a lovely, simple tattoo of, can you guess? A snowdrop blossom. The stem started at the bottom outside of her heel between two long leaves, tinted green. It curved around the back of her ankle bone and bent gently forward on the side of her foot into a blossom with three petals. It looked like the snowdrop from Kristers' painting over the fireplace. She disclosed she had one other tattoo, but to show me that one would require knowing each other a lot better. Would you be surprised if I told you that enticing information became a quest? Once a man, always a boy, ya?

My daughter had suggested I get a tattoo in Ireland so I floated the idea that when I returned for the concerto, I would like to get one, as an indelible reminder of my time in Ireland. No surprise, one of the best tattoo shops in Dublin was not far from her brownstone.

It was time to go. To my delight, she offered to pick me up when I returned and asked for my phone. She added all her contact info.

The next thing she said was the last thing I expected. Saoirse suggested I consider bringing my children for the concerto. She reasoned it would be so momentous that even my laudable word skills would be no match for experiencing it themselves. And meeting Aneska would be indelible for them as well. I was still savoring the word 'laudable' when she offered her cottage for their stay. Of course, I loved the idea, had secretly wished it. I hedged at the cost being considerable. She stopped me and said, "You must know by now, where there's an Aneska, there's a way." I said I would float the idea to them, pending their schedules.

Saoirse thanked me profusely for giving my valuable time and heart to writing her Mimi's story. How important it was for it to be told. We parted with a warm embrace, slathered in intrigue and anticipation. At least I was.

On the flight back, again in first class seating, I had time to reflect. Since Zuza's phone call in January, I was different. Under the spell of the Emerald Isle and Aneska's aura, something had shifted. Lifted. I knew what Aneska would call it: mending and hope. It felt like freedom.

The moment the plane touched down in Florida, I did what I always do, texted my children to let them know I landed. And added one more, to Saoirse, as she had requested.

The weeks trudged.

As I often do when writing, I sat in my car on the beach, feeling the breeze, hearing the surf. Looking northeast over the Atlantic toward Ireland was different now. Out of sight could not be out of mind. Listening to the recordings, editing, and reading Aneska's saga took me on her journey again. She loomed larger in my mind than ever, like a heroine from an ancient legend. But she and her world were real and just across an ocean, fierce real and vibrant. Aneska had held my hand, laughed at my quips. We ate together, cried and played music together.

Texts back and forth with Saoirse became daily. Often, multiple times a day. Quippy, wry and endearing. Sometimes she was so profound I swore it could be Aneska on the other end.

Here's a prime example. After we texted about going through difficult times, she wrote this prayer: "God, you have brought us through, time and time again, from enormous loss and heartache. And through these valleys, you continue to pour the riches of your tender heart through us to the world. While sorrow isn't a preferred path, we cannot deny the golden good we find there. Thank you for trusting us with this gift."

See what I mean? Who calls sorrow a gift? Besides the Apostle Paul. And who thanks God for the "golden good" found in it? Apparently, legendary faith runs in Aneska's bloodline. Saoirse concluded with: "Lord, be with us today as we navigate facets of our lives that were not on our bucket lists. Disappointments, griefs, losses, desires, longings, gifts, surprises, and deep callings calling to deep."

Captivating, ya?

Aneska texted as well. The pub gang wondered when I was coming back to play with them. Zuza kept me informed about preparations for the concert, as well as details and timing about printing the book in Ireland and releasing it.

Four weeks after returning to the States, Aneska texted: "Saoirse tells me you two have a 'very healthy text life' Ha! She's deep water, ya?"

I responded, "Ya, wonder where she gets that?"

A few days later, Zuza called to say all the arrangements, including plane tickets, were made for me and my children to make the return trip. Apparently, Saoirse and her late husband traveled extensively. Between her airline points and the gift in Brynn O'Cullen's will, four tickets were paid for. First class. All I had to do was choose the airports and dates. An unforeseen bucket list item? Indeed. I could endure navigating this kind of surprise.

To prepare my children for the experience, a week before our departure I forwarded a draft of the manuscript to them to read on the plane. At the same time, I sent it to Zuza and Aneska with the understanding the book would be completed to include accounts of the performances in Dublin and Hamburg. After proofreading and, of course, upon their approval, it would be published and printed in Ireland. Zuza informed me Aneska insisted the cover must be Kristers' painting hanging over the fireplace in the study. I replied, "Perfect."

* * *

The surreal and golden day arrived for all four of us to board an Air Lingus to Dublin. Eight hours later, we exited customs at Dublin airport about 9:30 a.m. to the broad smile and open arms of Saoirse. She hugged my children first, telling them by their looks and names they must be part Irish. She and Emmaline compared Claddagh rings. Saoirse finally got around to me. It was an effort not to hold the embrace too long.

We piled into her Land Rover. She and Emmaline chattered away. My sons, Will and Liam, nodded off. Aneska was at the National Concert Hall for rehearsal, so even though I would stay in the guest house at Snowdrop Manor, Saoirse's cottage was our first stop. The winter landscape of my first sleepy drive in January had surrendered to the new green of the Emerald Isle. My drowsy boys missed most of it.

We all agreed her cottage was right out of a storybook. I had only seen it in pictures attached to her texts. 'Cottage' was an understatement. A blue hue covered fields nearby. Bluebells. They lined the gravel driveway. Weathered stone masonry, climbing ivy, gray slate roof and arched green front door gave her cottage a Hansel and Gretel vibe. But inside it was a thoroughly modern home. In the entryway, a message on a chalk board greeted my children, "Welcome to Ireland, new friends, Dia dhuit," in Saoirse's beautiful handwriting. The place smelled of a wood-burning fireplace and something fresh-baked.

Saoirse showed us around. The kitchen was fully stocked, including Irish cheese, a growler of Guinness, Maja's bread and fruit preserves. Three bedrooms upstairs. A master on the main floor. A terrace overlooking the River Barrow. Firewood for the cozy stone hearth. Extra keys for the cottage and Land Rover. On the pillow of each bed lay an envelope addressed to each of them containing personal notes from Aneska and Saoirse, as well as crucial information, a simple map to Snowdrop Manor, but most important to my children, the Wi-Fi password, "Snowdrop2."

Bringing them was the right idea. How could I ever fully describe Saoirse, her cottage and the Irish landscape, much less Snowdrop Manor and the concerto? Meeting Aneska would be monumental for them. Reading may be a way of seeing, but actually seeing Aneska, Saoirse and Ireland would be tattooed on their souls for the rest of their lives. Not to mention hearing their voices, the music, and smelling and tasting Maja's magic. Throw in the still waters, new green pastures and an evening making music in the pub, the whole experience carried the prospect of making even the best of the rest of the world silver and bronze runnerups.

To be fair to the rest of the world, as Brynn told Aneska that November in 1945, "Everyone finds their own pot of gold where love is bound to lead."

Saoirse drove me to Snowdrop Manor before heading back to Dublin. Our caesura had been anything but silent. As a result, the emotional landscape had changed. Something had deepened beyond the easy laughter and witty verbal ping pong, as we called it. There was a common ground beyond our connection to Aneska and our affection for her. There was an ease that comes with friendship. And a mutual care. There was, perhaps, most important, a sense of rhyming in our heart journeys. And as a songwriter, I'm a sucker for rhyming. Granted, that had been fostered over long distance in a blizzard of texts and occasional phone calls, but there was no doubt - we had grown closer. Fierce close, at least in my mind. I couldn't help hoping I was closer to seeing her other tattoo.

CHAPTER FORTY-EIGHT

THE PRELUDE

Even amid a tsunami of details leading up to the realization of her lifelong musical dream, Aneska made time for my children. We spent an entire evening together after one of Maja's magical meals. Saoirse and Zuza were there as well.

Aneska also set aside one morning session for just the two of us, in our spot in the study. As usual, it was best to let her describe the anticipation and what I assumed was immense pressure. But that isn't what she wanted to talk about first.

First, my friend, your children are pure treasures. But you know that.

I thanked her for enabling them to be there. She credited that to Brynn and Saoirse. But I knew three more concert seats could not be easy to secure. All her family and much of Ireland wanted to attend, including the President and Prime Minister. There had been talk of an additional performance the night after, but logistics and schedules made that impossible. Aneska committed to another performance in the fall.

Second, Zuza has been reading your manuscript to me. I must tell you it thrills my heart how you've captured our story. And don't try giving me the line you gave Saoirse that you're just the scribe. It's your opus as much as mine. You've painted the characters and highs and lows with all the right colors, honestly and fearlessly, including your own vulnerability. You paid such attention to detail and honored all who deserved honor and need to be remembered.

I knew the honesty, fearlessness, coloring, vulnerability and honoring were almost entirely her own. I started to remind of her that, but she raised a hand to stop me.

And don't dare edit out my praise for you or I'll not approve the final version.

I responded in clumsy German to please her, 'Yawohl, mien freund.'

Danke. Allow me one 'I told you so' as well. I am especially grateful for the journey your own heart is taking. I told you, didn't I, at the beginning? We are part of each other's story now.

I thanked her, agreed and tried to redirect back to the joys and pressures of the concerto, but she wasn't done with private matters.

I hope in a few days you'll hear in the music what you captured on the page. Including a reflection of the movement happening in your own heart. And from what I gather, perhaps in someone else I love as well.

Like a skilled composer, she knew how to weave themes together with subtlety. The affirmation of her love for me wrapped around her wry implication like a duet. I could only smile and affirm, 'I love you, too, Aneska,' while ignoring the obvious reference to Saoirse. She seemed to enjoy my slight discomfort, but acquiesced to my evasive maneuver to steer her back to how she was handling the anticipation and pressures around the imminent performance of her life's crowning work. She quibbled with my choice of words.

Oh, my friend, I wouldn't call the concerto my crowning work. Remember Mama's early Latin lesson? On the sign in the music room? The concerto is an opus, to be sure. A vintage wine. I hope not over-fermented. But it's not my magnum opus. I'll leave that for you to work out.

I was fierce sure I knew what she considered her magnum opus, but she pressed on before I could surmise and laud her for it. Her story would make that clear.

As for the pressures of the past few months, and this week, fortunately, I guess I'm not only my Papa's daughter, but my Mama's as well. Now that the debut is nearly here, I feel her steady quarter note cadence in my spirit. From the outside, it may look like I'm carrying all this, but actually, I'm being carried. By Mama's faith and her belief in my gift. By Papa's passion. And Wilhelm and Jakob's protection and heroism. By the care of the Benedicts and Petra and the kind doctors. Certainly, by Dear Brynn and her family. But most of all, I feel the force of Kristers' indomitable spirit, and his sweet love and self-less sacrifice for me. Through the long process of composition, all I've hoped to convey is the beauty and power of all of them in my life. And the source of it, Gott's goodness and ultimate triumph in spite of all the pain and loss. My friend, Gott's direction, more than our plans, has led us both here, ya?

I couldn't agree more.

The same is true for Frieda Chidubem, my protégé. I haven't told you her story. Her great grandmother was a young nurse at a different munitions factory near Lübberstedt. She occasionally worked at my camp near the end of the war. Frieda remembers her greatgran talking about a young piano player there. That had to be me.

Like so many families in Germany after the war, her greatgran's family suffered severe poverty, so they immigrated to South Africa. Frieda's mother fell in love and married a black man at a time when that was very taboo. That's where her surname 'Chidubem' comes from. It means, are you ready for this? "Gott will guide you."

Like me, Frieda showed great promise on piano at an early age. Somehow, her instructor heard about our academy in Carlow. He raised the tuition and Freida entered our world when she was twelve. She and her mother lived in the guest house for three months until one of our sponsors took her in.

One day, Freida walked in while I was working on a piece for the concerto. The next day, I heard her playing it in the front room. Note for note! You will experience her gift. She never planned to be in that seat - in front of an entire orchestra - in Ireland.

My friend, never underestimate the calculus of the Lord. If he can put a gold coin in a fish's mouth and rise from the dead, it's no stretch for Him to seed a family tree across continents, oceans and cultural divides.

She gazed into the fire like I'd seen her do a hundred times.

No opus, no tribute, is too much for a Gott so great, so able and so…

She paused, perhaps to search for the right word or savor the one she had in mind.

…so, untamable, ya? A Gott who calls us 'friend.' Sacrifices everything for us. What else can we do? It only follows. We live to give his gifts away. To praise him. And like one of your songs says, never forget to be grateful. For life. For breath. For daily strength and bread.

Hearing my words from Aneska was always a high honor. I was glad my recorder was on.

We wrapped up with talk about the book cover, its release after the Hamburg performance and logistics around the day of the concerto. A familiar aroma pronounced a benediction on our session. Cornbread. Lunch and our daily bread were ready.

CHAPTER FORTY-NINE

THE DAY

The day arrived. April 29. Her concerto debut and liberation anniversary from Stalag X-B in Sandbostel, Germany, 1945. I knew Aneska's heart and mind had to be bursting at the seams about both. But that wasn't the first thing on her mind that morning. We gathered with her at Snowdrop Manor for a light breakfast. Zuza, Valor, me and my children. Maja did not disappoint. The aroma of Franzbrötchen filled the house. Aneska announced to everyone.

It's Saoirse's birthday. Let's throw a concerto for her!

No one had forgotten. Some plans and gifts were on tap.

We took two vehicles to Saoirse's place in Dublin. A dozen other Latvas, O'Cullens and Murphys would meet us there later. Instead of the complexity of eating out with so many, Saoirse was hosting a catered meal in the afternoon, on her own birthday.

Maja drove the Land Rover with my kids. Aneska, Zuza and I rode with Valor. Among other things, Aneska talked about the glorious day Saoirse, her Bluebell, was born. And the first time in October 1945 she and Kristers made that drive the other direction to the manor with Darby O'Cullen.

Kristers' head was shaved from surgery. It was cold. He held my hand the whole way. The trip was a little longer than the one from Sandbostel to Lübberstedt. My heart was heavy for different reasons, but I was curious about Brynn's world. Kristers stared out the window like a little boy. Until he fell asleep in my arms. We've come a long way. I like to believe the music tonight will rise to heaven so he can hear it.

Zuza assured her it would. She reminded Aneska of Psalm 150 which talks about praising the Lord with many instruments.

Before everyone arrived for the meal, Aneska planned a brief stop at Saint Patrick's Cathedral to pray. Saoirse met us there. We gathered in the back alcove where Aneska often went during her first weeks in Dublin. A priest led us in a beautiful prayer asking a blessing on the concert, that all who heard "might experience the awe of our Creator God." Aneska showed my children where to write prayers in the book on the brass lectern. They did, along with Saoirse. I was tempted to add my own just to read theirs, but resisted.

Back at Saoirse's, a classic meal of Irish stew and brown bread was perfect for the coolish April day. Maja made a chocolate Guinness cake for Saoirse's birthday. It matched her sweetness and the occasion. Afterward, Aneska lay down for a brief rest. When she emerged, Saoirse had done her hair like Aneska described wearing it the day she married Kristers, complete with snowdrop blossoms in it. My children and I presented Saoirse a large bouquet of mostly bluebells. About half five, four carloads of us headed for the National Concert Hall for a reception in the John Field room underneath the magnificent chandelier.

As we drove up to the hall, one of Aneska's best kept surprises revealed itself. A huge golden banner hung high across the massive columns. Emblazoned in deep purple lettering was the title of the concerto and a tribute that I knew thrilled Aneska:

Ireland's own, Aneska Latva

Presents

Piano Concerto Opus 1 in D major

UNTAMABLE

On the left side, a tall snowdrop blossom, the full height of the banner, bowed its head beside her name as in tribute. Aneska beamed at me.

I gave you a hint. Maybe consider that also as the title of the book? But you may have a better idea.

I slagged her saying I was thinking of a title like 'The Franzbrötchen Chronicles' but 'Untamable' wasn't bad.

We rolled up to the front entrance. Photographers, a TV crew and other reception attendees greeted Aneska like royalty. She walked arm and arm with Zuza and Valor. The rest of us followed. She stopped to look up at the banner and turned to take a picture. Cameras clicked all around.

The night of the Mahler symphony, momentous as it was, paled by comparison. We walked through the same massive columns, but this time for a world debut beside the composer. I kept one eye on Aneska. But also enjoyed the joy of Zuza and Valor, Saoirse, and my children, all of us trying to take the moment in.

Witnessing history being made has a dreamlike quality. You know you're awake, but there's an altered sense of time, an inability to process the import as it glides by. I wanted to rewind, slow it all down, exit the car again, see the banner for the first time, watch Aneska stop to look up at it. Having heard her story from her own lips, I could make instantaneous mental treks back to any moment in her timeline, but my senses snapped me back to the present. How much more intense for Aneska. The little girl, child musical prodigy, who saw the world turn black dark. The young woman so in love, now an old woman, still passionate, radiant, chatting with luminaries in tuxedoes and gowns under the glittering chandelier.

Musicians filtered through the crowd, some with instrument cases on their backs, heading to the stage to deliver notes meticulously harvested over decades from the river of Aneska's storyline. They couldn't possibly know the cost of the music.

I caught Aneska's eye across the room. Raised my glass. She lifted hers and gestured me toward her. She introduced me to the conductor and the manager of the Laeiszhalle, who wanted a preview for the Hamburg performance. A man approached to let us know it was time to open the doors and take our seats. Aneska, Zuza and Saoirse were led backstage to let the hall fill before Aneska's entrance. The rest of us wound our way up the broad marble stairs to the balcony. A large block of seats was reserved for us in her favorite location, center front row.

Crowd noise grew. We read through the program. I reminded my children who all the names were in Aneska's dedications and tributes. They recognized many of them from reading the manuscript draft. It was the cast of Aneska's life.

This music is dedicated to and inspired by the courage and kindness of my beloved German family, Deitrich and Miriam Pfieffer, brothers Wilhelm and Jakob, and true friends, Hans and Brigitte Benedict and Petra Neumann.

To my Irish family, daughter, Zuza O'Cullen, her husband Carl, children Sean and Amantine. My son Valor Latva, wife Cara, their children, Saoirse, Victory and Ben. And all the grandchildren.

The saints in heaven who welcomed me and my husband to the Emerald Isle just after WW2, Brynn O'Cullen and her son Darby.

More than anyone, this music rises up to heaven to Kristers Latva, the love of my life. You taught me what it means to be Untamable.

Special honor to Kristers' brother, Stephan Latva, an aspiring pianist, Valiant in life and death, and to all whose dreams are lost and sacrificed so ours can live.

My heartfelt gratitude for the help and support of the Royal Irish Academy of Music, Professor Johann Dichter, The National Symphony and Concert Hall and all the generous supporters who made my dream and this night possible.

Opposite the dedications was the title page.

Piano Concerto Opus 1 - UNTAMABLE

Composer: Aneska Latva

Guest Artist: Freida Chidubem

First Movement: Beyond Beautiful
Second Movement: Beyond Belief
Third Movement: Beyond Words

Caesura - Fifteen Minutes

Encore

Lieber Herr Jesus, Nimm Meine Hand - Aneska Latva

The encore was another well-guarded surprise. Adding such a personal touch delighted us all, especially Zuza, since she first suggested it.
A personal comment from Aneska appeared on the next page. It read just the way she spoke to me in our sessions:

Dear friends,

I am so honored and humbled that you are here. To hear my heart and journey.

Concertos and symphonies have movements and recurring themes. Our lives do as well. What you will experience tonight are the three movements of my life. My beautiful childhood. The darkness and agonizing losses of the WW2 years. And the redemption and rebirth of our lives in Ireland.

I hope you will hear your own journey in this music, the beauty and agonies leading to your own redemption and rebirth. If you are still facing the second movement of your personal symphony, hang on. Find a hand to hold. Call out to Gott. Believe for the third movement and a brave finale.

Soli Deo Gloria, Aneska Latva

It was safe to assume I was not the only one already moved, and the music had not even begun.

Farther back in the program were the names of the five Irish traditional instrumentalists and accolades to the conductor, a brief background of Freida's story and a list of primary financial supporters and sponsors. The name that stood out to me was the 'Brynn O'Cullen Memorial Trust.'

The house lights dimmed to half-light. Crowd murmur died out. An announcement began in the same faceless voice from the night of the Mahler symphony, the standard statement forbidding recording devices and flash photography. After a pause, the voice continued, Please welcome the President and Prime Minister of Ireland and their families. Everyone stood. Applause broke out. An entourage of seven or eight made their way to seats in the right wing of the balcony near the stage. The entire hall took their seats. After a brief pause the voice began again. The National Concert Hall, The Royal Irish Academy of Music and the National Symphony Orchestra are proud to present the world premiere of Piano Concerto, Opus 1, Untamable. Please give a warm welcome to the composer, escorted by her daughter Zuza O'Cullen and granddaughter Saoirse Murphy. Ladies and gentlemen, Ireland's own, Aneska Latva.

At a balcony door beside the massive pipe organ above and behind the orchestra, the three of them entered, bathed in spotlights The entire hall rose again to their feet, including eighty-five musicians on stage. Thunderous applause erupted. Spotlights followed them the length of the hall to their seats beside us. The applause never wavered. Aneska held both hands over her heart, turning and nodding to the crowd. Applause continued even after she took her seat. Saoirse sat down between me and Aneska.

As before, without introduction the conductor entered to enthusiastic applause. He turned toward the balcony, applauded and bowed to Aneska. He shook the hand of the Concertmaster violinist. As the crowd noise faded, the voice made yet another announcement, Please, welcome tonight's guest artist, Freida Chidubem. *Generous applause followed. Her green gown sparked in the spotlights. She extended both hands toward Aneska and bowed deeply before turning to the piano to take her place on the bench.*

The Maestro mounted the rostrum. The great hall grew silent.

CHAPTER FIFTY

THE OPUS

The Maestro raised his arms to begin. Saoirse took Aneska's hand. So did Zuza on her other side. I leaned forward to watch Aneska's face. I didn't want to miss that moment. That look. The first sound the orchestra made transported me back to where the young Aneska stood on the dock with her mother. It wasn't hard to picture the same look on her face as her Papa's boat set out to sea. Three rings of a ship bell launched the concerto into a playful romp in 6/8. It grew into layers of exhilaration.

As with Mahler's Symphony No. 1, there is no way to translate into words the music that sprang into the air. Like most art forms, music holds intangible, unseen, but self-evident realities and emotions of being a spirit in a physical world. Aneska's notes revealed and celebrated those realities and emotions.

My intimate knowledge of Aneska's journey gave me a distinct advantage. I had "seen" the film. Now I was hearing the soundtrack. In the music I relived her bright years in Hamburg again, the music lessons, the romance of her parents. Freida's first entrance was the same three notes and rhythm of the ship's bell. It grew into four octaves. Perfectly built into the score, the recurring triple notes of the ship bell, as well as a steady quarter note came and went, reflecting the family bonds and stability Aneska described to me. I would not have recognized these elements without hearing Aneska's recounting of their sources.

The piano part blossomed into melodic themes, arpeggios and cascades like a bird testing its wings, all set in a panoramic moving landscape painted by the orchestra. The music grew in delightful energy. A reviewer would later say about the first movement, "Its initial joy was akin to the Carol of the Bells with the rapid, right-hand flights and melodic beauty of Chopin's Minute Waltz." The momentum was contagious. Freida's own youth and vitality mirrored young Aneska's confidence, unbridled freedom, and fearlessness. Like teenage Anne Frank's soul, the music brimmed with passion and light. It made me feel free and fearless. More hopeful. The first movement clearly lived up to its title. It truly was beyond beautiful.

About ten minutes into it, the contra basses introduced a dark, pulsing motif under the brightness. They convinced the cellos and some horns to join them. The shadowy figure fought back and forth with the rising and falling piano. The two forces wrestled for dominance. One wanting to soar. The other out to clip its wings. The first movement ended with awkward rhythms and chord stabs, dissonance, on an unresolved chord cluster and a single, not triple, ring of a ship bell.

The conductor let the tension and foreboding hang in the air. No one dared move. A couple of muffled coughs added to the portent of what was to come. I reached around the back of Saoirse and put my hand on Aneska's shoulder. She patted and squeezed it with hers.

The second movement, Beyond Belief, lived up to its title as well, in complexity, power and angst.

The soul contains a myriad range of colors. Movement one had begun in bright primary colors invaded by deeper hues of dread and foreboding. Movement two brought a full range of both subtle and bold hues and emotions to the surface. It began dark and grew darker.

The rhythm section established a soft, steady cadence. An ominous theme in a minor key entered lock step, growing in volume to the feel of an army on the march. Against what felt like 4/4 time, the piano fluttered above in 6/8, like a butterfly running from a bear. The deep brassy pattern hammered in octaves as if demanding conformity or destruction. One by one, all the instruments joined it, eliminating any variations, nonconformity, individuality and beauty. All the while, Freida's fingers flew above and out of reach, tracing heartbreaking melodies with high strings and woodwinds. To any who knew Aneska's story, the passage so clearly portrayed the losing fight for freedom during the rise of the Third Reich. Tucked underneath it all, a steady quarter note voiced by various instruments came and went. The intensity grew, climaxing in a sudden pause. Like the boiling rapids of a river reaching the edge of a waterfall, the music leapt into the void. In the heightened anticipation of that space, Freida played the simple snowdrop pattern Aneska had sung to me two months ago. Dah-dah-daaah-dee-daaah-dah-daaah

Only a few in the audience could have known what point that was in the story. Kristers' bright soul and tender heart entered the music. Along with the innocence of their young love. The simple, pure melody shimmered against the strident monolith of the domineering theme.

The impact was palpable. I felt the tension between the beauty I knew in Aneska's story and the agonies she endured. Intense passages were punctuated by a restatement of the snowdrop theme in various instrumentations, and always as dependable as Kristers placing one beside her piano.

Rising to a dramatic high point, the music completely stopped on a single staccato hit from every percussion instrument, followed by a poignant caesura. The conductor kept his arms in the air, letting the silence speak. It felt like the whole audience held its breath. I knew the moment. Saoirse knew. Anyone who knew Kristers' story knew. It was the agonizing, defining moment. The shot.

But that moment wasn't exclusive to their story. It illustrated a precise moment of tragedy for anyone in the audience who had faced sudden, earth-shattering trauma. You didn't need to know Aneska's story to get it. Every life has decisive, defining turning points. Tragic or euphoric. Marked by great harm or great release, but in either case, life-altering.

In the pause after the shot, it felt like life and death hung, teetering in the balance. The next few soft notes from the piano signaled which had won. Freida played the notes of the snowdrop theme rubato, out of time at first.

Aneska was crying. Saoirse was crying. So was I. We were not alone.

The static tension felt like the moment in Acts just after Peter prayed and Tabitha came back to life. Her eyes fluttering open. Her breath returning. She sat up. Then stood.

Likewise, the tempo returned. The single violin of the concert master joined the piano. Then another string and another. Heavy brass and percussion restarted the strident theme. A steady quarter note pattern persevered in the maelstrom of it all. Like a pied piper, the snowdrop motif established a waltz feel. One by one, more instruments rallied to it with lovely embellishments. At one point, the opening melodic line to God Save the Queen wove into the mix. No doubt a tribute to the British liberators. Finally, against the swell of the entire orchestra, only a solitary piccolo remained on the vanishing defiant theme. It went out in a whimper. The full orchestra soared, embellishing the elegant melody like a celebration at a coronation. The finale grew to full volume with fortissimo stabs and flourishes, threatening to lift roof off before slamming to a full stop.

Normal protocol of no applause between movements was thrown aside. The hall erupted. It felt like the concerto could end there. I wondered how a third movement could top the second.

I leaned over Saoirse and whispered to Aneska, "I can see it all."

The Maestro waited, head bowed, his back to the audience. He gave the ovation its due. As soon as he raised his arms, silence reigned again. With one hand pointed to a spot in the orchestra, a dip of the baton signaled the third movement to begin.

I immediately recognized the solo melody that poured into the hall. The empathetic timbre of a solo uilleann pipe played the notes I heard standing at the door of the manor that first day. A 6/8 tempo was subtly implied. A concertina droned and an Irish harp arpeggiated chords beneath it. As before, the melodic phrase repeated over different chords. When it did, Frieda, the concertmaster and an acoustic guitar entered. The 6/8 time established itself and the tempo picked up slightly.

In my mind, I saw Aneska's flight from Göttingen to Dublin with her wounded love. But it easily expressed the feeling of my recent trips to Ireland. For that matter, it could serve as the soundtrack to a new chapter beginning for anyone, into an uncharted vista, opening on a brand-new day.

A lone bodhrán led the rest of the percussion into a lively, very Irish melody, like a jig, driven by strings and mandolin. It felt like a seafaring song or horses running free in slow motion.

The passage handed off back to the original melody, this time stripped down to just pennywhistle supported by acoustic guitars. As it repeated, the uilleann pipe and rolling piano joined. Instead of returning to the lively romp, a new third section launched. The undercurrent rolled like giant ocean waves. Long lines from French horns added a regal element. Over the top, a counterpoint began between the concertmaster's violin and Frieda's piano. Their instruments soared and rolled like two birds in a mating ritual. More and more instruments joined the dance. The pennywhistle and mandolin played distinctive patterns including the first line of the snowdrop motif. Every part was woven perfectly into the fabric of the whole canvas. It was like a Van Gogh painting come to life, swirling and pulsing with wonder.

Aneska and Saoirse's eyes glistened. Enthralled looks on my children's faces gave me as much joy as the music.

The entire hall felt like a ship on a rolling sea. Rising and falling, destined for safe harbor.

The score rose higher, gave the expectation of a finale, then dove deeper, sweeter before turning up again, this time to dramatic stabs based on the snowdrop pattern, but staccato, punched up by tympany and brass and string sections. All the while, Freida's fingers danced and reeled.

With unbridled passion and fortissimo exuberance, the finale came. I could feel my heart pounding. Saoirse grabbed my hand. The final crash left only a single note on the violin hanging in the air. Under it, Frieda delicately played the first line of the snowdrop theme in a high register. That was followed by a warm blossom of strings, uilleann pipe, woodwinds, full orchestra and piano, all landing on a nearly-home-at-last feeling of the five chord over the low tonic D in the contrabasses. At the Maestro's cue, three rings on the ships bell sounded. The chord under it settled to the tonic, D major, with a lush ninth added. The Maestro milked the chord to a pianissimo softness. With a fluid circle by both of hands and baton, he made the chord vanish like the last ray of sunlight in a spectacular sunset.

The effect was precisely what the title declared, like what I imagined the first step into heaven would be, beyond words. Out of the awed silence, applause exploded like a dam breaking. Everyone was on their feet, except Aneska. Even the orchestra stood and applauded. Saoirse and Zuza helped Aneska to her feet. The conductor lifted both hands toward her. The crowd roared. He directed Freida to take a bow to a surge of applause. She left the stage and had to come back to more adulation. She lifted her hands to

Aneska and bowed deeply, one hand on the piano, one on her heart. The outpouring did not abate. Each section of the orchestra stood in turn to receive their portion of the deluge. The Irish instrumentalists garnered a flood of whistles and cheers. The conductor acknowledged the Concertmaster. She turned the tribute back on him. He left the stage and returned together with Freida to yet more applause and bravos all around.

Every head in the hall turned toward Aneska. I was not the only one overcome with emotion.

She had done it! Lived to see the dream come true. As long as the world craved music to feed the soul, Aneska's music would live on. It was truly beyond beautiful, beyond belief, and beyond words.

The surreal sense of witnessing history returned. Reality shifted to another plane momentarily. I didn't feel born again again. But I felt more alive than I had in a very long time. Saoirse amplified the feeling even more. She embraced me. Tightly. And held on.

I could only imagine Aneska's euphoria, and couldn't wait for another session with her to hear about it.

The announcer's voice broke the spell and finally tempered the volume of the ovation. But the sense of exhilaration hung in the air.

"Ladies and gentlemen, after a fifteen-minute intermission, Aneska Latva will grace us with a personal encore."

Applause broke out again. The challenge became getting Aneska backstage quickly through a sea of admirers.

CHAPTER FIFTY-ONE

THE ENCORE

I sat in a state of profound bliss during the intermission. Like I had just won the national lottery. Saoirse took my kids to the lobby. About a fourth of the audience went, too. My body couldn't catch up with my spirit. I took out a small notepad from my coat and scribbled notes like a madman. No one but me would be able to decipher them.

The house lights flickered, signaling everyone to return to their seats. Members of the orchestra filed into the choir seating behind the stage just below the pipe organ. Zuza returned without Saoirse. The hall was still buzzing when the Maestro entered to warm applause. He walked to a microphone.

"Ladies and gentlemen, we will talk about what we experienced here tonight for the rest of our lives. I know I will. Save your ticket to show those who don't believe you. *Laughter ensued.* Now, imagine if you will, in an earlier era, you attended a Chopin or Liszt piano concerto. After the finale, the orchestra leaves the stage and the composer returns to the piano to play one more selection, just for you. That is what we are privileged with tonight. Ladies and gentlemen, Ireland's own, Aneska Latva."

Saoirse entered the stage with Aneska. The Maestro shook their hands and bowed his head to Aneska. Applause continued. Saoirse escorted her Mimi to the piano and exited with the conductor. Crowd noise finally trailed off as a stagehand adjusted a microphone for Aneska.

Her first words were, Dia dhuit.

Nearly the entire audience, except for me and my children, responded, Dia is Muire dhuit. "God and Mary to you."

Aneska had entirely won them over. Now, from a musical feast of the grandeur of her, they were about to fall in love with the great soul that her family, close friends and I knew.

I am gobsmacked, ya, truly. *More laughter.* Please allow me to thank a few dear souls. I would not be sitting here without the generous heart and hearth of Brynn O'Cullen. Her son, Captain Darby O'Cullen, flew us to Dublin just after the war in October 1945. God rest and reward their souls. My young husband needed special medical attention from the fierce brilliant doctors here. Brynn invited us to stay with her in Carlow for a bit. We did. For seven decades and counting. *More laughter.* Dear Brynn lived what she believed. "Do not merely look out for your own interests, but also the interests of others," as scripture tells us. That describes Brynn's life. Some of her family tree are here tonight. Would you stand, please?

More than a dozen stood to warm applause.

I was among the few who knew this night took so long to happen because Aneska lived by the same motivation. The interests of others, especially Kristers, took priority over the pursuit of her own dreams.

The Royal Irish Academy of Music took me under their wing in those early days. More recently, the National Symphony, beginning with the Maestro, as well as the kind staff of this spectacular National Concert Hall, they all believed enough to make this night a reality. Please, help me thank them. *Strong applause followed.*

And of course, my treasured family, by my side all the way. I was six months pregnant with our daughter Zuza on that flight to Dublin in 1945. Valor followed not long after. Both were born and raised on Irish soil. They are here with their families. Please stand and show your beautiful faces.

Aneska was doing her usual. Putting the spotlight on others. During the applause Saoirse entered the stage carrying two objects. Aneska was not expecting her. She set a glass of water and a small vase holding a single snowdrop on a stool beside the piano. Saoirse kissed her cheek and turned to leave, but Aneska made her stay. She pulled her around to sit next to her on the bench.

This is my remarkable granddaughter, Saoirse, Valor's daughter. Let me tell you what she has just done. At fifteen, I was required to work at a munitions factory. On occasion, I played dinner music for the officers. One day, I was practicing a Brahms piece. A tickle in my throat and slight cough made me stop and start again. A cook dressed all in white, the most handsome young man I have ever seen, bowed and handed me a glass of water. Our eyes met. After that, every time I played, he placed a glass of water and a flower in a vase with beside the piano. Almost always a snowdrop blossom, like these in my hair. Which Saoirse did for me today. Long story short, that young man became Saoirse's grandfather. So, that's what she brought me tonight. *Enthusiastic applause followed. Aneska wasn't finished.* Today is her birthday, and by the way, she's available. *Hearty laughter went through the hall. Saoirse kissed her Mimi again and exited. Aneska wasn't done aiming the spotlight away from herself.*

I hadn't planned on it but now is a good time to tell you. If you want to know the story that shaped this concerto, a new friend, musician, kindred spirit, and fierce good writer has graciously been listening to me drone on about my journey. The book is nearly completed.

Aneska had established such a personal rapport someone yelled out, What's the title? She turned the spotlight fully on me.

My biographer is here tonight. Let's ask him. *She pointed to me in the balcony.*

I answered in a loud voice, 'Untamable, just like you.'

She introduced me by name, asked me to stand and said to the audience,

Please, help me multiply my thanks to him.

Isn't it everyone's fantasy to have your name mentioned from the stage, by someone infinitely more impressive than you? That moment surpassed all fantasy. As I stood there, Saoirse returned to her seat beside me. Aneska could not have timed what happened next, but I would place a large bet she had her next comment in mind before it happened and wasn't about to edit it.

By the way, he's available, too. *That lit up the crowd. And I'm sure the color in my face.*

She rescued me from the spotlight by welcoming two musicians to the stage. A young cellist and a violinist. Both were students at the Academy in Carlow. The cellist was a young man from Kenya, Ashura Barasa. The violinist a young woman from Montana, Nelly Deere. She raved about them, of course, sharing the spotlight yet again. They seated themselves across from the piano, facing Aneska.

The song we want to play you was Kristers' favorite. As I said in the program, he is the untamable one and the central inspiration for the concerto. I believe he is listening in tonight. *Someone stood and applauded. Everyone stood, including Aneska. When the ovation crested, she sat again on the bench, pointed a finger heavenward, and said,* That was for you, miene Liebe, my love.

This song was written in Hamburg. In November 1938. I was nine. It's one of my first compositions. My mother was a fine pianist. She loved playing hymns. You will hear that influence in this piece. The shadows of tyranny were getting darker. I wrote this just after Kristallnacht, the Night of Broken Glass. That was the first of countless days the madness erupted in Germany. Papa was so angry. I didn't know this till much later. After that night, he began smuggling Jews to Sweden in one of his boats.

Fervent applause followed. After it subsided, Aneska said, That was for you, Papa.

My Papa loved the way this song calmed his spirit. It's a prayer, really. I've leaned on it many times, in the most trying situations.

One of the most memorable was at the munitions factory. By a miracle from Gott, the officer in charge was my dear friend from Hamburg, Hans Benedict. His name appears in the program. Gott rest and bless his soul. Hans made it possible for me to broadcast this song some evenings at lights out. The five-hundred workers were Hungarian women, prisoners doing forced labor. Many of them told me that lying on their beds, weary and hungry and a long way from home, this song comforted them. I took special delight in that. They were almost all Jewish and didn't know the song is called, "Lieber Herr Jesus, Nimm Meine Hand." 'Dear Lord Jesus, Take My Hand.'

Pleasant chuckles went round the audience. Someone uttered a "Hallelujah." *Aneska responded,* Amen. *She took a sip of water, raised the glass like a toast and said to the audience,* Tonight, this is my prayer for each of you.

I had heard the song more than a few times. But not in a magnificent concert hall arranged with cello and violin. The intro surprised me until I realized it was part of the bridge. When it rested to set up the verse figure, Aneska took it by herself. She still had a master touch in her aging hands. The arrangement was warm and comforting, like Kristers' cornbread. Violin and cello each traded off on the melody with the piano, and added lovely counterpoint embellishments. The whole thing was sweet and sad.

At one point, my daughter took my hand. She leaned toward me and whispered, Dad, you should write lyrics to that. *Her idea felt fierce honoring, but I knew what this music speaks is, to borrow Aneska's term, beyond words. Like the 'wordless groans' the Apostle Paul described, uttered by the Holy Spirit to intercede for us.*

As the elegant music poured out of Aneska and her accompanists, time suspended. I can't speak for anyone else in the audience, but I felt closer to heaven and a stronger connection and value for those I loved. It wasn't hard to picture Aneska playing it in the empty dining hall at the work camp, the music wafting over the laborers in their bunks. I knew many of them did not survive the war, but the ones who did never forgot this song. It conjured the scene just before Kristers took the bullet for her. How slowly she must have played it, hoping for a miracle. And I wondered if angels listening in, then and now, wished they were human just to know the beauty of such earthbound but boundless, untamable love, even with the suffering that comes with it.

Somewhere in the back half of the song, I reached for Saoirse's hand.

The ending circled back to half the bridge figure then poured into the main 'hook' line, as we call it, in Nashville. The masterful musicians repeated the hook rubato, out of time, retarding the last two notes in warm three-part harmony. The chord rang into silence. In the stillness, a collective sigh came from the entire hall. Like I had only seen one other time. In the middle of a Paul McCartney concert, out of complete darkness, his voice and acoustic guitar began the song "Yesterday." The arena gasped in unison. But this sigh was deeper, Holier, not dripping with nostalgia of lost love and lament for the passing of time. This sigh was a response to the assurance of divine intimacy and empathy in the universe. Contact had been made with God himself. He heard our pain, our plea and drew near as our Immanuel, God with us, here to carry us through to the other side of our earthly agonies. And receive us beyond this life.

Applause began like gentle rain. But soon grew into a thundering standing ovation. I hoped Aneska felt many times over what I was feeling, if not born again again, then washed in a Divine presence. And mended by it. Unburdened. Freer. More at peace.

Just as Freida had done, Aneska stood, stepped forward, put one hand on the piano, the other on her heart and bowed at the waist. She turned and led an ovation for Ashura and Nelly. She tried to exit but was met by the Maestro, who led her back out to more applause. Valor entered from a stage door with a gigantic bouquet. I hadn't noticed him slip out of his seat.

The explosion of blossoms looked like a mix of white lilies, snowdrops and bluebells. They exited. The flood of praise did not abate.

When she returned to the stage with Freida, I thought the roof might lift off the hall. Aneska bowed to Freida. They exchanged a long embrace and exited arm in arm as the torrent continued.

When she didn't come back a third time, we decided to let the crowd thin. Just as well. The magnitude of the experience left us speechless. In awe. Vulnerable, and at peace with that. Deep realities, normally smuggled several layers down inside us day to day, had surfaced. It felt akin to being naked and unashamed. To take it all in would require a larger soul and that's what the music had done. Enlarged us. All of us I presumed. How could it not? Isn't that what great art and authentic spiritual awakenings do?

After about twenty minutes, we made our way downstairs to a reception under the sparkling chandelier. Aneska and her triumph outshone it. We had to work our way through the crowd over to her. Between hugs and kisses she said the manager of the Laeiszhalle in Hamburg wanted to add a second performance, the following night. Tickets were already sold out and thousands were on a waiting list.

My time to talk with Aneska would come back at the manor in front of the fireplace, so I hung back as others thronged her. In the middle of a sea of admirers, she circled up with my children for a few minutes. I couldn't imagine them not being there. The sight was priceless and indelible, like Aneska. Saoirse was right. It was all beyond describing.

I overheard Saoirse say to Aneska, Mimi, I'm sure Jesus had to hold Kristers back from breaking through the veil to be here.

When Aneska's entourage finally walked out of the entrance, the world felt different. Not because the giant columns were drenched in gold from spotlights, or because photographers and a TV crew jockeyed to capture the monumental moment. The air felt richer. The stars burned brighter. Darkness was less dark. Evil, though surely still slithering about somewhere more insolent than ever, was a whimpering brat destined for defeat and extinction. And love stood more than a fighting chance to find safe harbor in a hazardous world.

Two carloads of us stopped for a short while at Saoirse's for drinks and Maja's apple pie from Miriam Pfieffer's recipe. As we left there, Aneska suggested Saoirse show my children around Dublin before they flew back to the states in a few days. I was staying in Ireland until the Hamburg performance. Saoirse agreed wholeheartedly.

On the way out her door, Saoirse made the comment to me, I don't envy you putting all this into words. But Mimi tells me you handle words like she plays notes. Zuza says the manuscript is fierce cracking. So, word Maestro, I look forward to giving it a lash as we say.

I deflected assuring her most of the fierce cracking came from Aneska. And added that her grandaughter plays more than a cameo role. She gave me a long embrace, thanked me again for telling her Mimi's story, and surprised me with a kiss on the cheek. It was accompanied by intoxicating aromas of Irish whiskey, apple pie and a lovely perfume.

The ride back to the manor was fierce different than my first one in January. I drove. I knew the way. Everyone was exhausted. Maja nodded off beside me in front. In the rearview mirror, I could see my boys out cold in the third-row seats. In the middle seat, Aneska slept on my daughter's shoulder. The quiet wasn't silent. Some of the melodies of the concerto and the encore ran through my head. I could still smell Saoirse's perfume on the collar of my coat.

Did I mention the air was richer? And the stars brighter?

CHAPTER FIFTY-TWO

THE CHALICE

In the days following, a steady stream of flowers and hundreds of letters began arriving at Snowdrop Manor and the National Concert Hall. Concert goers expressed how beautiful and inspiring the concerto was, and how much Aneska's personal touch in the encore moved them. There were a handful of attendees whose great grandfather or great uncle had been a prisoner at Stalag X-B and passed down stories of a piano player there. Aneska regretted not knowing of their presence at the concert. Many wanted to know when the recording of the concerto and the book would be available. Rave reviews poured in. Requests arrived from other orchestras in England and Europe to host a performance. A second performance in Hamburg was agreed to.

The morning after, everyone slept late. Maja served breakfast about half ten. Aneska and I resumed our familiar spot that afternoon in front of the fireplace in the study. It was raining. Besides our usual tea, per my request, Maja provided two wine glasses of Italian Chianti we were fond of. I toasted her, "Bravissimo." We both added, "Sláinte."

I had a question in mind to ask her. 'Having lived inside the journey of this music for so many years, what is it like to experience the realization of it?' But it sounded like something a reporter would ask, not a friend. And the answer, like most indescribable things, was likely beyond words anyway. So, I didn't ask it. Instead, we sat in silence. Sipped our wine. And listened to the fire crackle.

After a few minutes what was in Aneska's heart and eyes poured out.

I missed Kristers in our bed last night. More than ever.

I took her hand for a moment. And waited for more. There was always more worth waiting for.

I feel like I've been pregnant with this music since before the war ended. Now that it's born, it's like a pearl necklace of miracles from the hand of Gott.

Thinking 'good things come to those who wait,' I sipped and waited.

But I can see it for what it is. What it's all for. My friend, do you remember the day your first recording finally arrived, and you held it in your hands? And your first book?

I did. Of course.

Unforgettable, ya? I can guess you received two kinds of responses. Those who were impressed with the writing or singing, the playing or maybe the production. And those who expressed how much a song or something in your book touched them or helped them, maybe inspired or lifted them in some way.

I started to ask where this was headed, but knew better. She would get there.

If I know you at all, I'm sure the latter kind of response means more to you, ya?

Ya. The older I get.

We want to be impressive to the world, don't we? Especially when we're younger.

I sensed more pearls of wisdom ahead. Aneska delivered. Her thoughtful pace flowed like the River Barrow.

Craving validation can create an addiction to applause. The ovations last night reminded me how much I loved the attention my gift brought me at Konservitory. And even from the poor brainwashed sheep in the League of German Girls. I'm sorry, that was uncharitable. Who knows how many of those girls were faking it just like me?

I told you how Mama helped cure me with the difference between an opus and a magnum opus. Playing at the Stalag for the POWs and the Lübberstedt women broke my addiction. I experienced the deep satisfaction of how something in the music made a difference. And it was far better than applause. Mama was right. It wasn't about my gift, but about giving it.

You certainly gave it last night, I told her. It fed my soul. I don't think I'm alone in that.

Thank you. That means a lot.

But my friend, I think you would agree, the music is not the essence. Music is only a bucket. A bucket meant to carry something intangible, but essential. Food for a hungry soul, a key to a spirit locked in chains of fear or hurt, the hope of freedom, the shared agony of suffering. It can carry comfort for sorrow, the beauty of creation, the joy of loving and being loved, the possibility of redemption. Or the hollowness of missing it. Without that, like scripture says, it's only clanging cymbals, well-organized noise. But when music carries the living water of love, or points someone to the well where weary souls can drink and thirst no more, then the bucket, the gift, fulfills the purpose for which it was given.

I told her, I may be sitting here beside you, but inside I'm giving you a standing ovation.

She had a good laugh at that.

Oh, ya. that's marvelous! Thank you, again.

I added that I hoped my music might be a useful bucket, but hers is a chalice.

Oh, my friend, your kindness blesses my heart. But any vessel will do as long as it carries living water, ya? Your music feeds my soul. I've told you that. We like it, of course, when people like our bucket, our music. That's a fine thing. But not the main thing. The Lord's 'well done' is the real prize.

Ya, amen, I said. She had more wisdom about the bucket.

And the bucket doesn't have to be music. There's a variety of gifts. Mama showed me that in scripture. Gott gives them out as he chooses. An art or service or a calling of every kind can carry the love. From what I've read so far, your manuscript carries it. I'll read more of it before Hamburg.

I thanked her, but countered that most of the book was a bucket was filled with her water.

Let's just call it a vessel within a vessel, ya?

I agreed. We talked about what the next few weeks held before the trip to Hamburg. I planned to use the time to expand the manuscript to include the spectacular concert event we were still reveling in. She planned to rest and read and show my children Carlow Academy. Somehow, Aneska already knew I would be spending the following day in Dublin with them and Saoirse. Her next comment was quintessential Aneska.

Saoirse, my bluebell, now there's a chalice, my friend.

All I could do with that was raise my glass of Chianti.

CHAPTER FIFTY-THREE

THE INDELIBLES

Saoirse called after my session with Aneska to see if I was serious about getting a tattoo in Dublin the next day. The week before she made a reservation with a popular artist at a renowned shop, The Ink Factory. She needed to confirm or cancel. If you know anything about getting a tattoo, especially from an artist in demand, bookings are hard to come by, even a month in advance. Saoirse apparently had pull. I had a design in mind, so I told Saoirse, "Yes, what the craic."

She had a good laugh at my expense. Apparently, I comically abused the language. Again.

At dinner time I called her back to say both my sons wanted the same tattoo, if that was possible. Will's left arm already hosted a half dozen. It would be Liam's first. Saoirse had me text a picture of the idea to the artist. Emmaline surprised me. She wanted a snowdrop on her ankle like Saoirse, who was understandably thrilled by that. The artist responded that if the sizes were small, he and another artist, the one who did Saoirse's other tattoo, could make it all work.

Next morning, the four of us met at Saoirse's brownstone. We set out on foot first to Saint Patrick's Cathedral. I wanted to show them where I got the idea for the tattoo. On the grounds, in a group of headstones, stood a tall Celtic cross. Aneska told me in her first weeks in Dublin she prayed for Kristers there, touching that same cross. From there we headed to Christ Church, took in its magnificence and spent a few minutes walking the prayer labyrinth, where Aneska also prayed in those first weeks. We lunched in the bustling Temple Bar area. Fish and chips. What else? Though the main course for me was Saoirse's sparkling interaction with my children. After that, we showed up right on time at the Ink Factory directly across the street from the River Liffey.

Since I wanted a larger Celtic cross with more detail, the boys went first. The other artist began Emmaline's snowdrop.

Saoirse and I sat on a bench outside, checking in on their progress. We compared reactions to the concerto, finding our experience of it very similar, especially how it brilliantly traced Aneska's story. And how profoundly the music affected us. We talked about the upcoming Hamburg trip and the book. She wanted to help plan the release event, in the John Field room at the National Concert Hall.

Between creating an exact design and the inking process, the first three tattoos took about an hour and a half. They were spectacular! My sons' crosses were two inches tall placed on their inside left wrists. Saoirse declared she and Emmaline 'ink sisters.' My larger design was more detailed, a trinity knot inside the central ring, which represents the infinite love of God and Christ's nimbus or halo. I also wanted a traditional braided pattern on the beams, a sailor's Celtic knot. Traditionally, it represents remembering loved ones and a bond that can't be broken. The tattoo would be four and a half inches by three, placed inside my left forearm, and require at least two and half hours. So, while I got inked, the four of them headed out for more sightseeing.

When we went to pay the bill, Saoirse had taken care of it. Her gift to us. So we would never forget Ireland. That was not a remote possibility. More than ink bound us together. We tipped the artists and ended the day over leftover Irish stew and apple pie at Saoirse's, four out of the five of us with bandaged tattoos.

My children's flight home was the next afternoon. This time, no one slept on the trip back to the cottage. I stayed there with them that night. Needless to say, my kids were now like me, big fans of Ireland, Aneska, Saoirse and fish and chips.

Next day early we swung by Snowdrop Manor for a light breakfast, including scones, heavy cream and jam, and goodbyes to Aneska, Zuza, Valor and Maja. Freida joined us, too. Pictures were taken, possibly destined for a place on the crowded table in the study. Aneska secreted three envelopes to me to give my children at the airport. We left, as always, with hearts fuller than we brought in.

In Dublin, Saoirse took us quickly for one more dose of fish and chips to go. This time at U2's favorite "chipper," Leo Burdock's, serving fish and chips for a hundred years. Leo clearly had it down.

At the airport, Saoirse handed out goodie bags of Irish snacks for the flight. I managed to smuggle Aneska's envelopes into them. After a quick prayer and bear hugs from me, as well as Saoirse, my three crown jewels disappeared through the security doors.

Saoirse said exactly what her Mimi did, "Your children are treasures. I'm sure you know that."

She decided to make the drive with me back to her cottage. I was glad to have such good company. I drove. In the correct lane all the way. Supremely thankful for the rich memories made with my children. Memories more indelible than the new ink on my arm. And still more indelibles to come.

CHAPTER FIFTY-FOUR

THE HOMECOMING

I spent the next two weeks in early May bringing the manuscript up to the present, when I wasn't walking the estate with Aneska or Saoirse, sometimes both. Springtime was still repainting the Irish landscape, akin to the opening of Aneska's first movement. It was beyond beautiful. I could relate. I was going through a kind of repainting myself.

At mealtime, the main entertainment became reading the pile of letters and rave reviews of the debut. The second performance in Hamburg sold out in less than an hour. With its double balcony it seated two thousand. Eight hundred more than the hall in Dublin. Plane tickets arrived courtesy of the Laeiszhalle manager. First class for nine, which included Saoirse, Maja, Zuza and Valor with their spouses, me, Aneska, and Frieda. Plus, five coach fares for the Irish instrumentalists. Brilliant, world-class side musicians often go unheralded, apparently on both sides of the pond. But Aneska required Laeiszhalle to bring them over and made sure their names were in the program and per diem in their pockets.

I accepted an invitation to play one night at the pub with the regular gang. Saoirse and Maja brought a surprise guest, Nelly, the violinist from Montana. She lit the place on fire with her "fiddle."

The closer our departure drew, the quieter Aneska became. On one of our walks, a question I posed unlocked what everyone sensed was the reason. My question, clever but perhaps not completely sensitive, was out of my mouth before I could edit it. I asked if she felt like a homing pigeon returning to Hamburg. As usual, she was unflappable.

A pigeon? I should be so lucky. No, but a long time ago I used to feel like an albatross. Like I continually held my wings out, gliding over the ocean a long way from home. Ireland gave me a resting place. And a nesting place. It let me be a songbird. In Mama's native tongue, remember? Hemmet är där kärleken finns. Home is where the love is, ya? My home is here. I'm just feeling the flood of memories that wait for me in Hamburg, though I'm sure almost everything has changed since the last time I was there. That was 1955!

As you know our house there was destroyed during the war. The shiny years of my childhood were brief, but I still carry them with me. And so much heartache happened there, too.

My friend, as you know very well, life is a happy/sad song. Or a painting in process. Sometimes the colors choose us. Some colors we choose. Like Mama, I believe the colors we choose can prevail, even blended against the ones we don't choose. And Gott always has his hand on the brush with ours.

Another duet? I asked her.

Ya, precisely. Believing that makes things like this trip less daunting. And even full of possibility and good.

I told her, then color me a believer.

You've already chosen those colors, my friend.

* * *

The day came. We boarded our flight and took the same route across the North Sea as thousands of Allied bombers did to rain hell on Hamburg. We flew just north of the coast of the Netherlands. Darby O'Cullen piloted the same path a dozen times before getting shot out of the sky. The trek it took the Allied forces years to make, about six-hundred miles by air, we made in two hours, while drinks, finger food and hot towels were served.

What a difference winning the peace can make. But the cost in lives to secure our freedoms, and even the amenities, was incalculable.

Aneska was seated on the right side of the plane next to the window by Zuza, across the aisle from Saoirse and me. She got up once briefly and walked back into coach when we heard a penny whistle, squeeze box and bodhrán playing behind us. I was reading up on Laeiszhalle. I leaned across the aisle to tell Aneska that Pink Floyd and the BeeGees performed there. She countered that so did Strauss and Stravinsky and added,

I love Pink Floyd and the BeeGees. But I did recitals at Laeiszhalle before all of them were born. Kristers and I used to dance to "How Deep Is Your Love."

As the German coastline came into view, Aneska gazed out the window. The sky was cloudless and deep blue. She leaned forward and told us she could see the port of Bremerhaven, that Lübberstedt was only about thirty-five kilometers south. Twenty-two miles.

I could imagine some of the images stampeding through her mind. Singular among them, meeting Kristers. Falling in love. Their first kiss in the kitchen pantry, the first of many. The miracle of reconnecting with the Benedicts. Benca and Golda. The agonizing drive to see her dying mother. The evacuation. It was all down there in a mosaic most of the world had forgotten.

Aneska's music made it live again. As the book would. That was our hope. As she reminded me more than once: Remembering is revering. It makes what's lost along the way not as lost.

Zuza asked her mother what she wanted to see first.

The statue of Brahms in the foyer of Laeiszhalle. Mama and I stood there many times. The receptions after recitals happened in the Brahms foyer. My Opa and Oma from Sweden were there once. But before that I want Franzbrötchen!

We landed two days before the performances, for rehearsals with a completely different orchestra of fine musicians.

Laeiszhalle is lovely, Baroque Revival, no giant columns, and more ornate than the National Concert Hall. Just as in Dublin, a banner hung over the entrance, with one difference. Instead of "Ireland's own" it read, "Hamburg's own."

The day before the first performance, a TV crew interviewed Aneska, in German, sitting in front of the Brahms statue. Zuza whispered the translation to Saoirse and me. As usual, Aneska turned the attention elsewhere, paying honor to the Konservitory, Hans Benedict and even Dr. Nachtneder by name for nurturing her music. When the reporter asked her about the title of the concerto, she spoke briefly of Kristers and his untamable spirit. It was the only moment her emotions welled up. It was a good thing Saoirse thought to bring tissues. Aneska regained her composure by saying a book by the same title, soon to be released, would answer that question better. She pointed to me off camera as the author and suggested they interview me, too. Fortunately, the interview and camera stayed on Aneska.

"When will the book release?" *the reporter asked.*

Aneska looked at me. I shrugged my shoulders. I heard Saoirse say, July seventeenth. On Kristers' birthday.

Aneska's face lit up. She went with that. It had not been discussed or decided. Nearly eight weeks was plenty of time and it sounded so right. Besides, Saoirse leaned over and whispered to me.

I checked. The John Field room is available that day. They were glad to hold it for us.

Impressive? That's what I thought, too.

The reporter had a final question. "Having lived inside the journey of this music for so long, what's it like to experience the realization of it, in the place you were born?

Besides Aneska, I was the only one who knew her next words and didn't need a translation. Though you may.

Es ist wie eine Perlenkette der Wunder aus der hand Gottes. It's like a pearl necklace of miracles from the hand of God.

She spoke another minute about how God's gifts are meant to be given away. As usual, she was fierce authentic. Fierce endearing. Fierce Aneska.

* * *

Both performances confirmed it – music is a universal language. It not only goes beyond words, but beyond borders and cultures. It speaks the inexpressible to the soul of humanity and reaches places inaccessible except to the Spirit of God.

Both nights, Aneska addressed the audience in German. Her first words were, Guten Abend. Good evening. The only thing amended in the program were the thank yous to the Laeiszhalle and Hamburg Philharmonic.

Both nights, I heard parts and colors in the music I missed in Dublin in the rush and awe of the moment.

Both nights, tears flowed like before, sometimes in different passages. The ovations thundered like before.

Both nights, before the encore Saoirse delivered a glass of water and a snowdrop blossom to her Mimi at the piano.

And both nights Aneska mentioned the book, introduced me in the first balcony and made the same crack about both Saoirse and me being available.

Something spectacular happened that had not in Dublin. At the encore, after the Maestro introduced Aneska, he surprised her. There were half a dozen people in the audience whose relatives had been forced laborers at Lübberstedt. They were asked to stand. Aneska met them after at the reception. She delighted in their stories. The second night, there were a dozen who made the trip from Hungary because of their family connection to Lübberstedt and stories of Aneska playing there. Even more stunning, the Maestro escorted two older women onto the stage. One was an actual Hungarian laborer at the work camp. The other was one of the League of German Girls assigned there with Aneska!

Remembering and revering embraced under the spotlights.

Setting up the encore, Aneska talked about similar things as in Dublin, but added how she played at least half a dozen recitals on that very stage as a nervous young girl with a big ribbon in her hair. She welcomed back the Concertmaster on violin and introduced the young cellist from the Budapest Symphony. His connection to Aneska through his great grandmother, a forced laborer at the munitions factory, sparked yet more applause.

Both nights, as in Dublin, before Aneska played the encore she closed her eyes and paused. No one in the great hall stirred. It struck me she was doing what her mother instructed her to do to settle and focus before playing. I knew she was picturing one person in her mind to play to. I had no doubt who that was. She took in a long, deep breath. Exhaled slowly. Opened her eyes and nodded to the two musicians.

The tenderness and power of "Dear Lord Jesus, Take My Hand" poured into the hall. I could not imagine how the hardest heart could go untouched or unmoved, not only by the chalice of the music, but by the Spirit that poured from it through the weathered saint at the piano.

Both nights, after a second ovation Aneska walked to a standing microphone. The audience settled. For me, her final words of the evening echoed down the halls of her story. I wasn't sure anyone else understood the magnitude or felt the poignancy of them in her family history, spoken in a land scarred by so many hard goodbyes. The words nearly wrecked me. Both nights.

Gott sei mit dir. 'God be with you.'

Saoirse to my left, Zuza to my right, and nearly the entire audience responded in unison, Und mit deinem Geist. *'And with your spirit.'*

After the final ovations, Saoirse and I embraced. Both nights.

As in Dublin, there were dignitaries and supporters to meet at the reception. Aneska was gracious to them all, but spent most of her time talking and taking pictures with the people from Hungary and her barracks mate at Lübberstedt. My favorite image was her sitting with them in a circle talking and laughing and crying at the foot of Brahms' statue. Taking nothing from Johannes, icon to icon, I prefer a living saint. But freely confess my bias.

We exited Laeiszhalle through well-wishers, photographers and a TV camera crew. In the limo, Zuza told her mother our flight could be postponed a day or two if she wanted to see anything else. Aneska sighed and said,

Thank you, my lily blossom, but no, let's go home.

CHAPTER FIFTY-FIVE

THE CALL

News of Aneska's triumph traveled fast. The Hamburg performances confirmed her stature as a composer and the appeal of the concerto. Offers to host it began arriving from symphonies around Europe and even in America. A repeat performance for a live recording at the Dublin concert hall was in the works.

I told Aneska what an encouraging sign that was. In a world that can appear to be swiftly spinning off its axis into a morass of narcissism, immorality and subjective cut-and-paste truth, there is still an audience hungry for magnificent artistry created from a depth of soul and genuine faith.

She deftly and gently knocked me off my high horse.

My passionate friend, I hear your compliment in that, and I thank you. But self-centeredness, sin and truth twisting have been around a fierce long time. The persistent inclination toward darkness in the human soul just means job security for Jesus. Sadly.

I had to chuckle.

He's not finished, ya? Certainly not with me, or you either. Gott's grace stays busy editing us. Grace begets grace, ya? And let's not forget, he prefers harvesters and ambassadors to stone-throwers and pundits. Like Mama said, we play our part. For you and me our opus is making buckets and chalices to carry his water. His love and grace. Doesn't that seem worth getting up for in the morning?

She left me smiling and shaking my head. Her kind delivery and wry wisdom eased the sting of the chastening. Still, I had to ask, but some days don't you ever feel like ramming a submarine?

Oh, ya, I certainly know that feeling. Remember, I wanted to stop the monster that harmed my darling. By any means. And would have given the chance. But justice for him was delivered by other hands. As for me, the Lord just keeps saying, "Aneska, blessed are the bucketmakers, for they shall carry water to the thirsty."

How can you argue with that? I couldn't.

I found better use for my passion by forging ahead on the manuscript.

Since Snowdrop Manor began hosting a steady stream of visitors and meetings, Saoirse offered me her cottage for a change of scenery and a quiet place to work during the day. She was rarely there during the week anyway. Like the guest house, the cottage also had a lovely view of the River Barrow.

I had intended to return to the states and come back for the book release. There was likely only a chapter to write about the Hamburg performances, maybe one more leading up to the book signing and an epilogue. But if I stayed in Ireland, there were no doubt more gems to glean from Aneska, like the ones you just read. The deadline also loomed to get the manuscript to the book press in Dublin. It had to be proofread and formatted, which could be done online, but Zuza and Aneska requested a printed copy, even though it was unfinished. They preferred paper. Aneska wanted to read it, turning pages in the solitude of her bed at night or the solarium, since the days had turned so beautiful.

It made sense for Zuza to proofread. She was very precise and close enough to the story to catch inaccuracies. She also hired a trusted friend, a professional editor, to proofread it via software. I would need to work closely with both of them. And there was the annual birthday party and remembrance of Anne Frank coming up.

All of these things were more than ample reasons to stay. You may have noticed I haven't mentioned three other incentives. Guinness, music nights at the pub and Saoirse. Not necessarily in that order.

Much to everyone's delight, I stayed. With my children's blessing.

I finished the chapter you just read, The Homecoming, and made two copies of the manuscript to that point, putting them in binders at a shop in Carlow.

Saoirse came back and forth from Dublin overseeing arrangements for the book release on July 17. She even took the photo for the cover – Kristers' large painting of a snowdrop and barbed wire that hung in the study. She delighted her Mimi by using Petra's camera.

June twelfth arrived. Aneska hosted her annual birthday party and remembrance of Anne Frank. She and a few others read favorite passages to us in the music room. We prevailed on Aneska to play a couple of pieces. She chose Gymnopedie No.1 by Erik Satie. We chose "Dear Lord Jesus, Take My Hand." Halfway through it, she conscripted Saoirse to play the rest. Seeing the two of them side by side on the piano bench was, to borrow a phrase – beyond beautiful and words.

Early the next morning, as I put my things in the Range Rover to leave for the cottage, Aneska asked me to walk with her a bit. She was about to finish reading the manuscript and wanted to talk about it. We headed toward the cemetery. Near Kristers' marker, we sat silent on a bench for a few moments basking in the verdant beauty all around us. Nature had restored what winter temporarily stole since I first sat there in January. The serenity was exceeded only by the contented look on Aneska's face. She took my hand.

My friend, Gott directed our paths together. You were chosen for this. I know you have sacrificed time with your children and your circle of friends and pursuits in the states. I find it hard to express how truly grateful I am. The manuscript is, it's…

Beyond words? I said. She laughed.

I guess you should be able to finish my sentences by now, ya? Saoirse and Zuza do it all the time.

What she said next was no surprise after the party the night before. She quoted Anne Frank from memory.

One other thing before I let you go to work. Anne Frank wrote, at age fifteen mind you, "A person can be lonely even if he is loved by many people, because he is still not the 'One and Only' to anyone." My friend, the prayer I wrote for you at St. Patrick's is that you will find your one and only. Your rhyming heart. For your third movement. For the rest of your days. And I hope your experience here has helped ready your heart for that.

I mentioned her depth of soul before, right? Her words touched me deeply.

And who is to say on which side of the pond you may find her, ya?

Aneska's implication was not subtle. And fierce endearing.

One last thing. May I remind you? Do what Kristers did. Decide what you want. And pursue it with all your heart.

I responded, Yavohl. I will.

Now, what I want is to go finish the last few pages of your manuscript. And you need to go finish the finale. Will we see you for lunch?

I told her probably not, but dinner for sure. I knew Maja's Irish stew and cornbread were on the menu.

We walked back to the manor. Before I turned for the driveway, we embraced. As we parted, I said Dia dhuit in my best Gaelic, Jee-ah ghwitch. 'God be with you.'

Aneska responded, And with your spirit, my friend, and your writing. You're Gaelic has come a long way.

Driving to the cottage, I passed Saoirse. She had spent the night there instead of driving back to Dublin after the party. We stopped and spoke between cars. She was having tea with her Mimi before heading back to Dublin. I told her Aneska and I just had a wonderful walk and talk. As we drove away in opposite directions, she texted me, "God bless your writing today." *Thanks to her Mimi, the words of a fifteen-year-old Dutch girl echoed in my brain.*

At the cottage, laptop open, looking out on the River Barrow, the thought of penning the finale, and possibly an epilogue, was intimidating. It loomed as the biggest challenge of the entire project. How do you sum up an epic story like Aneska's? Without an orchestra?

Shelving that challenge for later, I dove in to writing this additional chapter, weaving in Aneska's most recent gems, the steps toward the book release and Anne Frank's birthday party. Several hours passed. Writing and rewriting. Because writing is rewriting.

I was just deciding to delete the previous paragraph and let this chapter end with: 'How do you sum up an epic story like Aneska's? Without an orchestra?'

My thinking was that would set up the finale nicely.

My phone rang.

I looked at the name on the screen. It was Zuza. Probably double checking on me for lunch. I took the call.

Dia dhuit, Zuza.

There was a pause. Her voice, nearly in a whisper, said,

Mama is with Jesus.

CHAPTER FIFTY-SIX

THE FINALE

I never imagined the finale would be so final. Or come when it came. None of us did. Aneska's abrupt and unexpected, I want to say 'departure' to avoid the sting of the word 'death,' was truly beyond words. But like I said at the very beginning, life can turn on a phone call. If you've grown fond of Aneska just reading about her, imagine how stricken those of us in her close circle were. I never imagined this entire book would become her eulogy. The previous chapter, "The Call," was originally titled, "The Release." That changed with Zuza's call.

Like Aneska's concerto, the finale had three movements: the earthquake, the wake and the homegoing.

The Earthquake

I raced back to the manor immediately after Zuza's call. I found them in the solarium. Maja had gone in there to tell Aneska lunch was ready. At first she thought Aneska had nodded off to sleep in her chair. But she was gone, the manuscript still clutched open against her chest.

Stunned, the three of us sat around her waiting for emergency services and other family members to arrive. On the rolling cart by her chair sat three cups and a tea pot. She and Zuza and Saoirse shared them earlier that morning. Nothing was spilled or disturbed, even though it felt like the ground was still shifting under our feet. Blue light from one of the stained-glass pieces shimmered on Aneska's face. She looked even more peaceful than when we talked just a few hours earlier.

But if you have been near death, you know the vacuum of its silence and the gulf that replaces the nearness of the one whose spirit has departed. The "peaceful" stillness is a mix of hollow and hallowed. One thing was certain, Aneska was not there. An immeasurable force had gone out of the world.

Maja cried softly. Zuza held her hand. "Let's pray," she said. "That's what Mama would do." So she did.

"Gracious and good Father in heaven, thank you that Mama's beautiful soul is at rest with you. We rejoice thinking of her looking into Kristers' eyes. And hearing him speak to her - in his full voice."

She paused. Tears came. Hers weren't the only ones. I realized Zuza had never heard her father's voice either. Beyond the whisper. She pressed on.

"We can only imagine the reunion with her Papa and Mama and brothers and dear friends. Lord, as she and I and Saoirse were talking to you this morning, you know how full her heart was of your mercies, her gratitude for your countless blessings, and how deeply she loved her family and all those she touched." With that, she took my hand, too.

"She's probably telling you all that now, face to face. We are glad for Mama, Jesus, but you know how her leaving us hurts on this side, so please carry our heavy hearts. Amen."

There was no doubt. Zuza was her mother and her grandmother's daughter.

Saoirse arrived less than a half hour after the med techs. Zuza had called her en route to Dublin. Valor came in shortly after her. Zuza insisted Aneska not be moved until after they both arrived. We watched as she lifted the manuscript from Aneska's grasp. It was open to a page in Chapter 25, The Look, describing her wedding to Kristers. That made me wonder if she had finished reading the whole thing. Saoirse scanned the pages. Many of them were marked in the margins with stars, exclamation points and comments, including chapter fifty-four, The Homecoming. Valor found a pen lying on the floor beside Aneska's chair.

Saoirse turned to the last page. She looked at me and said, "Mimi must have finished it this morning. She wrote a note to you on the last page." I was so shaken I asked her to read it.

Dear word Maestro, (I stole that from Saoirse),

Your writing honors Kristers. It rightly makes him the hero.
Bless you. You make me look much better than I am,
and the Lord far greater than all of us.

Bravissimo! And Sláinte. Can't wait for the finale.
My fellow bucketmaker, home is where the love is.
Should you ever want it, you have one here with us.

Aneska Miriam Latva (your first signed copy!)

Obviously, Aneska's generous words were written not long before she knew death was imminent. If she even had time to know. Hearing her final words to me from Saoirse, with Aneska's body resting there, in the spot we talked that first morning, was beyond surreal. It sent another aftershock through me. She was gone and I couldn't thank her. I had expressed many times how grateful I was to be invited into her world, to tell her story, but couldn't remember the last time I did. And didn't in our last conversation that morning.

"She got the last word," I said. "I can't even thank her."

"She knew," Saoirse responded immediately, "and you can thank her. By finishing it well. We know you will."

That was one of hallmarks of Aneska's family and close circle. They didn't leave the essentials unsaid. Whatever else might feel left unsaid now, love and care were never in doubt, in word or action. And it paid huge dividends. As far as I could tell, none of them felt more loved or favored by Aneska. The few family tangles she touched on in our sessions were treated with grace. She even asked me to turn the recorder off several times when she related those incidents, not wanting her words ever to be dishonoring or misconstrued. I followed her lead by not including any in the book.

"God's grace is busy editing us, ya? Grace begets grace," she said.

I avoided just now writing 'she once said.' It felt too painful. Made her absence more real. I'm sure she would think 'How silly.' Now I was even putting words in her mouth. No need, I reminded myself. Let Aneska's life and music and words speak for her. And besides, if I ever want to hear her voice, I have nearly a hundred hours recorded of her magnificent soul, wit, and wisdom. I made a mental note to offer the archive to her family. That felt like another way to thank her.

Over the next few days, plans were put in place for an Irish wake at the manor and memorial service to follow the next day. Zuza chose June 18 for the service. I was probably the only one who remembered on that date in 1944 Captain Darby O'Cullen waved at Aneska as his plane glided past her just before crashing outside Sandbostel. June 18th would leave only four weeks for me to complete the book and a first pressing printed in time for the release on July 17. Saoirse persuaded everyone not to postpone. It would be tight, but it could be done.

As to the cause of Aneska's death: aneurism near the brain stem. Her doctor said she probably just felt drowsy, bowed her head and drifted off. Like Brynn before her, in the study by whatever cause. My father went the same way, just from old age. One day after lunch at their rest home my mother kissed him on his head and went to take a nap. The staff found him in his chair, head bowed, gone. For the one departing, how merciful to go gently into that goodnight and the arms of the Lord. Not so gentle for us who remain.

Sometime in the fog of it all, I talked to the poet Brian. He said, "I hear she bowed her head and drifted away. Sign me up for that. Truth be told, lad, none of us know from day to day if we'll be having lunch here or in glory. That's why I tend to dine early and often at the Café Rose." That was his favorite café in his hometown, Portumna, in County Galway.

Flowers and letters arrived daily, not only from across Ireland but from Germany, Hungary and even South Africa, from Freida's family. My children sent white lilies set in snowdrops. Snowdrop Manor never looked more beautiful or felt more gloomy.

There was a slight disagreement about the location of the memorial. Aneska was not Catholic, but many in her extended family were. The Cathedral of the Assumption in Carlow seated more people than the Anglican church in Staplestown. The parish welcomed it. Both the priest and the pastor in Staplestown knew and loved Aneska. Both agreed to preside. So, even in death, Aneska brought people together.

Zuza and Valor asked me to deliver part of the eulogy. I was honored, but the question remained: How do you sum up an epic life like Aneska's? Equally surprising, they invited me to be a pall bearer. I declined, not wanting to take the place of any grandson or great grandson, of which there were plenty. Frieda gladly agreed to organize a few musicians to play. Offers to help in any way came from everywhere, including the symphony and the office of the President of Ireland.

I was included in the discussion about what should appear on

Aneska's gravestone. This was a topic she never addressed, and like so much of the proceedings, a conversation no one anticipated having, at least not this soon. One thing was unanimous, a snowdrop should be carved into it. The Royal Irish Academy of Music and the National Concert Hall graciously offered to pay for the stone, the sculpting and engraving.

I set to work on this chapter, but focusing didn't come easy. The guest house, which had been such a haven, delivered its own tremors. At first. Especially the words from Yeats on the wall, in Aneska's own hand, and the gallery of snowdrop paintings all around.

> We can make our minds so like still water that beings gather
> about us that they may see, it may be, their own images, and
> so live for a moment with clearer, perhaps even with a fiercer
> life because of our quiet.
>
> W. B. Yeats

My mind was troubled, not still water. Against the beauty of the setting and the bright paintings, so simple and colorful, the image of myself was thorny and pale. The possibility of anyone living with a clearer, fiercer life because of my quiet felt like a taunt. The only thing that was clearer and fiercer was the revelation that I had lived without the clarity and fierceness of the life and love like that of Aneska and Kristers. And I still longed for it.

I said, the cottage delivered its own tremor "at first." Over several days, the waves of inner noise lost some of their power breaking against the granite quiet and natural beauty of the place. An armada of sweet memories in Ireland floated by like the River Barrow. Many times I laughed out loud recalling them. Many times I cried.

Word by word, this chapter came. Day by day, the river and the world moved forward.

The Wake

The day of the wake, it rained lightly before noon. But cleared by early afternoon. Beginning at half three, family and friends streamed in and out of Snowdrop Manor for six hours. Aneska's body reposed in the solarium. Until the sun went down, refracted colors shimmered across the room, some moments across her dear face. Candles burned continually near her head and feet. In old Irish custom, all the windows were open, thought to allow the departed soul to move out of the house, and as a practical matter of temperature, helped preserve the body. Both the priest and pastor attended. They prayed and visited for some time and ate with the mourners.

After their prayers, a keening began around Aneska's open casket. I had heard the term but never witnessed it. A lead keener, the woman who sang the Gaelic seafaring duet my first night in the pub, began a refrain partly in Gaelic, partly in English, half sung, half spoken. Zuza told me it was an original composition heralding Aneska's life and speaking a final farewell. Her husband joined her. Sometimes they spoke or sang directly to Aneska in the casket. Other keeners, female wailers, joined in spontaneous emotional outpouring. It could have been unnerving if not so rich and authentic.

Even without understanding the Gaelic parts, I was swept up into an ancient, primal lament. At one point, the lead keener's husband began stomping one foot on the floor for three beats, then one beat with his hand on the casket. Others joined in the rhythm, including Zuza, Saoirse and other family members. I had wept in private down by the River Barrow and on the bench near Kristers' marker, but among such dear company a deep ache rose from my marrow. Tears flowed freely from the absence and love for my dear friend. I lost track of time. The keening rose and fell in waves until it settled into the brief Gaelic refrain that began it all, sung only by the lead keener. Embracing followed. It was time to eat and drink. Some more.

The buffet was not fancy but bountiful, like the spirits gathered to mourn and celebrate Aneska. Baked hams, casseroles, sandwiches, potatoes prepared half a dozen ways, a phalanx of breads and a chorus of desserts. Maja baked two apple pies. Just like Miriam Pfeiffer made them. And one picture-perfect Black Forest cake with cherry preserves and whipped cream. From Kristers' recipe.

Several original poems were recited or read, including one by Brian O'Kelly titled "Not Just a Measure." It described in fanciful detail the art of pouring a pint of Guinness, expounded its sacred quality, likening the beige head to the collar of a Bishop. Brian turned his ode into an homage to Aneska. After delivering the last line, he raised his glass for a toast, borrowing a line from his poem.

"To Aneska, like a pint, not just a measure, but a glorious sight to behold and surely the envy of every other drink." Clinking glasses rang like holy chimes.

And of course, there was music. Lovely and lively. An Irish harpist played in the front music room. The beauty of the instrument somehow heightened the pain, at least for me. Several times Freida honored Aneska with pieces she had loved, including Brahms' Intermezzo in A major Opus 118, No. 2 and Liszt's Consolation No.3. And of course, "Dear Lord Jesus, Take My Hand." Aneska's fellow pub musicians performed several sets under a large tent over the back patio and terrace. The typical Irish mix of joyful and forlorn songs perfectly matched the funny and poignant stories that went round. Tears and laughter flowed freely.

The last song of the evening under the tent was "The Parting Glass." I had heard it before at the pub. Now it struck a deeper nerve, yet buoyed me somehow. The chorus goes:

So fill to me the parting glass and gather as the evening falls
And gently rise and softly call goodnight and joy be to you all
But since it fell into my lot that I should rise and you should not
I'll gently rise and softly call good night and joy be to you all

The final words, 'joy be to you all' ends solemnly on a minor chord, a classic Irish blending of joy and sorrow. After the last chorus, without a word from anyone, every hand raised a glass. The holy chimes of clinking glasses sounded again.

Near the end of the evening as guests departed, I overheard many speak the simple parting, "God be with you," followed by the response, "and with your spirit." Most spoke it in English. More than a few in Gaelic. I would never hear those words the same again, or speak them without earnest.

Aneska's body remained all night in the solarium. In keeping with old Irish tradition, it was never to be left alone. Valor's sons, Vic and Ben, and Zuza's son, Sean, all volunteered to share shifts. Saoirse returned to the cottage for the night.

Before going to the guest house, I sat for a while in the study hoping to finalize my thoughts for the memorial service the next morning. Aneska's chair sat empty. Nearly every photo took me down a path we went together. Kristers' painting spoke volumes. Brynn's portrait drew my attention. Her warm gaze reflected all the grace and magnanimity Aneska spoke of her. I had seen before the Bible in her lap was open to the book of John, but for the first time I noticed her index finger pointed to a chapter number, fourteen.

I took a Bible, one of many on the shelves, and opened to John 14. I chuckled, thinking I chose to come into the study, but had somehow been directed to the John 14. Aneska would surely have commented on the duet nature of that. As I read the first three verses, something in my spirit eased. The inner noise quieted. The dread of tremors faded. Only Aneska's chuckle was missing from the moment. I spoke to the painting, "Thank you, Brynn." And decided to use the passage in my remarks at the memorial.

The Homegoing

The day came. Clear and sunny. None of us were.

For me, in spite of the assurances of John 14:1-3, the timing and abruptness of Aneska's departure, whether allowed or ordained by an otherwise good story-telling God, seemed at best questionable and at worst bungled. At least in a universe I would design. Why not allow Aneska to enjoy a fuller season of sweet triumph, savor more of her impact as it rippled out into the world? She would have forever in glory. What's a little more time here in the balance of it all? It struck me Aneska might answer my question with the same question. And all I could answer would be, touché.

I am sure she would have gently chastened me again for contending with the Almighty, while admitting she had wrestled with him about the same thing. And besides, I had learned a long time ago, more than once, I was not in charge of the universe or anyone's storyline, not even fully my own. Apparently, the "author and finisher of our faith" considered Aneska finished. No doubt I just made it abundantly clear he is not finished with me or my faith, as Aneska pointed out in our last conversation.

Maybe you've wrestled with this yourself. Otto Frank surely must have. Anne gone so young. And yet, her heartless death at the hands of the same tyranny arrayed against Aneska unwittingly insured Anne's legacy and impact. And the mystery rolls on. For us all.

Forgive me. Like Aneska, I've detoured to navigate internals instead of narrating the unfolding story. Maybe life is mostly an internal journey. I'll leave it at that. For now.

* * *

Half an hour before the eleven o'clock start time, the cathedral was packed. Standing room only. People in the narthex and an overflow room spilled into the hallways.

I was honored to be seated with the family on the front row. Thankful to sit by Saoirse.

Four altar boys came past us down the aisles, followed by the priest and pastor. The boys lit candles. The priest welcomed everyone to the celebration of Aneska's life. He asked us to stand for prayer. At the end of it, he led everyone in a confession. I was relieved it was written in the program. "May almighty God have mercy on us, forgive us our sins, and bring us to everlasting life."

Immediately, the organ in the balcony behind us played the familiar first line of the opening hymn, Beethoven's "Ode to Joy." Zuza chose it. A cantor stepped to a lectern on the dais to lead the song. The full throat of the organ, the cantor's rich baritone and more than a thousand voices filled the cathedral.

Two lines of the first refrain became my prayer, perhaps my dare to the Lord, "Melt the clouds of sin and sadness, drive the dark of doubt away." All four verses and refrains were printed in the program. By the time we sang the last refrain my grousing was tempered by the unflinching cadence and unbridled hope in the worship anthem sung full voice by the faithful, in the face of death itself. I couldn't argue my way around the song's unspoken declaration that death does not have the last word. And that God was the undisputed "Giver of immortal gladness." In the wake of the song, a private cloud of sadness remained, though not as dark. I knew Aneska was a "victor in the midst of strife." That she would say more than music led her "sunward in the triumph song of life." Without a word from her, I felt the reality of her triumph soften the flimsy bastion of my petulance. In life, she had softened so many places in my heart. Why not from beyond the grave?

The pastor from Staplestown followed. He delivered a brief and eloquent encouragement about God being near the brokenhearted and his ability to turn mourning into dancing. He highlighted how remarkably joyful Aneska was in spite of everything she endured in life. Many 'amens' rose from the pews.

As the pastor left the podium, Freida began a song on the grand piano. The cantor motioned all to stand and led all four verses of the powerful hymn, "It Is Well." Also chosen by Zuza. One of her mother's favorites. In the fourth verse, on the line "The clouds be rolled back as a scroll," the organist held nothing back. It went full, deep and regal. And there it was again. Clouds. And the Lord rolling them back. But not all of them till he returns, I supposed. When the powerful hymn ended, I was certain it wasn't all well with my soul, but it was better than when the service began.

The priest followed with the story of Lazarus. He focused on the sisters' grief and consternation that the Lord didn't show up in time to heal their brother. Honestly, while he spoke, I drifted a little. Saoirse's hands on her lap reminded me so much of Aneska's that a rush of emotion came as I remembered how many times she had reached out and taken my hand. That led to other memories. A unison congregational response, "Thanks be to God" brought me back to the present moment.

I haven't mentioned in a while the charming and eloquent effect of the Irish accent. Perhaps because my ear had grown more accustomed to it. In this setting, it colored every word with a timeless pathos of a legendary story and eternal truths being told.

The priest introduced Valor. He made everyone laugh with stories about him and his father playing pranks on Aneska, including putting tacks on the hammers in her grand piano to give it a honky-tonk sound. She wasn't angry. She just launched into a bluesy version of Beethoven's "Für Elise." He finished by describing her great love and care for Kristers, then introduced his sister.

Zuza followed with more stories of Aneska's tender love for Kristers, how and where they met. The glass of water. The snowdrop always beside the piano whenever her mother played. She even brought the last two notes they wrote to each other in their debate at Lübberstedt. Zuza read them, revealing how Kristers declared his love for Aneska. There weren't many dry eyes. Imagine my surprise when she ended her eulogy with the first three verses of John chapter fourteen. When she was much younger Aneska pointed the verses out in Brynn O'Cullen's portrait. I mentally edited them from my remarks. She closed with "Thank you Lord. For my dear mother. Make our love as untamable as hers."

My emotions had been under control to that point. Until Freida began the next hymn. "The Love of God." At the second verse, I could hear Aneska quoting it to me like she did on our first session.

> Could we with ink the ocean fill
> And were the skies of parchment made
> Were every stalk on earth a quill
> and every man a scribe by trade.

I lost it. Tears flowed freely. Saoirse handed me a tissue and put her arm around my back. The song ended. Saoirse went to the lectern.

If there was a dry eye in the place after Zuza, Saoirse made it unanimous. She told what most people close to the family knew, the sacrifice her grandfather made for Aneska during the war, and the enduring love returned to him by her Mimi. How Aneska had put off her dreams to care for him and so many others. I knew the story intimately, but hearing it from Saoirse brought the magnitude of their story into focus again. She ended by telling part of the prayer Zuza prayed as we sat with Aneska's body, waiting for the medical team. How happy it made them to picture her Mimi reunited with Kristers in heaven, hearing him speak to her in his full voice, perhaps greeting her like he did first thing every morning, "Good morning, snowdrop."

And I had to follow her.

Saoirse introduced me as someone her mother loved. That their family had come to love. She made a small joke that the only thing she had against me was envy that I spent more time with her Mimi in the last months than she had. But she added that, like the long wait for Aneska's concerto, having her Mimi's story written down so well was worth it.

I headed for the dais. As we passed, Saoirse gave me more tissues and squeezed my hand. In my other hand, I carried Aneska's copy of the manuscript and my remarks. I was glad I wrote them out. The emotions of the moment were unsettling. I stole my opening from Aneska's note in the concerto program.

'I am so honored and humbled you are here. To hear my heart and my journey.' Those are Aneska's words from the program for her piano concerto, which most of you know debuted only seven weeks ago in Dublin.

I am also honored and humbled to be standing here. God only knows why Aneska chose me to be the scribe of her magnificent story. I never imagined the book would become her eulogy. Or the concerto, her swansong.

I only had five months around Aneska. Like all of you who were privileged to be caught in her gravitational pull, I am much richer for that time. Some of you knew her heroic husband, Kristers. I envy you.

Even before her sudden homegoing, I have been asking myself, 'How do you sum up an epic life and great soul like Aneska?' One way is in her own words. I can't read you this entire manuscript, which is more like a transcript from our sessions together. But here is a glimpse of Aneska, in her own words.

"Never doubt your gift. Just keep giving it. God gives gifts as he sees fit. From Beethoven and the Beatles to the bard in the subway."

"Saying sincerely, 'Thy will be done' does not come easy in the crucible."

"Whatever you've heard about the luck of the Irish, Gott's providence never takes a day off to let luck have a play day." (laughter rippled through the cathedral)

"Remembering is revering. It makes what's lost along the way not as lost."

"No matter what you've lost. Give thanks. Bring all of you, even what's left of you, to life and to the altar. And lay it down. Live all in."

"There's a story being written and told in every heart. It will either be a story of redemption and freedom or one of decay and captivity. In this world where too often what matters is only who prevails, and less and less remains sacred, more than ever we need a Savior." (more than a few 'amens' followed)

"Gott, (as she pronounced it) prefers harvesters and ambassadors to stone-throwers and pundits. [His] grace stays busy editing us, ya? Grace begets grace."

About her music she said this:

"Music is only a bucket…meant to carry something intangible, but essential. Food for a hungry soul, a key to a spirit locked in chains of fear or hurt, the hope of freedom, the shared agony of suffering. It can carry comfort for sorrow, the beauty of creation, the joy of loving and being loved, the possibility of redemption, or the hollowness of missing it. Without that, like scripture says, it's only clanging cymbals, well-organized noise. But when music carries the living water of love, or points to the well where weary souls can drink and thirst no more, then the bucket, the gift, fulfills the purpose for which it was given."

I looked at Saoirse as I delivered the next quote. She returned a look and a smile I can't describe, but will never forget.

In our last conversation Aneska said to me:

"Like Kristers did, decide what you want. And pursue it with all your heart."

And finally, this is Aneska's heart from the concerto program:

"Concertos and symphonies have movements and recurring themes. Our lives do as well. I hope you will hear your own journey in my music, the beauty and agonies leading to your own redemption and rebirth. If you are still facing the second movement of your personal symphony, hang on. Find a hand to hold. Call out to Gott. Believe for the third movement and a brave finale.

Soli Deo Gloria, to God alone be the glory, Aneska Latva"

As I said before, I am richer from my time with Aneska. And I am also changed. When Zuza called me about writing her mother's story, I was questioning what difference another story, one more piece of music, one more painting could make in the world. I don't question that anymore.

I may never be as untamable as Aneska or her beloved Kristers, but I am more fearless now. My faith is growing. My heart is clearer, more unguarded. And my love is deeper for those I hold dear and wider for those who cross my path.

I suspect she changed you, too.

This manuscript is not finished. And neither is Aneska's legacy, not just the opus of her music, which will surely endure, but the legacy of her faith, endurance, self-sacrifice and generosity. No amount of pages can hold all of her.

Perhaps better than her words and music, the way to see Aneska is in the lives she touched. Her children, grandchildren, countless soldiers and work camp laborers and their descendants, a myriad of musicians. I'm certain you can see her touch on this community, in each of us here. And only God knows how many more her life. and music will touch.

Aneska Miriam Latva, mein Freund, my friend, made it clear every day what she lived for, not her gift, not the bucket, not the applause. We know what drove Aneska.

An untamable love. That is her Magnum Opus.

As I returned to my seat, Frieda took her place again at the grand piano. Ashura and Nelly, on cello and violin, joined her. As I sat down, Saoirse stood and walked to one side of the dais. She retrieved a glass of water and a vase. Pausing at the lectern she introduced the players and the song, "Dear Lord Jesus, Take My Hand." She briefly told its origin and history, placed the water and flower on a pedestal beside Freida, and returned to her seat beside me. She took her father's hand. With the other, she took mine.

The simple beauty of Aneska's song and heart poured out consolation and reassurance. When the last chord rang out into awed silence, it felt again like the entire cathedral sighed.

The priest and pastor came forward. Other musicians took their places near Frieda at the piano. An Irish harp, uilleann pipe, penny whistle, bodhrán, concertina and acoustic guitar. The pastor offered a beautiful prayer. He thanked God for the gift of Aneska to the world, exemplifying the Lord's untamable love. His 'amen' was followed by hundreds in the crowd. The priest gave instructions about the graveside ceremony. He thanked everyone for coming, asked us to stand and gave what seemed to me an off-the-cuff prayer, borrowing from Aneska's words.

"In the name of the Father, Son and Holy Spirit, go in peace, may we glorify the Lord by living a life worth remembering and revering."

Something told me he wasn't done. I nearly heard Aneska's voice in his final words.

"God be with you."

Every voice in the cathedral responded, "And with your spirit."

The uilleann pipe began the third movement of the concerto, Beyond Words. A funeral director and six pallbearers took their places around the casket. The music grew as they escorted it slowly down the aisle and out through the vestibule.

A large crowd attended the graveside service. There were chairs for about a hundred in three rows set in semi-circles in front of Kristers' monument and Aneska's resting place. Her gravestone, about five feet tall, was covered by a green shroud.

The pastor officiated. He began with a scripture, 1 Thessalonians 4:13-18, about the day of the Lord's return when believers will meet the Lord in the air together with all who have gone before. He kept his remarks brief, emphasizing the great heritage of faith represented by the grave markers nearby, and the "lasting legacy of faith present in their living descendants gathered here." He concluded with another scripture. Can you guess which one? Yes, he repeated John 14:1-3, then prayed, thanking God for preparing a magnificent place for Aneska and for all who believe. I spoke to him later. John 14 was not his original choice, but he changed when Zuza read it earlier.

After his prayer, the penny whistle player began, "Amazing Grace." It sounded pure and resolute. It had an Irish touch with lively trills and mournful bent notes. Again, Zuza's idea, a tribute to her father's obsession with the instrument. As the song played, each family member, including Maja, laid a snowdrop blossom on the casket. Saoirse handed me one to do the same. The Dublin symphony Maestro laid a conductor's baton. Last of all, Zuza placed a lily.

Valor retrieved a wooden box from behind Aneska's cloaked monument. As his sons Vic and Ben lifted the shroud, Valor released a white pigeon. I took Saoirse's hand. From the mottled gray and black stone iridescent flakes of blue sparkled in the sun. Blue pearl granite. Zuza and Saoirse's choice. Carved along one edge was a single elegant snowdrop. The stem curved over the top, the blossom bowing toward Kristers' column. Below Aneska's name and life dates stood the words:

Loved Beyond Measure
Dei magnum opus est amor

EPILOGUE

To detail the events leading up to and beyond the book release was logistically impossible. Zuza wisely decided, and we all agreed, the first pressing would end with Chapter 56 - The Finale. So, this epilogue did not appear in the first edition. Consider this like an encore. That's what Saoirse called it.

It probably comes as no surprise that the end of chapter fifty-five, The Call, and all of chapter fifty-six, The Finale, were the most difficult chapters to write. They were even harder to live in the midst of grief. The printing deadline and details for the release event added more weight for all of us. By the grace of God and perhaps Aneska's unseen but palpable influence, I amended chapter fifty-five and wrote chapter fifty-six over five days. Not without many starts and stops and walks around the estate, often sitting on the bench where we enjoyed our last conversation.

The monuments stood near like two sides of the same coin. "Loved beyond words" and "Loved beyond measure." The scientist beside the artist. Fused by love, faith, suffering and great sacrifice. Lives worth remembering and revering indeed.

Once the manuscript was proofed and delivered to the printer, and most preparations for July 17 were in place, Saoirse, Zuza and I went to the pub one evening, not to play music. Just to visit friends. Honestly, I went to drink. The kindness and camaraderie that met us there was like Guinness, rich and satisfying.

Brian, the poet, came in. He read us a new poem titled "Dine early and often at Café Rose." In his winsome Irish way, he credited Aneska dying before lunch as the inspiration. The poem was about seizing the day, seizing the pint, the moment, the kiss and most emphatically seizing the woman of your choice "before the day, the drink, the moment, the kiss and the lass all slip away." He wove a story of a lovely girl whose lips were as red as a rose. The expression "dine early and often at Café Rose" became a metaphor, meaning he kissed her as soon and as much as possible because life is short. The whimsy of it and Brian's delivery made us laugh. We hadn't done much of that. One verse was particularly memorable:

> Time, seasons, rivers and love, wait for no one, you see
> We're all always living on the fault line of mortality
> Whatever sunrise be our last, if afore sundown we go
> As for me I'll dine early and often at Café Rose.

My favorite couplet was:

> In my lassie's lovely eyes from early dawn to dawn
> The fire is always lit, and the Open sign is on

The poem was grand, as the Irish say, and especially poignant since Aneska's jarring homegoing had just reminded us of those realities.

As Saoirse drove us back to the manor, Zuza and I had to agree with her: church could learn a lot from a pub.

A series of meetings happened. One with the symphony Maestro and the manager of the National Concert Hall to map out a plan and date to record the Untamable concerto. Sooner than later was the consensus, a matter of weeks, not months, while the music was still fresh in the minds of the players. Capturing the passion drawn from such personal contact with Aneska was a factor as well. In another meeting, Zuza, Saoirse and I looked at proofs of the book cover and layout.

A third session just between Zuza and me was a precursor to the reading of Aneska's will. She was the executor. We sat in the study, which had become hallowed ground for me. She wanted me to know that a week after the Hamburg concerts, Aneska directed her lawyer to add specific and generous terms for my compensation, a portion of the copyright, and a share of royalties generated from the book. It included creative control, and a portion of film and audio rights. Aneska had discussed some of this with me. We were in agreement, but nothing had been formalized. Zuza let me know all that had been done.

Aneska's absence was keen in all these settings because she would surely have been present. But her legacy of music, love, and care was already in motion.

As Zuza and I wrapped up, my phone rang. Saoirse. She declared I needed a break. Does that remind you of anyone? She wanted the two of us to take a day trip to the Cliffs of Moher three hours west on the coast. I asked if Portumna was on the way, thinking maybe we could dine at the Café Rose. It was.

Next morning at half six, she 'collected' me, as the Irish say, in the Land Rover. To make the day less stressful for us both, and so I could enjoy the scenery, she drove. I have to say, the size of her vehicle on some of the narrow country roads still added occasional tension.

By half eight, we were sitting in Café Rose enjoying an Irish village wake up to a new day. It exceeded Brian's billing. A sign in the entrance proved fierce true, "This is a small house with a big welcome." The owner, Paul, served up Irish warmth and humor with a side of tasty scones and heavy cream, omelettes, bacon and lattes nearly as good as kisses. Strangers engaged us and came and went from our table like old friends. Saoirse told them we met Brian O'Kelly when I played at a pub in Carlow. They all knew him, called him a real "gas man." A funny bloke. A patron pointed out that Paul was a musician as well. Others chuckled, including Paul. He agreed, saying, "Yea, look it, if ever you need someone to clear a place with one song, I'm your man." Laughter and coffee cups rose in a chorus of "Sláinte!"

Café Rose put life in the land of the living. It wasn't listed on the menu, but they served us hope and resuscitation.

An hour and a half from Portumna, we arrived at the coast. Saoirse made a stop for a few edibles for lunch on the cliffs.

I had seen the Cliffs of Moher once before, but the power and grandeur spoke in a new way. We talked about how perhaps in grief, beauty and awe speak louder. If you've not seen the cliffs, they are like rugged, natural cathedrals, and make a magnificent visual backdrop to a symphony, grief or great love story. We sat on the ground by the observation tower, ate and watched people. As we left, we stood with a small group of tourists from Brooklyn, New York, to see a young couple be married. The pastor made a joke about "taking this leap." We congratulated them. Saoirse even hugged the bride.

She had one more stop planned before heading home, Gus O'Conner's, a pub in Doolin, a fierce colorful seaside village. It was her favorite on that side of Ireland for fish and chips. She had some details to attend to with her brokerage and about the book release. We broke out laptops. I began this epilogue. That's where she called it an encore. We worked side by side for nearly two hours.

Simultaneously, we got an email from Zuza. She was scheduling a reading of the will before the book release. It contained financial benefits to Carlow Academy, the RIAM in Dublin, and the symphony. We all agreed it would be fitting to announce that at the National Concert Hall.

As we worked, I wasn't the only one distracted by Saoirse. A quite tipsy fellow stumbled over to us. He told her she had the most beautiful smile he'd ever seen. He reiterated several times. Best smile of his whole life. In any country. I couldn't disagree. Saoirse wanted to bet me it wasn't the first time the 'bluthered clipe' used the line. I wasn't sure I wanted to know what that meant, but I didn't take the bet.

Hungry again, we ordered fish and chips. Spectacular. And of course, Guinness.

That evening about half nine she "delivered" me to the manor. I laid my head on the pillow that night, different from and better than when the day began. The Emerald Isle therapy worked.

* * *

A week later, nearly a dozen people attended the reading of Aneska's will in the front music room, including the Maestro, and directors of RIAM and Carlow Music Academy. Like Brynn, Aneska established funds for scholarships. This included a portion of royalties generated from the concerto and the book. It provided Maja's salary and living quarters until she married or moved on, including a generous severance when she did. Freida also received a portion of ongoing concerto royalties, though it was clear to everyone she was on her way to becoming a performing artist in her own right. Aneska's humorous side note to Freida emphasized how "instrumental" she had been in giving voice to the concerto.

The will gave Aneska's consent for some of Kristers paintings to be sold at Zuza and Valor's discretion. Any revenue from that she directed to the upkeep of Snowdrop Manor. Some of the royalties from the concerto and book copyright she bequeathed to all her children and grandchildren by name, to be distributed semi-annually, and be held in trust for the minor ones.

Snowdrop manor, which Brynn left to Aneska, was put in joint ownership of Zuza and Valor. Darby O'Cullen's son, Sean, retained title to the portion of land and the house on the estate Brynn bequeathed to him where his family lived and farmed.

Attached to the document was a very brief note from Aneska.

To all my dears, You know my love for you. My prayer for each of you is my mother's final one. "Dear Jesus, hold their hands."

Mimi

I continued to work on this epilogue, taking walks beside the River Barrow, sometimes to the dairy down the lane, often pausing on the bench in the cemetery.

* * *

The day came. The first copies arrived, July 15th, two days before the book release. We waited for Saoirse to come over from her cottage. Zuza gave me the honor of opening the box. The simple beauty and power of Kristers' painting on the cover struck me first. Because of the time crunch, the first pressing was a soft cover. It made no difference to me. I picked one up from the top of a stack of twenty. The rich time I spent with Aneska flooded over me. The magnitude of the moment was not like experiencing Aneska's concerto or seeing the Cliffs of Moher, but I must have slipped into a haze. Aneska's absence from this moment began to sink me. I felt a hand on my shoulder. Saoirse's. She said, "Mimi knows. She read it."

I handed her one. We embraced. I gave copies to Zuza and Maja. More embracing. And tears.

We sat around the room looking at the book. Flipping through it.

A thought ambushed me. *Saoirse is about to read everything I wrote and thought about her!* Zuza said something about presales in Ireland and Germany already exceeding twenty thousand. Fifteen hundred had arrived at the National Concert Hall for the book release. That exciting news helped mask my anxiety about Saoirse. But the hand had been dealt.

I didn't see Saoirse till late the next afternoon. A day before the book release. She came over in the Land Rover to load Kristers' painting for display at the event. After we loaded it up, she asked me to walk with her. She had stayed up all night reading the book and wanted to talk. I told her I had something to ask her, too. I'm not sure if she led the way, or I did, but we headed toward the cemetery.

As a diversion to cover my nerves, I had a question I'd been meaning to ask about her last conversation with Aneska that morning in the solarium. We were interrupted once before. She started in on the book. How much she loved it. How it captured her Mimi and grandfather and their story so well and for all time.

We neared the bench in front of their monuments. So we sat. The sun was sinking, turning the sky into watercolor. In that light, she looked more beautiful than ever.

She kept on about how she loved everything about the book, the italics to indicate my responses and inner thoughts, the song ideas I gleaned from her Mimi's inspiration. How she learned things she never knew about Aneska and Kristers and their families and friends, and the timeline of certain events. Not to mention the war details. She called the book epic and brilliant.

I said, "Begorrah, that's because your mother was epic and brilliant."

"Yes, she was, but no. It's a grand duet between you two, like Mimi said, between God directing and our choosing. Like you wrote on the first page, my too modest friend, this story chose you. And you chose to write it. I thank God you did."

She paused. We sat for a clean moment in the serenity.

"And," she began again, "I learned a lot about you. Besides the impressive fact that you shook hands with Margaret Thatcher. And Ringo!"

Uh oh, I thought. Here it comes. The vulnerability I risked in ink is about to leave me unguarded in the real world.

Her face turned serious. In a tone my mother used when I sensed trouble, Saoirse said, "I have only one melt with the book." I had no idea what a 'melt' was. Apparently, it's an annoyance. She left me hanging like a fly in a spider web.

"For the rest of my life, people will ask me about my other tattoo."

She chuckled. Then burst out laughing. I did, too. What self-awareness! What perfect delivery! She enthralled me more than ever.

When the delightful waves of that finally settled, she said, "Now, what did you want to ask me?"

I told her I wanted to hear about her last conversation with Aneska that morning. I really wanted to know. There was no personal fishing angle. At least no conscious one. I sincerely wondered if something between them might fit well in the epilogue that I was still working on.

She looked at her Mimi's monument.

"After Mimi prayed with me and Auntie Zuza, she walked me to my car. We talked about the book release and getting Kristers' painting to the concert hall for it. I told her I would take care of that. Standing at my car she quoted something out of Anne Frank's diary to me, about being loved by many but still lonely."

My full attention became fierce full.

"She told me about a prayer she wrote more than year ago for me, in the book at St. Patrick's about, well, about my future."

Though I was sitting still, my insides shifted and paced like a teenager at the door of his first date.

"The last thing Mimi said, besides 'I love you,' and 'God be with you' was something you quoted at her memorial service. She said, "My Bluebell, do what Kristers did. Decide what you want. And pursue it with all your heart.'"

I had to stand up. I walked a few steps away. Turned back and sat down.

"What is it?" she said.

I told her. All of it. How Aneska said the same things to me on that very spot the same morning, including Anne Frank's words.

She threw her head back and laughed. It was her turn to get up. She walked over to Aneska's monument. Embraced it. Laughed again and said, "That's my Mimi."

She returned, stood in front of me, looked me in the eye and said, "So, wordsmith, what is it you want?"

I knew. The words came. I didn't hesitate. I stood up, looked into her sapphire eyes and said it right out loud.

"I want to dine early and often at Café Bluebell."

Saoirse smiled her brilliant smile. And took my hand. By the look in her eyes, the fire was lit, and the 'Open' sign on.

 Dia dhuit 

ACKNOWLEDGEMENTS

My heartfelt thanks to:

My intrepid daughter who insisted we go to Ireland to research this story. That trip led to a cast of dear people who made our visit to the Emerald Isle rich and as indelible as the tattoo I got there. Thank you, new friends all. I hope to raise a pint with you again soon. Sláinte!

The O'Meara's of Lorrha, County Tipperary, who made Willow and I part of your family.

Dennas Davis, for playing the part of Kristers in paint for the cover art.

Brian Kelly, a.k.a. Brian O'Kelly, for excerpts from your poetry.

Café Rose in Portumna, County Galway, for the good cheer and lattes nearly as good as kisses.

The Ferry Inn pub in Lorrha, County Tipperary, for the music, camaraderie and Guinness therapy.

The Ink Factory of Dublin, for the fierce strong tattoo.

Karla Huitsing, stór mo chroí, for prayers, inspiration and encouragement all along the way.

My three muses with faces, Willow, Wyatt and Sawyer, who fuel and cheer on my creative habit.

The Holy Muse of heaven, who whispered beyond words into the ink.

ABOUT THE AUTHOR

William Luz Sprague was born in Tulsa, Oklahoma to Bill and Oteka Sprague. He grew up in West Texas, in Amarillo and Borger. He was graduated from Texas Christian University, studied literature at University of Texas for two years before spending a quarter of a century writing songs and recording in Nashville. His favorite title is "Dad" to a daughter and two sons, his "muses with faces."

Billy Sprague is an award-winning songwriter, recording artist and author. Previous titles include:

Letter to a Grieving Heart, a best-selling resource for those facing grief

Ice Cream as a Clue to the Meaning of the Universe, later retitled, *Is God Really There? (and is He Good?)* and his debut novel, *Music City Mayhymn,* a detective story set in Nashville, Tn.

Untamable is his second novel.

Soon to be released, a non-fiction title: *Sacred vs. Shinola, Letters to My Children from the Kitchen Table.*

Find other works at billyspraguemusic.com

Below are the piano pieces as they appear chapter by chapter. The year I spent writing *Untamable* was filled with these masterpieces. Now I return to them for inspiration. I encourage you to use the Spotify QR code at the beginning of chapters to listen as a soundtrack to the story. These titles can also be found wherever you source music.

If you have never experienced a symphony live, I highly recommend Gustav Mahler's "Symphony No. 1. Titan," written at age twenty-seven. Doing research for this story, my daughter, Willow, and I experienced it in Dublin, Ireland at the National Concert Hall where some of Untamable is set. Like Ireland, it was exhilarating and indelible. Enjoy.

Chapter 4:

Bach's Prelude in C, A Well-Tempered Clavier.
Gymnopedie No.1 by Erik Satie.
Bach's Minuet in G
Bach Sonata in D Major
Beethoven's Moonlight Sonata
Brahms' Intermezzo in A major Opus 118, No. 2.
Clair de Lune by Claude Debussy
Songs Without Words by Mendelsshon

Chapter 17:

Mozart's Rondo al Turca

Franz Liszt, his famous Rhapsody No. 2 in C# minor.

Liszt's Rhapsody no. 6

Chapter 18:

Chopin's Raindrop Prelude opus 28 No.15 in D flat Major.

Chapter 19:

Liszt's Consolation No. 3

Beethoven's Ode to Joy,

Angels We Have Heard on High by Mendelssohn

The chorus to Handel's Messiah

Chapter 20:

Liszt's Christmas Tree Suite No. 8 (Weihnachtsbaum, S186 VIII)

O, Come, O Come Emmanuel

O, Come All Ye Faithful

Chapter 22:

Liszt's Consolation No. 3

Chapter 23:

Chopin's Nocturne No. 20 in C-Sharp Minor

Chopin's Nocturne in E-Flat Major, Op. 9, No. 2.

Liszt's Hungarian Rhapsody

Chapter 24:

Reflection in A

Chapter 27:

Mozart's Air in A

Chopin's Nocturne in E Flat Major Op.9 No.2.

Tchaikovsky's Swan Lake

Chapter 28:

The first movement of Liszt's Rhapsody No.2 in C# minor

Mozart's Minuet and Trio in G major

Air in A, also my Mozart

Chopin's Nocturne in E Flat Major Op. 9 No. 2.
Chapter 30
Reflection in A
Chapter 33:
Reflection in A
God Save the Queen
Consolation No. 3 by Liszt
Chapter 35:
Mozart's Air in A
Chapter 36:
Ode to Joy by Beethoven
Chapter 39:
Ode to Joy by Beethoven
Chapter 41:
Reflection in A
Chapter 44:
Gymnopedie No. 1 by Erik Satie
Chapter 55:
Gymnopedie No. 1 by Erik Satie
Chapter 56:
Brahms' Intermezzo in A major Opus 118, No. 2
Consolation No. 3 by Liszt
Beethoven's Für Elise